Also by SARAH AHIERS
ASSASSIN'S HEART

THIEF'S CUNNING

SARAH AHIERS

HARPERTEEN
An Imprint of HarperCollinsPublishers

HarperTeen is an imprint of HarperCollins Publishers.

Library of Congress Control Number: 2016961163
ISBN 978-0-06-236383-1 (trade bdg.)

Typography by Kate Engbring
17 18 19 20 21   PC/LSCH   10 9 8 7 6 5 4 3 2 1

First Edition

To my mom and dad.

I know you always thought I'd make a good lawyer,

but I hope this is okay instead.

one

I DIDN'T FIT.

The night moon glowed overhead, cool and soft and bright. I'd slipped off the dark roof and into the darker room through the window, but my hips had gotten wedged, and try as I might, I couldn't pull my way through. I was stuck, half in and half out of the bedroom before me.

I stifled a sigh and instead held my breath, waiting, listening for any movement, any sign I'd been found. Nothing. The house was silent and still.

At least no one was around to see me in my amateur predicament.

I twisted, using my hips to push the window up a little more. I tumbled the rest of the way into the bedroom, catching myself on my hands. I lowered my body carefully to the floor. Even the slightest bit of noise on my part would attract attention, and that would be the end of it.

I adjusted my bone mask, decorated with raindrops, over

my face. A deep breath calmed the twitching in my muscles, my fingers, the blood rushing through my veins as it begged me to spring into action.

But this was not a time for action. This was a time of stealth.

I slipped out of the dark bedroom and into the darker hallway, closing the door so quietly it barely clicked as it latched. My ears strained for any noise. There was nothing.

I slid my feet across the hall floor, then gently stepped down the stairs, one after another, tiptoeing along the wall so the floorboards wouldn't squeak beneath me.

The common room spread before me, empty and quiet in the night. Moonlight from a single window cast beams across the dining table, motes of dust sparkling for an instant before passing from sight. Scents from the remains of dinner brushed over me—lamb, spiced with fresh herbs, and ripe summer fruit.

My mouth watered.

Down another flight of stairs, pausing every few moments to listen, to let my eyes unfocus, to catch any slight movements hidden in the shadows. My leathers creaked, keeping me snug in their tight embrace.

The shop on the ground floor stood empty and still like the rest of the house. Bottles filled with perfumes and concoctions lined the shelves, and though the shop had been scrubbed clean, the faint scent of goldencones and tullie blossoms reached me.

To anyone else, it would appear there was nowhere further

to go, that I had reached the end of my travels. But I wasn't anyone else. I was a clipper. My world was a world of secrets.

In the back room of the shop, past the flowers and herbs hanging from the ceiling and the jarred liquids waiting to be combined for later sale, I depressed a small, concealed latch. A hidden door slid silently open.

I crept through and closed the door tightly. Behind the hidden door of the shop was a hatch in the floor. I squatted and pulled a key from a pocket on my hip. The key fit perfectly into the lock. I twisted slowly until the lock turned over.

The hinges of the hatch were whisper quiet. They'd been well oiled. Beneath the hatch stood a ladder, leading deeper into darkness.

I exhaled, then stepped onto the rungs. I descended.

My eyes had adjusted to the night, but the room at the bottom of the ladder was so dark that blindness weighed me down like the heavy stones of the building above. It would be easy to panic, to let the crushing darkness and fear overtake me. I could scramble up the ladder to the shop and the fresh air and freedom that awaited me there.

But for once it wasn't freedom I sought, but answers.

And panic was for amateurs.

A breeze of fresh air brushed across my neck. I followed it. My senses stretched and pushed into the darkness for any signal or sign.

The room opened into a larger one. A small glow of orange light emerged from a hearth and the dying embers nestled in the embrace of the ashes. Hardly any light at all, really, but it seemed a noonday sun after the darkness at the bottom of the ladder.

The room was rectangular, with the hearth in the middle. Before the hearth rested chairs and a short table for reading or conversing. At one end of the rectangle stood the kitchen, with a dining table. At the other end of the room weapons leaned in racks, glinting quietly in the dying firelight, their edges well honed.

The room appeared empty.

It lied.

I inched forward.

I listened.

I watched.

My fingers twitched at my belt, the knives waiting for me to need them.

A blade pressed tightly against the skin of my throat. Then a breath, quiet, yet filled with arrogance and triumph all the same.

A voice whispered in my ear, "You lose."

two

I CLOSED MY EYES AND SIGHED, LIFTING MY HANDS INTO
the air.

"I thought this year would be the year." My voice sounded
loud in the dark.

The knife vanished and my throat seemed to ache for the
blade's presence. I fought against the urge to rub my skin.

Behind me, a lamp flared, filling the room with its muted,
yellow glow.

I turned. My uncle Les stared at me with a grin. "You'll
never be able to best me."

I pushed my mask to the top of my head. "One day you'll
be old, and I'll still be young. Or younger than you, anyway,
and I'll find you before you find me."

He held out his arms and I sank into his hug, feeling his
long arms wrapped around me.

"That day will never come," he teased.

I snorted and pushed free of him.

From the back hallway the rest of my Family appeared, carrying more lamps until the basement was filled with their merry glow.

"Happy birthday, Allegra." Les kissed me on the top of the head.

"How far did I make it before you caught me?" I asked.

"The ladder." My aunt, Lea, set her lamp on the kitchen table near the presents that awaited me. She pulled out a chair and sat. "The rungs were sandy and your boots scraped across the metal as you came down."

I grimaced.

Les waved his hand at me. "Don't punish yourself. We only noticed because we were expecting you."

"Still," I said.

My cousin Emile took a seat across from our aunt. He'd made it all the way to the table and his presents on his birthday two years ago. Granted, he was older than me, but it still stung.

Emile yawned and ran his fingers through his curly hair. "Let's get this started so we can go back to bed."

I sat beside him, shoving him with my shoulder. "Only some of us had the luck not to work tonight."

I'd been at the same job for over a week now. The mark was holed up inside his house and I was getting tired of watching and waiting, only for nothing to happen.

Five wrapped parcels and boxes, varying in size, rested on the table. I considered holding them, testing their weight, shaking them, maybe.

Behind me, Les placed his hands on my shoulders. "It doesn't matter how long you stare at them—they won't give up their secrets, *kuch nov*." Darling child, in Mornian. It was what he always called me.

Excitement made my finger twitch. Not so much at the presents, though they certainly held an appeal. But because it was my birthday and I was officially an adult. Which meant it was finally time for some answers.

My great-uncle Marcello took a chair across from me. "Another birthday," he grumbled. "Don't even see the point."

"You say that, Uncle," I said. "But there are five presents on this table, which means one is from you."

He scowled.

Beatricia waddled past me, belly stretched before her as she carried a tray of birthday tarts.

"That looks heavy," I said.

She snorted. "I'm not so pregnant that I can't carry a tray of tarts. Besides, look!" She balanced the tray on her stomach and I laughed.

Faraday, our Family priest, grabbed the tray and kissed her quickly on the cheek.

My aunt Lea hid a small yawn behind her hand. "Come, it's time for presents and tarts."

I grabbed my birthday tart and bit into its flaky crust. The berries popped in my mouth with bright flavors and the sugars they'd been boiled in.

"You've outdone yourself this year, Beatricia." Emile

7

brushed the crumbs off his shirt.

"If there's one thing I know, it's food." She patted her stomach and sank into a chair. Faraday sat on the arm beside her and clasped her hand in his. Neither Faraday nor Beatricia were clippers, but they were part of the Family and their baby would be the first born to the Saldanas in over twenty years. It was evidence that not only had the Saldanas survived the attempt to destroy them, but that they—we—were starting to thrive once more.

Eighteen years ago, a rival Family, the Da Vias, had set fire to the Saldanas' home. Lea had fled here, to the country of Rennes and the city of Yvain, looking for her uncle, Marcello, to help seek revenge.

Emile wiped his mouth with his napkin and then tossed me a box. I caught it and popped the lid open. Inside was a new push dagger. I slid it into my palm and closed my fist. The blade slipped easily between my knuckles.

"You've been complaining your old one is too big for your tiny hands."

I rolled my eyes, but not without a smile. "This one fits much better," I said. "Thank you."

He nodded and leaned back in the chair.

Marcello gave me a new pouch, the leather hand-stitched in a pattern of raindrops, like my mask.

Faraday and Beatricia gave me a journal, the cover made of thin calfskin, and with paper pressed so fine I could barely feel the grain. Faraday's favorite pastime was making paper, and he particularly liked to experiment with crafting it out of the myriad flowers found throughout Yvain. Those pages were splashed with color, and sometimes one could even catch a hint of fragrance from them.

The first few pages of the journal were filled with Faraday's neat script and a family tree for each of the nine Families.

From my aunt Lea I expected to get another weapon. A sword, maybe, or a new stiletto. It wouldn't be poisons, because she'd long ago accepted I would never have her skill with them. But instead she handed me a small bundle that, when opened, contained a delicate silk scarf. I held it before me and the lamplight caused the gold thread embroidery to sparkle.

My face must have registered my surprise because she immediately offered an explanation. "Just because we're clippers doesn't mean we can't own beautiful things."

Lea had once owned dresses and jewelry. But when the Da Vias attacked, Lea had lost everything, and everyone.

Only Lea had escaped their knives. Well, Lea and Emile and I, but Emile had been four, and I had been a tiny infant. We grew up knowing the Da Vias had killed our parents, leaving Emile and me as orphans. Or so we were told. I had no memory of it. Of my parents. Of the things I'd lost.

Sometimes, when Lea and I were in the market together, I would catch her staring wistfully at a particularly exquisite dress or necklace. And I knew she was remembering her home and the fashions of Lovero. I hoped one day to see them.

"Is it all right?" Lea asked.

I'd been staring at the scarf wordlessly. I clutched it to my chest. "I love it. Thank you."

"Last one." Les handed me a box, the smallest yet. He gestured for me to open it.

I slid off the lid, and inside rested a stone, a disc of agate with shades of blue radiating from the center, its three rings polished to a high sheen. Les's mother's necklace.

His mother had been murdered when he was a small boy, and his grandfather had abandoned him on the streets of Yvain. Before that, though, Les had taken his mother's necklace from her body. It was the only thing he had to remember his traveler life and family from before Marcello had taken him in.

I studied him and saw what I had overlooked before: the pendant was missing from around his neck.

I lifted the stone from the box and felt the heavy weight of it in my hands. "This was your mother's." My voice sounded quiet, even in the quiet room.

"And now it's yours. It's meant to be worn by a woman, and I want you to have it, *kuch nov*. The travelers say it has old magic, though it's certainly never done anything for me. But maybe it will bring you better luck." He smiled.

He wasn't my father. Les. He wasn't even related to me by blood, something I used to cry about as a child, especially on the days where I didn't seem to fit in with my Family, days that multiplied the older I grew. I was too rambunctious. Too rash. Too . . . everything. It wasn't fair to have parents who weren't really your parents. To have people who loved you who weren't even a part of you.

Lea would tell me it didn't matter. That Family comes before family in the world of clippers, but I knew she didn't really believe that.

But here Les had given me the only thing he had to remember his mother by, the only tie he had to the traveler child he'd once been, to remind me that maybe he wasn't my blood, but that it didn't matter. Anyone could be family. Anyone could fit, as long as you loved them.

I slipped the chain over my head, and the pendant came to rest on my breastbone. It felt warm against my skin. "It's perfect. Thank you." My voice broke, and I couldn't help the blush that crept up my neck.

Emile snorted, enjoying not being the blusher for a change.

Marcello grunted. "Did you get everything you wanted, then? Are the celebrations over so you can leave me in peace?"

Marcello was the only one who lived in the basement safe home. Lea and Les had tried to convince him they were in a new home and he was safe if he wanted to go outside again, but he refused. He said he'd spent the last few decades living underground and he wasn't about to change now that he was an old man.

The rest of us lived in the actual house, above the shop where we sold herbal remedies and perfumes, something Lea excelled at because of her expertise with poisons.

"It lends us an air of respectability," Lea had told me when I was younger. "It's harder for the common, and lawmen especially, to be suspicious of people who ply a trade in public view. As long as we have the shop, it will keep the lawmen's eyes turned away from our true work."

Murder, our true work. We were the mortal hands of Safraella, god of death, murder, and resurrection.

Sometimes Lea felt ashamed of the shop. She'd come from Lovero, where the common had treated her like royalty. And as the patron of Lovero, Safraella kept its cities free of the angry ghosts at night, and the people rewarded the clippers by practically placing them on pedestals. No clipper in Lovero had to work outside of their holy duties.

But the Saldana Family no longer lived in Lovero, and the rules and gods in the country of Rennes were much different. Secrecy was the only way to survive here.

"Almost everything, Uncle," I replied to Marcello.

Lea leaned back in her chair. "Out with it, then. What did we miss?"

I glanced around the table. Then I took a deep breath. "I want to know about my parents."

Emile groaned beside me and got up from the table to fetch a drink from the kitchen. "This again."

"Yes, this again," I snapped. It was easy for him. He remembered his father, though his mother had died when he was a baby.

But remembering a father was better than the nothing I had. All I knew was what I had been told, that my mother, a commoner, had died in childbirth. And my father, Matteo Saldana, Lea's brother, had been killed with the rest of the Saldanas when the Da Vias had carried out their plans to destroy the first Family.

"We've been over this before, Allegra," Lea said. The exasperation practically coated her voice.

"You never tell me anything specific," I said. "You know more about them, you just keep it secret from me."

"That's because I don't like to talk about it," Lea said.

It was always the same excuse. It was painful for her to talk about the Family she'd lost, her brothers and parents and cousin who had been murdered in their home, the house that had burned to the ground, leaving Lea alone and destitute, fleeing to Yvain to search for Marcello in her quest for vengeance.

But it wasn't true, her excuse. Lea spoke about Emile's father, Rafeo, all the time. If it was too painful for her to at least talk to me about my own father, Matteo, then why was she able to talk about Rafeo? They'd both been her brothers.

"I'm an adult now," I said. "I'm eighteen. I think it's fair I know everything."

Marcello snorted at this. "No one knows everything. No one except that one, anyway"—he pointed to Lea, who ignored him—"being favored of Safraella."

"You know that's not what I mean," I said.

"*Pah*," Marcello said. "The head of the Family always has secrets." He got up from the table and walked over to his favorite chair. He sank into its cushions and groaned. His knees pained him almost constantly.

And he was right, of course. Lea was the head of the

Saldanas. There were things only she was privy to, though I doubted she kept any secrets from Les.

"This isn't a Family secret," I countered. "This is about me. My life. My parents."

"Your parents are dead," Lea said. "We raised you. That's all there is to know."

"That isn't *all there is.*"

Les raised his hand. "*Kuch nov*, please."

Les had given me a beautiful gift for my birthday. I didn't want to ruin that by making him feel like I didn't appreciate that he had raised me.

I pressed my lips together. "Fine."

It wasn't that I didn't love them, that I wasn't glad to have been raised by Lea and Les. But when I thought of my parents, who they were, what they were like, my chest felt hollowed out. Maybe if I just knew more about them, I would finally understand how to belong. How to be a Saldana that they could be proud of, instead of the Saldana I was, the Saldana who got into trouble because I acted before thinking.

But every time Lea refused to talk about my parents, I pictured myself in a wire birdcage with a locked door, and the cage getting smaller and smaller the older I got.

More than anything I wanted to be free of that cage, and maybe knowing about my parents was the key to unlocking the door.

"Are we done with it, then?" Lea asked.

I shook my head. "No, but I'm tired. I'm going to sleep in

tomorrow. Birthday privilege."

"That's fine," Lea said. "But we have something else we need to talk about first."

She gestured at Emile, who hesitated before sitting down at the table.

I glanced at him, but he only shrugged slightly. Whatever was going on, he was as in the dark as me.

She clasped her hands and leaned forward. Lea opened her mouth, then closed it, struggling to find a way to start. Whatever she was about to tell us, it was serious. Bad news. Someone was ill. Or in trouble.

Les squeezed her shoulder and she visibly relaxed. "We've gotten an invitation."

I blinked. An invitation wasn't such a serious occasion.

"The king has entreated us to visit and swear fealty to the princess on her crowning with the rest of the Families."

"The king of *Lovero*?" I asked. We'd been invited to go to Lovero. Where everyone was fashionable and stayed out all night for revelry and refreshments and romance. This . . . this could be the best birthday present of my entire life.

I craved other places, other cities, other countries. I didn't hate Yvain. I loved it, its flowers and foods and canals. But it was small. Too small for me. I didn't fit here, either. And the world was a big place, just waiting for me to see it. All that wide space—surely I could belong somewhere.

"Yes," Lea said. "The king of Lovero. Camelia Sapienza has come of age. The Families must once again swear fealty to the Sapienzas, so they retain Safraella's favor and the ghosts

15

remain barred from Lovero."

Marcello snorted. "And this affects us how? We don't live in Lovero. The ghosts walk freely among our streets. We are only invited because you are the chosen of Safraella."

How luxurious it must have been to live in Lovero. They didn't have to watch their backs, or listen to wails and groans and wonder whether it was a ghost bemoaning its fate or just the wind over the canals.

Not that Lovero had canals.

"It affects us," Lea said, "because we are still considered one of the nine Families. We may not make Lovero our home, but that was our decision and not one I regret. And this is an opportunity for us. To show the other Families that there can be peace between us. That we can let the animosity go."

It was Lea's biggest platform. To try to finish the endless feuding between the Families. She had seen firsthand what it could do. Entire Families wiped out. Good clippers killed. Skills and knowledge and bloodlines lost forever.

She so desperately wanted there to be peace between the Families. Or, if not peace and goodwill, at least not war.

She had started with the Caffarellis and that had gone well. Of course the head of the Caffarellis, Brand, was her first cousin and they were on good terms. It was easier making peace between shared blood. That, and Emile was betrothed to Brand's daughter, Elena. She would join us and become a Saldana soon.

But the Da Vias and the Addamos still hated us. And the

Accursos and the Maiettas had been quarreling for generations, breaking into actual skirmishes every decade or so.

"If we go to Lovero," Lea continued, "and stay in Lilyan with the Caffarellis' welcome, we can show the other Families it can be done. That there can be peace."

"What about the Da Vias?" Emile asked. "Won't they try to kill us anyway?"

Lea shook her head. "I don't think so. Brand says their Family head, Bellio, is pious. He wants to regain Safraella's favor, the things they lost. He won't challenge us."

While Lea and Les had plotted vengeance against the Da Vias, the Da Vias had caught up to them and killed them both. But Safraella had resurrected Lea and given her Les back as well, and Lea had punished the Da Vias for turning to a different god by driving an army of angry ghosts into the Da Vias' home. The Da Vias had returned their worship to Safraella after that, and Lea remained Safraella's chosen one, able to drive away the ghosts and pass through the dead plains at night.

"You mean he won't challenge *you*," I said.

Lea waved her hand, dismissing my distinction. "Anyway, Costanzo Sapienza—"

"The king of Lovero," I interrupted.

"Yes, the king of Lovero has promised us safety if we attend his daughter's fealty."

"*Pah*." Marcello waved a hand at her. "Let them all rot, I say."

"Duly noted, Uncle." She turned her attention back to

17

the rest of us. "So the Saldanas will attend. Even if more peace cannot be brokered, swearing fealty to the Sapienzas, and through them, Safraella, is necessary and expected of us, even if we no longer call Lovero home."

Lovero held wonders and masquerades and foods and people I'd never seen before. It had other clippers I could befriend, or maybe more than befriend. Lovero was different from Yvain, and I wanted to see every inch of it.

But outside of all of that, Lovero held answers. My parents had died in Lovero. Someone there had known them, could tell me about them. And that was worth more than all the adventures Lovero promised.

"It's not as simple as all that," Lea said.

My stomach sank and I leaned back. "Not as simple" was Lea's way of skirting around telling us that we wouldn't actually get something we wanted, whether that was a new sword, a pretty dress, or a trip to Lovero.

"We can't all go."

And there it was, the final stab as my hopes and excitement slowly bled out. This didn't need to be such an ordeal. Lea could have just told us she and Les were going to Lovero alone and everyone else had to stay to run the shop and tackle any jobs that couldn't wait for them to return. It was the same thing. As always. Because nothing ever changed for me. Not even on my birthday.

"I'm expected to attend." Even if Lea hadn't been the chosen of Safraella, she was the head of the Family and therefore spoke for all Saldanas. If she swore fealty, it meant we all did.

"Les will come, too. He's my husband, and it will be a show of good faith if we both swear. Especially since he was not raised as a clipper."

Lea shifted and glanced at me quickly before turning her gaze away.

"And Emile," she said, avoiding my eyes. "You will be coming as well."

three

EMILE. EMILE WAS GOING TO LOVERO WITH LES AND LEA.

"What?"

I hadn't even realized I'd spoken until Lea focused on me. I swallowed. My cheeks felt flushed but I didn't know if it was from embarrassment or anger. "Only Emile?"

"Emile is coming because of our arrangement with the Caffarellis," Lea explained. "We've agreed to their terms for the marriage, but I know Brand would feel much better about sending his daughter away, especially outside of Lovero, if he met her betrothed. It's a courtesy we show them. That we don't take this agreement lightly, even though we are gaining a member and a dowry."

I shook my head. "That's not what I meant. I understand why Emile needs to go. But why can't I go, too? Why do I have to stay here?"

"We need someone to help Beatricia and Faraday in the store."

Beatricia looked between Lea and me. "I'm not so pregnant that I can't handle the shop alone, if Allegra went with you."

I smiled brightly at Beatricia, but Lea's shoulders stiffened. Beatricia's offer wouldn't change anything.

"And," Lea continued, "you're in the middle of a job. It can't just be abandoned."

"My mark hasn't shown himself in over a week. A few days won't change anything."

"You don't know that, and that's not the point."

"Then what is the point?" My voice had grown louder, and I felt a mixture of shame and strength from my anger. "I'm eighteen. Nothing ever happens here and nothing ever changes." And they kept me in the dark about my parents. "By the time you were my age, you'd already saved the Saldanas from oblivion and moved here to keep us all safe."

"I did all of that out of necessity." Lea clenched her hands together. "I would have gladly given anything to live a safe and happy life. The things I did when I was your age were not adventures. They were brutal and bloody and if I have to spend my entire life protecting this Family so none of us have to experience anything like it again, I will."

I closed my eyes, feeling the anger sliding through my veins. Feeling the mantle of my Family like an ill-fitting bone mask, or leathers. "You protect me too much. I'm cloistered away, except even Brother Faraday had more freedom when he lived at the monastery."

"Allegra," Faraday started, but Lea cut him off with a raised hand.

"The decision has been made."

"I just don't understand why!"

Lea and Les exchanged a glance, then she leaned back in her chair. "It doesn't matter why. Allegra, you will not be coming to Lovero."

Secrets. I could practically smell them.

"Of course not," I scoffed. "Happy birthday to me. I hope you all have a lovely time together."

I got to my feet and pushed my way past Emile, not caring that I shoved his shoulder.

"What have I done?" he asked.

I gathered my presents and left, ignoring Les's entreaties to return.

Upstairs in my room I locked the door behind me. Someone would try to talk to me—Les or Beatricia most likely. Maybe Faraday—and I didn't want to deal with any of them right now.

I flopped onto my bed and stared at my ceiling.

I was a prisoner.

I lived a life of relative luxury and ease with a family that loved and cared about me and wanted to keep me safe. But all I'd ever wanted was something different than the same old thing every day. My skin itched as I thought about my birdcage.

Emile was the exact opposite. He found comfort in things remaining the same, and the biggest reason he'd been fine with Lea arranging his marriage to Elena Caffarelli was that it meant he wouldn't have to step out of the little world of safety he'd built around himself. He liked his cage.

And yet, he was the one they were taking to Lovero.

I jumped off my bed and paced back and forth, any thoughts of sleep gone. There had to be a way to get to Lovero, even if I had to do it on my own. I needed answers. I needed my cage opened.

I paused and stared out my window at the stars in the sky, letting the night air pass over me. Lea had told me once that in parts of Ravenna in Lovero, the lanterns were so bright you couldn't even see the stars. I would give almost anything to witness it myself, to explore the night freely, to taste different foods and to drink different wines, breathe different air.

I clasped at my chest and felt a hard object beneath my leathers.

I looked down and found Les's necklace, still hanging from the chain. I shuffled to the mirror and held my hair out of the way, examining my reflection. The blues in the stone somehow made my brown eyes look richer, or at least it seemed that way in my dark room.

I dropped my hair. Maybe he'd just given me the necklace because he knew how upset I'd be that I'd have to stay home while the three of them went off to meet royalty.

I grasped the stone and it felt warm in my fingers. No. Les wouldn't do that. He meant what he'd said when he'd given me his mother's necklace.

I tugged my leathers off and threw them in the corner before climbing into bed with my gifts.

I paged through the journal Faraday had given me, looking through the Families. He'd written them in the current ranks: Accurso, Bartolomeo, Caffarelli, Maietta, Da Via, Addamo, Zarella, and Gallo. The first page, of course, was for us, the Saldanas, even though we were unranked.

I traced my fingers down the lines of my family tree to the very bottom. There was Emile, his line breaking apart at his father, Rafeo Saldana, Lea's oldest brother, and his mother, who had not been a clipper but a cleaner. And there was my line beside his, breaking apart at my own father, Matteo Saldana, and leading to nowhere for my mother. If Faraday knew the identity of my commoner mother, he hadn't included it in the journal.

I snapped the cover shut and shoved all my presents off the bed before curling up on my side under the blanket.

I would've loved to think morning would make things look better, but it wasn't true.

Nothing would be different in the morning.

———※———

I paced across the roof of the empty warehouse along a stripe of moonlight, listening to the sound of my breath beneath my bone mask.

When I'd finally fallen asleep after my birthday, I'd dreamed of a monster.

Or monsters.

Sometimes there were three of them, and sometimes they

would merge into one creature.

I couldn't quite see them. They were mostly hidden behind a veil of fog, and when I'd try to peer past, the fog would swirl and block my vision. But I knew the beasts were there, hidden, watching me.

Their whispers echoed in the dream, until they drowned out everything, even my own being.

Then I'd woken with a plan.

Seven nights.

Seven nights and seven days I'd been out in the southwest corner of Yvain, trying to catch Jonus Aix in person. He lived in the house across the street, the one that had remained locked and quiet. He hadn't even gone out for groceries or to meet a friend for a drink or a meal. He'd stayed locked inside his house and I'd stayed waiting and watching and itching to do something, anything, to end this horrible trap I'd found myself in.

This afternoon I'd skulked around outside his house, pretending to shop at the nearby market, innocently eating street food while I kept an eye on his door.

Which was the same thing I'd done the last week. But that was fine, because this time things were going to be different.

I bought a sweet pasty, the inside dripping with hot melted sugar. It burned my tongue and I waved cooling air at my mouth while keeping an eye on Jonus Aix's door.

"They're hot today," a voice said behind me.

I looked over my shoulder, then continued my surveillance

of Jonus's house, the pasty cooling in my hands. "They always are."

Denny stepped beside me. I could feel his gaze, but I kept my eyes away. If I looked at him, looked at the way the setting sun softened his russet skin, remembered the strength of his arms, the taste of his mouth, my chest would tighten unfairly. And I was tired of feeling things I didn't want to feel.

It had been fun, being with Denny. And more than fun. At least at first. And he'd been *my* secret, something I could keep from Les and Lea, just like they kept things from me.

But they'd found out. Of course. They always found out everything.

It wasn't that Lea and Les were against casual romances; they just had to clear him first.

Denny had black hair in tight curls and bronze eyes that seemed to peer right into me. I liked the way his strong hands gripped my thighs, how his mouth was as smooth as his skin. He could make me shiver by breathing on my neck and I thought I might have loved him, at least a little. And maybe it could have been more than a little.

But Lea and Les had to ask all these questions. Who he was, who his family was, what they did as a profession, how long they'd made Yvain their home. They'd even stalked him. Until being with Denny started to feel like another cage.

Denny and I had fought.

I'd said unfair things, and he had countered with his own.

And there was no reconciliation. We didn't fit anymore.

After that, it seemed easier to be alone. At least as long as Lea and Les were so adamant about their questions and concerns. Whatever they were protecting me from, they wouldn't tell me. And I didn't believe it was just from having my heart broken, like they said.

I had a strong heart. I wasn't afraid of a few cracks.

"How are you?" Denny's voice reached depths in me that made me tremble.

"I'm fine."

I bet there were plenty of attractive, available clipper boys in Lovero. Caffarelli boys dressed in black leathers with stark bone masks decorated in purple. Boys who weren't afraid of the night the way the Yvain boys were. Boys who could chase me and actually catch me. Boys who could keep up.

A shadow passed behind Jonus Aix's window. I narrowed my eyes.

"I just wanted to say hello. And happy birthday, Allegra. I hope you had a good year."

I looked at Denny then. He'd cropped his hair close to his scalp, and he smiled at me, teeth white and crooked. Then he inclined his head and went on his way.

I shoved the rest of the pasty into my mouth, not caring how much it burned me.

And when the sun had started to set, I returned home, changed into my leathers, and made my way back to Jonus Aix's house.

Jonus Aix was a bad man. He had hurt women. And girls.

But the lawmen hadn't done anything to stop him, since Jonus Aix was so rich he could pay them off.

But of course it wasn't the lawmen he should've feared.

The Saldanas didn't need huge amounts of wealth, just a fair payment and a fair reason for why someone should die. In this case, though, the families of the women and girls had pooled their money together, begging us in a lengthy letter to put an end to Jonus Aix before he hurt anyone else.

And the Saldanas were happy to comply.

Or, at least, I had been happy to comply seven nights ago when I'd thought this job would be either exciting or easy.

It had turned into neither. And now it was a reason—no, excuse—for why I couldn't go to Lovero.

Lovero had answers. Lovero offered freedom, the freedom I couldn't find here in Yvain, with my Family.

Lea didn't trust me to handle things my own way. She wanted me on a tight leash to control me. Control would keep me safe, she'd said more than once. But safe just felt suffocating.

If I finished this job tonight, Lea would have no excuse to keep me away from Lovero.

If I removed her excuse, then she would have to allow me to go to Lovero with them.

She would have no choice.

———◆◆◆———

The pry bar slipped easily beneath the lip of the window and I leaned on it until the window popped open with a crack. I waited for movement inside the house, but there was none.

Jonus had gone to bed like he had every night for the last seven nights. I climbed through the window and closed it quietly behind me.

We never entered people's homes. It was something Lea used to do, back when she lived in Lovero, but never here, in Rennes. Murder was legal in Lovero for clippers, but here in Rennes, entering someone's house just increased the chances of being caught. And the punishment for murder in Rennes was death.

But I'd be in and out quickly, and Jonus Aix would be dead and I would be on my way to Lovero.

Bookcases stretched to the ceiling, adorned with worn leather volumes, gold trinkets, and miniatures. My fingers twitched at his wealth so brazenly displayed, but taking anything would be breaking my aunt's biggest rule. Clippers weren't thieves. We didn't steal from the dead, or from the soon-to-be dead. That was not our purpose.

We were disciples of Safraella, god of murder, death, and resurrection. Every death we granted was in worship to Her. Every coin we left in the mouths of the deceased was a signal to Her that we had killed that person in Her name, and that She should offer them a new, better life.

And if people heard we were thieves as well as assassins, they'd no longer use our services. The common hired us because we murdered in the name of a god. It gave the grisly work a sort of legitimacy, relieved our clients of their guilt. If we clipped people for other, less than holy reasons, our clients would have to shoulder more guilt. And they didn't want to carry that weight.

A desk commanded the center of the room, and I quietly slid to the door. I cracked it open, staring into the darkness of the hallway, looking for any signs of movement.

My breath sounded loud behind my bone mask, but it was just a trick of the night. No one would hear me. I was proficient.

I stepped into the hallway and headed right, toward the bedrooms and my destination. Jonus Aix lived alone. There was no one else here.

Behind me, a muffled thump traveled down the hall. I pressed myself against the wall and scanned the darkness. A gray cat streaked across the doorway to the living room. I released my breath.

Jonus's bedroom stood before me, door closed against the cool night air. I eased it open, lifting up on the knob so the hinges wouldn't squeak.

A large bed filled the room, complete with a canopy and heavy drapes he'd left open. He lay on his back, snoring slightly.

I pulled a dagger from my belt and walked to the bed, measuring each footfall carefully. If he woke, I could take him, but better to be safe and end him quickly.

I exhaled slowly. He mumbled something in his sleep. Maybe he sensed my presence, dreamed of his imminent death.

I paused, then returned my dagger to my belt and opened a pouch instead. I ran my fingers over the etched corks sealing my poison vials until I found the one I wanted.

Poison would make his death less suspicious. Sloppy, violent murders always attracted more attention, especially from the lawmen. And though they certainly couldn't make any connection between the Saldana Family and the crimes committed, it never helped to raise their suspicion.

I popped the cork and tipped the bottle over Jonus's lips. The liquid dripped into his mouth. He fidgeted once, briefly, but then settled into a deeper sleep.

Behind me, the door creaked open.

I spun. The cat rushed through, tail puffed like it had seen a ghost. Perhaps it had.

Before I could stop it the cat launched itself in the air, landing on Jonus Aix's stomach before racing off again.

Jonus Aix shot up in bed at his rude awakening.

I held completely still.

Maybe he wouldn't notice me, in the dark. Maybe he'd drop back asleep.

"Dammit, Kela," Jonus Aix swore. He turned to his left and there I stood, vial clenched in my fingers, face covered by my bone mask, the left side decorated with black drops of water.

He blinked once, twice. Then his eyes widened.

Damn.

He shouted and lunged for me.

I leaped onto the bed, dodging his grasping hands. My feet twisted in the bedding, slowing me. I reached the other side and dashed to the door.

Jonus charged. I threw the empty vial at him. The glass shattered on the floor. He stumbled and I darted through the open door.

I sprinted down the hall.

Behind me, Jonus burst from the room. The rug beneath his feet slid. He crashed into the wall, but still he chased me.

I had to give credit: the man was brave, or at least didn't seem to fear me.

In the living room Jonus's cat yowled at the commotion and streaked in front of us. I dodged a chair, leaped over a table, shoving it behind me. A grunt expelled in the air. Jonus tumbled to the ground with a heavy thump.

I grabbed the knob to the front door and twisted.

My cloak jerked around my throat. I gasped and clutched the clasp. Behind me, Jonus struggled for a better grip as he tried to get to his feet. I hissed and pulled out a knife.

His eyes widened, but in a testament to his bravery he only gripped my cloak tighter.

I sliced at his hand. He let go. The sudden release of weight caused me to fall against the door and it swung open. I tumbled into the street, the cobblestones slick from rain earlier in the evening.

I kicked out and slammed the door shut. It thumped, and there was a groan, but Jonus didn't follow me outside. He'd either given up, or dropped dead. Either way, I'd won.

Another groan echoed down the alley. I blinked. This one hadn't come from behind Jonus's door.

I climbed to my feet, twisting.

A ghost floated between the buildings.

Its spectral white form bobbed silently in the night, back turned to me. It appeared to be a man, or what had been a man, once. But it hadn't noticed me. Yet.

Forget Lovero and answers and freedom. If the ghost caught me, I'd be dead.

It turned at the commotion I'd created and saw me. Its mouth opened, showing the empty blackness inside of it.

I ran.

four

†

THE GHOST SCREAMED. THEN CHASED ME.

It gained on me, was faster than I could ever be.

I sprinted right, down a side street. My boots pounded on the cobblestones and splashed in puddles. Left, through another alley.

The ghost continued to shriek.

The quick direction changes wouldn't work forever. The ghost would never tire. I needed a canal, or a crooked bridge.

A shadow fell onto me from above. A figure paced me on the roofs. He looked down and I caught a quick glimpse of a bone mask.

He pointed ahead.

Before me towered a pile of goods. I doubted it was stable, but it was the best option I had.

The ghost screeched, its breath practically on my neck. Not that they breathed.

I jumped onto the crates, climbing upward, fighting against my own legs as my feet sank into half-filled sacks of flour and empty crates.

A hand grasped my wrist and yanked. I kicked off the pile of goods and was pulled to the roof of the building, safe from the ghost, who couldn't climb or fly.

I fell onto my savior in a tangle of legs and cloaks. The ghost groaned from the street below.

Things hadn't gone perfectly, but Jonus Aix would drop dead very soon, if he hadn't already, from the poison I'd dosed him with. The lawmen would think his heart had given out. There would be no suspicion.

And with Jonus Aix dead, Lea didn't have an excuse to keep me from Lovero.

I sat up and caught my breath, pushing my mask to the top of my head. "I didn't need the help."

Across from me Emile pushed up his own mask, decorated in black hash marks. He brushed a stray piece of curly hair out of his eyes. "That's not what it looked like. And by the gods, Allegra, what were you doing?"

"The ghost wasn't my fault." I climbed to my feet. "I couldn't have known it was there."

"You were inside the mark's house. How dumb can you be?"

I shook my head. "Seven days I waited for him to leave. I had to make a move."

Emile held up his hands, finished with my excuses.

"What are you doing out here, anyway?" Scorn dripped

off my words. "Shouldn't you be home, packing?"

Emile stilled, which was something he did when trying to control his natural blush reaction. He always blushed when he was embarrassed. Or worried. Or happy. Or anything, really.

I narrowed my eyes. "Lea sent you as a spy."

Emile lost the fight with his body and his neck blazed red, bright beneath the light of the moon. "Allegra—"

"No," I interrupted. "You be quiet. You don't get to say anything to me about this."

"She's just worried about you."

"Worried that I'd do something she didn't approve of, you mean."

"Well, she was right!" Emile's raised voice echoed in the alleys below us. The ghost moaned in response. Emile stepped closer and dropped his voice to more respectable levels. "You didn't even think about it. You just crawled right into his house in your usual rash manner."

"Oh, I thought about it," I said. "And I don't have to justify that to you. Why don't you go home and pack your things and dream about meeting your precious betrothed, Elena Caffarelli, in a few days."

"Don't you bring her into this."

"Why not? She's going to be part of this Family soon enough."

I pulled my mask over my face and headed east.

"Where are you going?" Emile shouted, yanking his own mask down.

"Home," I said over my shoulder. "There's a conversation waiting for me."

———※———

"You what?" Lea asked quietly.

She didn't yell. She rarely yelled, and anyway it wasn't the yelling I had to be afraid of, but when her voice was quiet and still and empty of emotion. That was when she was really angry.

Like right now.

I'd made it home before Emile and found Lea in the common area of the basement, packing weapons with Marcello. And I'd told her I'd finished my job.

I didn't elaborate. But clearly the way I'd said it, or maybe the expression on my face—daring her to question me further—made Marcello shake his head and leave the space entirely.

"I dropped Jonus Aix," I answered. "He's dead."

She set down the sword she'd been cleaning. "How?" she asked. "I thought he hadn't stepped outside his house all week?"

Emile entered the room then, climbing down the ladder and shoving his mask to the top of his head when he reached the bottom. He saw Lea and me standing with the weapons between us and scowled.

"Why don't you ask Emile?" I crossed my arms. "He's your spy."

Lea closed her eyes and sighed. "That's not the way of things."

"Yes, it is." I could be quiet and still, too. "But it doesn't matter. I get to go to Lovero now, right?"

Lea's eyes snapped open. She glanced quickly at Emile, then back at me. "What?"

"You said the reason I couldn't go to Lovero was because my job wasn't finished. But here we are, and it's done. I have no constraints holding me back."

Lea blinked rapidly. I could practically see her mind racing. Trying to come up with another excuse.

And I should have been happy. I had proof now that she was keeping me in Yvain for some secret reason.

But I didn't feel happy. Instead my chest tightened and I dropped my arms to my sides. I was just tired of all of it. Of being caged by my own family.

"She went into the mark's house," Emile said into the silence.

My usual response would have been anger at Emile's betrayal, rage slowly burning through my veins at how easily he played into Lea's plots. But I couldn't even find the energy for that, either. It wasn't his fault, anyway. He was a rule follower when it came to things he thought were Family matters.

Lea looked at me then, her eyes heavy with emotions I couldn't read. Disappointment, though. That was definitely in the mixture.

"How could you be so unsafe?" she asked.

"It doesn't matter. I used poison. His death won't be suspicious."

"No." Lea shook her head. "Keeping this Family safe *is* what matters! Entering a mark's home always leaves evidence, no matter how careful you are. And evidence will stir up the lawmen, and the last thing we need is them investigating his death and poking around."

"You weren't ever going to let me go to Lovero," I said, "whether I had a job to complete or not."

There was another moment of silence, broken only when Les entered the room from the ladder. He paused at the tension and glanced around. "What's going on?"

From behind the hearth, Marcello snorted. "Oh, Allegra crawled into some mark's home and it will probably lead to us being discovered by the lawmen and we'll die. Just another day in the Saldana Family."

"What?" Les held my gaze and then turned to Lea.

"I asked Emile to check in on you," Lea said to me, "because I was worried you were getting too bored on the Aix job. And when you get bored, you do something rash. Case in point."

"It wasn't rash," I said. "I planned it out carefully before I went inside."

Liar.

"It doesn't matter," Lea said. "Going into homes is a last resort only. And something we discuss as a Family. Not something you decide on a whim."

"Well, I did decide. And it was fine," I said. "He was asleep and I dosed him with poison and now he's dead. And anyway, it doesn't matter. Nothing changed. Nothing ever changes. Not for me, anyway. You go on to Lovero and I'll go up to my room like I always do."

I turned away from Lea. Just looking at her made me want to cry, and I refused to cry in front of her.

"Wait," Les said.

I stopped and turned back around.

"The job's completely done?" he asked.

Something warm flickered in my chest. Hope, maybe. And if it really was just about getting the job done in time, and not some other sort of reason, then maybe Lea and Les weren't keeping secrets from me. Maybe I'd been too paranoid.

"Yes," I said. "Clean and quiet."

Not truly, but they would never know otherwise.

Lea shook her head. "Alessio, no," she said. "She went into his home. Alone. Unplanned. We're not going to reward that."

Les faced her and they exchanged an entire conversation through their expressions. They'd been together so long and been through so much that they didn't even need to use words.

My shoulders sagged. It wouldn't work, then. Lea was the head of the Family. She made all the final decisions.

"No," Lea said, shaking her head.

"Leaving town now," Les argued, "is actually safer for all of us. If the lawmen come with questions, we won't be here to answer them."

I blinked. Les was on my side, arguing *for* me!

"She was rash and dangerous!"

Les dropped his voice, speaking quietly to Lea, but I was so close I could hear him anyway. "She could be more rash and dangerous while we're gone."

I scrunched my nose. I had to remember that he probably didn't mean it. That he was using my character faults in support of me going with them.

Lea sighed and shook her head.

Les faced me once more. "Pack your things, *kuch nov.* You're coming to Lovero with us in the morning."

five

THE HILLS OF THE DEAD PLAINS BLURRED TOGETHER, IF one traveled them long enough.

After Les said I could go to Lovero, I'd gone to my room, packed my things, then tried to catch a few hours of sleep before sunup. My sleep had been restless, though. My excitement kept me awake, and when I finally drifted off, my dreams were filled with the same monsters behind the fog from the night before.

But then we'd left Faraday, Beatricia, and Marcello to run the shop, collected our horses and a cart, and left Yvain and Rennes behind us.

Lovero was a large country to the south of Rennes. Even its smallest cities were still larger than tiny Yvain, and I couldn't wait to reach it.

I let my stallion, Night, stretch his legs over the hills of the dead plains. The sun warmed my neck and the breeze smelled of the grasses he trampled beneath his hooves. We shared excitement: His was the call of the empty plains, urging him to run, run, run. Mine was Lovero, somewhere over the southern hills. Soon I would be in a new place, with new people, new cultures and foods and sights. And maybe I would finally belong, somewhere.

I laughed and Night kicked his legs beneath me, tossing his mane in the wind.

And by the time the sun was setting we'd reached a monastery, the same one Faraday used to call home before he'd joined the Saldanas as our Family priest. The brothers fed us and housed us overnight, while the ghosts pressed against the gates and fence of the monastery, held back not by the iron but by the holy ground and the faith of the priests. The ghosts could not walk on ground blessed by Safraella.

In the morning, after a dreamless sleep, we left the monastery behind and continued south to Lovero and the Lilyan gate.

Finally, as the sun sank toward the horizon, we crested a hill, and there stood Lovero and all her cities.

"Look!" I pointed, unable to help myself.

The last bit of sunlight sparkled on the river and Lovero spilling across the other side of it, just waiting for us. It seemed to fill me up with its light until my body warmed and I grinned.

Night trotted in place beneath me and I held him still.

"That's Ravenna." Lea gestured to a sprawl of city to the west. "That's Genoni to the east, where we'll find the palace and the fealty. And in between them, at least here on the northern border, is Lilyan, where we're headed."

I lingered on Ravenna. That's where the Da Vias lived. And that was where I would find the old home of the Saldanas.

But now that the Saldanas lived in Yvain, this trip was a homecoming for Lea only.

"There's a shrine in Ravenna, right?" I asked. "For our Family?"

Lea nodded, lips pressed together.

"Can we see it?" I asked.

Lea snapped her face toward mine. "No," she said. "There's no going into Ravenna, not for any of us. It's not our territory. We would not be welcome."

"But it's a shrine to us—to *our* Family. And the king promised us safety. Surely—"

"No," Lea interrupted. "Surely nothing. We cannot go into Ravenna, and that's final." I sighed. Everything was always "final" with Lea. From the small, inconsequential things like how many tullie blossoms to infuse in the perfume to what jobs we took.

But "final," I'd learned over the years, really only meant "don't get caught." It was better to beg forgiveness than ask permission with my aunt.

Les flicked the reins on the cart horse and we continued down the road toward the crooked bridge that would let us cross the river.

The final, small distance of our journey seemed the longest. It took less than an hour to reach the crooked bridge, our horses' hooves clipping on the stone, the cart creaking and moaning as Les maneuvered it over the sudden twist in direction—to prevent the ghosts of the dead plains from crossing the moving waters of the river—but it felt like days. And then we still had to reach the gates of Lilyan, which looked more rusted and useless the closer we got.

The sun had set now, and Night picked up on my excitement and trotted in place, mouth foaming as I kept him in check.

I looked over my shoulder at Lea. She stared to the west and Ravenna. Her thoughts probably bitter and sweet and complicated.

"They don't even try to keep the gates in working order?" I gestured ahead to the rusted metal on the ground outside the walls of the city. The walls were in a similar state of disrepair, large pieces of stone fallen to the ground, their mortar crumbled away. I wrinkled my nose. The walls and gates of Yvain were tall and clean and without breach. What if the rest of Lovero matched these walls? What if, instead of finding glamour and lavish parties, I found rot and ruin?

I squeezed the leather reins in my palms.

Lea shrugged. "There's no need. You rarely see ghosts on this side of the river, and why spend the money and manpower to keep walls and gates in repair when Safraella keeps the ghosts out?"

"Maybe because it would look better," I mumbled under my breath. Lea didn't hear, but Les barked a laugh from the cart beside me.

I cleared my throat and changed the subject. "Where are

we staying? With the Caffarellis?"

Lea snorted and shot me a look of disbelief before she managed to cover it. "No. We will not be staying with the Caffarellis. We're a different Family. It's not done."

"But we're kind of the same family. Emile and Elena are going to be married. And you're Brand Caffarelli's cousin. And there's all that 'peace between the Families' thing you're trying to do."

"He is my cousin, but when Elena leaves with us she will no longer be a Caffarelli, but a Saldana. And regardless of how fond I am of Brand, and he's easy to like as I'm sure you'll see, he's still a Caffarelli and we are Saldanas. Staying in their territory is a huge show of trust. A public display of how the Caffarellis are aligned with the Saldanas. It may seem small to you, but that's because you're unfamiliar with the ways of the Loveran Families."

She'd said all this while leading us away from the river. "I need you to listen and understand this like your life depends on it, because it might. Outside of the Caffarellis, you are not to socialize or fraternize with any other clippers. You are not to speak to any of them, except to respond, and I expect you to respond in a way that will bring an end to any conversation they may try to start."

Emile shook his head. "I know all this."

"You think you know it, but you don't. You were too young to really understand what it's like."

"I remember the fire," he snapped. Les and I exchanged a look. Emile rarely angered, and never at Lea. His nervousness over meeting Elena must have been getting to him.

Lea sighed. "I know you remember the fire. But as bad as that was, it was still only a single instance, a moment in a country filled with moments, any of which could be a spark that could lead to more moments like that in the future. Many of the Families don't like us. Many don't like me. There is nothing you can say or do to improve upon that and plenty you could say or do that could make things worse. This is why I'm struggling so hard to build a lasting peace. I tell you these things not because I think you're children, or prone to stupidity. I say these things because I don't want you getting hurt. And this is a place where people would desperately love to hurt you, and they would be celebrated for doing so in many cases. If someone hurts you, I will have to hurt them. And I'd really like to escape this visit without spilling more blood."

I wrinkled my nose. Sure, the Families knew we were coming, but really, there wasn't anything they could do about it. We would be staying in Lilyan with the Caffarellis, so if they wanted to reach us, they'd have to go through them. And the Caffarellis were the third Family. It seemed unlikely one of the lower ranked Families would risk a move against us, no matter how scorned they'd been.

And then, all thoughts of Families and politics and rules from Lea fled because we'd reached the gates of Lilyan and walked through them without hesitation.

We'd reached Lovero. Land of clippers and Safraella and freedom, for me.

six

THE STREETS OF THE CITY OF LILYAN WERE WIDER
than the streets of Yvain.

This was my first thought in a new country, and dumb
though it may have been, it seemed like the streets stretched
forever between the buildings, leaving plenty of space for
horses and carts.

In Yvain we used canals to transport goods and people.
There were no canals in Lovero, so they needed wider streets.

The streets seemed dull, too. The flagstones were smoother
than the cobblestones of Yvain, and there were no fragrant
mosses growing between the stones. No real flowers anywhere, actually.

And the people. I craned my neck as we passed a side road,
and then an alley that just ended at a wall instead of a canal.
I'd been raised to believe that once the sun set, the streets of
Lovero flowed with revelers, but here the streets were almost
empty.

Tonight was the beginning of Susten, a three-day holiday celebrating Safraella and how She had freed Lovero from the grip of the angry ghosts. The Sapienzas had timed the fealty to coincide with the festival. Maybe everyone was just waiting for the official start.

Or maybe it was only Ravenna where the night came alive.

I looked over my shoulder, to the west.

My knowledge of Loveran geography was not great, but I knew the cities weren't so big that I couldn't walk to Ravenna easily enough, if I found some time alone.

But a block later, people started to fill the streets. Many of them wore traditional Susten Day masks, colorful feathers and beads decorating half masks, but plenty went barefaced.

I resisted the urge to touch my own face. We'd elected not to wear our leathers and masks as a Family when we'd left the monastery. We didn't want to draw more attention.

Lea led us south, farther into Lilyan, until finally she called a halt in front of a small building with a fenced courtyard and a small stable in the back.

"This is it," she said, sliding from Kismet's saddle.

"We're staying here?" Emile looked up at the second floor of the boxy house.

"We got a good deal." Les stepped off the cart. "Brand knows the owner and they were happy to cut the price for clippers."

Les led horse and cart to the back of the house and I followed, securing the biggest stall for Night. There was fresh hay waiting for us and I filled his net before heading inside.

The ground floor of the house was made up of a kitchen, dining, and seating area. The upstairs held the bedrooms. The floors were worn, wooden planks, where Yvain floors were typically tile. Tile added more color, like the flowers found in Yvanese windows and streets.

"It's just for a few days." Les spoke behind me.

I turned and smiled. "I love it."

And it was true. It was so different from our home in Yvain. It was my first taste of freedom and all the tarnish in the world wouldn't hide its gleam from me.

Les squeezed my shoulder, then headed out the back door again just as Lea walked in, carrying bags.

A gust of wind blew through the house and for a moment I caught the scent of salt before it was erased by horse manure.

Lea set the bags down. "Do you smell that?"

"I smell horse."

Lea laughed. "No, the other scent, that sort of brininess. It's the sea." She inhaled deeply, closing her eyes. "In Ravenna you can practically taste the salt on the wind. I wish I could show you all that water stretching out to the horizon."

She smiled at me again, more wistfully this time.

The sea. I couldn't even imagine so much water. It was something that called to me, deep in my chest.

But the city of Lilyan was landlocked. Just one more reason Ravenna wanted to be my destination.

"I would like to see the sea," I said to Lea.

She took one more deep breath, then shook her head. "One day, perhaps."

A knock at the door interrupted our conversation. Emile, needing help with more bags. I walked to the foyer.

"Emile." I grabbed the handle and pulled the door open. "If you're able to knock I'm pretty sure you're able to open the door . . ."

It wasn't Emile, but a stranger. He had pale skin, like many of the Loverans I'd seen tonight, blond hair, and a nose that had clearly been broken more than once. He looked me up and down, and then smiled, creasing the lines by his eyes.

"I am indeed able to open doors, but it seemed a rudeness to simply enter without being invited in. You must be Allegra Saldana."

"I am," I answered. It seemed a safe response.

He watched me for a moment, then chuckled and looked at his feet. "Not much of a conversationalist, I see. You must get that from your aunt."

From behind me I heard the sound of footsteps. "Allegra, what are you—Oh."

Lea stepped beside me and the man's face split into a wide grin. "Lea."

"Brand. I didn't expect to see you so soon." She looked over at me. "Why didn't you let him in?" She pushed me out of the way and opened the door so Brando Caffarelli, head of the Caffarelli Family, could step inside.

"I would offer you some refreshments," Lea said, gesturing to a chair for Brand as she took the one next to it, leaving the couch for me, "but we've only just arrived."

I felt a bit like an extra dose of poison. I could have gone out back to help Les, but I also wanted to know what Lea and Brand were going to discuss. My curiosity won out and I sat down.

I could recognize some resemblance between Lea and Brand, mostly through their hair color, but also in the shape of their eyes. He was taller than her, which wasn't hard because I was taller than her, too. But Brand was almost as tall as Les.

"The Da Vias asked for permission to enter our territory tomorrow, pass through Lilyan for the fealty," he said to Lea.

I leaned forward. I'd definitely made the right choice to hear this.

"And?" Lea asked.

"We denied it, of course. They can make their way south to their own Genoni border. Even if you weren't here, I would have denied them. I'd say I feel bad for the Addamos having to grant all the Families access to their territory in order to reach the palace, but they can drink their own piss for all I care." He laughed at his own joke, and his laughter was so infectious that I found myself laughing along, and Lea, too. We'd never had guests at our house in Yvain. We didn't have friends, just customers in the shop and marks in the night. It would be so different, living in Lovero, not having to hide who I was. Making friends, maybe.

"So," Lea said, "tomorrow we have the fealty."

"The ball, yes. After that it's still Susten Day and your

time will be your own, though I hope you will have a meal or two with us? My wife, Robinia, is desperate to get to know you. I think once she does it will put her mind somewhat at ease over Elena leaving. She can be suspicious of clippers."

"Isn't she a clipper?" I asked.

Brand shook his head. "I stole her from the cleaners when I realized no other clipper would compare to your aunt."

Lea studiously ignored my gaze. "You two were betrothed?"

Lea shook her head.

"We put in an offer," Brand said. "Unfortunately, things didn't go my way, and not just because the Da Vias played their insane hand. Where is Les, by the way?" Brand craned his neck, looking around the room.

"Right here." Les stepped inside from the back door, arms full of bags from the cart.

I jumped to my feet and took the bags from him, grunting at their weight. I set them at the base of the stairs.

Brand and Les hugged, pounding each other's backs in the way that men always seemed to do.

"I wanted to tell you," Brand said, "that there's a traveler menagerie in town, taking advantage of the fealty and Susten Day, I suppose. Maybe they're relatives of yours?"

"What kind of animals do they have?"

"I haven't gone yet, but one of the children went and said he saw snakes, birds, and horses."

Les shrugged.

"Though he also said he saw a dragon, so I don't know

that we can fully trust his information. Going to need to work on his scouting some." Brand laughed and squeezed Les's shoulder.

"Even if they are relatives, they cut their ties with me long ago. I'm a Saldana now."

Brand nodded. "And a good addition you've been, judging by how well you and Lea have done in Yvain, even with all the required secrecy over there. I don't really know how you do it." He said this last part to Lea.

She shrugged. "We make do."

Emile walked through the front door. He saw me and scowled. "Thanks for the help, Legs—" He caught sight of Brand and stopped.

"You must be Emile," Brand said. "You look much like your father. Elena's excited to meet you in person. So am I."

"I—thank you—" Emile seemed confused by Brand's rapid-fire comments.

Brand nodded and then clapped his hands together. "Well, Saldanas. Let me or any of my Family know if you need anything. You're guests in our territory. Otherwise, I'll see you again tomorrow at the fealty."

And with that he strode out the front door.

"Who was that?" Emile asked, looking between the three of us.

"Brando Caffarelli," I said. "Elena's father."

His neck flushed and he closed his eyes. "I looked like an idiot."

"You could look like the biggest idiot in the world and it wouldn't matter because the marriage has already been agreed to."

"Allegra," Lea scolded.

"It's true," I said.

"Nothing is ever set in stone," Lea said. "Not even Family ties."

She walked to the bags at the bottom of the stairs and picked hers up, and I couldn't help but wonder if what she'd said was a clue to the truth of everything, if I had the courage to unravel it.

———

"I'm going to head out," I said from the bottom of the stairs.

"Allegra, wait!" Lea called from above.

I backed away slowly. If I made it outside without rushing, then I could claim I hadn't heard her.

Footsteps pounded on the stairs and I sighed.

"You unpacked already?" she asked me.

I pointed to my birthday scarf twisted around my neck as proof. Of course, unpacking just meant dumping all my things on a chair in my room, except my leathers and dress for the fealty, which I hung carefully in my wardrobe.

"I think maybe you should stay here," Lea said.

I snorted. "Stay here and do what? Sit in the house? Sharpen blades and mix poisons?"

"That would actually be helpful, yes."

I scowled. "I want to see Lovero! You've spent my whole

life talking about it and now that I'm here, I'm not going to hide from it. It's Susten! Shouldn't I be celebrating Safraella with the common?"

Lea hesitated. I knew throwing the worship of Safraella at her would trip her up. She was Safraella's chosen one, after all.

"It might not be safe," she countered.

"How so? We're in Lilyan. Caffarelli territory. You've spent years working toward building peace between the Families. How do you think it will look if you say you believe in peace but not enough to let your Family out of their house?"

"You're rash," she said, but once she jumped to my character faults it meant she was running out of logical arguments. "You don't think before you act. You could do something that will get you in trouble."

"Who would dare stand up to me? A clipper in Lovero, during Susten? None of the other Families can enter Lilyan. They can't reach us."

Lea blinked once. Then again. Her shoulders slumped slightly and I fought against smiling at my success.

"Only for a few hours," she said. "I want to see you back here before midnight."

I dashed out the door, letting it slam shut, cutting off the end of Lea's command.

Free. I was free to do whatever I wanted and Lea wouldn't be around to tell me no.

The streets were busier now that Susten was in full swing.

People were singing and dancing and drinking and making merry, and their enthusiasm spread to me. But my goal wasn't to dance in the street. My freedom wouldn't last, so I needed to use it while I could.

I headed west, toward Ravenna, and the answers it might hold for me.

seven

EVEN THOUGH THE SUN HAD SET, I WAS HOT IN MY dress with my hair draped around my shoulders and back. I tugged at my birthday scarf around my neck. Loveran women kept their hair covered or tied up and if this sort of heat was usual for them, it made sense.

Maybe it would be cooler in Ravenna, since it was closer to the sea.

I continued west, sometimes having to travel north or south a block or two to circumvent raucous gatherings or fenced-off courtyards, but I kept my eyes forward, even as the night seemed to fill with more and more people celebrating Safraella.

I assumed there would be some sort of marker for entering Ravenna, but if there was, I never saw it. Instead, the crowds just kept getting thicker and thicker, pushing me more north in my journey, where the crowd eventually seemed to thin out.

Once I reached Ravenna, I could discreetly ask around about my family, my parents. Find a church or a cleaner's guild who might remember them.

Finally, I pushed my way onto a street where the revelers were more sedate as they walked across the flagstones.

The crowd seemed to break apart, and there before me stood the remains of a house.

The house had burned down to the beams, which leaned against one another or lay collapsed on the ground, blackened. But there were no smoldering embers or ashes, no smoke or the scent of fire. This wasn't fresh destruction but an old ruin no one had removed.

I didn't understand why the common would leave this ruin here as an eyesore. If people had been inside they surely would have perished.

I swallowed and walked closer.

Across from the ruins, where the front door of the house would've been, stood a marble statue of a woman. My breath caught in my throat. The statue wore leathers. A bone mask covered her face and her fists held daggers at her side. The mask was patternless, probably so it could appear to be any clipper, but it was Lea who stood before me, Oleander Saldana carved out of stone, watching over the people who walked past the ruin of her home, her Family.

Eighteen years ago, almost to the day, this fire had been set by the Da Vias, killing the Saldanas. And the residents of Ravenna had left the destruction alone, to stare at it every day as a reminder of what had happened to the Saldanas

59

because the Da Vias had betrayed everyone and turned to another god.

And the statue was of Lea because though she had lost everything, she had emerged stronger with Safraella on her side.

"It's something, isn't it?" a voice asked me.

I turned and found a man, handsome and tall, though not as tall as Les, with blond hair he kept cropped short.

"It was unexpected," I said truthfully.

"It often is for those coming to seek it. There are always new visitors during Susten."

"Because of the festival?" I asked.

He shrugged. "That, or because it's the anniversary of Lea Saldana's victory over the Da Vias. It was a difficult era for Ravenna, losing the Saldanas. It was a long time before the common could once more trust the Da Vias."

I studied him. He wore clean, well-stitched clothes. Not too rich, but certainly well-off. A ruby ring sparkled on his pinky.

"And what about you?" I asked. "Do you trust the Da Vias?"

He stared at the statue. "Who knows who you can really trust in this life?"

I blinked slowly and took him in with new eyes. He had pale skin, like he didn't see the sun often. His stance seemed lazy and relaxed, but his weight remained balanced on his feet for quick movement. And though he wore expensive jewelry, his hands were scarred.

He was not of the common.

I smiled, infusing my eyes with all the false friendliness I could muster. East lay my salvation, but I had no idea how far away the Lilyan and Ravenna border was, and a Da Via would surely know the streets better than a foreign girl fleeing for her life.

He faced me then. "I think you need to come with me now."

He dropped his hand to his belt. It wasn't an overtly threatening gesture but the sense of danger was still present.

I dropped my own hand to my belt and the knife strapped there. "And how do I know if I come with you, you won't just slit my throat?"

"I can give you my word."

"Ah, but who knows who we can really trust in this life?"

"Well, family is a good place to start, Allegra Saldana."

My breath caught in my throat and my blood stilled in my veins. He knew me. Knew who I was. "How do you know my name?"

He shrugged. "Many clues. How you stare at the Saldana shrine different than all the common. The knives on your belt, your boots. Your fashion, clearly from Yvain. Mostly, though, the Family look about you. I've been waiting here, just in case you'd show."

I blinked. The Saldanas tended to be short statured, with dark, curly hair, or sometimes blond. I had the hair color, but had never been short. I didn't really look like Emile, Marcello, or Lea, and certainly not Les. I had never fit with the Saldana Family look.

But he had called me Saldana, not even mistaken me for a Caffarelli.

I swallowed. "I have no Family look about me."

He snorted. "Of course you do. You're just looking at the wrong Family."

I took a step away from him. He was speaking in riddles. "What do you know about it anyway?"

"Oh, that's easy. I'm Valentino Da Via. Your uncle."

Valentino Da Via led me deeper into Ravenna. I made sure to watch the streets as we walked past them, so I wouldn't become more lost, and though I was sure Valentino noticed this, he didn't say anything.

Family. He said he was my family. My uncle. I'd stared at him for so long after this pronouncement that he'd finally laughed at me. My skin flushed and I turned away, only to be halted by his hand on my sleeve.

He was smart. A stronger grip—his hand wrapped around my wrist or shoulder, maybe—and I would have taken it as a threat. But a few fingers on a sleeve could be easily escaped. It showed me he wouldn't stop me if I truly wanted to flee.

I paused. According to him I was somehow related to the Da Vias. The Da Vias were the enemy. And they were liars. But here he was, hinting at the answers I searched for. So I'd agreed to follow him in return for more answers.

I glanced over my shoulder, but the Saldana shrine was lost from sight. I stopped. "I think that's far enough."

He smiled and gestured to a restaurant ahead. "We're just going there. Not much farther now."

I hadn't eaten since that afternoon, and one more block didn't seem like it would make much difference. I followed him the rest of the way.

We were seated immediately on the patio at a table meant for four. The waiter poured us each a glass of wine. Valentino mumbled something in his ear and then shooed him away.

"So, Valentino. You're my *uncle*." I twirled my wineglass. "I don't know if I believe you. Though we share a similar appearance."

"People call me Val. And you sell yourself short. You have much of the Da Via look about you. The hair. The eyes."

"Some of the Saldanas are blond, too, from their Caffarelli lineage." Lea and me being the only ones.

"How is your aunt, by the way?" He sipped his wine, trying to appear as if he didn't truly care about my answer, but his fingers gripped the stem of the glass too tightly.

"Fine," I said. "Holy."

He snorted and then coughed on his wine. He set the glass down and dabbed at his lips.

"Do you know her?" I asked.

"Every clipper knows *of* her now, but yes, I do know her. Or did, anyway. A long time ago."

"Because you were enemies."

63

He examined the pattern on the tablecloth. "I suppose that was true, at the end. But before that, no, we were not enemies. I courted her and she let me. I'd hoped to marry her."

Lea, in a relationship with a Da Via? This Da Via before me? "I don't believe you."

He leaned back in his chair. "Why would I lie?"

"Because Da Vias are liars," I countered.

"Lea has kept things from you."

I turned away, so he couldn't see my face. If I'd had my mask, my expression would've remained hidden.

"And your reaction right there," he continued, "is how I know I've struck truth."

I ground my teeth together. He was right, of course. Because Lea kept me in the dark about so many things, I'd lost any advantage I had in this conversation. Time to regain it.

I loosened my shoulders and relaxed. "You courted Lea. So what? It doesn't mean anything to me."

"I guess not. But I do think those secrets of Lea's are why you agreed to sit down with me instead of fleeing. I would have let you go, you know. I wouldn't have chased you."

"So you claim."

He shrugged and finished his wine. A waiter poured him another glass. "Susten begins tonight, the ninth night after the midsummer new moon. A celebration of Safraella and all She does for us here in Lovero. But you're not Loveran, so why are you really here in Ravenna? Why did you agree to come with me? What questions do you want answered? Because I can see them there, in your eyes, wanting to burst free."

And I did have questions. So many questions. But now that I was sitting across from a Da Via, I found my questions drying up in my throat. I latched on to the first thing that came to mind. "Did you ever marry? Have children?"

He smirked. "Come, now. You didn't even know who I was until I found you at the shrine. I know this isn't what you want to speak about."

"Did you?"

He shook his head. "Never found the right partner."

"Why did you bring me here?" I gestured to the restaurant. "We passed plenty of other places on the way, why here?"

"Because I like their wine."

I didn't believe him. There was another reason he had escorted me this far into Ravenna. The back of my neck itched.

"You say you're related to me." I pictured the empty line on my family tree, leading to a mysterious common woman. "My father was a Saldana. Who was my mother?"

Val looked at me in surprise. "You want to know what happened to her, you mean."

"She died in childbirth."

A slow smile crept over Val's face. "Your mother, Claudia, was my sister."

For a moment, it seemed as if everything paused. The

waiters halted midstride, the diners stopped all conversation, the breeze held its breath.

A Da Via. My mother was a Da Via.

No. It couldn't be true. The Da Vias were the enemies of the Saldanas, had been so for generations. I couldn't be a child of a Saldana and a Da Via union.

But if Val spoke the truth, it would explain so much. It would explain why Lea refused to tell me about my parents, why they didn't want me to travel to Lovero, where I would possibly come into contact with family.

I looked Val in the eye. "I want to know about her."

"Claudia loved sweets when she was a child, the kind that make your hands stick together. Do you have something like that in Yvain?"

I shook my head, twisting this fact over and over in my mind. Claudia. My mother had a name. Claudia. She had liked sweets as a child. It was a tiny fact, nothing really, forgettable in a lifetime of facts and emotions and experiences a person lived. But it was also huge and wonderful and brilliant and the only thing about my mother that was real, that made her seem like more than a blank space on a Family tree.

So he claimed.

My throat tightened, and I reached for my wine, sipping. "You were her younger brother?"

"Yes," he said. "When we were children, she liked to think she was in charge just because she was fifteen months older. Gods, she was insufferable. So domineering. I think it's why she loved your father, though I never saw the appeal of their relationship. He liked to be in control, too. They were a mirror, reflecting themselves to each other."

Behind me waiters danced around the patio.

"You knew my father," I stated.

"Some. Not so much. He died young."

"A lot of Saldanas died young." At the hands of the Da Vias. "Do I . . ." I swallowed. "Do I look like her?"

He smiled again, a more genuine smile, and nodded over my shoulder. "Why don't you take a look yourself?"

I spun and there behind me was not a waiter but a woman, tall, with long blond hair she had twisted around her head and a nose with a bump in the middle just like mine.

"Oh," she breathed, looking at me. "Allegra. I'm so happy to meet you."

eight

I JUMPED TO MY FEET, THE LEGS OF THE CHAIR SCREECH-ing against the patio.

"What is this?" I looked back and forth between them. "Who are you?"

"Calm down." The woman held her hands before her, like she was trying to ease a frantic colt or steady a rocking canal boat. But I was neither.

I pulled my dagger from beneath my belt and held it before me. I didn't know what this was but I wasn't going to fall for it.

"Oh, put the knife away." Val finished off his wine and gestured to the waiter, who stood to the side, wide-eyed at the violence about to erupt around him.

"What is this?" I yelled.

"It's fine," the woman said, keeping her hands before her. "No one's going to hurt you. No one's going to do anything. We're just here to talk."

"Talk about what?" I snapped, but I lowered the knife a touch. She seemed to be unarmed, and judging by how much Val was drinking, he wasn't planning an attack anytime soon. And besides, he'd had me here the entire time and hadn't tried anything. Of course, maybe he'd just been waiting for backup.

"I'm Claudia Da Via," the woman said. She dropped her hands to her sides. "Your mother."

"That's impossible," I said. "My mother is dead. Has been dead for eighteen years."

"And who told you that?" Val asked, eyes wide.

Lea, of course. Lea had told me. My parents were dead. Emile's parents were dead. We were orphans, but not really because we had Lea and Les and Marcello and Faraday and Beatricia. We had a Family, even if our family had been broken.

Claudia slowly took a seat. "Why don't you sit down again and we can talk. We can explain everything."

I swallowed. This wasn't right. Something wasn't right here. I'd spent my whole life drowning in secrets and now I felt like I was drowning in lies.

Leave. I needed to leave. To put the Da Vias behind me. To forget all this.

But how could I forget it if I didn't get any answers?

I slipped my knife beneath my belt and sat down again. But I left my chair pulled out, in case I needed a fast exit.

I swallowed. "You can't be her."

"Why can't I be her?" she asked.

"Because . . ." Because if she *was* my mother, it meant Lea and Les and everyone had lied to me my entire life. And maybe more important, if they had lied to me about that, what else had they lied to me about? "Because my mother died when I was born."

She shook her head. "No, I didn't. I survived childbirth. I survived Lea's attack on the Da Vias. I owe my life to my brother."

Val toasted himself and drank.

"But everyone told me you were dead."

She shrugged. "I can't say why they did that. Well, that's not true. I can say, but without any real proof it would just be conjecture."

Val snorted. "Oh, please, Claudia." He turned to me. "Lea lied to you because she didn't want you to know the truth. Because she knows if you knew the truth she would lose you. And more than anything else in the whole world, Lea refuses to lose anyone."

"And why do you think that is?" I snapped. "Maybe because the Da Vias killed her entire Family?"

Val shrugged but didn't disagree.

"Let's pretend that you *are* my mother and didn't die in childbirth," I said, trying not to look at her. Because if I looked at her, I saw me looking back. An older me, maybe, a me with lines where I didn't have them, but a me nonetheless. "When your Family murdered my father with the rest of the Da Vias, you never thought to reach out to me? To find me? You just abandoned me?"

Val laughed until Claudia shot him a venomous look.

"I spent years looking for you," Claudia, my supposed mother, said. Something flashed in her eyes, dark and menacing, and I was reminded, forcefully, that she was a clipper, too. That she could be deadly. "Countless trips to Yvain and Rennes, searching for you, or a sign of any of the Saldanas. I was alone, though. Our Family head told the others to stay out of it since Lea was *chosen* by Safraella. And Lea knew how to cover her tracks. Knew what she'd done."

"What had she done?" Claudia's tale seemed vague and unspecific. Anyone could say they searched for someone, but who could say whether it was true or not?

"She took you from me," Claudia said.

The world slowed again, seemed to freeze as these words sank into me. "No," I said. "She saved me from the ghosts."

"She took you before the ghosts even appeared. She walked into the Da Via home, killed your father, her own brother, and stole you from your crib. She used the ghosts as a diversion to escape with you."

I shook my head. "No. You're lying."

Lea hadn't done it. She hadn't stolen me, and she certainly hadn't killed my father. He had died in the fire with the rest of the Saldanas. She and Les had gone into the Da Vias' home to rescue me and Emile and Marcello. It was the *Da Vias* who had stolen us.

"I suppose she told you we had stolen you and she was only taking you back?" Val asked.

I focused on my hands as they gripped the tablecloth. The

71

Da Vias were the villains. The Da Vias had turned to another god and killed the Saldanas.

"I would never have given up my child," Claudia said. "She stole you from your true Family. She is a child thief, and she hid the truth from you with lies and secrets."

"No," I said, but my voice was barely a whisper. "You don't know anything."

Liars. They were liars. But she looked so much like me, Claudia. I couldn't deny the familial resemblance. No one could. And Lea and Les had kept secrets from me, had not wanted me to come to Lovero, had left that side of my family tree blank.

And this made sense, what Claudia and Val had told me. This answered everything, revealed all the secrets surrounding me. Explained why I'd never fit.

Everyone knew the Da Vias were liars. But no one said they were the only ones.

"We were there, Allegra." Val leaned back in his chair. "We saw everything. If you don't believe us, just ask someone else. Ask Lea, if you want, or that bastard husband of hers. He was there, too, even though I'd done my best to put my sword through his heart."

I released the tablecloth. "You were the one who killed him?" I asked, staring at Val.

Even the common knew the story, of course. The Da Vias had killed Lea and Les in battle. Then Lea had stood before Safraella Herself and been granted a true resurrection, a return to the life she had left behind. And Lea had accepted, if Les could be brought back, too. And they were and it was a miracle and yet we still had to hide who we were in Yvain since they followed a different god.

"Yes," Val answered. "I killed him. I'd do it again, too."

I threw my wine in Val's face.

He spluttered, the red wine dripping onto his expensive silk. I ran from the table.

"Allegra!" Claudia shouted. But I didn't turn back, didn't look over my shoulder, just fled east, away from the Da Vias.

My heart pounded, filling my ears with its sound. But that was fine, that was good. If I focused on the sound of my heart, then I couldn't hear what it was whispering to me, trailing across my neck. *You don't fit. You don't fit. Don't fit. Don't fit.*

That maybe what the Da Vias had said was the truth. That maybe here were the answers to all of Lea's secrets, if I was just brave enough to see her for what she really was.

nine

†

I RAN THROUGH THE STREETS OF RAVENNA, SHOVING
past the revelers who'd emerged, not caring how angrily
they shouted after me.

I ran until my side ached with sharp pain and my chest
heaved for air. I ran until all my tangled thoughts and emotions had burned up, drifted away from me and left my head
and heart empty.

I stopped, hand pressed to my side, gulping. A woman
passed by me, dressed in red velvet, wearing a half mask that
covered her eyes with leather ivy.

"What city is this?" I managed to gasp at her.

She glared at me, and I knew what she saw: a strange
girl, out of breath, wearing outdated fashions, hair loose and
tangled about her face, barking questions.

She sniffed, and deigned to answer "Lilyan" before she
strode away.

I closed my eyes, relief easing the tension in my limbs. I was safe from the Da Vias. They couldn't reach me here.

I walked forward, letting my body cool, my heartbeat slow, the stitch in my side ease.

But it wasn't the stitch that was the source of my pain.

Liars. The Da Vias were liars.

But I'd long been privy to the fact that Lea was keeping something from me, keeping secrets. And the Da Vias, Val and Claudia—if that was even her real name—had been the only ones who had offered me any sort of explanation for those secrets surrounding me.

I found a wall and leaned against it, clenching my eyes shut.

I thought about Lea and Les and Emile, back at our house. Enjoying the festival, maybe. Or each other's company. Fitting together.

I couldn't face them. Not now. Not yet. I couldn't look in their eyes and search for the truth, ask them if they'd lied to me for my entire life. Ask if my mother was alive. If Lea had stolen me.

If I was a Da Via.

Because if I did, I would find the truth there, whatever it was, and I wasn't ready for it.

I needed time. The Susten Day celebration was just beginning. Now that I was safe in Lilyan, I could take in the sights until I was ready to see my Family again. Until I was ready to ask them questions.

My stomach growled. I'd never gotten a chance to eat at the restaurant with Val Da Via. Food always made bad situations better.

I followed the crowd, heading east. After a few blocks the street opened to a market area. The festival wasn't, say, one specific festival, but instead multiple little parties and revelries that ebbed and flowed throughout the streets of Lovero, and congregated where the food and music and entertainment set up shop. But in this market I couldn't help but think I'd stumbled across one of the hearts of the festival, or perhaps a heart of Lovero itself.

The size of the square meant there were dozens of stands with food and drink, lines and crowds of people at each one. Stilt walkers made their careful way through the crowd, fire breathers found corners to practice their trade to oohs and aahs. Children gathered around puppets, cloth and shadows alike, and I took note of the shows that seemed to attract the attention of adults, too.

The market square stretched farther south, but the crowd was so thick in that direction I couldn't see what secrets and delights it held.

The ache in my heart eased some at so much excitement, and I allowed myself a quick smile. Everything could be fine. I was in a different city, a different country! This was one of my dreams come true. I was seeing the world.

I had some money, enough for food and maybe something else. I headed to the nearest stand and stood in line. I didn't even know what kind of food I was waiting for, but judging how my mouth watered at the salty smell that wafted from the flames behind the stall, it didn't matter.

The crowd shifted and a girl in front of me jabbed her elbow into my chest. She turned and looked me up and down. She was very pretty, with dark skin and black hair twisted on top of her head in the Loveran style, a few tendrils artfully free to frame her delicate face.

She had two friends with her, and they, too, turned.

Elbow clearly didn't like what she saw because she sniffed once and her left eyebrow raised haughtily. Much of her prettiness fled. "I would appreciate it if you would keep your hands to yourself."

I blinked as my stomach flopped. I was trying to escape from my bad thoughts, not to find them somewhere else. "I'll keep that in mind the next time you decide to flail your elbows like a hooked eel."

Though it was hard to see in the dark night and past her dark skin, her face reddened ever so slightly. Her friend to the right couldn't control herself and let her jaw drop open. Guess they were used to getting their way.

Elbow narrowed her eyes and examined me up and down again, this time exaggerating it to almost comic effect. I stilled. Let her look. I was nothing if not proud.

"It must be hard for a country churl like yourself to understand the social niceties that come with a festival like this." She sniffed. "I mean, leaving your hair down and wearing such a simple dress? You poor dear."

My smile stretched thin and tight but before I could retort, or slap her across the face, which was what I really ached to do, a man shouted from an alley to our right.

The man raced into the crowd, shoving people aside in his haste, ignoring their cries and complaints. Behind him a shadow emerged from the alley, right on his tail.

I caught my breath and leaned forward. The man dashed, running alongside our line, and the clipper chased him, his cloak flaring out behind.

My heart raced. The clipper didn't care about the crowd or witnesses, he only cared about his mark.

The mark shoved past a woman and, seeing an opportunity, I stuck my foot out, catching the mark around his ankle. He shouted and fell to the street with a *whumph*.

The clipper wasted no time. The dagger was in his hand and with a quick jab the fleeing man was dead, the street collecting his blood.

Most everyone averted their eyes. Even Elbow and her friends, shocked though they seemed, dropped their eyes to their shoes.

Purple thorns decorated the clipper's mask. He studied me like Elbow had, but his bone mask lacked a sneer.

I inclined my head. "Allegra Saldana, brother."

His eyes met mine and he bowed his head.

"Sister Saldana." His voice was surprisingly soft behind his mask. "Welcome to our home. I hope you're enjoying the festivities."

The dead man's blood crept closer and I took a step away. No need to stain my boots. I glanced at Elbow and her friends, who kept their gazes locked on their shoes. "It's still early."

"That it is. You will be at the fealty?"

The fealty. The whole reason we'd come to Lovero in the first place. It was a ball, with food and dancing and maybe clippers trying to stab each other in the back.

Of course, who cared about what other clippers wanted to do when it turned out it was one's family who wielded the sharpest knife.

"Sister?" the Caffarelli clipper questioned.

I'd slipped into my dark thoughts. I nodded to him and smiled. "I will."

"Then I will see you there. Enjoy the night, sister." He crouched over the body of his mark and slipped a coin in the man's mouth, a signal to Safraella that this man had been murdered in Her name. Then he returned to the alley. Everyone gave him a wide berth, though they greeted him with respect and a touch of awe.

Elbow and her friends stared freely at me with a mix of horror and something else I couldn't quite decipher.

"It strikes me as strange," I said conversationally, "that you're so rude to strangers you meet on your streets when any one of them could be clippers. Do you value your life so little?"

Not that I would kill some stuck-up Loveran girls for simply playing to their stereotype, but still.

"We apologize so deeply, Lady Saldana." Elbow clutched her hands together and bowed her head. The other two followed her lead. "It's just, usually clippers are more . . ." She paused, unsure how to continue.

"I have my hair up all night behind my bone mask. If I want to leave it down, then I leave it down." Not that I needed to explain myself.

"As is your right and privilege."

To show her true and utter support of me, Elbow reached behind her head and unpinned her own hair. It tumbled to her shoulders in a free wave. It didn't necessarily make her prettier, but it did make her seem friendlier. The girl on the left immediately copied Elbow, but the one on the right widened her eyes in shock. She glanced at me once before staring at Elbows and her other friend.

"Mebba," Elbow snapped. The remaining friend unclipped her own hair and let it fall around her shoulders.

"Next!" the man at the food stand yelled. Elbow and her friends were next but they ushered me forward. I wasn't going to complain. I was starving, and any chance to get food sooner was an opportunity I was willing to take. It turned out the stand was selling skewered fish, fried in oil. But when I went to pay, the man waved my money aside. "No charge for clippers."

When I turned around, Elbow and her friends had vanished and I wouldn't have been surprised to see them later, hair carefully repinned.

Two cleaners appeared beside the dead body and loaded it

onto a stretcher. They would identify the body and contact his family. Loveran death was quick and efficient.

I headed south toward the heavier crowds of the market, blowing on the pieces of fish on the wooden skewers, willing them to cool so I could ease the pains in my stomach. Finally, burned tongue be damned, I bit into the fish.

My mouth filled with steam, but the fish was meaty and flaky and tender and the oil made the skin crunch between my teeth.

I finished the rest of the skewer and the next one, trying to savor the fish as much as possible while fighting the urge to shove it down my throat as quickly as I could. I was mostly successful, though, and wondered what kind of food I could find elsewhere in the market.

To my right a loud roar filled the night. People screamed and jumped. I turned and before me, separated by stakes and ropes from the rest of the festivities, was a traveler menagerie.

Travelers hailed from the country of Mornia in the east, and were called travelers because their gods let them travel across the dead plains unharassed by the angry ghosts. They were menagerie people and some of them visited different countries and cities with their exotic animals.

The roaring came again from deep within the menagerie and my feet carried me to the entrance. A man watched the crowd dispassionately. He was tall, like Les, and shared the same sort of olive skin and black hair, but outside of that they didn't look much alike. The man smirked at me. He held up a single finger for the price and I didn't even hesitate, fishing for the coin in my purse and handing it over. The man swept his arm forward, ushering me inside.

I took my coin purse and shoved it down the bodice of my dress, then used my scarf to hide my necklace. I knew from Les that travelers worshipped Boamos, a god of thievery and wealth. Better to be safe.

The menagerie was set up with what seemed to be portable cages, the backs and sides made of solid wood and the front metal bars latched tightly together. Whether that was to keep the animals in or the people out, I couldn't be sure. The cages pointed away from the marketplace, no use giving the crowd a free look, and snaked around, creating little pockets of different sights and types of animals.

Immediately I found a cage of colorful birds. They were no bigger than the canal sparrows in Yvain, but each was a different color: jewel green, bloodred, night black, bone white. They flitted around, making little peeping sounds. I watched them for a few moments and then drifted to the next cage. More birds, loud parrots that screeched and squawked and snapped at each other. I didn't linger.

I continued past the birds and found monkeys with humanlike faces, their eyes wide and sad. A child to my right flung a piece of fruit into the cage and the monkeys raced for it, all seeming humanity erased as they hissed and screamed at one another, fighting for the food.

Loverans ambled around, drifting from cage to cage at their leisure, spending more time in front of the animals that caught their eyes. And travelers stood guard, seemingly bored with the entire thing, though Les had told me travelers often made enough from a single menagerie to support several families for several years. Once the money ran low, the families would gather their animals and head out for another city to earn money.

I skipped past the lizards since I could smell them from a distance and didn't relish getting closer. There was a ring of horses, each one exquisitely bred. Lea would've appreciated them more than I did.

My stomach flopped. I moved away from the horses. I didn't want to think about Lea. I was here to enjoy the menagerie, to take my mind off my Family. Off everything.

A crowd bustled in the next alcove. I slipped past people so deftly they barely even noticed until I'd reached the front and the animal that had drawn so much attention.

A tiger paced in the cage, mouth slightly open, panting, yellow eyes staring at the crowd. It walked back and forth, back and forth, its eyes unseeing, lost in its own thoughts, maybe.

What did tigers dream of when they were awake and trapped in a cage? I couldn't even imagine.

I swallowed.

Les had told me about them, how their stripes were orange and gold and black. This one's stripes tapered to white on his chest and stomach, his cheeks, and the end of his tail, which flicked every time he turned. And he was so beautiful. But as I watched him, my chest tightened, and I blinked my eyes rapidly at the tears that crept up on me.

I couldn't stand to see something so beautiful, something that only longed to be free, trapped and caged like he was.

I slipped back through the crowd, not even pausing when the tiger roared. Even if it seemed like he was roaring at my retreating figure, I knew he was roaring at something only he could see.

A home and family lost, maybe. Or his freedom.

ten

I FOUND AN ALCOVE OF MENAGERIE CAGES THAT WERE blessedly empty of Loverans and I caught my breath. It was cooler without so many bodies pressed together.

The animals, while distracting at first, were losing their hold on my thoughts.

These cages in this alcove were smaller, some even stacked on top of one another, and there were no bars, but instead tiny, thin wires, woven together to make a sort of lace big enough to see through, but too tiny to fit even my smallest finger through the gap.

Tiny cages, like mine, growing smaller every day.

I leaned closer.

A snake struck at me, smashing against the wire lattice. I jumped back and the snake coiled around itself, yellow eyes watching me as its tongue flicked in and out.

"Do not be scared," an accented voice said behind me. "He cannot hurt you."

I turned. The traveler boy had hazel eyes. It was the first thing I noticed about him, mostly because they were at the same level as mine, but also because they were striking, set against his olive skin. He wore a strange, red-and-blue cloth hat, circular, that sat close to his scalp, allowing room for his dark hair to be tied at the base of his skull.

"I'm not scared." I looked back to the snake. The scales above its eyes made it seem like it had horns.

"Hmm." The traveler boy took a step until he stood beside me. "That is not what your jump said."

"I was startled. There's a difference."

"Hmm," the boy said again. I got the feeling he said it frequently, a noncommittal noise that was yet, somehow, completely committal. "You are not from around here."

I faced him. He was nice to look at. His cheekbones were a bit too sharp for my taste, though it may have just been the lanterns hanging from the ropes above the menagerie to better illuminate the animals. "Neither are you."

"I am a traveler," he said. "I am never from *around here*."

"Except for Mornia."

The boy smiled slowly, his teeth very white in the dark. He reached out and his fingers lifted a strand of my hair and tugged. I let him.

"You leave your hair down when all the Loverans pin it or cover it. And your dress is more practical. Rennes, I would say. Yvain."

My turn to smile. "Oh, I can dress impractically if I choose."

Flirting. We'd slipped into flirtation and I hadn't even noticed. I took in the boy as a whole. Close to my age and my same height. He seemed fit and strong. His left forearm had scars along the length of it. From tiger claws, I knew, which meant he was trusted enough to handle the large cats.

This. Maybe this was what I needed. Maybe this would help me forget everything.

The boy spread his arms wide. "Do you like what you see?"

I nodded. "Yes."

He laughed, a single bark, seemingly amused by my brazenness. "Well, I am Nev." He wore a coin pouch on his hip and something inside set the bag squirming.

"Allegra." I pointed at the pouch. "It seems your coins wish to escape."

Nev untied it from his belt. "It is not for coins."

He loosened the drawstring and carefully slipped his hand inside. When he pulled it back out he had a small snake draped across his fingers. The white snake had black eyes and a sort of pearlescent sheen about it. It looked very delicate and almost . . . cute, if something cold and scaly could qualify. "Her name is Kuch."

"'Darling,'" I translated, and he looked up at me with wide eyes, surprised. "My . . ." I paused, never quite sure how to refer to Les or even Lea to strangers. "My uncle is half traveler."

He raised his eyebrows. It was uncommon for travelers to have children with people who were not other travelers.

I kept my eyes on the snake and reached out a finger. "Can I touch her?"

Nev yanked his hand and the snake away. My fingers floated in the air between us, awkward.

"No," he said. "She is venomous. She looks sweet but she is only that way with me." He slipped Kuch back into her pouch and cinched it tight once more. "She tries to bite anyone who does not smell like me."

I dropped my hand to my side. "Then why do you keep her?"

He blinked, like he'd never been asked the question before. Maybe he hadn't. Or maybe he didn't actually show his deadly little viper to that many girls.

"I am really good with the snakes, and I like her."

He shook his head. The way he said *like*, though, made me think he actually cared about his little pet more than he was willing to admit to a strange girl wandering around his menagerie.

I pointed to the horned snake that had struck at the wire. "What about him?"

Nev stepped beside me, close enough that I could feel the heat of his skin against mine. "He is venomous, too, and angry. He does not like the lanterns." He pointed a single finger at the rope lights above us.

"Then why don't you blow them out for him?"

"Because then all you paying guests would not be able to see him, and if you could not see him, you would not pay to come back tomorrow with your friends and all their money."

"Huh."

He looked at me, the shadows hiding his expression. "What?"

"It just seems because you're responsible for him, for all the animals, you'd want to make them happy."

He shrugged. "They are happy. Most of the time. We take good care of them for their entire lives, and every now and then they have to come traveling with us. How do you think we earn enough money to feed them?" He pointed behind me at the crowd of people I'd left behind. "The tiger needs a whole goat every five to ten days."

I grabbed his hand and traced my fingers along the scars on his arm. I felt more than heard him catch his breath. I couldn't help my smile. I liked being able to catch him off guard. "You take care of the tigers, too," I said. "That's what these scars mean, right?"

He looked me directly in the eyes, and then grabbed my fingers with his own. His hand was callused, but not like a clipper's. Our calluses were from weapons. Nev's calluses were in different spots, and I suddenly felt a desperate need to explore every inch of his hands to find each one.

"Yes. Tigers and snakes." He leaned closer to me. "It can be very dangerous. *I* can be very dangerous, so maybe you do not want to get so close."

His statement sounded more like a question. Or an invitation. I grinned, his fingers warm in mine.

"Oh, I know all about danger, and about getting closer." I tugged him toward me and he smiled again, the same slash of white teeth in his wide mouth.

"Come." He pulled me away from the snakes.

"Where are we going?"

"Away from here."

He drew me past another row of cages. A traveler woman shouted a question to Nev in Mornian and he responded, but I didn't know enough of the language to understand all that was said.

Nev pushed aside a curtain of colorful fabric and then we were away from the menagerie and the Loverans and everyone else and instead behind the cages in an area the travelers had crafted as their own space, safe from prying eyes. There was a small table, made from a barrel and a piece of wood, and stools encircling it. A bottle of what appeared to be wine sat corked on the table with tiny glasses beside it. Canvas had been draped overhead, to protect them from too much sun, or rain.

But Nev pulled me past the table, into a darkened area made by the backs of two menagerie cages. I stepped into the corner, spine pressed against the wooden walls, and pulled him after me into the shadows.

He leaned closer, but then paused, his grin slipping. "This is fine? You will not have friends looking for you?"

By friends, I knew he meant a suitor, someone who would take offense at the two of us sneaking off together. But I couldn't help thinking about my Family. I'd been gone awhile.

I shook my head. "No. No one to worry about—"

He pressed his mouth against mine, cutting me off. His lips were warm and he tasted like oranges and something else I couldn't name. I tried not to think about how I probably tasted like the fish I'd been eating.

He pulled away for breath but I tugged him forward again. This. This was what I needed. Knowing it was temporary, that the lanterns at night, the festival, this boy who kissed me, would all simply be a memory in a few days made me want him even more, made me pull him closer, to keep him with me forever if only I kissed him hard enough.

Nev made a noise against my lips and slid his hand from my hip to the front of my bodice. The coins I had stashed there clinked together.

Nev's hand paused, lips still pressed against mine. Then he pulled away. He reached two fingers past the top of my bodice, purposely not touching my skin, even though my skin practically ached for him to touch me. He hooked the loop of my coin purse and pulled it free of my bodice.

He held it in his palm and then looked up at me. I couldn't read his expression. It was dark, but I also didn't know him well enough to know what he was thinking as he held my coins and stared at me.

"Did you think I would steal them from you?" His voice was quiet and still. Offense. That was what his expression meant.

I grabbed my coin purse and tugged it off his palm. He lowered his hand.

"Yes," I answered truthfully. Lying would get us nowhere,

and anyway, I'd had enough lies today.

His eyes narrowed.

"Boamos is a god of thievery and wealth and it didn't seem right to leave any of my wealth so open to thievery," I said. "I meant no insult by it."

"We follow his tenets of wealth. We do not steal. Only children steal. It is permitted because they are children."

I shrugged one shoulder, hooking my coin purse back on my hip. "I didn't know. I meant no disrespect. If I thought you a common thief, I wouldn't have come back here with you."

He dropped his gaze to the ground.

"Do you regret bringing me back here?" I asked quietly.

He shook his head. "No."

"Do you want me to leave?"

"No." More forceful this time, and he raised his eyes to meet mine again.

"I'm sorry," I said.

"People think we are thieves. We are not thieves."

I grabbed his hand and slowly pulled him toward me again. "Why do you care what the common think?" I asked. "You do not share the same god, and if one of your gods commands that you steal, then steal and be not ashamed of it. Let them worship their own gods."

He pulled his fingers free and stepped back. "You are one of them."

I exhaled and leaned against the corner. I'd wanted distraction from my life, from the thoughts and truths that were twisting around inside my head, not more problems. "One what?"

"Murderers. Have you come here to murder me?"

I laughed. I couldn't help it. He frowned.

"I'm sorry," I said. "I'm not laughing at you. Not really. But yes, I am a disciple of Safraella. A clipper. And no, I haven't come to murder you. A clipper wouldn't murder in the name of Safraella without their bone mask." I pointed at my face. "No bone mask. No death."

"How do I know you will not come and find me later?"

I fought against a sigh. "Has someone paid to have you killed?"

He shook his head slowly, not taking his eyes off me. "Not as far as I know."

"Then you're fine. I'll tell you a secret." I leaned closer to him. "Most clippers don't kill unless they're getting paid."

I tapped my coin purse and the coins clinked together. I leaned back.

Nev took this all in. I could practically see him rearranging me in his mind, taking what he thought I'd been and changing me into what I was.

Lea had explained how some people could never really wrap their heads around the idea that clippers could be people, too. Even Loverans who made their home side by side with the Families and welcomed their dark work. If Nev was one of those people, there would be no continuing with him.

"One last time," I said. "Do you want me to leave?"

"No. No." He must have come to a conclusion because he rubbed the top of his head, adjusting his hat, before he stepped closer once more. "It is just, I have never met a clipper before."

"That you know of."

His eyes widened and I wondered if I'd pushed him too far. But then he nodded and smiled. "That I know of."

"What gave me away?" I asked.

"You called everyone the common. Like they are below you. And then your talk about the gods."

I hooked my fingers around his belt and pulled him against me again. "Clippers are simply people, you know. For the most part." I whispered this against his throat and he swallowed. "Sometimes we're just looking for distractions."

He tilted my chin up. "I can help you with that."

And once more his lips tasted like oranges and when he pressed his body to mine again he somehow felt closer, with fewer secrets between us.

eleven

†

A GROUP OF MEN ENTERED THE BACK AREA, AND WHEN they spied us, they jeered good-naturedly until Nev grabbed my hand and pulled me away from their common room.

We entered a sort of hallway, with curtains draped everywhere. A few travelers peeked out at us as we walked past, but when they saw Nev they went back to whatever it was they'd been doing.

We reached a blue curtain on the right and Nev held it aside, gesturing me in.

The room was tiny compared to the common area we'd just left. A small bed stood to the left, a pallet, really, on top of some crates, with blankets and pillows, and a single stool sat beside a table that wasn't much bigger than the stool itself.

Nev lit a lamp and the yellow light filled the small space, illuminating its tininess even more. He set Kuch, still in her pouch, on the table.

"Is this where you live?" I sat on the stool.

He sat on the pallet across from me. "This is where I sleep."

The walls and ceiling of the room were made of more curtains. They had been secured to the ground but gaps in the corners allowed surprisingly fresh air to circulate. The lamp flickered on the table.

"The stool is not comfortable," he stated. And he wasn't wrong.

I snorted and slipped off the stool to sit beside him on his bed.

He gave me a strange look I couldn't quite decipher. Like maybe he was surprised I had so easily capitulated.

And maybe I should have been surprised, too. I had come to the menagerie to try to forget the things I had learned. And it was working, at least as long as I was focused on Nev.

And I was focused on him. I liked him. I didn't know I could like someone so quickly, and yet here I was, in his room, my leg pressed against his in the warmth of the night.

I slipped my hand behind his neck and pulled him toward me, ending the distance between us.

Kissing him was everything I wanted it to be. Better than before, if that was even possible.

We kissed and kissed and kissed in his room, only breaking apart for breath, or to shift position, or to draw closer to each other. I had no idea how long we spent like that, tangled together. It could have been minutes, or hours even. The sun could have risen and set again and I would have known nothing of the outside world. Just this tiny world of Nev's room and Nev's hands and breath and hoarse chuckles as he pressed his lips against my throat.

He slid his hands up my ribs and across the stiff bodice of my dress. He grumbled in frustration, at the lack of access.

I laughed and pulled away. My lips felt hot and I was sure my hair was a tangled mess.

"Sorry." I tapped the front of my bodice.

"Before now," he said, "I really liked the dress."

I smiled. "Me too. But a break does sound nice. I could use something to drink."

"That I can help you with." He stood and offered me his hand, pulling me to my feet.

"Don't you need to bring Kuch?" I pointed at the bag on the table.

Nev shook his head. "She is fine."

Then we were out through the curtain door and heading back down the hall toward the common room.

The men from before sat around the table, smoking and drinking and playing cards.

They waved Nev over and he snatched two of the small glasses and the bottle from the table. The men complained but Nev waived them aside, pouring the liquid into the glasses and handing one to me.

"What is it?" I sniffed it dubiously. I expected it to have the dry, burning scent of strong liquor but it didn't smell anything like that. It actually smelled slightly earthy.

"It is *ahlo kheel*. It is good. You will like it."

Nev drank his in one swift gulp. The rest of the travelers watched, waiting to see if I'd back out. But I'd never been a coward, and certainly not when it came to food. Or drink.

I poured the liquid into my mouth. It was thicker than I thought it would be, more viscous. I swallowed, then coughed. "It's oil!"

The men laughed at my surprise and Nev smiled, taking the glass from me and putting it back on the table. "Yes." He nodded. "It is good for you."

"I'm sure it is," I said, "but I didn't know you could drink it."

Nev nodded and pulled out a chair for me to sit at the table. The other men scooted over, making room for both of us. "We do."

Nev gestured at one of the men, who scowled but then got up from the table to rustle through a crate. When he returned it was with a wooden plate filled with what looked like cured and salted meats and another bottle with more oil, this one not as green.

Nev poured me another small glass of the new oil.

"More?" I asked. "Doesn't all oil just taste the same?"

The men laughed, but there was no malice in it. A few of them speared slices of meat and shoved them in their mouths. My stomach growled.

"Try it," Nev said.

I took my glass and sipped gently. The men cheered at my surprised expression. The oil had a sweet, fragrant taste to it. "Like della fruit," I said.

Nev passed me the tray of meat. "Many things can make oil. Some oils are better for breakfast, and some for dinner or dessert. And some for playing cards while traveling with Culda's blessings."

The slice of meat was heavily salted, but it was tender and sweet beneath the salt and I helped myself to a second slice.

Nev grabbed the deck of cards and dealt to everyone.

I swallowed, and took another small sip from the della fruit oil. "I don't know how to play."

"It is easy," Nev said. "Even children play."

"Well," I said, gathering my cards before me, "I certainly hope I can best a child."

The game was indeed easy to play. There were ghost cards and king cards and a single god card. Some kings could beat some ghosts and some ghosts could beat kings and the god card could beat everything. We took turns laying down our cards, attacking the other players, defeating cards that had been played against us until only one player remained to take the pot of coins wagered before the start of the round.

The men were competitive but friendly, with good-natured jokes and jeering. A few of them only spoke Mornian, but we were able to communicate easily with gestures and help from the others.

When we finished another round, Nev got to his feet and pulled me after him.

The men complained, asking us to stay, but Nev patted his empty coin purse and then we were free of the common room, out among the menagerie once more.

Nev took my hand as we walked past the cages and something trilled in my stomach. I bumped his shoulder with mine and he chuckled. Lovero was so different from Rennes, from Yvain. It had brought me this night, which had been full of Nev and his hands and lips and smile and laugh, and the company of the other men and games and salted meats and oil to drink, which I'd actually started to like by the end of my second glass.

And this was nice. Kissing Nev had been nice, too, and fun. But this, walking with him in the night, in comfortable silence, was almost better.

I glanced over at him. He smiled at me.

The menagerie, the travelers, Nev, all were temporary things, of course. They no more called Lovero home than I did. They chose where they wanted to go, and just went.

I had a choice, though, too. Yvain or Ravenna. Saldana or Da Via. Family or family.

My hands shook and I pulled my fingers free from Nev's. The usually crowded menagerie was surprisingly empty. Empty enough that I began to wonder what time it was. I frowned as Nev led me through the menagerie and toward the exit.

The tiger roared and Nev paused. It roared again, and Nev sighed, pinching the bridge of his nose.

"What is it?" I asked.

"I must deal with something." His voice was low and resigned. I followed him as he strode to the far side of the menagerie where the tiger was displayed.

The space was empty of Loverans for the time being. But there was someone in front of the tiger cage. A traveler woman with strong shoulders and hair almost as short as Brother Faraday's, her skin brown even beneath the menagerie lanterns.

She spoke quietly to the tiger. But he pinned his ears and bared his teeth. The whites of his eyes shone brightly and he crouched in the back corner of the cage.

"Perrin!" Nev barked at the woman.

She turned, and when she found Nev she smiled slowly.

Nev asked her something in Mornian. It was too quick and complicated for me to work out. The woman, Perrin, responded.

They conversed, Nev using short, clipped words and Perrin speaking slowly, almost languidly. She glanced at me once, but otherwise paid me no mind.

Finally, she laughed and strode away.

The tiger kept his ears pinned, but I could read the tension easing from his shoulders as Perrin left.

"One moment," Nev said to me.

He walked behind the tiger cage and returned with a tarp. He tossed it over the cage and the tiger made a sort of growling sound before Nev covered him from sight.

"What was that about?" I asked as Nev returned to me.

He shook his head and led me back toward the exit. "She teases the tiger."

"Why?" I asked. Teasing a caged animal seemed cruel, especially for a traveler who raised and cared for animals.

"Because she knows it will anger me. He is my tiger. I take care of him."

"Why does she want to anger you?" I asked.

Nev exhaled slowly. "She is . . . angry with my family. She does not let me forget it. She is a bully."

We'd reached the entrance to the menagerie and he led me outside. "I have had enough of Perrin, though," he said. "Come."

Then he slowed his pace, content to walk beside me as we strolled through the streets.

"I'm jealous of your life."

His eyes creased in disbelief. "Why?"

"You surround yourself with these amazing animals. You travel wherever you want. You see the world. You're free."

He tilted his head. "I travel for my family. Earn money. It is my role. I do not feel free. But I do not want to talk about the menagerie. I live with it all the time while we are here."

He inhaled deeply, then turned and faced me. "Tell me. What is fun to do outside the menagerie?"

I twisted a piece of my hair. I hadn't actually done much, besides visit the menagerie and then have fun with Nev. I supposed we could explore together.

I smiled, but before I could answer another voice spoke up.

"Yes, Allegra. Please enlighten us about what could be so fun."

I turned and found a man directly behind me, arms crossed over his chest, scowl on his face.

Les.

twelve

LES STARED AT ME AND NEV. I COULD PRACTICALLY hear his teeth grinding.

Les was angry. Les never got angry, not really. Sure, sometimes he swore when he hurt himself or one of us got in a good shot while sparring, but actually angry like this? Never. That had always been Lea's expertise.

"Who are you?" Nev stood in front of me. It was kind of endearing, how he thought he was going to protect me.

Les spat in return, something in Mornian that made Nev bristle.

I stepped between them before things could get out of hand. "Everything is fine, just calm down."

"Calm down?" Les narrowed his eyes. It seemed I was playing with a delicate bomb here. I needed to defuse the situation.

I faced Nev. "It's fine, he's my family." Nev relaxed. I leaned closer and lowered my voice, well aware Les could probably still hear us. "I'll see you later."

He grabbed my hand and kissed my knuckles. "*Will* I see you again, *kalla?*" Beautiful.

I leaned forward and kissed him, quickly, to leave him wanting more. "Yes. Until the festival ends."

He nodded. "Until the festival ends."

Les shifted behind me.

I had no idea if I was lying to Nev or not, but I wanted it to be the truth. Nev had been the single bright spot in my life since I'd reached Lovero. It had only been a few hours, but my life had been completely overturned in that time, and Nev had been warm and simple and sweet and I suspected I would want more of that in the next few days.

Nev nodded briskly to Les and then headed back into the menagerie.

I watched him go, knowing as soon as I faced Les, his anger awaited me. Finally, I couldn't hold it off anymore. I took a deep breath and turned.

And there he stood, arms still crossed over his chest, jaw still tight, even tighter than it had been, maybe, if that was possible.

"You're angry." Sometimes stating the obvious could end the situation. Or it did with Lea, anyway. She didn't like to think she was too predictable.

"What do you think?" he asked.

"I'm not sure," I said carefully. "I guess it all depends on why you're angry at me . . ."

"Ghosts weep, Allegra," Les swore. "Can you honestly be so blind?"

I didn't respond. I didn't want to make him angrier.

He dropped his arms to his side and his fingers twitched like they searched for something to do. Strangle me, perhaps.

And then he hugged me, arms wrapped around me tightly, chin pressed against the top of my head.

"We didn't know where you were," he whispered to me harshly. "This isn't Yvain, where we only have to worry about ghosts and lawmen. There are people who would hurt you. Clippers who would hate you purely because you carry the Saldana name." Les released me.

"We're safe in Lilyan," I said. "I wasn't in any danger." Lies. I hadn't stayed in Lilyan. If the Da Vias had wanted to kill me, they could have.

Les shook his head. "You told Lea you would be back by midnight. Dawn is approaching."

"I got distracted by the menagerie."

We walked down the street. "Just the menagerie?"

I scowled. "No," I said. "That wasn't the only reason."

Les sighed. "You should stay away from him. He is dangerous."

"How can you say that, *you* of all people?"

"I say that because I used to *be* one of them. I have very few memories of my childhood in Mornia. But I know when they travel, it is a chance for them to make as much money as possible, and they won't shy away from that. But it's also a chance for them to spread their wings, so to speak. They will be needlessly reckless. It is dangerous. Every time they travel, some won't return, for whatever reason. He could bring trouble."

I looked at Les then. Really looked at him. Had Nev seemed safe to me because Les had always seemed safe to me in the past? Les was only half traveler on his mother's side, but still. They clearly shared a heritage.

But I knew what it must be like for the travelers. To feel bound and trapped and then want to live wildly while you had freedom, even if it was just for a moment, really. A small breath in a lifetime of feeling unable to breathe.

And anyway, what right did he have? Lea and Les had lied to me my whole life. Had stolen me from my true Family. They were the ones who were dangerous. Who I needed to stay away from.

"He's not like that," I countered.

"They're all like that."

"You don't know him."

Les glowered. It didn't really matter. We'd reached the house and I knew this argument between us was just a glimpse at what was waiting for me inside when I faced Lea.

I swallowed.

"Come," Les said gruffly. He was trying to remain angry with me, but he, too, knew the yelling and the arguments that awaited me.

I couldn't escape this confrontation. I couldn't escape

what they had done to me. They couldn't keep lying to me. Not when I told them I knew the truth.

There would be no more secrets between us.

———————

"I told you to not stay out later than midnight," Lea said as soon as I entered the house.

Les leaned against the kitchen counter. I slumped on the couch, feeling my body relax. I tugged at my scarf, freeing my necklace. I was tired and more than anything sought my bed.

I stared at Lea, all righteous anger. Like she had any right to it.

You stole me.

"It was an accident," I said instead. Mostly true. "I'm sorry." Not true at all.

My whole life is a lie.

I glanced around the room but it was just the three of us. "Where's Emile?"

Does he know? Was he complicit in your lies? Your secrets?

"Don't change the subject—" Lea said at the exact same time Les said, "Out with Elena Caffarelli."

Caged. I remained caged while he got to fly free. Yes, I'd had my own time with Nev, but I'd had to take that, steal the time to be with him.

It had been worth it.

I narrowed my eyes. "So, Emile gets to go out and enjoy the Susten festival with his betrothed as long as he wants.

But I'm only given a few hours, and then am scolded like a child when I forget the time?"

I didn't belong here.

Lea's cheeks reddened. I'd scored her.

"Emile gets more freedom because he's shown us that he can be responsible with it."

I shook my head. "No. Emile gets more freedom because he's Emile and he doesn't want it. Because he does everything you ask and tell him to do, like a good little Family member, like a perfect-fitting Saldana."

You're the reason I never belonged. I'm a stolen child.

Lea pinched the bridge of her nose.

"Allegra." Les sighed, the fight draining out of both of them. "We're only trying to keep you safe."

No. They were only trying to keep me caged, with lies and half-truths and betrayals.

But I knew the truth about it now. My whole life I had felt like I didn't belong with them. That all I did was disappoint them, and all they did was disappoint me. And now I knew the reason for that was because I wasn't a Saldana. Was never supposed to be a Saldana. I was a Da Via.

Lovero, Ravenna, this was where I belonged. With my true family and Family. With them I would finally fit.

My skin flushed. I opened my mouth, ready to confront them about everything.

"I know," I said instead, the fight leaking out of me. Maybe I could keep secrets, too. Maybe I could be the liar for a change. "I know."

I slept through the next day, only waking once the sun was sinking past late afternoon and into evening once more. My sleep had been heavy, and dreamless. Everything I had experienced the day before—the fight, the Da Vias, the emotional upheaval, the relief with Nev—had exhausted me more than I would have guessed.

I hadn't done it. Hadn't confronted Lea and Les. I was a coward, maybe. But now the power lay with me. I controlled the lies, the secrets. And I could decide when to break it all apart.

Food awaited me downstairs in the kitchen, as well as my family. They sat around the table, conversing quietly. My chest constricted tightly and all the questions and lies and feelings flooded over me once more.

Was this what it was like for them? Did they feel this way every time they looked at me? Every time they lied?

I couldn't stay with them. I couldn't continue to be Allegra Saldana, not when I knew she was built on lies, built on a foundation of betrayal, of stealing me from my real family.

"Glad to see you're finally awake." Les's bright smile was like a dagger to my chest. His lies seemed worse, somehow. Lea was at least the head of the Saldana Family, and like Marcello had said, Family heads always had secrets. Les couldn't claim the same excuse.

Not that being Family head was an excuse, either.

"You missed Elena," Emile said. "She stopped by with her parents for a visit."

That explained the flush of Emile's skin. "You could have woken me."

But of course they hadn't. Why would they want to parade me around? The Saldana who didn't belong.

Les waved that aside. "You needed the sleep."

"Besides," Emile said, "she's coming back with us. You'll have the rest of your lives to get to know each other."

I turned away, using a choice from the pastry selection to cover my own flush.

I couldn't do it. If I went back with them after Susten, back to Yvain, I would be culpable in my own kidnapping. I would be shutting the door on my little cage and throwing away the key.

"We're leaving for the fealty once the sun sets," Lea said.

I shoved a pastry in my mouth, too hungry to try to savor it. The dough was flaky on the outside and chewy in the middle and stuffed with sugared figs and herbs.

I could stay, here in Lovero. Return to Ravenna, the Da Vias, my mother. Become who I was truly meant to be. Finally find out what it felt like to fit somewhere.

I brushed my hand free of crumbs. "I guess I should start getting ready, then."

"I'll come with you," Lea said.

My stomach twisted and I regretted eating the pastry so quickly.

Upstairs we changed into our dresses and then met in my room to pin up our hair in the Loveran style.

"This is the nicest dress I've ever worn." I petted the embroidered fabric. If I just focused on talking about minor things, like my dress, I could keep from thinking about what Lea had done.

"I know." Lea twisted my hair and shoved pins into the mass to hold it in place.

"We can't ride in these."

"We're taking a carriage to the palace." As she slid in another pin, it scraped against my scalp and I hissed.

"Sorry." She cleared her throat and grabbed another pin. She avoided my eyes in the mirror. She was preparing to say something to me. I dug my fingers into my palms. She couldn't know the truth. There was no way.

"Did you have fun last night?"

I blinked and turned to look at her, but she grabbed my head and made me face the mirror once more. She slipped another pin into my hair.

"I thought you were angry with me."

She scrunched her nose, then pulled out one of the pins and moved it to a different spot. "I can feel more than one emotion at a time, Allegra. Les told me you met someone?"

I scoffed. It was Denny all over again. She only cared when she thought there was someone who could pose a threat. She only ever cared when she thought I might escape from my cage. "His name is Nev. He's a traveler. But I did other things. I met a Caffarelli. I ate delicious food."

Lea laughed. "I remember Loveran food."

I cleared my throat. "They have a tiger at the menagerie."

Lea's eyes found mine in the mirror. "You're sure you saw a tiger?"

"I know a tiger when I see one." I paused. "Do you think they could be Les's family?"

I hadn't made the connection while there—I'd been too busy kissing Nev. My arms prickled with guilt over not considering it before now. I didn't want to think that Nev could be part of the family that had abandoned Les to the streets of Yvain, not caring if the ghosts took him or he starved.

"I don't know." Lea twisted one last piece of hair around my face. "He's probably the only one who would know."

She paused, hands stilled over my hair. "You're being safe, right?"

I rolled my eyes. "It was absolutely safe out there. The only clippers I saw were Caffarellis."

"That's not what I meant."

I pressed my lips together. She always saw the heart of things. Maybe it was because she had seen a god, once. "Don't worry about that."

Nev and I hadn't slept together, and anyway, I was always good about taking the concoction Lea had made to prevent pregnancy.

"That's also not what I meant."

I turned in my seat and faced her. "I'm not going to let anyone break my heart."

"Hmm," she said. "That's the thing about broken hearts, though. They sneak up on you."

We fell into silence. Sometimes it was nice, spending time alone with Lea, just the two of us. But now I measured everything she did and said against the truth I'd discovered.

We could never go back. Things could never again be the same between us. Between me and my Family.

Leave. I had to leave. Return to the Da Vias.

I looked at her in the mirror. She hummed as she finished my hair.

I would wait until the end of Susten, to enjoy these last few days before telling them I wouldn't be returning to Yvain with them. A few days more of being a Saldana. I owed them that, at least. But only until Susten ended.

And then I would stay here where I belonged.

I would be a Da Via.

thirteen

†

I STOOD IN FRONT OF THE MIRROR. MY DRESS WAS silver, with black embroidered flowers covering the bodice so barely any silver slipped through. The flowers then trailed down to the skirts. I slipped on my necklace from Les, the stone sliding beneath the bodice. My hair had been twisted behind my head and I couldn't help but remember Elbow and her friends and how they'd looked down their noses at me for letting my hair hang freely. They probably wouldn't even recognize me now.

Neither would Nev, for that matter. My stomach thrilled pleasantly at the thought. My skin flushed as I remembered the feel of his lips on my neck. And then his laugh, when I'd scored a winning hand in the card game. I wanted to hear more of his laughter.

Lea stood beside me, her own dress black and cream. "Everyone will be wearing their Family color, to make it easier."

"And so lines can be drawn."

"Yes."

We found Emile and Les in the living room, also dressed in black and silver and cream. Outside, two carriages waited for us. Les and Lea took the first one and Emile and I the second. The driver cracked his reins and we were off.

I sighed, much of my tension fading now that I'd made my decision. And any lies I'd been told probably didn't involve Emile. It was easy to be around him now, just the two of us, like when we were children.

The enclosed carriage protected the passengers from rain, or perhaps rowdy revelers. I bounced on the seat, testing it out.

"Legs," Emile admonished, "I doubt very much Lea and Les are jumping on the seats in their own carriage."

I stopped. "I bet they're taking advantage of their privacy, though." I would've. If I'd been in this carriage with Nev.

"No." Emile scoffed and looked over at me.

"You wait and see. They'll look rumpled by the time we get there."

Emile turned away but he couldn't hide his red ears.

"How about you?" I asked. "Did you and Elena do some rumpling yourselves?"

"Of course not," he snapped.

"Why not? Look around you!" I leaned over him and pushed aside his curtain. The colorful lantern lights filled the carriage. "You'll probably never experience anything like this again. This festival is made for excitement and fun, and what's more fun than taking a girl, the girl you're going to *marry,* by the way, and slipping off together to get to know each other a little better?"

Emile rolled his eyes. "Well, with the first night, we'd just met. And then Lea and Les and her parents were with us the entire time. It would have been obvious had we left."

"Don't you think they'd be happy to know that you two were . . . compatible? I mean, you do want to—"

"Yes." He cut me off. "I do. I like her very much and I'm excited to get to know her better tonight without everyone else listening in."

I leaned back. "Well, good, then. I'd be disappointed if I was the only one getting to know someone a little better." If he was happy with Elena, if everyone liked her, then maybe she would fit better than I ever had.

"By the gods, Allegra, really?" Emile said. "When did you even have—you know what"—he held up a hand—"I don't need to know. What will Lea say when she finds out? And she will find out. She finds out *everything.*"

She hadn't found out I'd been with the Da Vias yesterday.

"Don't worry your handsome face about it," I said.

Emile sighed and leaned his head against the window. "You and I are so different."

"Yes," I agreed. "Why do you think that is?"

He shrugged. "Our mothers, I suppose."

I leaned back against the seat, trying to settle my nervous stomach.

I'd heard enough small remarks from Lea, or quiet

conversations between Lea and Les, to know that my father, Matteo Saldana, and Emile's father, Rafeo Saldana, had been very different and hadn't gotten along, even if they had been brothers.

But Val and Claudia told me that Lea had killed my father, and that made the least sense to me. Lea was loyal to her Family like no other. She would never have killed one of them.

But then, maybe I didn't know her as well as I thought I did.

Emile's mother had been a cleaner, but she had died when he was just a baby. Anything that made us not *Saldana* came from our outsider mothers. My mother, who was still alive. Who maybe I'd see tonight, again. Who I would return to, after the festival.

My hands trembled. I clasped them together, keeping them still.

Emile sat with his eyes closed, either trying to doze or lost in his own thoughts. Emile and I *were* very different, but we still got along, were still friends, still loved each other. I could never imagine killing him.

I would miss him, when he left to go back to Yvain. We were the opposite in many ways, but he was more brother to me than cousin. I loved him.

I watched outside my window as we drove toward the palace. Already people packed the streets, even though the sun had just set. Food vendors were preparing for the crowds, their wares filling the air with strange scents that made my mouth water.

"Good clipper!" a man called to our carriage as we passed. He bowed deeply. "You grace us with your presence!"

I snorted and looked over at Emile. "It's a little early to be drinking."

"He's not drunk," Emile said. "He hopes to gain favor from Safraella. Expect this response from most of the common."

And he was right. When people saw our carriages heading toward the palace, they bowed and moved out of our way. Or they called out greetings from down the streets, raising their hands as if we were old friends.

"We're not even Caffarellis," I said.

The carriage turned down a side street, away from the slowly filling main roads. "Purple can look an awful lot like black in the right light. And there haven't been Saldanas in Lovero in over fifteen years. People see what they expect to see."

This was true. It was why it was so easy to work jobs. People didn't expect a person to be waiting for them on the roof, so they didn't even think to look up, to check for danger. A person's routine could get them as killed as straying from the course.

Which was one of the reasons I couldn't stand a routine. Emile liked things just so, liked things to remain the same so he knew what to expect and could prepare himself accordingly.

But there was no freedom in that. A routine was just another trap, one you forced yourself into. I refused to trap myself. I was already caged enough.

It was one of the things that drew my thoughts back to Nev. He'd gone along with me, a strange girl he'd just met. He had the sort of freedom to do what he wanted, and he took advantage of it.

Our carriage turned another corner and I gasped.

The palace of Lovero stretched into the sky, its stone walls sparkling against the torches and lanterns lighting its grounds. "Wow," I said.

The carriage rolled through the gates of the palace, then pulled to a stop. Footmen opened our doors, and then we were escorted inside the palace.

The floors were smooth wood, polished until they gleamed like a mirror. The ceiling soared above us, and windows stretched equally as high, letting in the stars and the light from the colored lanterns outside.

My dress was brand-new but I still felt too dirty to walk these halls. Like this place was only made for royalty, or dainty women who never had blood staining the corners of their fingernails or men who preferred pipe smoke instead of bomb smoke.

A servant led us down the halls, the floors changing from polished wood to thick carpets that my shoes sank into, leaving an impression behind. We reached a set of double doors, propped open.

The ballroom was packed with people, and not just clippers. Many of the higher-born common and nobility had been invited as well. It wasn't just a clipper event, but an event celebrating Camelia Sapienza's fealty.

In hindsight, it seemed like a bad idea.

We entered and stood off to the side, surveying the room. There were plenty of people dancing, and more people hovering around the food tables, but there were also pockets of people like us, studying the crowd. These pockets of people all wore matching colors. Members of the nine Families.

Lea sighed. "Let's just get through this without anyone dying."

She led us to the east end of the room, where the king and queen and princess sat, welcoming guests, accepting congratulations on the princess Camelia's oath of fealty to Safraella. We stood in line behind an old couple dressed in expensive clothing that looked too young for them. They glanced back at us, then did a double take.

"Family Saldana." They bowed deeply. "Please, don't wait on our behalf." They stepped to the side.

"It's quite all right," Lea said in her voice I'd come to call her *common tone*. She always sounded different when she was speaking to the common as a clipper. It wasn't the same as when she spoke to customers in the shop, or even to the Family. Lea wore more masks than only those crafted from bone.

"We insist," the old couple said.

And so we stepped forward to take their spots. And the same thing happened again, and again, until we found ourselves at the front of the line.

"At least we'll eat sooner," I mumbled to Emile. His mouth twitched.

When the royal family of Lovero saw us, they got to their

feet and more than one person in the ballroom took notice.

"Lea," Costanzo Sapienza, the king, said as he approached us. "It has been too long."

I don't know if I was more surprised that he hugged her, or that she hugged him back.

"It has." She pulled away from him. "But we're here now." She turned to face Camelia. "Congratulations on your fealty."

She nodded her head primly. "Thank you. It is my honor to serve."

Clearly she had been coached in what to say. Lea introduced us, and there was some bland conversation about how much Emile looked like his father, Rafeo, and subtle glances in my direction that they thought I wouldn't notice. But I did, and I knew what they meant—that I looked like my mother in the way that Emile looked like his father. But they couldn't talk about it because they thought I didn't know about my mother.

I resisted the urge to run away from the entire ordeal. But then we were done conversing with the Sapienzas, and we took our leave while they returned to their seats and their greeting of the rest of the guests.

I made straight for the food tables. Food always made me feel better. Food would help cover the twisting in my gut that had grown as I stood there, feeling the lies press in on me.

I grabbed a plate and filled it with tiny cuisines from the table, each made to be eaten in one bite, and then filled my other hand with a glass of red wine so dark it was almost black.

"The wine matches our Family," I said, turning.

But Emile was gone.

I searched the crowd behind me, then the dance floor. And there I found Emile, hand in hand with a girl. She had dark skin, as dark as my old suitor Denny's, black hair plaited at the base of her neck, and a stunning purple dress.

Elena Caffarelli. Emile's soon-to-be wife.

Lea stepped beside me, her dress brushing against mine as I sipped my wine and watched Emile and Elena dance.

"Sometimes, things change quickly," she said, rather enigmatically.

I understood the truth behind her words, though. Yesterday morning I'd had an identity. Maybe I'd worn it like a secondhand dress that didn't quite fit, but it had been mine. And soon I would shed that dress and don a new one, tailored for me, with a new Family.

I set down my glass and shoved a little piece of bread spread with something pink into my mouth. Fish, it seemed, delightfully delicate and sweet. "I was mostly just thinking about how they look good together," I replied. "They're the same height, which is nice."

I glanced at Lea, knowing full well she couldn't measure up to Les. I pushed more food in my mouth. "Where's Les?"

She pointed behind her, never taking her eyes off Emile and Elena. I looked over my shoulder and found Les speaking to Brand Caffarelli. They were laughing together like they were old friends. Maybe they were.

I ate the rest of the food and then set the empty plate on the table, clutching my wineglass as if it were a canal boat and a ghost was pulling at my cloak. My chest felt . . . strange. I couldn't quite figure out what I was feeling, watching Emile and Elena dance, watching the rest of the nine Families whisper and look at us, some of them surely hoping for our demise. Lea may have been the chosen of Safraella, but no one ever liked losing power.

Les appeared at my side and kissed me quickly on the temple before he turned to Lea. "Dance with me."

He held out his hand and she only hesitated a moment before she accepted, and I was alone, watching the rest of my Family dance with someone they loved.

The food felt heavy and cold in my stomach. I downed the rest of my wine in a single gulp.

A man approached me from the left.

He was a clipper, that was apparent even without the elegant yellow clothing marking him as a Maietta. He had close-cropped silver hair and dark eyes that were almost black.

"You are Allegra Saldana, yes?" he asked.

I kept my left foot in place and slid my right foot back, giving me more space while keeping the illusion that I held my place. Not that I thought he'd try anything, with my Family so close, in such a group of people. And as far as I knew, the Maiettas weren't one of the Families who particularly hated us, but still. It seemed dumb to throw caution completely to the ghosts.

"I am." I resisted the urge to rub my face and just had to hope there weren't any crumbs.

"I am Tulio Maietta," he said, as if this should mean something to me. He waited a moment for a reaction, and then when he didn't receive one, sighed and reached into his pouch.

My fingers twitched at my side, begging for me to take out my stiletto, or a push dagger or something.

But his hand returned from the pouch with a sealed letter. "I was hoping Marcello Saldana would be with you tonight."

"Oh," I said, before I could help it. "He doesn't like to travel."

He nodded, like this made perfect sense to him. "I understand. But perhaps you would give this letter to him? It's not from me, but my brother."

He passed it to me and I looked down at the soft paper in my hand. The ink had faded and the paper was worn from time, but the name on the front still clearly read *Marcello*.

"I've had it for a long time. Too long," he said quietly. "But I don't think it's too late to do the right thing. At the very least, perhaps my conscience will be lighter, though I suspect it will still be weighing me down when I stand before Her at the end of my life."

I looked up at him, and it did seem something weighed him down. But when I nodded and slipped the letter into my purse he smiled quickly, and it brightened his face.

"Lea Saldana strives for peace between the Families," he

said. It wasn't a question, but I nodded anyway. "It is a noble endeavor. One worth fighting for."

He inclined his head to me and then strode off, leaving me alone once more.

"The Maiettas can be a strange lot," a voice said behind me.

I turned and found a Caffarelli. He wore an elegantly embroidered purple vest and though he had black hair instead of blond, it had been slicked back with oil until it nearly shined in the lamplight.

"So it would seem." I glanced once more in the direction that Tulio had disappeared. I faced the Caffarelli. "I'm Allegra."

"I know," he said. "We've met."

I examined him more closely. Older than me. Older than Emile, too. But his face didn't strike me as familiar. I shook my head in apology.

"You helped me with a well-placed foot." He pantomimed tripping someone.

"Ah!" I said. "Thorns, yes?" I gestured to my face and where my bone mask would be if I were wearing one.

"Indeed. Would you care to dance?" He held out his hand.

I hesitated, though I wasn't quite sure why. He was a Caffarelli and therefore no threat. And he was handsome enough.

I shook off my hesitation and took his hand. He pulled me onto the dance floor, where we joined the spinning and twirling people.

"That mark was trying his damnedest to get away," I said.

"I'm sorry if I interfered. I just couldn't help myself."

"No, it's fine, actually. It meant I returned home all the sooner and could start enjoying the festival."

"I'm surprised you were working at all."

He spun me and my dress flared out. He was a good dancer. Light on his feet. I wondered if Nev would be a good dancer.

"The jobs don't stop just because of Susten Day. I'd been waiting for that mark to make an appearance for two weeks now. The festival drew him out."

I nodded. "I know what that's like. Well, not the festival. We don't have these kinds of events in Yvain. But the mark that just won't make an appearance."

I remembered slipping into the window of Jonus Aix's house, fed up with waiting for him to leave. Not that that had ended as well as . . .

I blinked. "I'm sorry," I said. "I never got your name."

He laughed and I joined in. Seeing the face behind the mask was just as intimate as knowing a name, so it hadn't even occurred to me to wonder who it was I was dancing with.

"Dario Caffarelli." He led me past a tight group of dancers. "And have you had much time to enjoy the festival yourself?"

I thought of Nev's lips pressed against mine, his hands sliding up my legs. I couldn't help the grin that spread across my lips. "Yes. The traveler menagerie is especially interesting."

"I haven't had a chance to take it in yet," Dario said. "But I hope to rectify that before they leave. I heard they have a tiger."

"They do. Though I found the snakes more enticing." Specifically a little white snake, twisting around the fingers of her master.

My skin warmed beneath my dress and my heart sped. But Nev wasn't here, couldn't ever be here, and I was dancing with Dario, who was a Caffarelli.

"And are you related to Brand?" I asked. Most clippers were related to other clippers in the same Family, but sometimes blood ran thin, especially in the larger Families and the ones more committed to bringing in outside blood.

"Second cousins," he said.

"Hmm," I said. "I'm not really good with extended relationships. Does that mean you're related to my aunt? Or me?"

He smiled slowly, a grin that suggested something more. And too late did I realize how my casual conversation could be taken as something else. As flirting perhaps, though there had been nothing flirtatious in the way I had asked my question. I had truly wanted to understand his lineage, not because I wanted to know if we were too closely related to court.

We danced on the outside circle of the floor and we spun past a group of clippers in brown, who glared at me with the kind of hatred reserved for someone who had personally destroyed them.

"No," Dario said suddenly, and I snapped my attention back to him. "We are not related. Or at least, not closely related."

"I don't see the Da Vias here," I said, changing the subject.

Dario scanned the crowd and then shrugged. "They're probably late so they can make an entrance. If they're the last ones here, it means everyone will notice them."

I smiled at Dario, but couldn't bring myself to continue the conversation. The dance had lost its appeal, and the room was hot, filled with people. I gently pulled my hands from his. "I think I need a drink."

"I'll come with you," he said brightly, but I held up a hand, forestalling him.

"Sorry," I said. "I was trying to be polite. I said drink, but I really meant lavatory."

A lie, but a simple one to spare his feelings. He had been nothing but kind to me.

Dario nodded and bowed graciously. I slipped past the dancers and once more found myself on the sidelines by the table filled with foods.

I snatched another glass of wine and gulped it while I stared out at the floor. The Da Vias hadn't shown. I wasn't sure what it meant, but it had to mean something.

Emile and Elena were still dancing, and the happiness in their faces seemed real enough for people who had only recently met each other in person.

I wondered if that was how my face looked when I was with Nev.

But Nev wasn't here. And neither were the Da Vias. And I was alone.

I finished off my wine but it suddenly tasted sour in my mouth. I set the glass down and held my stomach.

"Are you not feeling well?"

I turned to find Les behind me, the concern on his face quickly vanishing behind a more stoic facade. No reason to attract any attention from the other Families.

"No," I said. "My stomach is queasy. I think maybe I'll go home."

Of course, if I went home now, it meant I had plenty of time to find Nev.

Thinking of Nev made my nausea vanish and my heart pound. It could be Allegra and Nev, then. At least for a little while, anyway.

And it wasn't even a lie, really. My stomach *had* been queasy.

Les blinked and looked me over slowly. "You do seem a little flushed."

Just thinking about Nev was helping with my cover story.

Les snatched a glass of wine from a passing servant and sipped it thoughtfully. More, I thought, to make it appear as if we were having a polite conversation about nothing important. "I can return home with you."

I shook my head. "You should stay here, enjoy the ball. You and Lea never get to have any fun. Not that this is necessarily the most fun, since I'm sure there are more than a few clippers here who would like to see us dead, but still.

The food's free and the music is pleasant. And there's actual royalty over there."

Les frowned.

"Really," I said. "I'll just take the carriage back. I'll be perfectly safe. There's a driver so I won't even be alone."

"Are you armed?"

I nodded. "Knives on both ankles. Biggest I could fit."

Les sipped the wine again. "All right," he said. "But make sure you keep the curtains closed. I don't want anyone catching sight of you alone in Genoni and making an attempt for you."

"I will," I said, trying to remember that I was supposed to be ill and not excited to leave the ball. "You don't have to tell Lea, either. She'll just worry."

Les snorted. "Thank you for your permission. And I will tell her," he said. My stomach sank. If he told Lea, she'd definitely make Les go home with me. Or she'd go herself. "But I'll tell her after you leave. I don't want to spoil the fun. So don't make me regret this, Allegra."

Guilt rose in me at how easy it was to lie to him. But all I had to do was remember the truth, how I wasn't supposed to be wearing black tonight, but red, and my lie didn't seem to hold much weight.

He winked at me. I smiled, making sure my lip trembled just enough so he'd believe my sick angle but not enough to change his mind about the escort.

And then he was gone, looking for Lea, and I was slipping around the outside of the dance floor, sliding past people and other clippers until I found myself at the door to the ballroom once more.

The hallway was blessedly cooler than the ballroom and the air chilled my skin as I walked down the hall. My dress rustled pleasantly around my feet.

Maybe I was making a mistake. I'd probably never get a chance for another ball like this. And my dress was very pretty and I'd have no reason to wear it again once I left.

I stopped. Maybe the Da Vias would still show. I looked over my shoulder to the ballroom. The party continued on without me. A man at the doorway peeked out at me, but then returned to the ball. He was the only one to even notice I'd left.

Nev noticed me, though, at the menagerie. Nev wanted to see me again. And I wanted to see him.

I turned away from the dance and stepped out into the night.

fourteen

†

THE CARRIAGE WAS WAITING WHERE WE'D LEFT IT AND the driver didn't even blink when I told him to return me to Lilyan.

The nightlife of Lovero was amazing, especially with the festival.

I would never tire of this place. I would never tire of people walking unrestricted at night, not harassed by ghosts, their lives free and safe.

Well, safe from the ghosts, at least.

When I lived here, I could have clipper friends who understood what our lives were like. When I lived here, I wouldn't have to run the shop, to mix perfumes and colognes as a cover for our real business. People would respect me on sight.

Lovero offered so much more freedom than Rennes.

The carriage stopped and my body jolted forward.

I looked out the window. We'd halted on a side street, off the main route of the festival. There were lanterns here, but no revelers nearby. In Yvain, this would have seemed completely out of place. Here it also seemed out of place, but because everything was so quiet.

I pulled my knives from their ankle sheaths, then pounded on the wall in front of me. "Why did we stop?"

No answer. Which could mean a great many things, but none of them good.

I stood, my head hunched over in the cramped space.

If I stayed inside, there were only two ways to come at me: from the carriage doors. But it didn't offer a lot of space for defense. If I left, I would gain the space lacking in the carriage, but I didn't know what I faced outside, and I was a stranger to this part of the city.

A round canister punched through the curtain of the window and crashed to the floor of the carriage. Smoke immediately billowed around my ankles. The air filled with its acrid scent and I covered my mouth and nose with my forearm, knife clutched in my fingers.

Outside it was, then.

I kicked open the door and jumped from the carriage to the flagstone street. My shoes clicked loudly on the stone. I spun, knives held in a defensive stance. My dress twirled around me, the silver and black fabric flashing in the colorful lantern lights.

They were here. Somewhere. I just had to find them.

But there was nothing. Or seemingly nothing. It was a lie, of course, that the streets were empty. The smoke bomb had come from someone, but it seemed they were biding their time. Assessing me, perhaps.

I glanced to the front of the carriage. The horses waited placidly, but the driver was gone. Taken? Or fled? Not that it really mattered.

Maybe I should have agreed to Les's escort. Two clippers were always better than one, especially in unfamiliar circumstances. I could handle myself, but Les by my side would've made the dark seem brighter.

"If you wanted to dance," I shouted into the night, "you could have just asked me at the ball."

"But you fled so soon," a voice answered from behind. I spun. No one.

"And besides." Another voice, to my left. "Now we have our own private dance."

They appeared then, from the shadows and roofs. Seven of them, the darkness of the night turning the brown on their masks to the color of pitch. Addamos.

Of course. I was still in Genoni, in their territory.

They wore no leathers. Instead they were dressed in the same high fashion I'd seen on the clippers at the ball. An image flashed through my mind of the Addamos glaring at me as I danced with Dario Caffarelli, the hatred in their eyes. And the man in the ballroom, watching me as I left alone.

All seven were men, not a single ball gown between them. It was a calculated move on their part. My own dress would do me no favors in a fight.

They were well armed. My daggers wouldn't do much

against their swords, certainly not against all of them.

I had been in tough situations before, with some of my clipper jobs, but this . . .

I swallowed.

"So many of you," I said, pleased my voice hid the fear that traveled up my spine, that squeezed my chest. "Who would like to dance first?"

"Oh," one said. "This isn't that kind of dance."

They charged me.

Lea had killed three Addamos when she was my age. Younger, actually. She'd said the Addamos were sloppy, with no grace about them.

If that had once been true, it was no longer the reality.

They circled around me so quickly I had a hard time keeping them all in sight. And that was the most important thing I needed to do. If I lost track of even a single Addamo, that would open me up to an attack I couldn't block or evade. A misplaced Addamo would be my end.

One of them lunged at me with his sword. I blocked it with my knives and pushed him away. Nothing fancy from either of us. Him because he was feeling me out. Me because this wasn't the time for anything fancy. This was a time of blood and death and desperation and only these things would save me.

An Addamo at my back. I kicked my leg out, my dress swishing pleasantly but slowing me down. The Addamo jumped back, dodging my counter.

Then nothing but movement. Jabs. Blocks. I almost lost

sight of my own knives in the flashes of steel.

Another attack from my left. A ruse, to distract me from the real attack on my right.

I slid to the left. Let them think I bought their ploy. Then a sharp stab from my knife to the right and an Addamo's gasp turned into a gurgle. He dropped his sword and tried to stop the blood that cascaded from his throat.

A brief twinge of regret flowed across me. His vest had been handsome and now his blood had ruined it.

Six Addamos left. They circled me, more wary now that I had dropped one of them.

I flicked the blood off my knife and onto the street. It shone wetly between us. A line for them to cross, if they were brave enough.

"I am in your territory legally," I said. "I have Costanzo Sapienza's protection. There's still time for you to let me leave. No more of you need to die." Or me, for that matter.

"We don't care about that," one of them snarled. "A long time ago, Lea Saldana took people from us. Now it's time to take people from her."

I snorted. "Even if you succeed here, which is still up for debate"—I gestured to the dead Addamo to my right—"she will never let you get away with it. She will come and raze your Family to the ground, until the only thing remaining is the memory of your name."

Maybe I was bluffing, but I didn't think by much.

"She and who else?" one of them scoffed. "You number barely a handful."

"It was she alone who killed your Family members in the past. It was she who toppled the Da Vias. You're willing to take the chance that you could stand up against her, Safraella's chosen, where the Da Vias could not?"

"The Da Vias were traitors to Safraella. We have always been loyal servants. She will not help the Saldanas against us like She did with the Da Vias."

They were right. Even if Lea could once again rouse an army of ghosts to use as a weapon, there would be no way to set them on the Addamos. They were safe behind the protection of Safraella. No ghosts could harm them while they were in Lovero.

My face felt naked between all these clippers with their bone masks. The fear wouldn't have gripped me so tightly if I'd had my mask to wear.

The Addamos stirred. I could practically hear their grins behind their masks. "No, sister. You are alone here and your aunt can't do anything to save you or avenge you. Little birds shouldn't fly so far from their nests."

"Then come on!" I snarled, brandishing my knives before me.

The Addamos took a step, then stopped as one. They held their swords before them defensively.

It hadn't been me who had caused them to pause.

I glanced over my shoulder. Two clippers stood behind me, neither Saldanas nor Caffarellis.

I spun so the Addamos were on my right and the newcomers on my left, a knife pointed at each group.

The newcomers' masks shone bright red in the lanterns, one with a pattern of feathers, the other with checkers. Bellio Da Via, head of their Family, along with another Da Via.

Bellio Da Via faced the Addamos. He was a big man, even bigger up close, but it seemed that neither he nor the other Da Via had come prepared for a fight. At least, they didn't carry swords like the Addamos.

"This is none of your concern." The lead Addamo pointed his sword at Bellio.

"She has the right of passage like the rest of the Families," Bellio replied. "Your attack here breaks the truce created for the fealty."

Relief flowed through my veins like a cool breeze. The Da Vias were on my side. The Da Vias were protecting me. Because I was family, even if I wasn't Family. Not yet, anyway.

"She has the right to die!" the Addamo snapped.

If the situation I'd found myself in hadn't been so serious, I would have snorted at his retort.

"Everyone has the right to die," Bellio said in his deep voice. "Just like you and the rest of your brothers here. And even if you succeed, do you honestly think there will be no repercussions? It won't just be the Saldanas who will come for you. You, who have broken a truce agreed upon by all the Families. A truce requested by the king. If you turn your back on him, perhaps She will turn Her back on you. You endanger everyone with your foolishness."

"Foolishness," the lead Addamo spat. "Lea Saldana has

killed our brothers. She owes us blood."

Bellio stepped closer, and even the evening breeze seemed to hold its breath. "Don't speak to me, *brother*, about the blood Lea Saldana spilled. But she is the chosen of Safraella. It is not blood you owe her, but reverence."

I could practically see the Addamos twisting this point around in their heads. They must have felt truly threatened by the presence of these two Da Vias if they were weighing Bellio's words so carefully. Six well-armed clippers against three lesser-armed clippers were still odds that leaned heavily in the Addamos' favor if they made the decision to continue the attack.

The lead Addamo lowered his sword, and the night seemed to breathe again.

"Just because you found yourself some friends, Allegra Saldana, doesn't mean this is over," he said. But then he motioned to the others and they grabbed their dead brother and dragged him away, vanishing in the shadows once more.

I pulled my arms in and faced the Da Vias fully. They wore exquisite garb, mostly reds, but sprinkled with black-and-gold embroidery. Their boots were crafted of the finest calfskin, and looked both comfortable and strong. They wore cologne that I could smell from where I stood. Expensive stuff. I could tell from the scent alone. And the Da Via with the checkers on his mask wore a ruby ring, which flashed on his left pinky. Val. My uncle.

"Thank you," I said. I wanted to say more, to talk to them about my plans, to join their Family once Susten was over.

But Bellio turned his back on me. "Go home, Allegra Saldana. Before you find yourself in more trouble with no one to save you."

He dismissed me so easily. And Val, my own blood, just followed behind, like a dog to heel. Maybe they had saved me, but I'd dropped one Addamo before the Da Vias had even shown up. The only reason they were able to save me at all was because of the weight their name carried.

Claudia had asked me to join their Family, but here their Family head showed no interest in me. As if I was below his notice, even if he had chosen to back me up in a fight.

Maybe I wouldn't be as welcome as Claudia and Val had made it seem. Or maybe I didn't know much about Bellio Da Via and shouldn't presume anything based on the few words we'd exchanged.

"Enjoy the ball, brother." I curtsied with a smile that didn't quite reach my eyes. "And uncle."

Val looked over his shoulder at me then, but his expression remained a mystery behind his mask.

I turned my back and walked away.

I felt, more than saw, Val watching me as I strode toward the safety of Lilyan.

fifteen

MY FEET HURT.

My little silver shoes had been made for dancing across marble or wood flooring, not striding the rough flagstones of the streets.

At least now I'd made it to the safer streets of Lilyan. Once I crossed out of Genoni, the signs on the streetlamps proclaiming the border of the cities, my shoulders relaxed and I was able to find a bench to sit on and sheathe my knives. I used my dress to clean the one I'd bloodied, which was a shame, but the knife came first. It had done its job and saved my life. The dress, though beautiful, had just put me in danger.

Still, I used one of the hidden underlayers. No need to show the blood to everyone.

Then it was back on my sore feet to head deeper into the city.

I could have gone home. I could've changed into

something more comfortable, but the menagerie, and Nev, were closer, and besides, I wanted him to see me in the dress.

And the sooner I got to Nev, the less I would have to think about the Addamos' attack and Bellio Da Via's dismissal of me and what it meant.

I swallowed and pushed forward.

I'd been warned, of course. So many times, by both Lea and Les. And I'd known, objectively, that it could be dangerous in Lovero in ways that were unfamiliar to me. I knew how to handle ghosts in the darkness—run, hide—I knew how to handle suspicious lawmen—lie, bribe—but even though I'd handled the Addamos as best I could, I was the only one to blame for even being in that situation in the first place.

The attack took some of the shine away from Lovero. Made me remember that freedom wasn't necessarily safe.

It was fine, though. Because I'd rather be free and in danger than safe and suffocating. I'd come out the other side of the attack unharmed. Granted, that was because of the Da Vias, but still.

I turned down another street, avoiding large crowds of drunken revelers.

Thinking about the Da Vias set my stomach twisting again. Bellio had dismissed me without hesitation. And Val, my uncle, had followed suit.

If I wasn't welcome with the Da Vias, if they didn't want me, regardless of what Val and Claudia—my mother—had said, and I was forced to return to Yvain and my cage— tighter, now that I knew the truth of things—I would start to scream, and I didn't think I would ever stop.

But Nev would halt these thoughts twisting in my head. Nev would be a balm to my worries, helping me to cast them aside, if just for a time.

Nev would welcome me, even if no one else would.

The revelers that passed me on the streets gave me a wide berth, many of them bowing as I slipped by. Whether they recognized me as a clipper, or just someone dressed for a party at the palace, didn't really matter. The space was a luxury I gladly accepted.

By the time I found myself outside the menagerie, my feet begged for me to rest.

A traveler man stood at the entrance, taking payment before letting people inside to see the animals. He had a stick of something in his mouth. The end of it smoldered and every now and then he would exhale and smoke would escape from between his lips and his nose. I stepped beside him. The smoke from his black stick smelled sweetly pleasant. He glanced at me and then held up a single finger for payment.

"I was here before," I said.

He smirked and the stick slipped from the middle of his lips to the side of his mouth. "Princesses still have to pay."

"I'm here to see Nev."

He blinked slowly, showing no sign he even recognized the name. He exhaled a pulse of smoke, and then looked me up and down. Finally, apparently meeting with his approval, he nodded me forward and I slipped into the menagerie once more.

The birds were still beautiful, the horses still elegant, the tiger still ferocious and sad, but I paid them no mind as I weaved past people and made my way back to the corner with the snakes.

Empty. Though the cages were filled with their usual hissing occupants, there were no traveler boys with strange hats and tiny, venomous serpents trailing across their fingers.

I looked around slowly. He had to be here somewhere. The traveler at the entrance wouldn't have let me in if Nev wasn't here, or if Nev had really been some strange figment of my imagination.

For some reason that thought made me remember the nightmares I'd suffered back home in Yvain. Since we'd left, I'd gone without a single interruption to my sleep. Nev only gave me sweet dreams.

If Nev was here, but not visible in the menagerie, that meant he had to be behind it somewhere, like where he'd taken me before so we could kiss in private. I headed to the curtained entrance. I heard voices and hesitated.

I didn't need to be afraid. It wasn't a band of clippers behind the curtain waiting to ambush me. That had already happened once tonight, and I'd come out unscathed. Surely I could face a group of travelers.

I pushed the curtain aside and stepped into the gloom of their tented area.

Four men sat around a table, smoking more of the black sticks like the traveler at the entrance. The smoke floated above them in a gray haze and before them sat tiny glasses, no bigger than my thumb. In the center of the table stood a tall bottle with a green liquid inside. More oil.

They stared at me, any conversation between them forgotten at my entrance.

Once again I missed the safety of my mask.

One of them stood. Thoughts warred in his eyes. He wanted to tell me to leave, but my dress caught him off guard.

"No animals back here," he finally said. He pointed at the exit behind me.

"I'm looking for Nev."

He glanced over his shoulder at the rest of the men remaining at the table. They said something in Mornian between them, and then the man faced me again. "So, you are his little *lob*. He did not mention the dress."

The smoke from his stick swirled around my face and I waved it away. "I came from the palace."

The men laughed, shoving one another and smiling. But they kept their comments in Mornian, still. Maybe I would have to ask Les to teach me more of the language.

No. He wouldn't be able to teach me anything again, not when I joined the Da Vias.

"Is Nev here or not?" I snapped.

They laughed again and the one in front of me grinned. "He is somewhere. Sit down, have a drink. He will come. You play kings and ghosts?" He gestured at a pile of cards stacked on the edge of the table. "We can teach you."

He reached a hand toward my face and I grabbed his wrist, twisting it sharply.

The man gasped and the other men laughed at their friend's discomfort. "Did I give you permission to touch me?" I twisted a little more so he grunted in pain. "I don't believe I did."

To my left a figure walked into the room from behind another curtain. Nev, adjusting his pants before he looked up and saw me and the other travelers. He glanced at the table and the grinning men there, then looked more closely at me and the man whose arm I still gripped.

He smiled slowly. "I see you have met Mart. But maybe you could let him go before you break his wrist? He needs that to help clean the cages."

I released Mart's arm and he gasped in relief. His friends at the table roared in laughter. Even Nev laughed, and I smiled sweetly at Mart, who frowned at me.

"Come." Nev grabbed my hand and pulled me from the common room and the men. He led me once more behind the curtains to his room.

It was dark inside, almost too dark to see, but it didn't matter. The space was so small I remembered where everything was. Remembered the feel of Nev's skin beneath my fingers, the taste of his mouth, the scent of him.

Nev lit a lamp and we sat on his pallet together, side by side. He watched me, a strange expression on his face.

"What?" I asked.

"Just, your dress."

"I was at the palace."

"You were at the palace."

"I was. There was a ball. All the Families were invited."

"You were at a ball. Which explains the dress. But now you are here. Still in the dress."

Something fluttered in my chest. An emotion I couldn't identify. "Is this a problem?" I asked. "Because I can leave if it's a problem."

He shook his head. "No, it is not a problem. You surprised me."

"The menagerie was closer than going home. And my feet were sore from walking here." I lifted my leg so he could see my feet.

He leaned forward suddenly and grabbed my leg. "You are bleeding!"

"What?" I saw a streak of blood from when I'd used my dress to clean my knife. "Oh. It's not mine."

He looked at me again, another expression I couldn't begin to untangle. He was a prince of looks tonight.

"Where did it come from?"

I pulled my leg from his grip. "Do you truly want to know?"

I remembered how he'd reacted when he'd found out I was a clipper. But knowing something and *really* knowing something were two different things. Telling him the details of my night would definitely push him into the second category. And once he was there, everything between us could just fall apart.

"Did you kill someone?" he asked.

"Does it matter if I did?"

He paused and frowned. "I am not sure."

His honesty was like cold water on a hot summer morning. "Yes, I did."

"You said you were here for the festival, not as a murderer."

"Clipper. And I am. But I'll defend myself, if needed."

"You were attacked." This was more of a statement than a question, almost as if he was trying this idea out.

"Yes." And even though I was sitting in a small room, being questioned by a traveler boy I'd only known for two days, I still felt comfortable with him. And I hadn't felt this way in, well, never, really. Not even with Denny.

I didn't know why, though. Nev made me feel welcome beside him, even when questioning me. Questions usually made me want to shut down, to lie. I'd been trained to be evasive when questioned, and I'd learned long ago that it was better to keep quiet or lie when Lea asked questions if I knew she wouldn't like the answers.

But Nev asked questions and I wanted to be open. Truthful with him. I liked the honesty between us. It settled deep in my chest, warm and comforting. I'd never had that before.

Nev was different. And I was different with him.

"Who attacked you?" Nev finally asked. "And why?"

"Another Family. The Addamos. They said they attacked me because they owe my aunt a blood debt, but I'm sure there's more to it than that."

"And you killed them? These other murderers?"

"Clippers. And just one. Then some other clippers inter-vened, and they ran off. That's it."

"Will they try to kill you again?" His eyes flicked to the curtains surrounding us.

"Maybe," I said. "But they can't set foot in Lilyan, which means I'm safe as long as I stay here. And after tonight there's no reason for me to leave Lilyan again."

Until I went to the Da Vias.

"They can't come here, Nev." I shifted on the pallet. "They won't."

Nev slid over, to make more room for me, but then it just became easier to lie down on the pallet, side by side, staring at the curtain ceiling.

"So," he said. "You would kill anyone who threatened you?"

I shrugged. "I do what I need to do."

"Would you have killed Mart?"

Mart. The man who had tried to touch my face. I looked at Nev then. Really looked at him. He did seem to simply be curious about my lifestyle. "Mart didn't threaten me. Not seriously. He didn't mean it."

"What if someone did mean it?"

"There are plenty of things to stop someone before mur-der. Sometimes a well-placed knee will drop a man faster than a well-placed knife. I can take care of myself."

"Yes." His fingers traced lines on my arms. I shivered.

"I have never been to Rennes," he said.

"It's pleasant," I said. "Well, I can only speak for Yvain.

149

But there are flowers everywhere. And canals that make travel easy. No need to shove past crowds of people like Lovero. But there are ghosts at night."

"There are ghosts everywhere at night."

"Not here."

"They sacrifice people to be free of them."

I scrunched my nose. "It's not like that. Safraella is a god of murder, yes, but also death and resurrection. She comes for all of us in the end, and gives a better life for those who follow Her."

Nev slapped at a bug.

"Travelers have three gods, right?" I asked.

"Meska, Culda, Boamos."

"Tell me about them."

He exhaled. "We have a song. Let me think."

He hummed a bit under his breath. Then began to sing.

"We sing a song about the Three, of Meska, Culda, and Boamos. Boamos gives us wealth and thievery, while Culda sings us safely home. And great Meska with her animals, wraps us in our mother's warmth."

It was a nursery rhyme of sorts, something to help children remember when they were very young. "It didn't exactly rhyme," I teased.

Nev laughed. "It does in Mornian."

"What does 'mother's warmth' mean?" I asked.

"She is a god of motherhood."

"So of mothers? Like fertility?" The Da Vias had turned to Daedara, a god of light and fertility, when they hoped to increase their numbers. And it had worked until Lea had led ghosts into their home, killing many of them and forcing the rest to return to Safraella.

"Yes and no," Nev said. "I will tell you the story of Nula. She is the first to have worshipped Meska."

I snuggled against him, prepared for the story.

"Nula was a mother. Her daughter was named Bema. One day they were on a boat together, fishing. But a storm came and their boat sank, leaving Nula and Bema stranded in the water.

"And Nula knew they would drown. They could not return to shore without a boat. But Nula could not stand to see her daughter die. So she held Bema above the water, using all her strength as long as she could to keep her daughter from drowning.

"And then Nula drowned. Her body sank below the waves until it finally came to rest on the bottom.

"Bema wailed long and hard, for even though she knew that she, too, would drown, she did not fear her own death. Instead, she wailed out of grief and sorrow and loss for her mother.

"And then Bema drowned. Her body sank below the waves until it, too, finally came to rest on the bottom, settled in her dead mother's embrace.

"And Meska looked down at them, together even in death, and felt the depth of their love for each other. Meska had been a child, once, and She knew what it was to love a mother. And Meska had been a mother, once, too, and She knew what it was to love a child.

"And because Meska is a god of mercy, She sank to the bottom of the water, gathered Nula and Bema in Her great arms, and breathed life back into them, returning them to the shore.

"And for the rest of her days, Nula thanked Meska for saving the life of her daughter. And Bema thanked Meska for saving the life of her mother. And one day Bema became a mother, too, and passed her love for Meska on to her children."

"It's beautiful," I said.

"Yes," Nev agreed.

"All our stories about Safraella have a lot of death in them, too. Just not as much resurrection." Though Lea's story did.

He pulled me closer and I let him.

"Is it hard, worshipping three gods instead of just one?"

He pressed his lips to my throat. His hands fiddled with the ties on my bodice. "It is our way. Is it hard to kill people for your god?"

"Yes," I answered. "Sometimes. But who said faith was supposed to be easy?"

He chuckled at that, and the sound traveled across my skin, sinking lower in my body.

"Nothing is easy in life," he murmured. "Not faith. Not family."

A flash of Les and Lea appeared in my mind. My whole body tightened, thinking about their lies, thinking about my life, thinking about the coming confrontation when I would reveal to them that I knew the truth.

My breath sped up, but then Nev's lips trailed lower, anchoring me in this moment again.

I rolled on top of him, kissing him over and over.

"What is wrong?" Nev asked when I paused for breath.

"Nothing," I said. "Everything. I don't want to talk about it."

I slipped my hands down his pants and he gasped in surprise, but he wasn't unwilling.

"Are you sure?" he asked. But whether he was asking if I was willing or if I really didn't want to talk about it, I didn't know. Either way, the answer was the same.

"Yes," I said.

He pulled his shirt over his head and I yanked the ties on my bodice until it had loosened enough for me to wriggle free. I threw my shoes, knives, and jewelry on the floor but I wanted to touch him so badly that I forgot the rest of my clothes and instead reached for him, pulling his mouth back to mine, running my hands along his skin, his flesh, touching every inch of him.

This was what I wanted, what I needed.

The weight of him on top of me didn't feel like a trap; it felt like freedom, a freedom I could never seem to find.

And even though Nev was warm and willing and good, I still couldn't help but think about everything, about my family, both of them, wondering which one deserved my love and which one deserved nothing.

Tears rolled down my cheeks. I couldn't stop them.

Nev paused. "Am I hurting you?"

I shook my head, jarring the tears free from my cheeks. "Don't stop," I said, and clung to him, wishing this moment would last, so I wouldn't have to face the people who thought they loved me but instead had hurt me, so I could stay here forever, with him, in the safety of the dark.

We lay side by side, pressed against each other in the smallness of his bed. His skin warm against mine.

"Where is Kuch?" I asked, breaking the silence between us.

Nev leaned over me and pulled her pouch off the table. He opened the drawstring and slipped his hand in. Kuch slithered out, twisting over his fingers.

"Wait," he said, then slowly placed his hand over mine. Kuch slid across my skin, smooth and soft and warm, so unlike what I thought she would feel like.

"I thought she would bite me?" I asked, watching her as her tongue flicked in and out.

"You smell like me," he said.

We fell back into silence as Kuch explored our fingers. The lull in the conversation made me sleepy. I briefly wondered at the time. Finally Nev put Kuch back in her bag and returned her to the table.

"Do you want to talk about it now?" he asked quietly.

"I don't know," I said. Which was the truth.

"Did someone else hurt you?" he asked.

I laughed, I couldn't help it. "I think I've been hurting all my life, I just didn't know why."

And then I told him. Told him how I'd come here with a plan to learn about my mother only to discover that my mother was alive after all, and that I had been born to the Da Vias, but Lea, my aunt, the woman who had raised me, had stolen me as an infant from my mother.

"She killed my father," I said. And this was the hardest truth to bear, that she could kill her own brother. And for what reason? To steal a child? How was his life worth less than mine?

Nev made a noncommittal noise.

"What?" I asked.

"It is just . . . you do not know if any of this is true yet, yes? You have only heard one side, and you yourself said they are not trustworthy. So maybe you need to give your family, the ones who raised you, a chance to explain. Maybe it is true and maybe it is not."

"What if I ask her, ask them, though, and they lie to me? Deny it all?"

"Then . . . then I guess you cross those plains when you get there. Either way, it seems a lot of people want you in their life."

"Do you want me in your life?" I asked quietly.

Nev shifted beside me. "Yes."

"Why?"

He turned his neck to face me. "You are . . . different," he said after a pause.

I snorted. "I'm not a traveler, if that's what you mean."

"Yes and no," he said. "You are strong. You do what you

want. You are never frightened."

I looked at the top of the tent. "If I was more afraid," I said, "things would probably go better for me in general." Maybe I'd be less rash.

"No." Nev shook his head. "You would not be Allegra then."

"Yes, but being me doesn't always work out. This me never fit with my Family. I know now why that is, but I spent so long trying to be someone different."

"Did it make you happy? Did it work?"

"No."

"Be you," he said. "Everything else will fall into place."

I closed my eyes. "I don't think it's as clear or as well-meaning as all that. I love Yvain. But it also felt . . . wrong. Like I didn't belong there, either. What if I don't belong anywhere?"

He fell silent then, thinking about something.

"Do you kill a lot of people in Yvain?"

I paused. What qualified as a lot? "I don't know," I said. "I've killed in the past. I'll kill in the future. Most of the people I kill are not good people. They are killers themselves, maybe, or some other sort of villain."

"And killing them gives you enough money to live on?"

"Sometimes. But I also sell perfumes and concoctions."

"Ah," he laughed, and pressed his face against my neck. "No wonder you smell so good."

I snorted. "The Saldanas used to be rich," I said, "but that was before I was born."

"Riches come and go. When they go, we travel once more."

"Do you travel a lot?" I ran my hands over the skin of his stomach and he twitched, ticklish.

"Yes."

"Do you not like being home?"

He paused, weighing his answer. "When I travel, things are different. I have more . . . space, maybe."

"Freedom?" I asked.

He shrugged.

I looked up at the dark canvas roof over our heads. "I would love to travel like you. See the world. Be free."

"No one can be free." He shook his head. "To be free is to have no one. To be alone. The more people we love, the less free we are."

"We can be free and have our family, too," I said.

Nev made a noncommittal hum.

"My Family keeps me caged," I said to him. "They say it's to keep me safe."

"They keep you safe because they love you. If they did not, they would not care about your safety."

I rolled my eyes. He sounded like Lea. Nev shifted and I moved my shoulder so his elbow wasn't jabbing me in the ribs. "Do you have family?" I asked.

"A sister. Older. She is in charge of our status. She is pregnant, which is good. She lost a baby last year, so a new one will help."

"I don't have any siblings. Just a cousin. Emile. He's getting married soon."

"The son of your aunt and uncle?"

"No. They have no children."

I'd heard Les and Lea once, discussing it when I was young and prone to eavesdropping. There were no children for them. They'd died, once, killed by the Da Vias, and been brought back by Safraella, and maybe dying and returning meant one got another chance at life, yes, but one didn't get to bring any new life into the world. "Emile is my aunt's nephew," I continued. "I'm her niece. Children of her brothers, who are dead."

Murdered. One at the hands of the Da Vias. One at the hands of Lea.

"My father traveled six or seven years ago and did not return. My mother died a few years after that. Wasting illness."

"I'm sorry," I said.

He shrugged again. "Who can say why Meska, or any of the gods, take who They take, eh?"

"My aunt probably could. At least with Safraella. She's Her chosen one. She met Her, once."

"Truly?" Surprise colored Nev's voice.

"Yes. She died. Safraella resurrected her."

Nev made a noise I couldn't decipher. "Well," he continued, "those of us not chosen must make do with our small knowledge. *Chorav dend e alo postia chorev.*"

I worked it out. "What we have is all we have?"

He laughed. "Close enough. Your Mornian is not terrible."

"I only know a little," I admitted. "My uncle doesn't speak it all that much."

"Your uncle yesterday." He shifted again.

"Yes." Thinking about Les made my chest hurt. Lea . . . Lea doing what she'd done made a small sort of sense. Her Family had been murdered. She'd been killed and resurrected. Her life had become a madness. But Les . . . I'd thought I was his favorite.

"He had some of the features of a traveler," Nev continued.

"He's only half," I said quietly. "He's lived in Yvain since he was a child."

"Still, though," Nev said. "He must have spoken enough Mornian for you to learn some."

"My great-uncle raised him. They speak it, sometimes."

"Hm. Well, what about this? *Mos phel skornu sir?*"

I turned it around in my head. "Something like, 'are you . . . ready or eager . . . to try again?'"

"Close enough," Nev said, and pulled me to him, lips on mine once more.

sixteen

†

WE FELL ASLEEP, PRESSED AGAINST EACH OTHER IN HIS small bed. My sleep was restless, though, with dreams of fires and monsters and other things that reminded me of the nightmares I'd had at home. When Nev's stirring woke me, I was glad to be free of them.

"What time is it?" I mumbled.

Nev climbed over me and stumbled to his feet, swearing softly in the dark. "Dawn, soon."

I closed my eyes. I'd stayed out too late. My Family would be wondering where I was. And maybe I should have felt bad about it and worried about the trouble I'd be in, but I didn't care about any of that anymore. I needed to confront them about the truth. I needed to know why they had done what they'd done, and why they'd lied to me for so long.

And then I needed to tell them I was staying.

Nev fumbled with something and the lamp on his table flared to life, filling the room with its warm, yellow glow.

"I have to go," I said, though I didn't move. Leaving was the last thing I wanted to do.

He sighed and sat down. I sat up, making room for him.

"Is this it?" he asked quietly.

"I don't know." It was a lie. I just didn't want to say good-bye to him. I thought Lovero would be adventurous and fun, but in the end it hadn't been much of any of those things. The one bright spot had been Nev, and though he would be here as long as the menagerie was, I wouldn't be able to step foot in Lilyan once I joined the Da Vias.

I leaned against his shoulder.

"Maybe you could return someday," I said. "Travel to Ravenna. To visit."

He nodded. But we both knew it wouldn't matter. There would be no waiting for each other. This wasn't some romantic story performed by players. This was real life, and I'd known what I'd gotten myself into when I'd first met him. I just hadn't known what else would befall me and how easy it had been to fall for Nev.

"You . . ." he started to say, then rubbed his face, scrunching his eyes. "I travel," he started over. "I travel so much. I see places. I see people. But I do not ever really *see* them. Yes?" he asked, and I nodded.

"I see you, Allegra. I see you. I see your strength. I see your heart. I do not want to stop seeing you. You are the best travel. There will never be another like this one."

I kissed him again, soft and quiet in his room. Maybe, if Safraella was kind, or if Meska, Culda, and Boamos were kind, we would find each other again.

But I'd never known kindness like that from the gods.

I grabbed my clothes from the floor. My necklace slipped out of the pile and tumbled to my feet. I slid my dress over my head.

Nev gasped.

"What?" I ran my fingers through my hair.

"Where did you get this?" He held my necklace in his palm, staring at the stone and the blue color radiating from the center.

I reached for it. "Why?"

He snatched his hand away.

I paused. "Nev—"

"Allegra, where did you get this?" he repeated more forcefully.

"It was a gift." I held out my hand, waiting for him to return the necklace. The mood had shifted dramatically, and not for the better.

"Who gave this to you?"

"Why does that matter? What are you going on about?"

"This cannot be," he said to himself.

I snatched the necklace from his hand and slipped it over my head.

He looked at me then, and his expression was a mixture of many things, but mostly fear.

I relented. "My uncle gave it to me for my birthday."

He blinked, then grabbed his pants, dragging them up his legs. He snatched his hat. "You must leave. Right now."

"What?"

He was frantic, shoving my shoes toward my feet and tossing me my bodice.

"I said you need to leave." He straightened, and this time his expression had hardened. "Do not come back, not to see me, not even to the menagerie."

"What are you talking about?" I tugged my bodice over my head. The ties had mostly stayed laced and I pulled on them now, tightening the stiff fabric until I could knot it into place. "Have you gone crazy?"

He shook his head. "It does not matter. This is the end between us. There cannot be anything more."

"I thought you *saw* me?" I asked.

He dropped his eyes to the floor, wringing his hat between his hands.

This was it? This was how we said good-bye after everything, with him shoving me out of his room after we'd slept together, telling me not to come back?

It was too warm in here, too warm and too tight. His room was a trick, like his kisses, pulling me in until I was trapped.

I shoved my feet into my shoes. I needed to leave, needed to get out of here.

I twisted my hair at my neck.

He stared at me, some sort of emotion flickering through his eyes, then he looked away.

I turned and shoved past the curtain. If there had been a door I would have slammed it.

I walked down the hallway and out of the common room to find myself in the middle of the bustling menagerie.

I pushed my way through the crowd, not caring who my elbows jabbed, until I was free of it completely and on the streets of Lilyan once more.

The traveler at the entrance did a double take as I exited. He glared at me, and even after I merged with the crowd, I felt his eyes on my back.

I took a deep breath, urging my body to relax, my mind to calm. But my throat felt tight and my eyes burned with unshed tears. I fought against the urge to look back, to peer into the menagerie, to see if Nev was there, standing by his snake cages, with Kuch twisting around his fingers like nothing had happened, like nothing had changed.

But I didn't. Because it wasn't true.

Everything had changed.

I fled from the menagerie, fighting against my tears. If I started to cry, I wouldn't be able to stop, and then I would just be some strange weeping girl.

The streets were still full of people, though not as packed as earlier. People were heading home, to their beds, to sleep the morning and afternoon away, only to continue with the festivities for one more night. And then, their lives would return to normal.

Not mine, though. Mine would be different. Even if I changed my mind, decided to go home to Yvain, continue with my caged life where I didn't belong, things would never be the same for me. I knew truths I hadn't before. They altered everything.

I reached the house without even really being aware that my feet had carried me there. The windows were filled with the warm glow of lamplight. They were home, and awake. I wouldn't escape a confrontation.

I picked up my dress and pushed my way through the courtyard gate and then into the house.

Lea and Les were in the living room, dressed in their leathers, loading their pockets with knives and swords and poisons.

We stared at one another, the house still, the only sound our breaths, until finally Les exhaled loudly. He took two long steps and pulled me into an embrace. He smelled like his leathers, and the ball still, warm wine and tiny little foods.

"We didn't know where you were," he whispered to me harshly. "There was a rumor at the ball, after you left, that the Addamos had carried out some sort of plot in the street that had led to one of their deaths. We saw your abandoned carriage, and the blood in the street. Not enough for two people, but still, when we arrived home expecting to find you, you weren't here."

Lea set her sword on the counter and pushed her bone mask to the top of her head. Each movement was precise, carefully controlled. It was just a cover, a way to actually control her emotions. She thought the mask disguised them, but she was wrong.

"I can't believe you lied to us," she said slowly. Les released me.

"I didn't lie," I said. "My stomach hurt. I wanted to go home."

"But you didn't go home." Still no yelling. Still just calm.

"I had intended to. There was no lie."

Lea glared at me then, but I stood my ground.

"This, right here, is why you can't just walk alone in Lovero." Lea started to pace. "The Addamos could have killed you."

Les sat down on a chair, pulling his mask off the top of his head and setting it on the end table. He rubbed his face.

"Well," I said, "it seemed they were planning on it, but here I stand, unharmed, while one of them lies dead." I waved at my body, dress and all, showing them how unharmed I was.

Of course, I hadn't really expected the rest of the Addamos to fall so easily, but Lea didn't need to know how close it had been. How much fear had rolled through me.

"Don't joke about this," Lea snapped. "It isn't funny."

I sat on the couch, my dress puffing out around me. "I'm not joking," I said. "I understand how serious it was."

"Do you? Really?"

"Yes!" I yelled. "I'm not a child anymore, no matter how much you treat me like one. It was a bad situation with the Addamos, but I didn't bring it on myself. You have a right, maybe, to be angry at me for not going home, but it's unfair to be angry with me because I was attacked. I handled myself well in the fight, without leathers, without a mask. I dropped one and kept them away from me until they were scared off."

I closed my mouth with a snap. I hadn't meant to bring that up, hadn't meant to mention the Da Vias' interference at all. At least not yet, not when I didn't have control of the conversation. If Lea knew about their help, she would grab that and hold on like a ghost with a body.

Lea tilted her head. Les leaned forward in his chair.

"Scared off how?" Lea's voice was deceptively smooth.

"It's nothing." I leaned back against the couch.

"Allegra," Les snapped.

I ground my teeth. "I had some help."

"Help from whom?" Lea stopped her pacing. She stood loose, easy, and anyone who didn't know her would think she was at peace. But I knew this calmness, this looseness was how she looked before she killed someone. Lea was her most dangerous when she was calm.

"Another Family."

"The Caffarellis?" Les was offering me an easy way out of this mess. Because he knew it couldn't be the Caffarellis. They would have told Lea and Les if they had helped me.

"The Da Vias," I said.

Lea inhaled sharply. She and Les exchanged one of their glances, their glances that said there was a secret here, right in this room.

But I knew those secrets now. The truths behind the glances.

"I'm so tired of this." My time to be calm. To be deadly.

167

"You keep secrets from me, and then are disappointed when I keep secrets from you. Where do you think I learned it?"

"You!" Lea shouted at me, her face filled with rage and frustration and something else. Fear? I reeled back. "You have *no idea* about this. The Da Vias . . ."

She paused and closed her eyes, trying to gather her thoughts. And I wondered if any other Family would have been acceptable. Had it been the Maiettas or Gallos or Zarellas who had stepped in to face the Addamos with me, would she react as strongly?

I suspected not.

Lea opened her eyes and turned to Les. "What are they doing? What are their plans here? I can't work it out."

"I didn't even see them at the ball," Les said. "What were they doing in the streets of Genoni?"

I shifted on the couch. "They were on their way to the ball," I said. "There were two of them. One was Bellio Da Via."

Lea blinked a few times rapidly. "Did he speak to you? Did he"—she paused, like she was weighing her words carefully—"try to convince you to do anything?"

This was the time. This was the moment to speak up. To tell them I knew everything. How they had stolen me as a child. How Lea had killed my father, her own brother, and taken me from my mother and escaped with me to Yvain. How she was the reason I didn't fit. She was the reason for all of it.

I swallowed. Opened my mouth to tell them everything.

"No," I said instead, my voice barely more than a whisper. "They didn't ask anything of me."

It would be a fight, when I told them. When I shared that I knew the truth, and that I wasn't going home with them. And I couldn't do it now, not after the fight we'd just had. Not after Les had been so frightened for me.

And I had said the end of Susten. That I would give them these last few days together. I would wait. There was still time.

Lea's shoulders slumped in relief. Because as far as she knew, nothing had changed.

"No more festival, Allegra," she said to me. "You've lost the privilege to leave the house alone."

"What?" My breath caught in my throat.

"You heard me," Lea said. "You don't tell us where you're going means you don't get to go anywhere alone."

My bodice squeezed my chest harder than it had before, making it difficult to breathe. I stood, trying to bring more air into my lungs.

Trapped. Everywhere I went I was trapped.

I stumbled to the back door.

"Allegra," Les said at the same time Lea asked, "Where are you going?"

"To get some fresh air," I mumbled. "Unless I need an escort for that?"

Lea scowled, but her cheeks reddened.

I pushed the back door open and stepped outside into the cool night.

The fresh air had an immediate effect and I took a deep breath, palm pressed against my stomach. Breathe. The first step in any sort of conflict was to breathe. With enough breath I could remain calm, could make rational decisions. Strength only came from a cool mind and heart.

Of course I had learned all this from Lea.

I squeezed my eyes shut. I wouldn't cry. Not for this. Not for them.

But it didn't matter how much I slowed my breathing, the tears still trickled down my cheeks. "Be calm and make rational decisions" was a jest. There weren't any decisions for me to make, rational or otherwise. I had no power. I had no control over my life. I was trapped, caged. I was the tiger in the menagerie.

From the stable in front of me I heard a noise. A rustle that sounded too much like cloth to be one of the horses.

I rubbed my cheeks and picked up my dress, walking across the stones to the stalls. In the far corner I found Emile and Elena pressed against the wall together, kissing. Her hands had slipped beneath his shirt, pushing it up, exposing the bare skin of his stomach.

I gasped in surprise.

"Legs!" Shock colored Emile's voice. Elena removed her hands and he tugged his shirt back into place. "You're home."

Anger and jealousy flared up in me. Emile did whatever he wanted. He didn't need an escort. They trusted him when they didn't trust me. And maybe sometimes I wasn't trustworthy, but maybe sometimes if they just loosened my reins, I could show them that they didn't need to hold on so tightly.

But of course they held me tight. If they loosened their grip on me, they might lose me altogether.

"I see you were looking hard for me," I snapped at Emile. I'd wanted it to come out harsh and strong. But instead my voice broke and my eyes filled with tears again and I just couldn't stand to see the surprised looks on their faces, which faded to something like pity.

I turned and fled from them.

"Allegra!" Emile called after me, but I ignored him. It didn't matter, anyway. What could he possibly say or do that would change anything? He got everything. He lived a life of safety and control and it was exactly what he wanted, so he could never understand me. Had never really understood me before. And when it had just been the two of us it was easy to ignore our differences. But now he had Elena so he didn't need me.

Inside, Lea and Les sat together on the couch.

Les looked like he wanted to say something but I ignored him, too, walking up the stairs to my room where I closed the door, trapping myself inside.

Just another cage, really.

Even if it was a cage of my own making.

seventeen

†

I DIDN'T SLEEP.

I couldn't sleep.

I stripped off my dress, and stood there, clutching it in my hand, while I stared at the mirror, lost in my own thoughts.

Les's necklace hung against my breastbone, its blue stone pale in the dawn light that crept through my window.

Nev had rejected me. Had sent me away like I was nothing, just a fling he'd had while traveling. Less than that, really.

I pressed my fingers against the necklace, feeling its warmth from my skin.

I had just met him. We barely knew each other.

But it didn't feel like that. We'd talked for hours. Shared memories, plans, hopes for the future. I'd thought, here was someone who understood me, truly. Here was someone who felt the same way I did, but who had an access to a sort of freedom I would never know.

And he had thrown it all away for nothing.

"Don't let it hurt you," I said to myself in the mirror.

But it did hurt. Everything hurt because everyone betrayed me.

I dropped my ball gown on the floor and found a clean dress. I slipped it over my head, tugging it into place. I draped my scarf on my shoulders.

Lea and Les had stolen me. Had taken me from the Family I belonged to, the person I was supposed to be, had caged me in Yvain and called it love. And family. But it was all lies.

Love wasn't supposed to hurt.

I wrapped my scarf too tightly around my throat and was forced to loosen it.

The Da Vias hadn't hurt me. Hadn't caged me. Val and Claudia—my mother—had let me go when I'd run from them. Val had helped to save me from the Addamos, and then let me go on my way. They trusted me to be safe. They let me have my freedom.

I was meant to be a Da Via. I belonged with them.

I closed my eyes, trying to ease the pain behind them. My breaths sped and I pressed my hand to my chest, trying to slow them. The air in my room was stale, trapped. I needed . . . I needed . . .

I stumbled to my bedroom window and shoved it open. A small morning breeze puffed in my face, but it wasn't enough. I was suffocating. I needed more.

I climbed out of my window, sliding down a drainpipe until my feet touched the stones of the courtyard. But it was too much, the building behind me. It loomed over me.

I walked. I walked away from the house, from my Family, inhaling deeply, trying to find enough air, trying to ease the ache in my chest.

I walked down the empty streets, past the square where I had eaten the fish skewers. Past the shadow puppet stages, stagnant in the dawn light. Past everything until I found myself at the Ravenna and Lilyan border, the street running between them neutral territory.

I stopped. My breaths, my heartbeat had returned to normal again. I stared at Ravenna. The city that was supposed to be my home.

If I crossed the line now, I could find her again. My mother. Become a Da Via. Return to the life I was always meant to lead.

If I crossed the line now, maybe I would belong, finally. The door to my cage would open and I would no longer be trapped.

If I crossed the line now, there was no going back.

"Allegra," a voice called.

Claudia Da Via stood across the street from me.

She looked beautiful in the morning sun, with her blond hair pulled neatly back and her gray dress highlighting the smoothness of her skin. Seeing her like this, I could understand why my father had loved her.

No. That was dumb. I didn't know my father. I didn't know anything about him, so I couldn't begin to guess why he'd loved Claudia Da Via. And I didn't know her, either, nor what about her was worthy of love. She said she'd searched for me in Yvain, when I was a child, but here I was now, and she wouldn't even cross the street.

"Come home with me." She extended a hand, like she wanted me to take it, like I was a child and she could pull me back into her arms.

But I wasn't a child.

"Did you kill the Saldanas?" I asked her. I thought about the Saldana shrine, the statue of Lea, yes, but behind it the house a charred ruin, a testament to what the Families could, and would, do to one another if given the chance. "Did you burn them in their beds while they slept?

Her hand dropped slowly to her side. "No. I was in labor. You were born that night."

I closed my eyes. I couldn't decide if it was fitting or not that I had been born the same time the Saldanas had been dying. But it was just one more lie I'd been told. My birthday wasn't even the right day.

"You were worshipping Daedara," I said.

Daedara, a god of light and fertility. The Da Vias had turned their worship to Him in secret. It was why their family had grown so large. Why Estella Da Via had ordered the murder of the Saldanas, lest they find out.

"We all were. We were commanded to by our Family head. I don't regret it, Allegra. He brought me you."

I snorted. I couldn't help it. He hadn't brought her anything, then.

Val appeared beside her. He said something to her, then

glanced across the street and saw me. He scowled.

"Come home with us, Allegra," Claudia said. "You're a Da Via. You should be with your Family."

"You've given the Saldanas eighteen years," Val added. "Don't you think that's long enough?"

I blinked. It seemed so logical, so straightforward when he said it like that.

But that wasn't how the Families worked. We didn't get to go back and forth between Families. When Elena married Emile, she would move to Yvain with us and become a Saldana. She couldn't just return to being a Caffarelli whenever she wanted, not unless the marriage completely fell apart, and even then, if they had children together, the children would be Saldanas and remain in Yvain.

And I'd promised myself I'd stay a Saldana until the end of Susten.

Across the street, Claudia and Val stiffened, focusing over my shoulder.

I turned.

Behind me stood Lea, still dressed in her full leathers, bone mask covering her face, knives held in her hands. With the morning sun cascading over her she looked like a replica of the marble statue at the Saldana shrine.

"Allegra," she said, her voice slightly muffled behind her mask. She kept her eyes focused on Claudia and Val across the street.

"Lea," Val called. "So nice of you to join us."

"Let's go home," Lea said to me.

"She's coming with us," Claudia said.

Lea tilted her head slightly. "And yet she stands here in Lilyan."

Which was true. I hadn't gone to the Da Vias yet.

"Allegra," Claudia said. "I'm your mother."

My chest burned at that, because she *was* my mother and I'd spent my whole life wanting one and wanting to know about her and now here she was before me and I couldn't bring myself to cross the street.

"I won't stop you," Lea said quietly to me. "But if you cross that street, it is a final decision. You know this, right? There will be no wedding for Emile and Elena for you. There will be no celebrating Faraday and Beatricia's baby. There will be no more time with me and Les. You will be gone from our Family. You will be gone from us."

I took a step away from the Da Vias. Susten wasn't over yet. I'd told myself I was a Saldana until the end of Susten. To have time to say good-bye.

"You can't take her again," Claudia shouted at Lea.

Lea spread her arms. "I don't see you stopping me."

"You're by yourself this time. No ghosts. No Marcello. No fake clipper by your side."

"These are all truths, Claudia," Lea called. "And yet, you still haven't crossed the street."

Val spoke quietly to Claudia. She narrowed her eyes.

Lea inclined her head and turned her back on them. I went to follow but from the corner of my eye I saw Claudia shove Val, and then she was after us, racing across the street so quickly I barely had time to react.

"Claudia!" Val shouted.

Lea reacted. She hadn't even sheathed her knives so when Claudia leaped at her, daggers in hand, Lea spun and blocked her strike.

Claudia was taller than Lea, and just as fast, but Claudia wore a dress instead of leathers and Lea had come prepared for a fight.

I stared at the two of them, utterly frozen. I didn't know what to do. I didn't know who to help. If I stepped between them and one of them backed down, the other could use the opportunity for gain. But if I didn't step in, they could kill each other.

Their fighting pushed them down the street, toward a market specializing in baked goods. Barrels of flour and sugar stood beside stands displaying loaves of bread.

"Stop!" I raced to them. I watched their hands, their arms, legs, looking for an opportunity to disarm them, but they were so fast. Had it been me in the fight, I would have lost already.

Running footsteps behind me. I spun. Val charged, having gained the courage to cross into Lilyan. I yanked my dagger from my belt. Val dashed to the right, nearly crashing into a flour barrel. He sprang toward me, fist flying up in my face. Flour exploded in my eyes.

Blinded, I lunged toward where he'd been. My knife struck air.

I frantically cleared my face. He wouldn't kill me, but I

couldn't be sure about Lea.

A woman screamed. I gasped and blinked. Through muddy vision I spotted Val between Lea and Claudia, his own knife brandished before him. He sprang at Lea, forcing her to defend against both him and Claudia.

I coughed and rubbed my eyes. Lea needed help.

And then we were no longer alone. Clippers dropped from the roofs around us, beautiful in their black leathers, their bone masks decorated in purple patterns. Five Caffarellis come to stop the invasion on their territory.

Val saw the Caffarellis behind Lea and grabbed Claudia's arms. He yanked her behind him and sheathed his knife. He held his hands before him and pushed Claudia backward, toward Ravenna.

"You are outside your territory, Valentino and Claudia Da Via," a Caffarelli called. He wore metal claws on his hands and his mask had purple flames. Brand had come himself.

Val waved his empty hands before him and continued to push Claudia back, though she struggled against him, trying to get past him to attack Lea again.

"I apologize on behalf of myself and my sister," Val said. "It will not happen again."

The Caffarellis strode closer to Val and Claudia, forcing him to push her back even more. I stepped behind them and rushed to Lea's side. She hadn't sheathed her knives yet, and I kept mine out as well. Anything could still happen.

Finally Val turned and grabbed both of Claudia's wrists, squeezing until she gasped and dropped her knife.

Val gave a hasty bow to the Caffarellis and then dragged Claudia back toward Ravenna.

She fought against him, all wrath and rage until finally she screamed, a loud, high-pitched sound that grated against my ears. "You can't have her again!"

This was not the calm woman I'd met at the restaurant. This was someone completely different, lost in her fury.

Val pulled Claudia across the street until they were safe in Ravenna once more. They disappeared around a corner.

Beside me, Lea sheathed her knives. I did the same, and then brushed more flour from my eyes.

Brand approached Lea and she conferred quietly with him. He nodded, and he and the other Caffarellis returned to wherever it was they had come from.

Then it was just me and Lea, alone together on the street.

eighteen

†

WE WALKED HOME IN COMPLETE SILENCE, NEITHER OF us knowing what to say.

Or, more likely, Lea had been trying to decide where to start because when we finally reached the house, she stopped me before we went inside.

She stared at me from behind her bone mask. I knew she wanted to take it off. She never liked to have serious discussions with the Family behind the mask, but she couldn't remove it in public. She wouldn't let the common see her face. It was too much of an ingrained habit with her. Sometimes it seemed the bone mask was her true face.

"You . . ." she started to say, but then paused. I didn't offer her any help, mostly because I knew if I started talking first, I would either break into tears or start screaming, and neither of those seemed like good things.

"I don't even know where to begin," she finally said.

I licked my lips. They tasted chalky and dry from the flour. "Don't you?"

Behind the mask her eyes narrowed. "You snuck out, put yourself, the Caffarellis, our Family in danger."

"Family," I said slowly. It tasted strange in my mouth, the word. Or maybe it was because I was speaking with Lea. I looked at her again, at the bleak starkness of her mask. "I was thinking about entering Ravenna."

"You . . . what?" Lea asked. I'd had rare opportunity to see her so shocked before this moment. "How could you do that? You could have been killed."

I shook my head. "No. And don't pretend like you believe that, either, especially not after that little skirmish."

"That little skirmish could have ended with you or me dead, so maybe try not to treat it so cavalierly."

I shrugged. I couldn't find it in me to take it more seriously. I felt strangely empty and raw, like my insides had been scooped out. "It wasn't me they were trying to kill."

And I'd suddenly had enough of all of it, of talking to Lea, of dancing around the point of everyone and everything.

I strode to the house.

"Allegra!" Lea snapped, but I ignored her and pushed my way past the front door.

It was cool and dark inside. The lamps needed to be lit.

Lea stormed into the house beside me and I could practically hear the anger in her sharp breaths. Les came down the stairs at the same moment and when he saw me his shoulders slumped and he closed his eyes.

"Ghosts weep, Allegra."

"She was on the Ravenna border," Lea practically spat. She strode around me and yanked off her mask, setting it on the table.

"What?" Les asked, caught between shock and anger. "How could you do something so careless? What if the Da Vias had found you?"

"They did." Lea rubbed her face.

And then because this little event hadn't been enough, Emile entered from the back door, smiling. But when he saw the three of us, he stopped. "What's wrong?"

"We have to leave," Lea said.

"What?" he asked. Even Les looked at her in surprise.

"We have to leave. Immediately. We can't stay here any longer. The Da Vias . . ." She pinched the bridge of her nose. "The Da Vias breached the Caffarelli territory to try to get to Allegra and me. If they did it once, they could do it again. We can't take that chance and we can't let the Caffarellis face such a burden on our behalf."

"But what about Elena?" Emile asked, and he sounded so worried that for a moment I felt guilty, until I remembered that none of this was my fault.

"She'll come with us. We're leaving at first light. Sooner, if we can pack fast enough. If I have to keep ghosts off us, I will."

"I just . . ." Emile looked between Lea and Les, bewildered. Then he settled on me. "What happened?"

"It's complicated," Lea said. "There have been some

183

developments with Allegra."

"With Allegra?" he asked.

"Emile—" Lea started to say but something bubbled up inside me and I couldn't contain it anymore, couldn't stand that they were talking about me like I wasn't there, couldn't stand the rage coursing through me.

I screamed. Loud and long and it felt so good just to let it out.

When I stopped, everyone stared at me, shocked.

"What the hells?" Emile asked.

I whipped around until I was facing Lea. "You stole me."

She closed her mouth, pinching her lips together. Silence echoed around us.

"Allegra . . ." Les finally said.

"Your stole me from my mother," I continued.

"It's not what it seems," Lea said.

"Don't lie to me!" I yelled. "You've lied to me my entire life. Everything about me is a lie and you kept it secret from me for eighteen years. Eighteen years! All this time I thought I was an orphan, that my father had died in the fire and my mother had died in childbirth, but she's alive and you're the one who killed my father and now you want to stand there and tell me it's not the truth?"

I was panting, staring at her, daring her to deny it.

Emile looked at all three of us with wide eyes.

Lea exhaled slowly through her nose. "I took you," she said. "I took you from your crib and we walked out of that house and I never once looked back and never regretted it.

You want to call me a child thief, then go ahead, but it was the right thing to do and I would do it again."

Her words hit me like a bucket of canal water. I closed my eyes and rocked back on my heels. Dumb. I was so, so dumb. All my life I'd been living a lie. I was a stolen child, and now to have any sort of relationship with my mother, with the Family I'd been stolen from, I would have to give up the Family I was raised in, give up the people I'd spent my entire life loving.

It was unfair.

But I'd never fit with them. And I never would.

I took a deep breath, then walked up the stairs to my room. No one tried to stop me.

As I turned the corner, Emile finally spoke up. "Allegra has a mother?"

I couldn't even take any satisfaction from knowing he'd at least been in the dark. Hells, maybe he had a mother somewhere, too. Nothing would surprise me anymore.

In my room I looked at my things. I hadn't brought much. I hadn't thought I wouldn't be returning home. I hadn't thought this would be the end of my time as a Saldana. I would have said good-bye to Marcello, Faraday, and Beatricia if I'd known. Now I would have to send them letters.

I remembered the letter Tulio Maietta had given to me at the ball. I found my purse and pulled it out, setting it carefully on the table. They could bring it back with them.

I needed to pack my things. I picked up my gown from

where I'd left it on the floor and spread it on my bed. It was beautiful, but I would never wear it again. I would forsake Saldana black for Da Via red.

My eye caught the brown stain of one of the underlayers and I remembered the blood I had wiped there, and the way Nev's hands had felt against my ankle when he thought I'd been injured. Which made me remember the way the rest of him felt, too, in the darkness of his room.

He'd sung that nursery rhyme about the Three.

We sing a song about the Three, of Meska, Culda, and Boamos. Boamos gives us wealth and thievery while Culda sings us safely home. And great Meska, with her animals, wraps us in our mother's warmth.

And then he'd told me that story about Nula and Bema, wrapped in each other's embrace after they had drowned, loving each other endlessly, even in death.

Soon I would be with my own mother. I wondered if I would love her as much as Bema had loved Nula. Or was it too late for that? Had Lea stolen that chance from me, too?

I turned away from the dress and pulled out my empty bag from under my bed. I caught a glimpse of myself in the mirror.

Flour still coated me, except in spots where I had rubbed it away. Tears had traced vertical lines down my cheeks. I hadn't even realized I'd been crying. But the white powder and the tear tracks made it almost seem like I was wearing my bone mask. I'd always thought of the water droplets decorating my mask as rain, but maybe they'd been tears all along.

I took a rag and scrubbed the flour from my face and throat and neck. I probably needed to bathe, but I just didn't care enough to make the effort.

Someone knocked on my door. I studied it, wondering how to respond. The choice was taken from me when Lea pushed the door open.

I stared at her and she stared at me.

"What are you doing?" She finally broke the silence.

"I need space," I said. "Can't you just once give me space?"

"You were attacked by the Addamos mere hours ago, and you think it's a good idea to go off on your own because you want some space? I thought you were smarter than that."

A cold flame of anger burned through me. "Yes, well, I thought you were someone who didn't steal children and lie to them, so I guess we're both disappointments."

Lea made a noise, some sort of angry, exasperated groan. "What do you want me to say? I did what I thought was right."

"How could it have been right?" I shouted at her. "You *stole* me! You stole me from my mother and you killed my father, your own brother! How could any of that be right?"

She shook her head. "I hope and pray that you never have to understand what it's like to have your hands coated in the blood of your family, Allegra. None of the decisions I made were easy. And I've certainly made mistakes in my life. Mistakes based on love. On anger. Mistakes that had grave consequences. But taking you out of that home was not one of them."

She paused and sighed. "Do you hate your life so much? Did we treat you so poorly?"

She sounded honestly concerned and sad and for a moment the anger inside me melted. But then I remembered the sound of Claudia screaming as Val dragged her away from me.

"How can you ask me that?" I asked. "I have nothing to compare it to, because you took me away from the life I was supposed to lead."

"This is the life you are supposed to lead." Lea jabbed her finger at her feet. "Safraella is not a god of fate. You can't look at the past and imagine how your life would be if things had been different. That way lies madness and no comfort comes from it. Believe me, I know."

"Believe you?" I raised my eyebrows. "How can I ever believe you again? My whole life has been based on a lie."

Lea glanced around the room. "Maybe. Maybe we lied to you—"

"There's no maybe!"

"Fine. Yes, we lied to you. We lied about the manner of your father's death. And I lied about your mother and your heritage. And I lied about taking you. But I did these things because I wanted to keep you safe. Because the Da Vias were a nest of vipers, and I couldn't stand to leave you with them."

I shook my head. "But I'm a Da Via," I said. "And if you hate them still, after all these years, then you must hate me, too. Because I'm one of them by blood. I'm Allegra Da Via as much as I am Allegra Saldana."

"I can never forgive the Da Vias for what they did," she

said. "For what they took from me. From Emile. From you, even. It's why we kept you confined. Why we didn't want to bring you to Lovero. I knew the Da Vias would find you. I can't let them take something else."

Everything in my body stilled. "You were going to continue lying to me?"

Lea shook her head. "It's not that simple. We hoped you would find something to ground you, to take your edge off. If you had found a reason to keep you with us—marriage, a child maybe, devotion, anything—we would have told you the truth."

"You would have told me the truth only after I was forever trapped, you mean," I said. "You speak about what the Da Vias took from you, but here you are, taking from me."

"It's not like that."

"Isn't it?"

"Allegra—"

"I'm done." I cut her off. I was done listening to her lies. Her excuses. "When you leave, to go back to Yvain, I'm not going with you."

She paused, her eyebrows a sharp V as she tried to reason through what I had said. "You can't just stay in Lilyan with the Caffarellis."

I grabbed my bag. "I'm not staying in Lilyan."

I pushed my way past her, out into the hall.

"No," she said after me, racing to catch up. "Allegra, no!"

I walked down the stairs and dropped my bags at the bottom. Les and Emile had lit a fire in the hearth and their conversation fled when Lea and I appeared.

"I'll come back," Emile said, and glanced at me quickly before heading for the front door.

"What's going on?" Les asked.

"Tell her that she's coming back with us when we leave," Lea said, pointing her finger at me.

Les looked at me, eyes wide in surprise.

"Umm," Emile said from the front door. "There's a package out here if someone wants to open it . . ."

"Not now, Emile!" Lea snapped.

I strode to the front door.

Emile gave me a tight-lipped smile, and then left, heading off to find Elena, no doubt.

A small package sat on the front step. It hadn't been there when Lea and I had returned so it must have just been delivered.

It wasn't very big, the size of a large block of salt, maybe. It had been tied with a string, but there were no markings on it and it wasn't addressed to anyone. There was a small, single hole on the side where a postman had mishandled it.

I picked it up and walked back inside, setting it on the kitchen table. I took a seat. Les sat beside me.

"What thoughts are tangling in your head, *kuch nov*?" he asked me quietly. Les never yelled like Lea, or got angry like Lea. He just got calm, and quiet. And maybe disappointed.

"I have to leave this Family."

Lea threw her hands up in the air, and stomped up the stairs to busy herself in their bedroom.

Les looked at me, not trying to hide the pain in his eyes. "You would go to them? You would become a Da Via?"

"Did you really think you could hold on to me forever?"

He shook his head. "You were always a wild one. Always breaking the rules, wanting to play the games your own way. But if I pictured you leaving, I thought it would be with the Caffarellis, maybe. So you wouldn't be lost to us forever. If you go the Da Vias, we will never see you again."

"I could write letters." And though I meant it mostly as a joke, Les shook his head.

"Letters are just empty shells of the person you really miss. Ask Lea about that. She can tell you."

I didn't need to ask Lea. All I had to do was think about the letter Tulio Maietta had given me for Marcello. That letter was just an echo of Marcello's long dead lover. That letter would not return him to Marcello. "I don't want to ask her anything."

Les sighed. "You can't shut her out forever. She raised you. She loves you."

"Does she?" I asked. "She stole me from my mother. She killed my father."

"No," Les countered. "She didn't."

My face must have registered my doubt because he continued.

"Your father, Matteo Saldana, died that night in the Da Via's home, yes, but I killed him, *kuch nov,* not Lea. I'm not sure Lea could have brought herself to do it."

I closed my eyes. I felt like I was drowning in a canal, that

191

no matter how much I stretched, I couldn't reach the glassy surface above me. "I don't believe you," I said. "You're just trying to protect her. Cover for her."

"Lea Saldana has never needed my protection," he said. "And I'm not lying to you in this. Your father attacked us. Lea didn't know who he was at first, but when she discovered the truth, the fight drained away from her."

"So you killed him. My father."

I grabbed the package on the table, twisting it around, looking for the knot in the string to open it.

"Yes. I killed him to save Lea. To save her life. To save her from the grief of doing it herself. But also I did it because Safraella told me I would have to."

I paused, the package forgotten in my hands as I looked at him and saw he was earnest. Les never spoke about meeting Safraella the night they'd been killed, but here he had given me something, a small truth from his experience.

"We didn't go there to steal you," he continued. "We went there to save Marcello. And to kill the Da Vias. But after your father was dead, we found a nursery with you and Emile inside. And Lea couldn't leave you there. You were so tiny. And you and Emile were all that remained of her brothers, of her family. I think she would have rather died than leave you there.

"So we freed Marcello and went back for you."

"And then you killed all the Da Vias," I snapped, slamming the package on the table. Something shifted inside it, sliding across the inside of the box. "Let's not forget that slaughter."

"Safraella took the Da Vias. If they hadn't turned to another god, the ghosts would have never been able to enter their home. The deaths of the Da Vias are on the Da Vias alone. We would have left them alone had they not tried to stop us."

"I don't believe you," I whispered.

He leaned closer to me. "I didn't grow up with parents," he said. "I never knew my father. My mother died when I was very young. All I had was Marcello, and you know how he is. But I tried to do my best by you and Emile. More than anything we wanted to keep you safe. To keep you free from heartbreak. I didn't want you to grow up knowing I had killed your father. That I didn't even hesitate. That I would do it again. I didn't want you to grow up thinking there was something wrong with you because you were a Da Via, a member of a ruined Family. We wanted . . . we wanted better things for you."

"You still could have told me the truth. You have no idea what it's like to find out that you have a mother you thought was dead."

My whole life I'd wanted to know about my mother, and in reality I could have actually *known* her.

"You're right," he said. "I don't. And I'm sorry for that. But I know how you often act or make decisions before you fully think things through."

"This is not one of those times," I said. "I've been thinking about it since I learned the truth the day we got here."

He paused, seemingly collecting his words before he continued. "At the very least just know it was a rash decision that made us take you from the Da Vias that night."

I tugged at the knot securing the string around the package.

"If you'd had time to think about it," I said, "would you have changed your mind? Or would you have still taken me?"

"I would take you," he said. He didn't even hesitate. "I would take you a thousand times over, *kuch nov*."

The knot securing the package came apart. The string tumbled off and coiled on the table. I flipped open the lid.

Sound.

A slither, maybe. Or a hiss.

A flash of movement.

A white stick sprang from the box. Les grabbed my hand and jerked me away.

The stick hit Les on the wrist.

But it wasn't a stick. Hadn't ever been a stick.

It was a snake. Small, white, with pearlescent scales. I'd last seen it twisting around the fingers of a traveler boy who'd had callused hands and tasted like oranges and who I missed more than I wanted to admit.

Les yanked it from his arm.

She's venomous, Nev had told me.

Les threw Kuch into the fire.

She bites anyone who doesn't smell like me.

nineteen

SILENCE BETWEEN US. WE STARED AT EACH OTHER, IN shock.

"What?" I finally managed to utter.

Les clutched his arm, using his right hand to tightly squeeze his left wrist. He closed his eyes for a moment and seemed to slump. Then he stood, kicking his chair away from him. It screeched loudly and a moment later Lea appeared at the top of the stairs.

"What's going on?" she asked as she came down.

Les grabbed his cutter from its sheath, still keeping pressure on his wrist. He set his cutter on the table before me.

I blinked rapidly, staring at the weapon. He kept it well honed, and it was heavy. Heavy and sharp. It was made for doing violent damage.

A weapon strong enough to cut through bone.

"What is going on?" Lea repeated, her voice firm and sharp. It was a tone of voice she used when she wanted answers. She hadn't seen what had happened but she could sense the tension in the air.

Les looked at me and nodded to the cutter that still sat before me on the table.

I picked it up. The handle felt smooth and worn after years of Les gripping it.

"I asked a question!" Lea shouted behind us. She sounded almost panicked. But Lea never panicked. Panic was for amateurs. Lea had been the one to teach me this.

"It was a snake in the box," Les answered. "It bit me. It's venomous."

Les put his arm on the table, right hand still squeezing his left wrist. Two tiny puncture marks, no bigger than a pin, leaked blood. But we lived with Lea. We knew our poisons, our venoms. Sometimes it didn't matter how big the needle was.

"No." Lea shook her head. "We are not doing what I think you're doing."

"No choice," he said.

"No!" Her arm sliced the air before her. "There's an antivenin. I can find an antivenin! Where's Emile? He can help!"

Les shook his head. "No time."

"We're not just going to hack you apart!"

"No time," he repeated. Then he closed his eyes and exhaled. He looked over his shoulder at her.

I'd never seen Lea scared before. But she was frightened now, my aunt. She, who could make the common flee with just a glimpse of her mask, who had destroyed the

196

entire force of the Da Via Family.

Who had died and faced a god once, and returned.

So much fear poured from her, I could practically taste it.

"There's no time, *kalla* Lea," he said. Then he leaned over and kissed her and she pressed her hands to either side of his face. And my chest burned and ached until I had to look away from them, look away from their love and tears and everything because it was too much. Everything was too much.

Lea grabbed on to Les's shoulders, holding him in place.

"*Kuch nov,*" Les said to me.

I rubbed my eyes, nodding.

Then I chopped Les's arm off.

⸻ ❈ ⸻

Blood.

So much blood.

And I was used to blood. I'd seen blood since I was a child. My life was practically a ballad of blood.

But this was different. This was Les.

And I was the one who had made him bleed.

There was movement, shouting, orders, and Les's pale, pale face before he passed out. But I couldn't focus on any of this because all I could see was the blood coating the table, and his left arm, no longer a part of him. He'd brushed my hair when I was a child with that arm. He'd taught me how to throw a knife with that arm. Les was left-handed. He'd probably never use his cutter again.

I looked at the weapon, still in my hand. I dropped it on

the table. I couldn't stand the feel of it anymore. It had been his favorite weapon and I'd used it to destroy a piece of him.

I closed my eyes and took a deep breath. And then the sounds surrounding me clarified into words.

Lea had wrapped Les's arms tightly. The white bandage was already soaked through with blood.

"I need to find an antivenin in case any venom got through." Lea was back in charge once more, though her cheeks were bright pink, the only sign of her emotions. "I need to know what kind of snake it was." She tied off the bandage with a grunt.

"He's bleeding too much." My voice was quiet and empty. It sounded like a different person's. Les was so pale. He could die from the blood loss. He could die from infection. He could die if we hadn't been quick enough to stop the venom. "We need a doctor."

"Allegra," Lea said. "What kind of snake was it?"

I shook my head. "It's too much blood."

I took a step away, toward the front door. A doctor would stop the bleeding. A doctor would save his life.

"Allegra!" Lea shouted, and I looked up at her and took a deep breath.

"I'm going to get help," I said. "To get a doctor."

And then I turned and fled out the front door.

I stumbled in the courtyard, trying to get my feet to work right. My body seemed so far away. I reached the gate. The wrought iron slammed into my palms. Everything snapped into focus.

Les could die.

No. I wouldn't allow it. I took a deep breath, clearing my head even more. I ran down the street. Looking for a sign that would signal a doctor, or someone who could point me in the right direction.

I turned the corner, my boots slapping the street. A trickle of water in front of a fountain reflected white, pearlescent from the morning sun. Like the snake that had bitten Les.

Like Kuch.

My chest constricted, as if Kuch was wrapping her scales around my heart. It didn't make sense. Where had the box come from? And why was Kuch inside?

It was an attack. It had to be. An attack from our enemies. The Addamos. The Da Vias.

No. That made no sense.

Nev had told me Kuch was a rare snake, and only found in a certain part of the world. The Addamos and Da Vias wouldn't know anything about that. And they didn't even know how to find us.

I clasped my necklace. The necklace Les had given to me. My throat tightened and I gasped for air.

There was something going on here. Some mystery I couldn't solve right now, not while I was running, looking for help. Where was a doctor?! But that snake had to have been Kuch. That was the only logical conclusion. Which meant Nev had to be involved.

My stomach churned and I barely managed to stumble to an alley before I vomited.

I spat and wiped my mouth, loosening my scarf, trying to breathe. But I couldn't catch my breath. I couldn't do anything but lean against the wall, head bowed, and gasp for air while tears poured down my cheeks.

I was going to leave him. Les. And now I might not even get the choice anymore, not if he left us first.

A sob escaped me but I straightened and took a deep breath. The mystery, the why and how of it all could be solved later. Right now his life was the priority.

A scraping sound reached me from the alley entrance. I turned.

A whisper in the morning air. A pinch on my neck.

I touched the skin beneath my ear and my fingers came back with a small dart between them, a tiny, white down feather attached at the end.

A blow dart.

Clippers used blow darts.

I spun, searching the alley behind me but it was dark. Too dark. I raised my hand but I couldn't see it. I was blind.

Fatigue swept over me. The ground heaved beneath my feet. I stumbled

Shuffling before me. Hands on my arms. Callused fingers.

A man's voice. Words I couldn't understand.

Then nothing.

twenty

†

CREAKS AND GROANS FLOWED OVER ME. MY BODY bumped and moved outside of my control. Blackness.

My stomach churned. I rolled and vomited.

A voice. Male. I couldn't understand his words.

Another voice. Another man. This one familiar. Their words tangled in my head.

I forced my eyes open. A shadow hovered over me. Something pricked my neck.

Blackness.

———⊰⊱———

The creaks and groans returned.

I woke slowly, regaining my wits. Memories came back to me. Of what had happened the last time I tried to wake. I kept my eyes clenched shut. I would not give myself away again.

My stomach fought me once more, but this time I seized control of it, willing it to calm, to ease its nausea.

I'd been attacked. Pricked by a blow dart. Someone had taken me.

I breathed shallowly and sank into my senses.

Wooden planks beneath me. And movement. A canal boat.

Something snorted. No, not a boat. A cart or a wagon being pulled by horses.

No sounds of people. The rolling wheels below me were muffled. No streets. No city. The dead plains. Which meant it was day and not night.

I'd been out for at least a few hours, then. Long enough for them to get me on a cart and out of the city.

No heat on my skin. Stale air. A covered wagon, blocking the sun.

I shifted my wrists, slowly moving them apart. Then did the same with my ankles. No bindings. I was free to move.

A mistake on their part.

The cart stopped.

Muffled voices outside as people conversed. At least three, maybe more.

A noise beside me. Someone was in the cart with me.

They shifted and stepped over my prone body.

I chanced a quick look.

Shadows covered everything, leaving any clues hidden from sight. Then a beam of light burst into the cart. The person inside with me had pushed aside a curtain. They stepped outside and the curtain flopped closed, sending me into darkness once more.

I held my breath and listened. Nothing. I was alone.

I opened my eyes fully and tried to sit up.

My body was sluggish. It felt heavy, like it weighed more than a horse, or a house. I groaned and bit my lip, but finally managed to pull myself to a seated position.

My head spun from the movement. I paused, reorienting myself.

The cart had two long benches on either side of where I sat on the floor. There were some supplies at the front, behind my head, but nothing else.

My fingers twitched against my pockets. All my weapons had been removed, including the needle I kept sewed into the hem of my dress. They'd searched me thoroughly.

Voices outside again, still too muffled to make out what they were saying. They drifted closer, then farther away.

The curtain on the back of the wagon snapped open. I covered my eyes from the flash of light.

"You are awake."

I lowered my arm, blinking until my eyes adjusted, until I could better see the figure silhouetted at the end of the wagon. A traveler boy with a round hat on his head.

Nev.

"What's going on?" My words slurred. I pressed my hands together, trying to regain control of my body. Something was wrong with me. I wasn't working.

Nev climbed into the wagon and the curtain closed again, slipping us into darkness.

Nev dug through a bag behind me, then pulled out a

bottle. He popped off the cork. "Here." He handed it to me, but even with both hands I didn't have the strength to hold it.

"Something's wrong," I said, then Nev helped me tip the bottle to my lips.

Cool, refreshing fruit juice poured into my mouth, sweet, but with a hint of heat that tasted unfamiliar to me.

I drank as much as I could, letting the fruit juice ease the ache in my mouth and throat. Finally, Nev lowered the bottle and I took a deep breath.

I stared at him, trying to remember how I had gotten here with Nev, where we were, what was going on.

Nev wouldn't look at me. He kept his eyes on his hands as he replaced the cork in the bottle and then the bottle back in the bag.

Something wasn't right. I wasn't seeing things clearly. Seeing things.

I looked at Nev again. "You said you saw me. Really saw me . . ." The memories of what had happened were coming back to me. How Nev had kicked me out of his tent. How I had wandered to Ravenna, only to witness Claudia and Lea fight. How we'd gone home and argued and then Les—

Blood. Les's blood. Les's arm.

My stomach heaved and I barely managed to crawl to the end of the wagon, shoving the curtain aside, before I vomited up all the juice I had just drunk.

Nev sat beside me, rubbing my back as I emptied my stomach.

I wiped my mouth and sat up, looking at the landscape before me.

Late afternoon sun seemed to set the world on fire. Everything looked . . . wrong. Different. Not the dead plains I knew. There were no green, rolling hills. Instead the grass was gold, and everything looked flatter.

A man appeared to the far right. He was tall, with a shaved head. I'd seen him before, at the entrance to the menagerie. He'd glared at me the night Nev had sent me away.

The travelers had taken me. They'd tried to kill me, and when that hadn't worked, they'd taken me from the streets of Lovero, secreted me away in this cart, and fled.

I closed the curtain and leaned back against the bench in the cart. Nev sat across from me, glancing at me from time to time, his neck flushed with some sort of emotion.

"You took me," I said, my voice a hoarse croak. I rubbed my mouth again.

"I am sorry," he whispered, looking anywhere but at me. And when he did lift his eyes to meet mine he looked genuinely confused and sad and I was so, so angry when my chest constricted, when a part of me wanted to press my lips to his, to kiss away his sadness.

But Nev was not the person I'd thought he was. If he'd ever been. All I had to do was think of Les, of the blood on the table, the sound of his cutter in my hands, slamming through his bone and flesh. To remember that.

Rage flowed over me.

I lunged at Nev. I didn't have a weapon, but I didn't care. I

205

would make him bleed, would make him hurt the way he'd hurt me.

I hit him in the face.

Pain bloomed across my fingers, but Nev's grunt was like music.

I punched him in the stomach.

He gasped and bent over.

I rained punches and slaps and scratches and anything I could think of on him, until he covered his head with his arms, until he finally managed to shuffle away to the other end of the wagon.

"Stop!" he shouted. Blood dripped from his nose. His left eye was already bruising and his lip was split and oozing blood.

My chest heaved and my body trembled like I was recovering from a long illness. But none of that mattered. I smiled at the damage I'd done.

"What are you doing?" Nev raised his fingers to his lips and then scowled when he pulled them away and saw the blood.

"You took me!" I said, the anger gripping me again. "You kidnapped me."

Any anger he felt at my attack seemed to fall away from him.

"You can't deny it," I said.

He shook his head and turned to face me. "Of course I cannot. You are here."

"You sent Kuch," I said, "to try to kill me."

And though my voice rang strong and accusatory, I couldn't help the pain that lanced through me at this.

"What?" he asked. "No."

"I saw her, Nev! I opened the box!"

He took his hat off and crushed it in his hands, before he rubbed the top of his head. "I thought . . . I hoped maybe . . . maybe you would still smell like me. That she would not bite you."

I stared at him. Ridiculous. Everything about him was ridiculous. "I slept with you hours ago, Nev! You think I didn't bathe? After you kicked me out of your tent, it was the first thing I did!"

Lies. I was a liar. But I didn't care about the truth. I cared about causing pain.

His face flushed red at my words.

"She would have killed me!"

Nev closed his eyes and shook his head. "You do not understand."

"Nev!" Someone shouted from outside the wagon.

Nev groaned and got to his feet, hunched over. "Stay here." He slipped out the back of the wagon.

Stay here. If he thought I was going to stay here, he really didn't know me at all.

I slid out of the wagon, greeting the warm afternoon sun.

My legs collapsed beneath me.

I crumpled, grabbing on to the wagon at the last second to prevent a complete fall to the ground.

Sweat coated my forehead and my whole body shook.

Weakness spread through my limbs and I was reminded of a time when I was a child and fell ill. When the illness had finally passed, it was still days before I regained my strength.

Someone shouted and a moment later Nev was at my side, trying to help me back into the wagon. I slapped his hands away.

"I told you to stay here," he said as I climbed back into the warm darkness of the wagon.

"What did you do to me?" I gulped air, trying to catch my breath and ease my trembling.

"It will wear off," Nev said as an explanation. "Another day. Maybe two. You will be back to normal."

"What did you do to me?" I hissed at him.

He swallowed but before he could respond, the curtain at the end of the wagon was yanked open. A woman with brown skin, wide shoulders, and short hair glared at us. Perrin, the woman from the menagerie who had teased the tiger. She snapped at Nev, speaking Mornian so quickly I couldn't pick out a single word.

"No," Nev replied, shaking his head. She repeated her question and Nev continued to shake his head.

Perrin slapped him in the face with the back of her hand.

Nev's head rocked back, and he stumbled before regaining his balance. He took a deep breath before calmly looking at Perrin again. She had reopened the split lip I had given him, and blood trickled down his chin. He wiped it away without a thought.

"No," Nev repeated.

Perrin's jaw tightened. Another traveler shouted. Perrin's eyes flicked to the dead plains and then she slowly smirked.

"How long do you think you can last?" she asked him, speaking so I could understand her.

Nev responded in Mornian, and though I couldn't work through what he said with the pounding in my head, I could hear the resolve in his words.

Perrin snorted and retreated, dropping the curtain.

Someone shouted, and the crack of reins snapped through the air. The wagon lurched forward, causing me to tumble backward until I grabbed the bench.

We were on the move again. I pulled myself onto the bench, sitting up, trying to calm and ease the illness raging though my body.

Nev hopped into the back of the wagon and sat across from me, resting his head against the wall and closing his eyes.

"She was angry at you," I said.

"She is always angry." He sounded tired. I was sure I did, too. "She thought you were trying to escape."

"I was," I said.

"I know."

Silence between us then, filled only by the creak of the wagon.

"Where are we going?" I asked.

"Mornia." He sighed and looked at me then.

Mornia. It wasn't unexpected, really. But then they were travelers and could go wherever they wanted. And I didn't know what was going on, which made it hard to plan.

I needed to get out of this wagon. I needed to get back to Lovero.

"Why am I even here?" I pulled my knees to my chest. My trembling had stopped, but I still felt weak. I wasn't going anywhere until my strength returned.

"We are not like you," he said.

"No one's like us," I hissed. "We're disciples of Safraella. We are Her hands in the world and perform Her dark work."

"That is not what I mean. Travelers are not like Loverans, or people from Rennes. We have more gods than you."

"Meska, Culda, and Boamos," I said. "Yes, I know. People can worship whomever they want."

"Yes, but they worship a single god. We worship three. They are equals among us. It can complicate things. I told you to hide the necklace," he mumbled, glancing at the entrance to the wagon.

"What does my necklace have to do with anything?" I snapped.

"You were seen with it, when you left the menagerie. They think you are a thief of our ways."

"What ways? And how I am the thief? It's your god who asks for thievery. It's you who have stolen me from my home."

"This is not only a matter of Boamos," he said. "You do not know what you do by wearing the *singura*. The necklace."

"And you do not know what you do by taking me from

my Family," I snarled. "Do you think they will let you keep me? Do you think they will not come for me? The Saldanas are favored of Safraella. My aunt is chosen by Her. She will come for me and you will rue the day you ever took me in the night."

Lea had told me what it was like, standing before Safraella in the land of the dead. Safraella had greeted her amid of forest made of bones.

The bones of gods, Lea had told me. The bones of Safraella's enemies.

"I have no choice in the matter." He pulled his hat off and rubbed the top of his head. "I have little status and everything I do have I used to save you."

"To save me," I stated. I didn't feel very saved.

"Perrin wanted to kill you."

"I'm harder to kill than I look."

"I know."

I scowled. He knew I was trying to escape. He knew I was hard to kill. He knew all these things about me, and yet here we were, together because he had taken me.

"You can make this right, Nev," I said. "There's still time. You can let me go. You can tell the other travelers you lost me. No one would need to know the truth."

He shook his head. "No. We are in the dead plains. There are ghosts. And even if there were not ghosts, it would not work. We would just look for you again."

Of course, it wouldn't just be a single ghost in the dead plains, and I'd only escaped with Emile's help.

"I need to go home, Nev. I need to be with my Family. It's only been a day. If I return now they won't even be angry . . ."

"Allegra—"

"We can forget everything. Forget all of this and just go back to our lives."

"Allegra, no," he said. "It has been more than a day."

I blinked. More than just a day. "How can that be possible?"

"We kept you drugged. We only woke you for short times, for water. Some small foods."

"How long?" I whispered.

"You probably cannot remember," Nev said. "The drug causes that. Same with your weakness. You will recover."

"How long?" I said louder.

Nev sighed. "Over fifteen days."

Fifteen days. Fifteen.

I closed my eyes. I tried not to think about Les, or my family and what they thought about my disappearance. But I couldn't help it. My chest squeezed me once more and I gripped my necklace, trying to calm down. But there was no respite from this. I'd been gone so long, they had to think me dead.

"Allegra . . ." Nev started.

I shook my head. "Don't. Don't talk to me."

They couldn't save me. My family. Either of them, the Saldanas or the Da Vias. They probably had no idea what had happened to me. I had left the house looking for a doctor and never returned.

I couldn't count on them. I could only count on me now. I had to escape, to return to Lovero. To be free of the travelers.

To find where I fit.

twenty-one

†

THE WAGON STOPPED ONCE THE SUN TOUCHED THE horizon.

Nev hopped out, and as soon as I was alone I tried standing again, but my wobbly legs shook until I was forced to sit.

Not yet, but soon.

Of course, even if I was in top form, I wasn't sure how I would cross the dead plains. I wasn't Lea, who was the chosen of Safraella and could command the ghosts away. But that was a problem for later. Right now I just needed my body to recover.

I scooted to the edge of the bench and pushed the curtain aside.

There were three other travelers besides Nev and Perrin, two men and a woman.

They untacked their horses and settled them down for the evening with bags of grain and mash. One of them lit a fire that roared to life when the sun disappeared below the horizon.

The ghosts rose.

There weren't many, but the handful I spotted—their white, luminous forms drifting across the dead plains—were certainly enough to end every single one of us.

And they would. The angry dead always found the living.

The travelers separated, spreading out to four corners of the camp.

A ghost caught sight of us and screamed. The others followed suit, until the night was filled with the shrieks of the ghosts as they sped for us, eager to steal our bodies for themselves.

I clutched my necklace.

The travelers began to sing.

I didn't understand the words. They were in Mornian, maybe, or perhaps another language. I was closest to Nev. He was a tenor, and his smooth voice made something twist in my stomach, until I had to look away from him.

I focused on the others, but they all sang the same song.

The ghosts continued to charge, their voices growing louder, until they covered the sound of the traveler song. But the travelers simply kept singing.

If I warned them, what could they do about it? There was no stopping ghosts. And if I kept quiet, maybe the ghosts would take them instead of me.

But Nev . . .

The travelers stopped their song. A light flashed between them. The ghosts halted, their screams dying away.

"What happened?" I asked one of the passing travelers. She ignored me and continued on her way. A necklace bounced on her chest, a twin to the one that hung around my neck.

I grasped the stone of my necklace in my palm, then slid it beneath my dress.

Nev returned. "They cannot see us. The *singura* and Culda's song blind them to us, pushes them away in their travels."

As he said that, the ghosts turned and headed back the way they'd come.

"This is how you travel?" I asked. "With a song? And a necklace?"

"Yes. Culda protects us as long as we stay in camp." He paused, and studied me before adding, "If anyone leaves camp, the ghosts will take them."

It was a pointed warning, so I wouldn't try to run off in the middle of the night.

He headed to the fire, where one of the others appeared to be roasting two animals—rabbits, by the look of them.

A song and a necklace. *While Culda sings us safely home.* The travelers used magic to keep them safe from the ghosts at night. It was how they traveled so easily.

Nev spoke with one of the others and then Perrin stomped next to him. She spoke and the other traveler slipped away from the confrontation.

Their traveler magic could be my escape. I tapped my necklace on my chest. I already possessed one part of the equation—the necklace, the *singura*. All I needed was the second part, the song. If I learned the song, then as soon as my body recovered, I could flee back to Lovero and the people waiting for me.

I would save myself and return to the Da Vias, triumphant. They would welcome me with open arms.

My mind drifted to the image of Les's arm on the table. I coughed and shook my head.

Perrin jabbed her finger toward the wagon and where I sat, watching. Nev replied, but she just pointed again until he headed my way.

I dropped the curtain and scooted back on my bench. Nev entered a moment later. In the evening shadows of the wagon, his bruises looked even darker.

"You can't stay out there with the others?" I asked.

Nev grabbed one of the bags and began digging through it. "I must stay in here with you tonight, to watch you."

I narrowed my eyes. "Isn't that dangerous?" I asked. "Couldn't I kill you in your sleep? Or is that why you're watching me?"

"Yes. Perrin would be happy. No more Nev, and a reason to kill you before we reach Mornia. With you dead, she takes your *singura*. She gets everything she wants."

He pulled a blanket from the pack and spread it on the floor of the wagon, then grabbed two of the softer bags and put them at the top, to use as pillows. He was making a sleeping space for two people.

"No." I shook my head. "I'm not sharing a bed with you."

"There is nowhere else for you to sleep," he said, his tone suggesting he wouldn't argue with me.

"No," I said.

"Fine." He lay down on the blanket, back turned to me, shoving the makeshift pillow under his head until he was comfortable.

I sat on the bench instead, curling my legs beneath my dress. The bench was too short to use as a bed, but I was fine just like this.

Until I wasn't.

Until my legs started to cramp and my back ache from my hunched-over position as I tried to get comfortable.

Finally, I had to admit defeat. I stepped onto the bed Nev had made and lay down beside him, back pressed against his. The muscles in my body relaxed, thanking me. I tucked my scarf under my head, adding more fluff to the pillow. Anyway, I would need to be well rested if I was going to flee.

Nev was still awake, by the sounds of his breath. We didn't speak. But that didn't mean the air between us was quiet. Instead, it was filled with a thick tension. I could practically taste it.

I closed my eyes, trying to concentrate on sleep. The warmth of his body sank into mine. I tried not to think about the toned leanness of him, pushed against me. Tried not to remember the feel of his skin beneath my fingers, the weight of him on top of me.

His fingers stroked my hair.

"Don't," I warned. "You don't get to touch me like that anymore."

"It was in my mouth. That is all."

I couldn't read him from my position. Couldn't see his eyes. Couldn't tell if he was lying.

But apparently I had read him wrong the entire time we'd been together. I'd thought he was someone different. I'd been wrong.

"I thought you loved her," I whispered.

He stiffened behind me but didn't respond immediately. Finally he asked, "Who?"

I closed my eyes.

"Kuch. I thought you cared for her. Was it all a lie? Just a show to trick me? To entice me to your bed?"

He shifted again but I refused to look at him. "There was no trick, Allegra. And if I remember, it was you who began everything."

"Oh, that's right. You're just an innocent who went along with it. You had no say at all."

"That is not what I meant."

"Then what did you mean? What did you mean when you told me you liked her? Does that mean something else to travelers?"

"No." I felt him shake his head. "It is the same."

"But if you liked her so much," I said, "how could you be rid of her so easily?"

I swallowed, waiting for his answer.

He cleared his throat and fell silent.

I'd started to drift off to sleep when he finally answered.

"It was not so easy," he said softly. His breath brushed the back of my neck. I hadn't realized he had rolled over. I fought against a shiver. "She was beautiful. And strong. And unique. And some people didn't understand her. But I did."

He exhaled slowly.

"Why did you try to kill me?" I asked again. He'd never answered me the first time.

"She was not for you."

"Then who was she for? And what did my Family ever do to you to engender such hate?"

"It is not your family," he said. "It is . . . complicated. But you are unhurt, so everything is fine."

"Everything is not fine," I hissed at him. I felt like Kuch, and wished I could have struck out at him. Could have sunk my fangs into him, let my venom kill him slowly from the inside.

"Did you kill her?" he asked.

"Of course we killed her!" I snapped. "What did you expect us to do?"

He rolled over again, away from me. "I expected nothing. I put her in the box for him like I was told to do."

"For him? My uncle, you mean?" Les. Kuch was meant for Les. But that made little sense. He had nothing to do with Nev and me. He had nothing to do with any of it. "Why, because he's a half traveler?"

"No."

There were traveler mysteries here involving Les that I wasn't privy to. Secrets. "What did he ever do to you?"

"Nothing," he said quietly. "He did nothing to me. It is complicated, Allegra. I had no choice. I do not want to talk about it."

I looked over my shoulder at him, twisting in the floor of the wagon. Even in the shadows of the wagon I could see how the olive skin of his neck blazed red from some hidden emotion he felt. "There's always a choice, Nev,"

He didn't respond, and I slipped into familiar nightmares and shadows that whispered my name from a gray fog.

twenty-two

†

IN THE MORNING WE PASSED A LAND WHERE NOTHING grew. Little golden foxes played together, but hid inside their burrows when they caught sight of us. Dust puffed into the air with every footstep, with every creak of the wheels. It coated everything and I was glad when we were free of it.

The strength of my body slowly returned. By afternoon I could stand without problem, and even walk well, but running was out of the question. Soon though, I knew. Soon.

"We will reach Mornia before night," Nev said as I watched the passing landscape.

I was full of wrath and rage and despair and worry over everything that had happened to me, to my family, but a tiny part of me was still excited. I was seeing the world. Granted, it was nothing but dead plains filled with golden grasses, but still. It was more than I'd seen before. More than I'd ever hoped to see.

Of course, thinking about that just made me even angrier

at Nev. I couldn't enjoy these new lands because I had been brought to them against my will. I had exchanged one cage for another. At least for now.

The sun was setting when we crossed over a hill and the home of the travelers spread before us.

Nev pushed the wagon curtain aside and pointed ahead. "Mornia."

I tried not to look interested, but I was. Outsiders rarely visited the traveler home. Its location was not quite a mystery, but neither were the travelers eager to share it.

I didn't know what I had expected, but it wasn't what I found outside the window.

There were no walls. Mornia sat in the middle of nowhere, golden dead plains surrounding it, and yet it remained wide-open for any ghosts or even people to walk through it.

It was terribly small, too. Maybe around the same size as Yvain. There was a small grouping of buildings to the left, none more than two stories high, but that was all. No castles, no cobblestone or flagstone streets, few fountains or gardens or squares.

I didn't know how many travelers there were, but surely there were not enough houses here for all of them.

"That is the New Mornia." Nev pointed at the buildings. "Most of Mornia is behind it. Old Mornia."

"There's nothing behind those buildings."

"Everything is behind the buildings," he said.

The wagon continued to roll east. The first buildings passed us on the left. They weren't made out of stones and bricks like Rennes or Lovero but instead smooth rock, with no joins or breaks anywhere. Mud or clay, maybe.

The streets seemed to be the same, pressed into shape by feet and hooves and wheels. Even as we passed New Mornia, it seemed ancient, as if centuries of animals and people had worn these roads to their present state.

We continued deeper into Mornia, travelers glancing at us curiously as we passed. Then we were through the buildings of New Mornia and a flat expanse stretched before us.

Unlike the dead plains I was used to, though, there was no long grasses here. Instead, colorful curtains dotted the landscape, thousands of them, two adjacent corners anchored to the ground, the other corners hoisted into the air on wooden poles, creating a sort of lean-to of fabric.

Farther to the east, past the fields of curtains, water sparkled in the setting sun. Silhouetted figures bathed in the waves.

I leaned closer. "Is that the sea?"

Nev smirked, but there was no malice in it. "It is a lake."

A lake. Yvain had no lakes. Just the canals that twisted throughout the city. I wished we were closer, so I could gaze across its waters, looking for the other shore.

I knew how to swim. Maybe I could find my freedom on the other side.

To the south and north of the curtains, huge pastures and orchards flowed in all directions, fences and walls separating them from one another. We passed one on the right, and I peered past gaps in the wooden, slatted wall to see a strange deerlike creature, with horns that twisted into the air above its head.

"The animals," I said aloud, "for your menagerie."

We passed a paddock of horses and mules and other pack animals. I made note of their location.

Nev nodded. "Yes. Many pens hold goats—they are food for us and the animals—but some are for the menagerie."

I scanned the pens for a glimpse of stripes. "Where do you keep the tigers?"

"In a pit."

I looked at him then. "You keep them in a pit."

"Tigers jump very high. It is safer for them, for us, and all other animals if they are in a pit. It is fine. They were born here. They know no other way."

I remembered the tiger in the cage at the menagerie and his unseeing eyes. Surely he hadn't been dreaming of a pit in the ground, of another cage . . .

The wagon stopped. Nev exhaled slowly and glanced at me before he pushed the back curtain open and stepped out. I followed. There was no point in waiting. The sooner whatever was going to happen happened, the sooner I could make a plan for my escape.

The setting sun turned everything orange and yellow. Even the blue curtain we'd stopped at, flapping gently in the evening breeze, had a yellow tint to it.

Below each curtain seemed to be a hole. A large hole, rectangular in shape, but smaller than the curtains. Maybe they were one of the tiger pits Nev had mentioned.

Two women stepped out of the hole beneath the blue curtain. The first one was heavily pregnant, and my heart sank, thinking about Beatricia back home. Maybe the baby had been born already. Maybe she'd had a boy, maybe a girl. Maybe everyone was so happy.

The pregnant woman walked to us, hair pulled back in a tight plait. She had tanned, olive skin, sharp cheekbones, and hazel eyes. I looked at Nev. He had mentioned a sister who was pregnant. This had to be her.

Behind Nev's sister stood another woman, with curly brown hair that matched the color of her eyes, and brown skin. She smiled brightly at Nev and the other travelers, but when she saw me, her smile melted away.

Nev's sister strode to him and grabbed his chin. She turned his face to the left, then the right, examining his bruises and his cuts. She spoke to him in Mornian and he answered quietly back.

His sister stared at me, expression unreadable. I returned her stare.

Behind me the three other travelers dismounted.

Nev's sister released him and she strode to them, bypassing me completely. She confronted Perrin, barking at her in Mornian.

Perrin looked askance at me, then spoke so I could understand her. "He let that one try to escape, Metta."

I snorted and glanced at Nev. If falling out of a wagon constituted an escape attempt, they were going to be pretty shocked when I gave it my all.

"No one let me do anything," I said.

Nev's sister—Metta—Perrin, and the other woman studied me.

Nev stepped beside me. Part of me wanted to recoil from him, but another part was glad for his presence. He was a familiar stone in this field of uncertainty. Maybe I didn't know him, not truly, but I certainly knew him better than I knew any of these strangers.

"It was no escape," Nev said to his sister, speaking so I could understand. "She was too ill."

"Lucky for all of you," I said.

"Why lucky?" Metta's eyes focused on me. I fought against fidgeting, stilled my fingers from trying to pull a mask I didn't have over my face. I tugged on my scarf.

"She is one of Lovero's murderers," Nev said. "Clippers," he corrected, eyes flashing toward mine.

The woman with the curly hair stepped beside Nev's sister and spoke quietly to her in Mornian.

Metta continued to study me, as if I were a puzzle she could unlock if she only tried hard enough. Her mouth tipped in a slight smile, eyes narrowed.

Plotting. This woman was a plotter. I would have bet money on it.

"Yes," Metta finally said to the other woman. Metta turned back to Perrin and spoke so I could understand. "Do not touch my brother again."

Perrin had been grinning during the entire whispered exchange, but now her smile vanished. She replied in

Mornian but Metta cut her off.

"I do not care. He is not yours to discipline. Find your own men if you must hit someone."

Perrin scowled and shot such a look of venom at Metta that I was surprised she didn't flinch. Metta stood tall, shoulders back, head held high. She carried an air of pride about her, like she was someone important and Perrin was below her thoughts.

Perrin strode to her horse. She mounted and called the other travelers after her. They left silently, heading northwest toward New Mornia and the buildings we had already passed.

"Isha," Metta said to the curly-haired woman, "the wagon." Isha nodded without a word and led the horse and wagon away, until it was just me, Nev, and Metta standing together.

Nev watched his sister, but she and I stared at each other.

I understood pride. Pride offered strength of will. Pride offered strength of body. I let my own pride command me, lowering my arms to my side, looking down my nose at her.

Around us, travelers climbed out of different holes in the ground, each beneath one of the colorful curtains. They skirted the pens and pastures with the animals. A few of them openly gaped at me—my blond hair made it abundantly clear I was a stranger—but most just went on their way.

"My Family will come for me," I finally said to Metta, "and when they get here, people will die."

It was a lie. Mostly. No one knew where I was. I was on my own.

"Our gods protect us," she said.

The Three. Gods of song and safe travels, motherhood and animals, wealth and thievery.

"My god is a god of murder and death," I said. "How will yours of wealth protect you from that?"

Metta rubbed her belly and smiled, but it didn't reach her eyes.

She faced Nev, who'd been watching the exchange quietly. "She will stay with you. Answer her questions."

Nev stared at his sister. "There will be talk. People will not approve."

"People never approve. It is how we will win." She grinned, though it didn't seem to hold much joy. She placed her hands possessively on her belly, then headed back to the hole under the blue curtain.

Nev rubbed his face, his palm tugging his skin. His chin was rough with stubble. He needed a shave.

Finally, he sighed. "Come."

I shook my head. "I'm not going with you."

"Then what will you do? Sleep out here in the dirt? Sleep in a pen with the animals?" I'd exasperated him again. It was getting easier to do.

"I could kill you in your sleep. Walk home. No one would even know."

He nodded. "Yes. But there are still ghosts, even out here. And like you said, your god is not Culda, She of safe travels."

Around us, the soft sound of music began to grow. I looked out past the pens and the curtains over the strange holes in the ground and saw a line of travelers, evenly spaced. They sang the same song I'd heard Nev, Perrin, and the other travelers sing on the way here. I watched them, listening to the song, memorizing the lyrics even though I didn't know their meaning. When the song reached its end, a light flashed between each person, but this flash stretched on and on, until I lost sight of it as it encircled what seemed to be everything.

"All of Mornia?" I asked Nev as I turned the lyrics over and over in my head, committing them to memory.

"Culda keeps us safe in the night."

I exhaled, then followed Nev.

But I looked once more, out at the dark sky, past the curtains, the pens, and the buildings of New Mornia.

There were always ghosts in the dark.

I clutched the necklace—the *singura*—hanging from my neck, thinking about the traveler song.

But there was freedom in it, too, for those willing to take it.

twenty-three

†

NEV LED ME TO A RED CURTAIN AND THE HOLE THAT hid beneath it. Stairs had been carved into the earth, leading downward.

Nev descended, and I watched as his head twisted around, the stairs spiraling into the darkness below.

But I'd grown up underground, in the safety of the tunnels below the streets of Yvain. The darkness beneath the earth held no fear for me.

The steps were even under my feet, like generations of travelers had used them, their boots and feet smoothing the stone until it was soft and flat like glass.

I reached the bottom of the stairs just as a light flared in front of me. Nev had lit a lamp. He covered it as it flickered, lighting the space.

It was small. Smaller even than my room back home, the one above the shop with its window that let the moonlight spill through.

Wait. Not home. Back in Yvain.

The rectangular space stretched before me. At the other end was a sort of kitchen, with bowls and plates and pots. The cook space was blackened with years of use, and the char had embedded itself so firmly in the stone and clay surrounding us that I could smell it from where I stood.

There was a small seating area, reminiscent of Nev's room at the menagerie. Two stools and a table almost the same size were tucked beside the spiral stairs. Clearly he didn't expect many guests for dinner.

To the left a curtain hung over a door. A bathroom of some sort, I supposed. And to the right were two more curtains, though they were pushed aside to show niches carved into the walls. One of them was empty, but the other was filled with a plush-looking mattress and colorful pillows tucked into the corners.

Shelves were attached to every empty wall space, and they were stacked with more supplies and food stores. Nev dug through a basket on a shelf, pulling out more pillows and blankets. He looked to the left and came face-to-face with a small wire cage. He paused, pillows seemingly forgotten as he contemplated something.

I cleared my throat, and he turned away from the cage.

"This is your home?" I asked.

He nodded, then held up the pillows like they were some sort of explanation. "For your bed." He pointed toward the empty niche.

"Your sister—Metta is your sister, right?" He nodded.

"She said you were to answer my questions."

He scowled and walked to my niche, throwing the pillows and blanket inside. "It is not my place."

"I don't care whose place it is," I snapped. "I want answers."

Nev pressed his lips together in a thin line, then returned to the shelf, digging around again until he pulled out a dark, thin bottle and two small glasses.

The glasses were the same as the ones we'd used at the menagerie, when we'd played cards. I frowned, remembering that night. How fun and exciting it had been, kissing him in the dark of his room, befriending the travelers as we gamed together.

It seemed like a lifetime ago. And clearly the travelers hadn't been my friends.

He pulled a knife off a shelf, using it briefly to pry the cork out of the bottle. He put it back and turned around.

I yanked my gaze from the knife.

Nev set the glasses and bottle on the little table and sat on the stool, gesturing for me to take the other one.

I sat across from him and he poured oil into the glasses before corking the bottle once more.

"I don't want any oil," I said. "I don't want your hospitality. I want answers. I want to know why you took me, what you plan to do with me. I want to know why you sent Kuch to my home to attack my uncle."

I wanted to know why he'd sent me away, after the intimacy we'd shared in Lovero. I wanted to know if he'd never felt anything with me. If it had been easy to end it all, like

233

it had been nothing more than dinner with an acquaintance instead of what it really was.

Or what I had thought it was, anyway.

I wanted . . . I wanted a lot of things, but for now I would settle for answers.

"There are different oils for different times," he said. "This one is for sharing yourself with others. Drink."

He pressed his own glass to his lips and tipped the liquid into his mouth. The oil coated the sides of the glass when he set it back on the table. He motioned toward my glass again, and from the look in his eyes I knew he wouldn't answer any questions until I drank.

I dumped the oil into my mouth, swallowing it all with a single gulp.

It tasted rich, with a slight hint of something earthier. Mushrooms, maybe. I crossed my arms and stared at him.

He exhaled slowly and leaned back on his stool, until his spine rested against the wall of his home. "I am not sure where to begin."

"Why don't you begin with why you took me?" I snapped.

He shook his head. "That is not the easiest place to start."

"Try."

He rubbed his face, carefully avoiding his healing lip. "Your *singura*. The necklace your uncle gave you. He should never have given it to you."

I slipped the necklace out from under my dress and held it in my hand. The three concentric circles swirled around the center of the stone. "Keep going."

"That necklace is holy. It is reserved for . . ." He paused.

"Reserved for what?" I couldn't help the impatience in my voice. The sooner I got answers, the sooner I could make my plans to escape.

"There is not really a word for it in your language. What do you call yourself again?"

"Clippers?"

He shook his head. "The other word. When you speak about your place with your god."

"Disciples of Safraella."

"Yes, that." He smiled, like we were friends, conversing before we sought our beds.

"The necklace is for your priests?" I tried to get the conversation back to what was important.

"Close enough. Only they can wear it. It means they are the ones who commune with the Three. The Three look to them, speak through them."

I shook my head. "Les wore this necklace for years. There were no gods speaking to him. It's just a stone he took from his mother."

"He is a man. Only women speak to Meska, Culda, and Boamos."

"So because I'm not a man, and because I'm wearing the necklace, that's why you took me?" The *singura* was my key to escape. But if it was the reason I was taken in the first place, then I didn't need it.

I slipped the necklace off, dropping it on the table before me. "You can have it, if it's that important to you."

Pain struck my stomach. I gasped.

I clutched my ribs and leaned over as my stomach rolled and my body shook.

Poison. I had been poisoned. It was the only explanation. But how? I hadn't eaten or drunk anything that Nev hadn't sampled first.

Nev jerked forward, panic on his face. He grabbed the necklace and yanked it over my head, painfully twisting some strands of my hair.

My stomach calmed. The pain eased.

I swallowed and took a deep breath, sitting back up slowly.

"What was that?" I rubbed my mouth with the back of my hand.

Nev looked up at the top of the stairs nervously, but there was nothing there. Just a black emptiness where the stairs led above and outside.

"Do not offer to give up the *singura*," he whispered to me.

"Why?" I didn't bother to whisper. I didn't care who heard me.

"It can only be passed on in death. If you give it up willingly before then, the Three will take your life. You will die." He gestured at me, and I knew he was referring to the immediate pain I'd experienced when I'd given him the *singura*.

I licked my lips. So I couldn't just give it up, then. Fine. That was fine. I was an expert in death. Surely if someone could avoid it, it was me.

"Once you have worn the *singura*," Nev continued, "it is your burden to bear for life. You are a *samar*. One who wears a *singura*. A true *samar* can use the *singura* to sing the ghosts away."

Sing the ghosts away. Travel anywhere, across the dead plains at least, to return to Lovero.

I exhaled. "So what? I'm wearing this necklace. Why did you take me from my home for it? And why did you send Kuch for my uncle?"

"Your uncle was a thief." Nev said it matter-of-factly, leaning back once more, avoiding my gaze.

I laughed. I couldn't help it. "You serve a god of thievery!"

"He is a man and should not have possessed the *singura*. And I told you only children steal."

"He was a child when he took it!"

Nev paused at that, then pressed on. "We do not steal from each other. Do you kill other clippers?"

"Yes! I told you that in your bed!"

Nev blinked at me in surprise.

"Safraella is a god of death and murder and resurrection. Every death at our hands serves Her, regardless of who it is or how it's done."

"Our gods are different," Nev said.

That was clear. "So, because my uncle was abandoned as a child, and took one thing to remember his mother by, that was enough to earn him a death sentence at your hands?"

"He was a snake. We sent him a snake in return."

"He was a child!" I was shouting now and I didn't care if anyone heard me. "He was alone and frightened!"

"No true traveler would have taken the necklace."

"Oh," I said. "Oh, I see the truth now. He wasn't *really* one of you. He never belonged because his father wasn't a traveler."

"That is not—"

"And because he never belonged," I continued, "he never learned things that other traveler children learned. And then when he did something that is anathema to you, to your gods, you punish him for it."

Nev shook his head but he refused to meet my eyes. "It was not my decision."

"It was someone's decision. And you were the only one who knew where I got the necklace."

"If you had just kept it hidden—"

"This is not my fault," I interrupted. "You can't blame this on me."

Nev raised his voice over mine. "If you had just kept it hidden"—he leaned forward and dropped his voice—"I would not have had to tell anyone anything."

"But *you* knew about the necklace."

"I would have kept quiet," he said. "For you."

Silence then. Silence thick with tension and spoken words and words that remained hidden between us.

"You would have kept it secret," I said, "from the others. Even though it belongs to your gods."

"Yes."

"But you made me leave." My voice sounded tiny, beside his sudden conviction.

He sighed. "I made you leave because I was trying to protect you. I knew if anyone else saw you with the necklace, they would kill you."

"They would have tried."

"Yes. But even if they failed, someone else would have tried. We would have kept trying until you were dead."

"But I'm not dead now. I'm here."

"Someone saw you with the *singura* when you left. Perrin wanted you dead. I told her no. I told her it was not her decision, that you were a *samar* and so only the other *samars* could decide if you live or die. I convinced them to take you instead." He said this quieter. "We sent a bird to Mornia, to tell them we were returning with you."

"So it is your fault."

"I was trying to protect you."

I snorted, and Nev's face fell. And my stomach jumped unpleasantly. I looked away from him. "I don't need your protection."

"It does not matter anyway. Now that we have returned, I have no protection to offer you. I have no wife or mother. I have no status."

Above us footsteps sounded on the ground, and a moment later the woman with the curly hair walked down the spiral stairs. Isha.

She carried with her a mattress practically bursting with

stuffing. "Oh," she said when she saw us sitting at the table together.

She stumbled down the remaining stairs, and then stood there, shy, unwilling to make eye contact with me.

"Isha," Nev said in greeting. *"Ahlo kheel?"* He held up his glass, offering her the oil.

She shook her head and then spoke so I could understand, her voice quiet like a mouse and her accent so heavy and thick it was hard to understand her. "I remembered you do not have two mattresses so I brought you this." She pushed the mattress toward him and he gathered it in his arms, grunting.

Isha spun then, seemingly eager to leave. But she paused at the empty wire cage on the shelf.

"Oh," she said again. This time quieter, like she was saddened. "Oh, Nev."

"Good night, Isha," Nev answered roughly.

She nodded without looking at us, then scurried up the stairs, leaving us alone again.

Nev rose. He pushed the mattress into the second niche, adjusting it and tossing pillows around.

"Who is Isha?" I asked.

"Isha is my sister's . . ." He shook his head. "You do not have a word for it. They are together. *Ashka.*"

"She's your sister's wife?"

Nev gave a halfhearted shrug, punching the lumps out of the new mattress. "There are some similarities. It is not

240

as permanent, I think. Isha stays as long as she wants. If she wants to leave, or Metta wants her to leave, she will. But they love each other. She will not leave. They fit together."

"But Metta's pregnant," I said.

"Yes. The father is Abel. A friend."

"He was her *ashka* before Isha?"

Nev laughed, and the amusement eased the lines and bruises on his face. My skin warmed at the sound. I scowled.

"No." He shook his head. "Metta does not enjoy men. But she needed a child, and Abel agreed to help." He shrugged once more, then stood and pronounced my bed made.

"Now what?" I asked.

"We sleep."

"And then?"

He took a deep breath. "We see what happens."

"Whether the others decide to kill me or not, you mean?"

"Yes."

"If they don't, what does that mean?"

"I do not know," he answered truthfully. "You would stay here."

"Forever?"

"No one lives forever."

I knew this probably better than he did. "And if they decide to kill me," I said, "would you help me flee?"

He rubbed the back of his neck. "Where would you go that the ghosts would not find you?"

"You didn't answer my question."

Nev sighed. "There is no point making decisions for things that have not happened yet. Things will be better in the morning."

He slipped off his boots and before I could question him further he jumped into his alcove and pulled the curtain shut.

I stared after him. It didn't matter if he agreed to help me or not. It didn't matter if the travelers decided to kill me or let me live. None of it mattered. I was leaving this place the first opportunity I found.

I'd take my chances with the ghosts.

twenty-four

THE BED WAS SURPRISINGLY COMFORTABLE, EVEN IF I felt a bit like a mouse, tucked into a tiny hole to nest. But the mattress was stuffed with wool, or some other soft fiber, that enveloped my body. After sleeping in the wagon, the mattress was a moment of brightness in the dark night my life had become.

I rolled onto my side, facing the curtain. Footsteps sounded outside my alcove, soft and quiet. Then a puff of breath and the lamp went dark. It wouldn't take long for Nev to fall asleep. Maybe I wasn't fully recovered yet, but stealth wouldn't require running.

I needed to escape. I needed to steal a horse and head west. Or south to the sea, which would lead me to Lovero eventually. I needed to get out of here.

Nev had told me the travelers would simply come for me again, but if I reached my Family, they would protect me. Lea would—

No.

I wasn't going back to Yvain. To Lea. I was going back to Lovero. To the Da Vias and where I fit. They would protect me as well as Lea would, I was sure of it.

Claudia Da Via . . . my mother . . . had screamed at Lea, told her she couldn't keep me. Would she look for me in Yvain? And what would she do if she didn't find me?

Of course I didn't know what anyone was doing.

I tried not to think about what had been happening the last time I'd seen them. Les's blood everywhere. Kuch's venom could have killed him. Removing his arm could have killed him. Infection could kill him.

I closed my eyes, but it wasn't any darker. When I'd been younger, sometimes I'd catch Lea and Les having whispered conversations and I would hide and listen in. I'd heard them talking about death, what it meant for them.

There had been no children for them, and Lea was convinced this was because they had died, once, and been resurrected by Safraella. She had offered Lea a new life, but Lea had chosen to return to her old one instead, to return to being Lea Saldana instead of being born as someone new.

And Lea and Les spoke quietly, thinking they were alone, about what would happen if they died again. Would Safraella offer them a new life then? Or had they given it away, to stop the Da Vias, to do Her bidding? To save Emile and me?

But of course, all that had been a lie. I hadn't needed saving.

Maybe they had given up any chance at a new life,

sacrificed it to return as they were.

I pressed my face into the pillow, letting my body relax as I waited for Nev to fall asleep. I couldn't waste any more time here. The sooner I left, the sooner I returned and my new life with the Da Vias could begin.

I would have freedom with them. I would belong.

I fell asleep.

I dreamed of monsters.

The same monsters. Over and over again. Hidden behind the gray mists, watching me, whispering.

"Allegra . . ." one of them called to me. I peered at the shadows behind the mists. "Allegra . . ."

I woke with a start. My heart pounded. My surroundings were strange, foreign. I felt around in the darkness for anything familiar and found smooth stone above me.

It came back to me then. Mornia, with their homes buried beneath their colorful curtains. The alcove in the wall Nev had given me. The taste of the oil on my lips.

I felt for the necklace, the *singura,* on my chest, squeezing its familiar weight as I slowed my breathing.

I twisted, pushing aside the curtain that covered my alcove. Nev's little house was so dark, it reminded me of home, our hidden space below the shop, and how dark it would be when the fire in the hearth had burned down. How dark it had been when I'd crept through its silence on my birthday, trying to reach the table with my gifts.

It was late. Nev was surely asleep by now.

I crossed my legs and held the *singura* in my hands. It didn't seem special, no more than a pretty stone necklace, but I had seen the traveler magic with my own eyes. And Nev said I had become a *samar* just by wearing it, so surely that meant the magic would work for me.

I sang the song quietly, the lyrics and tune barely more than a whisper. If I woke Nev, if he saw what I was doing, he would know immediately why. He would try to stop me. Tell his sister, maybe. And then they would lock me up.

It was what I would do, anyway.

I finished the song and nothing happened. The *singura* rested in my palms. There was no flash of light, no sign that anything at all had happened.

I leaned closer to the *singura* and started again, my words and breath brushing across the surface. I needed this to work. I needed to get home. I needed to travel safely across the dead plains.

I needed . . .

The necklace flashed, the light filling my alcove so suddenly that I gasped and dropped the *singura*. The light vanished, plunging me into darkness again.

Only the knowledge that Nev still slept soundly stopped me from cheering at my success. I felt around my covers until I found the *singura* and slipped it over my head once more.

Time to go.

I slid out of my alcove quietly. I curled my toes at the cold stone beneath my bare feet. I had slept in my dress. Not because I didn't trust Nev, but because I didn't want to waste any opportunity for escape by having to find my clothing.

I slipped my boots on. The darkness was not as heavy in the upper left corner of Nev's home, where the stairs led outside. I walked to the opposite wall and felt around the shelves until something sharp slid against my fingertips. I paused and carefully removed the knife. I tucked it into my pocket and then headed toward the exit, walking softly. The stairs were steep and seemed treacherous, blind as I was, but then my head was through the hole and the rest of me followed.

It was no longer night.

Outside, the sun had risen hours ago and travelers went about their errands and chores in the early afternoon sun, blocked by Nev's curtain. I'd greatly overslept, and my stomach dropped at my missed opportunity.

I'd never slept so long before, through the night and through the morning as well. It had to be due to the remnants of the drugs in my system and the trip through the dead plains.

Behind me, hurried footsteps erupted from the stairs and I turned to find Nev, scrambling up the stairs in a panic, until he spotted me and stopped his mad rush.

"Allegra." He glanced around, as if he was looking for something, or expecting to find someone. He was barefoot and shirtless and I watched his chest heave up and down, breathless. I wasn't the only one who had overslept. "What are you doing?"

"I don't sleep well."

He stood beside me, his breath returning to normal.

All my senses were focused on him, on the smoothness of his bare skin beside me. My fingers twitched, begging me to run them over his flesh.

I crossed my arms, keeping them to myself. He wouldn't be able to watch me every moment. As soon as he took his eyes off me, I would disappear.

"How long have you been up here?" he asked conversationally.

I didn't bother to respond.

To the south, the animals set up a racket. Loud hoots and hollers came from one of the pens far to the southeast. Perhaps it was so far away because it was so noisy. Birds began to sing and squawk and other animals made strange sounds I'd never heard before. I strained my ears, wondering what they could be.

"Everyone is excited to be fed," Nev said beside me, his breath brushing across my neck and ear. I gasped, startled by his presence. I'd been so focused on the animals I hadn't noticed him move closer.

Nev smiled, and I tried not to remember that same smile when we'd hidden behind the cages and kissed the night away in Lovero.

Beneath the blue curtain to the left of Nev's, Metta and Isha climbed up their stairs. Isha wore a plain brown-and-gray dress that draped to her ankles, her arms bare. Metta wore a vest and loose trousers, her round belly stretching them outward.

Lea would have found their garments too plain, but to me

they looked comfortable and cool. The sun was high, and I could already feel its heat spilling over everything.

My own dress felt tight and hot in comparison.

Metta strode to Nev and me, Isha following behind, avoiding my eyes. I wondered briefly if her shyness was just because of my presence, or if she was like this with other travelers.

Nev muttered something under his breath, and scratched the back of his head.

"Nev." Metta's greeting was sharp and staccato.

She looked at me, her gaze trailing from my feet to my head. Whatever she found, her expression kept it hidden.

"You slept so long"—she spoke so I could understand—"I thought maybe you were dead. But it seems she has not killed you."

I smirked. "Yet."

She blinked, but didn't respond, turning instead to Nev once more. She spoke to him in Mornian, rapidly and sharp, like her greeting. Nev responded, but she cut him off. Nev dropped his gaze and nodded.

"We will speak to Bedna soon," Metta said to both of us. "She will be the best one to help. If she joins us, we will hold the *singura*. If she is against us, you will die," she said to me, "and the *singura* will go to someone else."

"Metta," Nev said, but she held up her hand, stopping him from speaking.

He closed his mouth and I could practically hear him grinding his teeth.

"Keep her close," Metta said to Nev, nodding at me. I narrowed my eyes. Did she know about my plans to escape? Or was she referring to something else? "She is my chance for status. I need her."

And with that said, Metta left and Isha followed quickly behind.

I watched Nev as he watched Metta and Isha walk away. He was different, here in Mornia. Weighed down.

At least the bruises I'd left on his face would fade.

I cleared my throat. "What was she talking about?"

Nev rubbed the back of his neck. "It is too much on an empty stomach. Come."

I followed him down the stairs into his home. He lit the lamp. I sat at the little table, watching him in his kitchen. He spread a loaf of bread on the table, followed by nuts and fruit and a tiny jar of golden honey. He brought out two small glasses and more oil.

"We had some last night."

"This is different." He poured us each a glass and then sipped his. I did the same. This oil had a sweetness to it, lighter than the earthier oil he'd served me last night.

I spread my bread with honey, then topped it with the nuts and fruit. The food we'd eaten in the wagon had been dried biscuits and meat for traveling. I hadn't realized how much I missed fresh, good fare until my teeth sank into the soft bread. The bite of the honey was smoothed over by the fruit, and the nuts added contrast.

"Our status is very low," Nev said suddenly, sipping from

his oil again. "Metta. Me. Isha now. Since our mother died. Even before that, but mostly since our mother died. I am lucky I have Metta."

But the way he said this made me think he didn't actually feel lucky. "Are you sure about that?" I asked.

"Things would be much worse without her," he stated.

I thought about Lea. Her lies. How she had stolen me. How I had never fit as a Saldana and had felt my whole life that it was my fault. How it turned out that it wasn't. That it had been her fault, and she had known why, all along, and hid it from me.

"That doesn't mean things are good with her," I said.

Nev gave a small nod and then poured more honey on another piece of bread. "Metta holds the status for our family. If she was not here, I would have none."

"What about those?" I pointed at the tiger scars on his forearm.

"They are old, from before my mother died. The tiger is not enough. Any wealth from traveling is not enough. We need mothers, daughters. Meska holds the most status of the Three. It is why Metta needs the child. Even if it is a boy, she will still be a mother then. Isha helps, too. Though her mother was not happy when she joined with Metta. Metta had little to offer her."

"But they love each other."

"Yes. People tell Isha all the time it was a bad decision. Her mother and grandmother and sisters try to get her to go home. But she does not. She will not. Not unless Metta asks her. She would do anything for Metta, I think."

His eyes flicked to mine for the briefest moment.

"And what does this have to do with me?"

"The families that have the *singura*"—he pointed at my chest and the necklace—"have much status. Right now, Metta has your *singura*. But if you die, then someone else will have it. Probably not Metta. Their status will rise, not hers."

"I have the *singura,* though. Not Metta."

Nev busied himself by pouring another glass of oil.

"Nev," I said.

"She has it," he said, corking the bottle slowly, "because you are with me."

Nev's cheeks blazed red and I tried not to picture Emile and how easily he blushed.

"I'm not with you, though," I said.

He shrugged. "She knows this. Others do not."

It all started to come together then. "And that's why she sent me here to live with you. To continue this idea that I'm *with* you."

He nodded quickly, focusing on the last bite of his bread.

I leaned back, thinking this over. Nev had said it was complicated, and though some of it was, much of it was familiar. I understood the intricacies of status. The Families ranked themselves and one another. Rank was important, worth dying for sometimes.

Metta was playing a dangerous game if she thought she could use me to fix her family's status. Not the least because I wasn't staying. If she was relying on me, her plans, whatever they were, would crumble around her.

And anyway, I would not let her cage me, as a tool in her machinations. I was a clipper. We bowed to no one other than Safraella and the king of Lovero.

Metta would not find me an easy pawn to control.

twenty-five

A HORN SOUNDED. LONG AND DEEP. A SINGLE STRIDENT note.

Nev looked up from his lunch, concern etched on his face.

"What is it?" I asked.

The horn sounded again, and Nev jumped from his chair. "Stay here," he commanded, running up the stairs.

"Nev!" I shouted, then scrambled after him.

Aboveground, the wind whipped through the air. The curtains around us cracked and snapped and everywhere travelers ran, like angry ants when their hills have been disturbed.

I shoved my hair out of my eyes, my mouth. "Where are you going?"

He spun and saw me aboveground. "I must see to the snakes. Stay here!" He shouted. The gusting wind stole his words. "It is a *bol*!"

He pointed west and I turned.

The horizon was gone.

In its place stood a wall of dust and sand, rushing its way right toward Mornia. A dust storm.

Around me the travelers climbed into their underground homes, unhooking the ends of their curtains and using them to cover the entrances, so the dust wouldn't pour inside.

I watched Nev run south with other travelers who were rushing to tend to their animals. The air tasted of dust.

This was my chance.

I dashed back down into Nev's home. Silence seemed to echo everywhere, even as the winds from the approaching dust storm howled above me. I grabbed a satchel and stuffed it with everything of use I could find: dried meats and fruits, bottles of juice and water, anything that would help keep me alive in my journey back home. Then I scurried up the stairs.

I glanced at the sun. It was afternoon, yes, but still hours before the sun would set. I didn't know how long the *bol* would last, but there was no point in worrying about things I couldn't control.

I took off toward the animal pens. I needed to find a horse. Without one, it would take me weeks to get home.

The wind buffeted me, trying to push me off the path I followed. Once the sand and dust arrived it would only get worse. I had to hurry. I had to be gone from Mornia before Nev returned to his home and found me missing. He would know what it meant. He would know I was escaping and not just lost somewhere in the storm.

I made it to the animal pens as the first grains of sand

stung my skin. The taller pens blocked the wind and sand, but between the cages I had to keep my face turned away from the west, to keep the sand out of my eyes. If I'd had my bone mask, it would have at least protected my mouth and nose.

A left, then another right, and before me stood the paddock with the horses and other cart animals. The paddock stretched before me, the other end disappearing in the rapidly worsening storm.

There were wooden lean-tos at the east end and I climbed over the fence and headed there.

The mules and cart horses were pressed tightly together under the lean-to, facing east, away from the oncoming storm.

Most of them wore halters, which made my plan easier. I could ride bareback, but I didn't relish the idea of trying to control a strange mount through a storm by only tugging on its mane.

I grabbed the closest animal, a mule with almost comically long ears. She looked at me, and though she was only an animal, I was sure I read scorn in her eyes.

I led her from the lean-to and into the storm.

It had grown darker now, the storm blocking out the afternoon sun. I headed back the way I had come, until the fence posts of the paddock appeared before me, rope wrapped around the gate, holding it shut.

I unlatched the gate, pushing it wide open. It was fine if

the other animals escaped. It meant their owners wouldn't immediately suspect this one had been stolen.

I tied the rope from the gate to the mule's halter, fashioning a set of reins, which I tossed over her neck.

The mule pinned her ears back, snorting and shaking her head in the sand that pelted our faces.

I looked west, but couldn't sustain my gaze in the force of the wind and sand. That was my escape, that was my way free of this cage. But there was no way we could travel like this. We would be blind, or the storm would choke us.

Lea's scarf whipped around my neck. I pulled it off.

It was beautiful still, and reminded me of my birthday, one of the last days that everything had been good, had been normal.

I ripped the scarf into three pieces.

The first I tied around the nose of the mule. It was thin enough that she could breathe through it, but thick enough to block most of the sand and dirt. The second piece wrapped around the mule's eyes. And the third piece was for me.

I tore the bottom of my dress and used the strip of fabric to tie the scarf over my face.

It was hard to see through, but I wasn't blind, and the scarf protected my face from the sand.

I used the fence and climbed onto the mule's back, then kicked her forward. She pinned her ears, but followed my command, jumping into a canter as I leaned forward, driving us into the oncoming storm.

My escape reminded me of the Jonus Aix job, the rush when I'd fled from his house, dodging his grasping hands. But here, it wasn't Jonus Aix's house I fled but all of Mornia. And it wasn't his hands that grasped at me, tried to hold me in place, but a storm of wind and sand and dirt.

I pushed the mule until her chest heaved beneath me, until her steps started to falter and her head drooped. Only then did I let her slow to a walk, slipping off her back to lead her farther west.

The scarf mostly did its job, but sometimes a gust of wind would find its way beneath the covering and the dry graininess of the dust would coat my lips and mouth.

I craved a sip of fruit juice, or water, but if I drank now, there was a chance the dust would sneak into the bottles, fouling the liquid.

Finally, after hours of travel, the storm began to abate. The sand and dust fell to the earth and the wind died until the mule and I stood together under a still night sky, the stars spreading over us like a comforting blanket.

I sighed, and pulled the scarf off my face and the face of the mule, stuffing the pieces beneath my belt. "I think you need a name." I patted her neck. "How about Flee? Since that's what you're helping me do here."

Flee didn't seem to care one way or another about her name. She probably only spoke Mornian.

The moon provided light enough to see by and we pressed forward once more. I only looked over my shoulder once, but we'd made it so far that not even the lights of Mornia could reach us out here.

We made no noise as we traveled. Flee had no tinkling bridle, I had no creaking leathers. The only sounds were our footfalls and the night insects, buzzing and singing love songs to one another in the dark.

Nev would have known of my escape for hours now. I wondered if he'd told Metta and Isha or kept it to himself—waiting for morning, perhaps, when it was clear I wasn't returning. My thoughts focused on him, what he was thinking, if he was angry or disappointed.

He said he saw me, in Lovero. Saw the person I really was. If that was true, he couldn't be surprised by my actions. He knew my desire to go with the Da Vias, to belong.

Thinking about Nev made my stomach ache and I shook my head, trying to clear him from my mind. When the sun rose, I would head south. Sooner or later I would reach the sea and its shores would eventually lead me to Lovero. Where the Da Vias would welcome me with open arms. To home.

Movement on the horizon to my left. I paused, and Flee stopped beside me to lip at the sparse grass peeking through the dust from the storm.

A ghost. It meandered west as well, traveling a parallel path to ours.

I pulled Flee's head up and turned us northwest. We were quiet, so the ghost hadn't noticed us, but the more distance between us, the safer I'd be. I'd have to keep my eyes open, though. In fact, height would only help me.

Ahead stood a large rock formation. Three stones jutted from the earth, like fingers, one of them leaning against the other two. If I could get to the top of one, I'd be able to examine my surroundings.

I pulled Flee after me, picking up our pace. Running would only make more noise and draw attention, but a fast walk was better than a slow one.

Finally we reached the rocks and I tied Flee's rope to a stunted, dry shrub. I began to climb.

The rock's surface was smooth beneath my fingers, worn even from the weather and years of dust storms and wind. But I'd chosen the leaning stone and it was at such an angle I could almost walk up it. Instead I crawled, using my hands to brace me or pull me forward when a boot started to slip.

When I reached the top, I stood straight and surveyed my surroundings. My breath caught in my throat.

Ghosts.

Ghosts everywhere.

Their glowing white forms dotted the landscape. I swallowed. It had been sheer dumb luck that Flee and I hadn't come across any until now. Perhaps Safraella had been watching out for me.

The ghosts wandered aimlessly, endlessly looking for a body they could steal to try to make their own. Their slow, sad wails drifted to me on the night breeze and I was surprised I hadn't heard them before now.

My stomach churned. There were too many ghosts, and no way safely past them. I couldn't go any farther tonight—at least, not without some traveler help.

I pulled the *singura* out from under my top. Its magic would help me now.

To my right, a flash of white appeared behind the tallest rock. I dropped to my stomach, flattening myself as much as possible.

The ghost hadn't seen me, but it turned to the left now, searching the darkness. It drifted closer, attracted to Flee's movement as she tugged at some weeds. If it looked up, if it saw me, there would be nothing stopping it from reaching me. Nothing stopping it from screaming at me and attracting all the other ghosts.

I clutched my necklace, the *singura,* my weapon against the ghosts. Its weight felt comforting and made me think of Les and then Nev and the sound of his voice when he sang.

I opened my eyes.

I sang quietly, softly. The ghost was so close, I couldn't risk anything louder. As it was, the ghost stirred when I began to sing, looking for the source of the sound.

I stumbled through the Mornian lyrics, my eyes locked on the ghost. It spun beneath me, searching.

I reached the end of the song and a ray of light burst from my spot on the rock. But instead of encircling me like it should have, it just sped off into the night, a straight line that continued for a few moments before it faded away.

It hadn't worked.

Yes, the magic had worked, but I wasn't protected. I wasn't safe from the ghosts.

I'd done something wrong. I should have asked Nev more specifics about how their magic worked, about how to make the light encircle me so the ghosts couldn't see me. But I'd only experimented once and judged myself fit to escape.

The ghost below wandered back to the other side of the rock. It wasn't gone, but it was far enough away that I could adjust my position. My boot kicked a small pebble off the stone and I watched as it dropped to the ground below me. There, at the base of the middle standing stone, was an indentation. An alcove, almost. It wasn't large. In fact it was mostly squat and shallow, but if I could squeeze my body against it, and get the beam of light to return, it would create a wall between me and the ghosts, and the rock would protect my back, hiding me from sight.

I hoped.

I got to my hands and knees, craning my neck to try and spy the ghost. It had wandered even farther away now, but I couldn't trust that it wouldn't return. This could be the best opportunity I'd have.

I slid down the rock, keeping my eye on the ghost until I got low enough that it dropped out of sight. I went slowly and carefully, trying to remain as silent as possible.

I reached the ground and stepped down one boot at a time, my toe sinking into the sand and dirt before I stood on my full weight.

Flee watched me, her ears tall and proud, as I slipped beneath the leaning rock I'd just descended. I pressed my back into the alcove.

Too small. It was too small to fit all of me.

I pulled my legs into my chest, turning sideways in the alcove and crunching myself into a flat, small ball.

Flee brayed at me, her mouth wide and her call loud and echoing across the flat, Mornian dead plains.

The ghost on the other side of the rock screamed.

I grasped my necklace and began to sing. I didn't have to be quiet now, or careful. Flee had given away my advantage, and I let the Mornian lyrics pour out of me as fast as I could sing them.

A glimpse of white to my right, the ghost rushing to find the source of the song.

The necklace flashed. The beam of light spread before me, covering the opening of the alcove like a traveler curtain and hiding me inside.

The ghost sped past me. It didn't stop, it didn't grab my limbs, pull me from my body. It didn't even see me.

My plan had worked. I was safe as long as I remained in this alcove, invisible to the ghosts.

I closed my eyes and thanked Safraella.

The necklace grew warm in my hand.

twenty-six

I REMAINED CROUCHED IN THE ALCOVE ALL NIGHT. MY
muscles cramped and screamed for release, but I pushed past
the pain, the discomfort. It was the only way to stay safe.

At one point I drifted off, and only when I fell out of the
alcove, landing with a thump at the sandy ground beneath
the stones, did I come awake. I scrambled back to the alcove
and sang the Mornian song to reset the barrier I'd disturbed.

After that I forced myself to stay awake, concentrating on
the pain in my limbs, picturing my new life in Ravenna,
picturing Emile and his wife and how happy they'd be without me mucking things up, and anything else that would
distract me from thinking of Nev.

Finally, as dawn appeared, I tumbled out of the alcove,
my muscles and limbs crying in relief. I felt almost feverish
from the respite and I curled in the shade of the stones and
fell instantly asleep, dreaming of monsters.

Something jostled my shoulder. I snapped my eyes open at the same moment a dark figure grabbed me, dragging me from the shade into their arms.

I shouted and shoved at them, my open palms connecting with their chest and pushing myself free of their hands.

I scurried to my feet. Nev sprawled before me, an expression of disbelief on his face.

"What were you doing?" I shouted.

"You are alive . . ." he said, eyes wide.

"I'm standing here, am I not?"

He got to his feet, brushing the sand from his legs. "When I saw you under the rock I thought . . ." He swallowed. "I thought you dead. Claimed by the ghosts."

"And what were you doing?" I snapped. "Trying to gather me into your arms so you could wail at the gods?"

Nev dropped his gaze.

Oh. *Oh* . . .

He'd sent me away in Lovero. He was the one who had told me to go, had told me we were over.

"Nev," I said, then stopped, unsure how to continue.

He looked at me, a flash of something in his eyes, then he stomped over. I stood my ground, prepared to weather whatever he would do, but he grabbed my shoulder and pulled me against him.

And then his lips pressed against mine, kissing me.

And I let him.

And then I was kissing him back, remembering the nights spent in the menagerie, remembering how I'd felt warm and safe, how simple and easy things were with him, in the dark of Lovero, when he'd been the only sanctuary in a life that was crumbling around me.

Nev pulled me closer, wrapping his arms around me. If kissing him hurt his lip, his bruises, he made no show of it. And more than anything I wished I could sink into his arms, into him, and forget everything else. Forget my new life waiting for me, forget my problems.

But he was the source of those problems. And I was long past forgetting anything.

I pushed away, untangling myself from his arms while he tried to keep me close.

"Stop," I said.

He caught his breath and dropped his arms to his side.

"We can't do this." I brushed my hair away from my face. I wished I still had my scarf to tie it up.

"Why?" Nev asked.

"Because of everything, Nev!"

"Forget everything," he said. "I want to be with you. When I found you gone last night, I . . ." He paused, rubbing the top of his head. "I thought you were gone from me. That I would find you dead. I want you with me, Allegra. We are here, together. We can start over."

"We can't simply start over here."

"Why?" Exasperation threaded through his voice.

"Because the only reason I'm here is that you stole me!"

"I told you I had—"

"No choice, yes, I remember what you said. It doesn't

make a difference, Nev. All my life people have stolen me. I was a stolen child and now you've stolen me again. I'm never where I'm supposed to be."

Nev shook his head. "You are where you are supposed to be. You are supposed to be where you are."

I shook my head but he continued. "Your god is not a god of fate. Neither are the Three. Your life is your life. If you keep searching for where you are supposed to be, it will pass you by."

I scowled. He sounded like Lea. "Can you not see it from my point of view?"

"I see it," he said. "But I think you should let it go."

"You don't see it, then," I said. "Not truly. What if I had come here, to Mornia, and I had tried to kill Metta. And then I took you away from your home, your family who desperately needed you. And from a new life with people you were supposed to be with all along. Would you just let it go? Start over?"

He looked at me then, really looked at me, until he dropped his gaze to his boots, which had sunk into the sand. "No," he said. "I would not."

"That is why this"—I gestured between us—"can't happen."

"But you do not see it from my side, either." He locked gazes with me again. "If your aunt, or your god, asked you to hurt my family, to take me from my home, and you did not want to, but you knew it was the only way to save my life, would you have not done it?"

I blinked. He was right. I would have done what Lea told

me to do, even if I disagreed. She was the head of my Family. I would have done what she commanded. "You took me," I said again. "You took me after you sent me away. After you rejected me."

My voice broke. I looked away from him, trying to control my emotions.

"I am sorry," he said, his voice quiet, earnest. "I sent you away, yes. But I did not reject you. I did not want to send you away. I did not want you to leave at all."

He could be lying, of course. But he had never lied to me in the past.

"I wanted to stay with you, Allegra," he continued. "I wanted you to stay with me. But mostly I did not want you to be hurt."

"That's what everyone always says to me," I said. "They all say it after they've already hurt me."

He closed his eyes and took a few breaths. "I have . . ." He paused, searching for a word. "I have regrets, Allegra. I wish for things to be different. But they are not. I cannot undo the things I have done. You are here. I am here. That is how things are. Wishing for the past will not change that."

Marcello had once told me that the past was a fixed point, that nothing could change it. And maybe that was true, but it didn't mean I couldn't strive for a different future. I was tired of everyone controlling me. Of keeping me caged. I wanted to make my own choices.

I rubbed the tears from my eyes. "How did you find me, anyway?"

"The stones." He gestured to the standing stones where I'd spent the night. "It is the closest landmark. I knew you would go there."

"And so you set off to bring me back, a prisoner."

He shook his head. "No. I went to find the mule." He pointed over at Flee, who was drowsing in the late morning sun. "No one knows you are missing."

"You kept it secret." He was protecting me from the others, from his people. He was choosing me over them.

"Nothing good would come from the others knowing you escaped," he said. "I will tell them you went with me to find the mule."

"I can't return with you."

Nev's shoulders slumped and he suddenly looked exhausted. If he'd truly been so worried about me, he'd probably gotten little sleep last night. "You must."

"I'm tired of people telling me what to do."

"Where will you go?" He gestured at the sparse dead plains surrounding us. "You have little food. Little water. The ghosts will find you. You will not find more stones like this, to hide you from them."

"I won't need stones," I said. "The *singura* will protect me."

He scoffed, but then looked at me closer when he realized I wasn't joking. "You sang the ghosts away? The *singura* protected you?"

"Yes."

His face blanched. He blinked rapidly, trying to come to terms with something. He shook his head. "It does not matter," he said. "There is no protection with only one person. You need others to make a circle."

I remembered back to my first night with Nev and the travelers who had taken me from my home. They had stood in a circle, and when they sang the song, the barrier connected between them. I had been alone last night. The barrier had no one else to connect to, which was why it had just traveled straight into the night.

"I could dig a hole each night," I said. "Hide myself inside, let the barrier cover me.

"Dig with what tools? There is clay and stone beneath the dirt and sand. And you will be starving and dying of thirst. No. You cannot reach your home this way, Allegra."

"I don't have to reach my home. I just have to reach the sea."

Nev looked over his shoulder, facing south. "The sea? The sea is farther away than Rennes or Lovero from here. You would surely die."

Something inside me crumpled. If the sea truly was so far away, then I really had lost my way home. I couldn't blindly head east and hope I'd stumble across Lovero or Rennes. I had been unconscious during the first days of my kidnapping. I had no idea how far north or south we could have traveled on our way to Mornia.

I pinched my eyes shut, trying to fight against the tears that threatened to overwhelm me.

"Allegra," Nev said quietly.

"You have caged me," I said to him. "You have trapped me

like you have trapped your snakes. Like your tiger. Everywhere I turn I am caged by those who profess to love me."

"Love is a cage," Nev said. "And you are not the only one who feels this way. Why do you think I travel so much? Why do you think I leave my home every chance I can?"

"It's not the same."

"It is the same!" His voice echoed over the dead plains. "Love and family and duty trap us all. We are all caged. You would have to give it all up to be truly free. You say freedom is what you want but I know it is not true. If it was, you would not be trying to return home, return to your family and the cage waiting for you there."

"It won't be a cage," I said. "It will be different, with the Da Vias. It will be different."

"How?"

"Because . . . because I belong with them!"

"You could belong with me!"

He stared at me, breathing heavily. "You . . ." He paused, then rubbed his eyes. "Everything is better with you. This—" He gestured between us, and the fight we were having. "Even this—" He pointed at the bruises on his face. "When I made you leave in Lovero, it was wrong. I wanted to take it back. But I could not. Because it was not safe, but also because I knew you would not let me. But you are here, with me once more. I will not watch you walk away from me again."

He crumpled his hat in his hands. "Allegra, come back with me."

"If I return with you, your people will want to kill me."

"I will not let them."

I sighed. It wasn't as easy as he made it seem. "I'm sorry," I said. And I found it to be true. I was sorry. Nev made me feel . . . Nev made me feel things I hadn't before. I didn't know how to categorize these feelings, how to categorize him. He had taken me from my Family, just as Lea had done. But he had done it to save me.

But that was what Lea had said, too. That she had taken me to save me.

It was different, though, maybe. Nev had never lied to me about it.

I shook my head. "I have to keep going."

Nev sighed and rubbed the back of his neck. "Fine," he said. "Then I will come with you."

He pointed over his shoulder and there, hidden behind the standing stone was a horse and a tiny, covered wagon.

I blinked. If he had really come to look for me only to bring me back, he wouldn't have needed the wagon. The only reason to bring the wagon was for a lengthy trip, like across the dead plains and back to Lovero.

I looked at him and my face must have shown the confusion I felt because he chuckled and shook his head. "I see you, Allegra. I see you."

My body thrummed. I changed the subject. "Where did you get that wagon?"

"It is mine. It used to belong to my father. Sometimes I travel with it. I will travel with you, now," he said. "We will leave together. You and me. We will travel safely and make Culda happy."

Nev smiled then, but unlike his wide, bright smile, this one was small, and sad. And I couldn't help but love him there, in that moment. Love his sadness.

Perhaps we were caged, but maybe if we were caged together, we wouldn't be so alone.

twenty-seven

†

THE LAND PASSED BEHIND US AS WE TRAVELED IN silence.

"I don't think you should travel with me," I'd said to Nev, even as I climbed up beside him on the wagon seat. We had tied Flee to the back of the wagon, then Nev had snapped the reins and we had set off to the west, toward Lovero.

"I know," he said. "But I am."

"What about Metta?" I asked. "And Isha? They're your family. Don't they need the money you earn from traveling? What about your snakes? And your tiger."

"Metta and Isha can take care of the snakes and the tiger. They have each other. And soon a child. They do not need me."

He said this with a touch of bitterness.

"But she's your sister," I said.

"What about your family?" He looked sideways at me. "You are leaving your family, too, yes?"

"That's different." I shook my head. "They lied to me, stole me—"

"They did those things to protect you. Even you said so."

I shook my head again, but didn't respond. He didn't understand.

We continued on in silence, watching the empty dead plains and the tall golden grass as it swayed in the wind.

The morning air was warm and the sun hot. I fanned myself with my hands, but I continued to sweat.

I leaned my head against the back of the wagon and tried to let its rocking motion soothe me but instead it just seemed to agitate things. I felt too hot, tight.

Birds appeared around us, flitting from blade to blade, chirping to each other.

I watched them, their little motions, their tiny squabbles.

Two of them flew around us on the wagon seat and I swatted them away.

Nev glanced over at me.

I wiped the sweat from my forehead and closed my eyes. The birds continued to chirp and flit around us.

"You could lie down in the back of the wagon," Nev said to me.

I nodded and stumbled inside. The wagon was tiny. There was room for a single person to sleep, two if they really crammed together, and space for storage. I barely noticed any of that as I collapsed onto the bed made up of blankets on the floor.

My thoughts twisted and spun around me.

The birds flitted in and out of the wagon and I tried to wave them away from my face, but instead they sat around me, on little wooden perches like they belonged in the wagon with me.

Because they did. Because the wagon was a trap, just another cage.

Their chirps changed into a melody. A slow, soft song, like a viola. I'd heard the song before, but I couldn't remember where.

"Nev," I said, trying to call out for help, but my voice emerged as a croak and he didn't come, didn't free me from my cage. "Nev."

I slipped into darkness.

My head pounded.

I awoke hours later. The wagon creaked and rocked below me, but it was quiet otherwise. I lifted my arms to rub at my eyes, but they were too weak. I was too weak.

"Nev," I said. My voice emerged as an unintelligible croak. Still, the wagon stopped and then Nev appeared above me. His eyes were wide and frightened.

"What's going on?" I asked, my words still slurring. Nev shook his head, like he was having trouble understanding me.

"You are ill," he said. He grabbed a water skin and pressed it to my lips so I could drink. The water tasted cold, even though it had been sitting in the skin.

I drank my fill, then put my head back down, exhausted.

"Sleep some more," he said.

So I did.

--- ❦ ---

When I woke again, it didn't feel much later. I sat up, prepared for more fatigue, more hallucinations, but there was nothing. The sickness had passed as quickly as it had come. I had recovered.

I pushed my way past the curtain and climbed back onto the seat beside Nev.

He looked at me, concerned.

Ahead of us, Mornia spread on the horizon, the afternoon bright overhead.

My stomach sank. I glared at Nev. "You brought me back. You lied to me."

He shook his head. "You fell ill."

"You should have just kept going! I would have been fine."

"Allegra, no. You were ill. I could not wake you. There was a fever. You got worse and worse. I had to return. I thought you might die."

I scoffed. I hadn't been that ill. It had just been a passing sickness, from too much sun, maybe. Or the strange Mornian air.

"You lied to me," I said. "You said you would come with me, to go to Lovero, and as soon as I fell asleep you turned this wagon around." Betrayal. Everywhere I went people lied to me, betrayed me. Said they loved me and

277

then did what they wanted anyway.

My breaths sped, until my chest heaved, until I had to clench my necklace and close my eyes, trying to get everything under control again.

"Allegra," Nev said. He pulled on the reins and the wagon came to a stop. Behind us, Flee brayed loudly. "Breathe," he said, watching me.

"I am breathing," I gasped.

"Listen to me," he said. "You grew worse and worse." He faced me. "It was bad."

Breathe in. Breathe out. Slowly. Take my time.

"You got worse the farther we went. I did not lie to you. If you want to go to Lovero, I will go with you. But I had to turn back, for help. You . . ." He paused, then swore. "I do not know the word. Your body shook, yes? With the fever."

"I seized?" I asked. I'd been so ill that I'd had a seizure?

The tightness in my chest eased. I took a deep breath, and then released the necklace.

Nev rubbed the top of his head, sliding his hat around. "I turned around and you got better. The closer we came to Mornia, the better you grew."

"I don't believe you," I whispered.

"I have never lied to you," he said.

I thought over everything, every moment of our time together, every word he had spoken to me, in the darkness, yes, but also in the light, and he had always been truthful.

"So you're saying leaving Mornia made me ill."

"I do not know what it means."

I bit my lip, thinking. Then I hopped off the wagon and marched west, away from Mornia.

"Allegra!" Nev shouted after me. "Where are you going? You cannot walk to Lovero!"

I knew that, of course. I certainly couldn't walk there without supplies, anyway, and those were all in the wagon. But Lovero wasn't my goal.

I walked west, leaving Nev behind as he watched me. Leaving Mornia behind once more.

The afternoon sun beat down on me. Sweat broke out on my forehead. I brushed it away. My hand shook.

I paused. Maybe it was just the sun. I had to keep going.

"Allegra!" Nev finally yelled at me, his voice carrying over the flat dead plains. "Come back!"

The farther I walked, the weaker I seemed to get. As if my strength just poured out of me. My limbs shook, my feet practically dragged in the dirt with each step, my skin burned and flushed. Lights sparkled in the air, like little ghosts, maybe, dancing in front of me.

I tripped.

The dirt felt surprisingly soft beneath my body. Maybe the best thing to do was to take a nap right there.

Footsteps pounded behind me. Nev slid to a stop at my side.

"Are you hurt?" He placed his hands under my arms and pulled me to my feet. "Come," he said, and tugged me back toward the wagon.

It only took a few steps before my mind began to clear, my limbs to stop shaking.

I rubbed my face, trying to brush away the last of the cobwebs in my head.

I didn't have the strength to keep going toward Lovero. It was as if my body couldn't physically do it. And when Nev had tried to bring me there on his wagon, I'd passed out, then had a seizure. If he'd kept going, kept heading away from Mornia, would I have continued to get worse until I died?

"All right," I said. "I believe you."

Nev exhaled slowly. "I am sorry."

"What for?"

"I know you want to go to your home. Your new home. I am sorry you must go back to Mornia now."

I pulled free of his support. My strength was returning, I could walk on my own.

"What does it mean?" I looked over my shoulder to the west, to the freedom that seemed even farther away now. "Why is it that your people can wear the *singura* and travel around the world, but something keeps me from leaving Mornia?"

"I do not know," he answered. "It is not good."

"No, it's not. Not if I ever want to leave Mornia." Leaving Mornia was the crux of everything.

"I have to get rid of it," I said to Nev. "We have to find a way for me to get rid of the *singura* without my death."

Nev nodded but remained silent.

It didn't take us long to return to Mornia. It stretched out on the horizon, the buildings of New Mornia growing closer and closer as we headed east, the afternoon sun hot overhead.

Things seemed easier between Nev and me now. Much of my anger and blame for him had drifted away when I'd truly put myself in his place. I still wanted to be free of Mornia, of the travelers, but my previous plan of just running home was no longer feasible.

I was aware of every move he made, each twitch of his wrists, directing the wagon, every breath, when he stretched his legs before him.

My senses strained as if I was in a dark room, searching for someone.

Nev sighed beside me and I caught his eye. "Metta will know, of course," he said, answering my unspoken question. "She and Isha will have noticed we are missing. That my wagon is gone, too."

"But they wouldn't tell anyone," I said.

"Who would they tell?" He shrugged.

It must have been hard, just the three of them together, Metta trying anything and everything to regain their lost status. She reminded me of Lea, in that sense. Lea, who would kill anyone to protect us. And Nev had so easily put Metta aside for me.

I clutched the *singura*. "How many *samars* are there?"

"Twenty-four. Counting you now."

"Who did this *singura* belong to?" I asked. "If my uncle hadn't taken it, who would have it now?"

Nev paused, glancing at me quickly before looking off to the sky.

"Nev," I said. "Who would it belong to? Please don't tell me Perrin."

He snorted and shook his head. "No. Not Perrin. No matter what she thinks, she will never be a *samar*. The Three will never pass it down to her. She wants it too much."

"Then who?"

"Metta."

I twisted on the seat until I was facing him fully. "What?"

"If things had not gone wrong, if the *singura* had never been lost to us, it would have passed down to Metta. Maybe. It is not a for sure thing. But it did go wrong, and the blame lies with our family."

Metta. Metta was the true owner of my *singura*. The *singura* Les had stolen from his mother as a child. Which meant . . . "You're his family. My uncle. You're the family that abandoned him when he was a child."

Nev scowled. "We were not born yet, Allegra. It was before our time."

"How are you related to him?"

"His mother was our grandmother's cousin. When his mother died, the *singura* would have probably passed to our grandmother." Another one of his traveler shrugs.

"Is that why you tried to kill him? Because he was related to you?"

Nev sighed. "I did not want to try to kill him at all. But yes, that was Perrin's reason. But even if he was not a traveler, she still would have made me send Kuch. He was not a traveler and he stole a *singura*. Punishment for that is often death. Metta would have never agreed to it. But she does not travel and Perrin was in charge."

Perrin, then. Perrin was at fault for what had happened to Les. What I'd had to do to Les.

"Why is Metta keeping me alive, then? The *singura* could be hers. She would regain your status, right?"

"Our family lost the *singura*. Now that it has returned, Metta does not think she will be rewarded as a result. She thinks the gods are angered. Her first baby died before it was born. Sometimes it happens to women, but Metta believes the Three were punishing her for our family losing the *singura*. She will not take the chance.

"Also, she does not find death to be an answer. And she likes a challenge."

Metta hadn't been kind to me, but neither had she been unkind. I squeezed the *singura* around my neck. "How does it work?"

"What?"

"The *singura*. How does it pass between women? How does one become a *samar*?" I needed to know as much as I could about the *singura* if we were going to find a way for me to be rid of it.

"A *samar* chooses who they want to pass it to. Almost always it is a daughter. Or sister. Maybe the daughter of their sister or brother. Almost never is it someone outside the family unless their line has ended or there are no women. No women in a family is a sign of Meska's ill favor."

"So they pick their successor, and then they pass it on and just . . . die?"

Nev shook his head, tugging the reins so the horse would head more south. "They choose someone, but they continue to be *samars* for all their days. Then, when they die, the *singura* is passed on to their chosen. Mostly it works."

"What does that mean?"

"Sometimes the chosen will put on the *singura*, but the Three do not approve of the choice. And so someone else will be chosen instead. If the family has done something to anger the Three, maybe none of their women will be able to be *samars,* and the *singura* will pass to another family."

"This is what Metta is afraid of," I said. "If I was to die, and the *singura* passes to her, she is worried she will be rejected by the Three."

"Yes," Nev said. "She tries to do much to appease the gods. She is having the baby, to be a mother, to appease Meska, the strongest of the Three. She sends me traveling to appease Culda and any money I earn appeases Boamos."

"But if I choose someone to be the *samar* after me, and I just give them the *singura* early, I would still die?"

"Yes."

That didn't solve anything. There had to be a way to get rid of the *singura* without dying. It was the magic of the gods, anyway, and gods could change their minds and do what they wanted. Lea was a living example of that.

"Look!" Nev pointed to a line of wagons rolling into New Mornia. "The menagerie has returned!"

He snapped the reins and the horse picked up her pace, the wagon creaking behind us and Flee grumbling about the increased speed.

"There will be much work," he explained to me. "But after the work is done, there will be a festival."

A festival.

My emotions warred inside me. On the one hand, a traveler festival sounded exciting. Something new, something I'd never seen and I bet few outsiders had.

But the part of me that knew I was still trapped in my cage recognized it as a delay to figuring out how to get back to Lovero.

It didn't matter how decorated the cage was if the door was still locked with me inside.

twenty-eight

WE SNUCK INTO MORNIA WITH THE MENAGERIE. NO one noticed one more small wagon with the chain of large ones, filled with travelers and animals. There were still some areas, especially around the corners of curtains, where piles of dust and sand had collected from the *bol,* but mostly it seemed like nothing had changed.

We returned the wagon, the horse, and Flee and then we headed back the way we'd come.

Travelers rushed to the menagerie, laughing and shouting, and we followed in their wake. Nev shot me a rare smile, and my stomach tightened.

I let his pull on me linger. He would help me. It was nice, not being alone in this.

Ahead stood wagons and carts, each pulled by horses, mules, or oxen. A crowd had gathered, and travelers stood on the carts and waved and called to the friends and family they'd left behind while they'd traveled.

We weaved our way through the growing throng until finally we stopped before two carts. One was stacked with the small, wired cages I'd seen the snakes in. The other was a covered wagon, with small slits carved into the wood at the top for airflow.

Suddenly the cart roared and many of the travelers laughed and cheered. The tiger I'd seen in the menagerie. He'd come home, for whatever it was worth.

There were two women and one man standing by the mule that had pulled the tiger from Lovero to Mornia. "Nev!" the man called when he saw us. They clasped forearms and spoke in rapid Mornian, too quick for me to make out a single word.

Someone stepped beside me and I turned to find Metta and Isha. Isha pushed a flat cart before her, a single wheel in the front. But Metta was unburdened, aside from her expanding belly.

Metta blinked at me slowly, studying me through slitted eyes. Isha refused to make eye contact with me.

"You are back," Metta said to me quietly. When they had discovered us gone, I couldn't imagine the sort of scramble she'd found herself in. All her plans and plots to regain her status revolved around Nev, and now me.

"Yes," I said.

But Metta seemed the resourceful type. The kind of person who, when faced with crumbling plans, would use the pieces to simply build stronger ones.

Metta sniffed, then looked at the cart with the wired

cages, before turning back to me.

"You can help us," Metta said as Isha wheeled the cart over to the smaller wagon with the snake cages. "You will have to speak to Bedna soon," she added.

"Who's Bedna?" I asked.

"She is leader of the *samars*." And that was the only explanation she gave as she stood before the cart with the cages.

A woman greeted them and wasted no time handing down a snake cage, handle on the top to keep her fingers away from the gaps in the wire and the venom of the snake.

Metta took the cage and placed it on the cart, then took another and stacked it on top.

I reached out for the next cage, but the woman yanked it away from me. "*Ghoshka*," she said to me.

I didn't know much Mornian, but I knew enough to understand the insult as it was meant. I was not a traveler. I was an outsider in their midst, gifted with the magic of their gods. I understood the woman's animosity.

"Delka!" Metta shouted, and the woman looked at her. Metta said something in Mornian and the woman looked at me anew, her eyes settling on the *singura* around my neck. Then she reluctantly passed the cage down to me.

"Keep your hands on the handle always," Metta said. "They sometimes try to bite, even through the cage. Meska will not protect you if you are bitten. Even if you are a *samar*."

I remembered the horned viper that had struck at me that first night in Lovero, when I'd fled from Ravenna and the ugly truths the Da Vias had told me. When I'd found shelter and sanctuary behind the cages of the menagerie, in the arms of a traveler boy with a wide smile.

I looked over my shoulder and saw Nev speaking to some other men, all of them standing around the wagon of the tiger.

"Will they return him to his regular cage?" I asked Metta of the tiger. "It's a pit, right?"

Metta nodded. "Yes. First they must wait for things to calm. Tigers are mean if things are not calm."

We continued to take the snakes from the wagon, stacking them on the smaller pushcart until it was full of cages. Then Isha picked up the handles and led Metta and me away from the menagerie caravan.

We headed east and south, toward the pens and cages that held the traveler animals when they were not traveling.

I kept my eyes open while we passed cages of deer, rodents with long legs, monkey-like animals with striped tails. There were large pastures reserved for goats, though the goats did what they wanted and jumped in and out of their pens. There were also pastures for stunning horses, and they cantered around together, welcoming back the ones who had gone traveling with the menagerie.

Isha and Metta spoke quietly together, their Mornian drifting over me. Metta chuckled at something Isha said, and Isha placed a hand on Metta's belly.

I looked away, giving them their privacy. Nev was right. I didn't see Isha ever leaving Metta. They clearly fit.

I thought about Nev and the way he had chuckled, late in

the night. My skin tingled at the memory.

Isha pushed the cart to the right and then stopped. We stood by a small alcove, built out of wooden boards that stretched over six feet into the air, creating a sort of half circle. A canvas stretched across the tops of the boards, keeping the interior of the alcove shaded and warm.

Metta grabbed two cages and walked inside. I followed.

Shelves had been built inside the half circle, and some already had cages stacked on them. I leaned close and found more snakes, different from the ones that had been in the menagerie.

Metta stacked the two cages on a shelf and gestured for me to do the same. We continued until we had emptied the cart of all the snakes.

"This is where they live?" I couldn't help the surprise, touched with scorn, that coated my voice.

"Snakes," Metta said, "like the dark and the warmth. And they do not need space. They like small cages as long as they have food. They are not like you or me. They are snakes."

I eyed the small cages and the snakes inside, and they did seem comfortable, even if the wires were just tiny bars, really.

I rubbed my arms and stepped back. "What do they eat?"

"Mice. Rats."

I grimaced. "Where do you even get the rats? Do you have ratters to catch them? Terriers?"

Metta shook her head. "No. There is a rat family. They breed them. Their status is very low, though."

"Because they're rat people?" I asked. "Even though so

290

many of you rely on them for your own animals?"

A traveler shrug in response.

"What's the highest-status animal?" I asked. "The tigers?"

"Goats," she said.

I laughed. "Truly?"

She nodded. "Everyone needs and uses goats. Not just the animals, but us, too. Milk and hide and meat and food for the meat-eating animals. Isha comes from goat people."

Isha peeked her head inside at the sound of her name and Metta said something to her in Mornian. Isha nodded and smiled. "Goats," she said. "They are very smart and very kind."

It was the first time she had spoken to me, though she still refused to make eye contact.

"Do you miss them?" I asked her.

She shrugged. "They are everywhere. If I miss a goat, I go find one."

"Come." Metta gestured me out of the snake nook. "We must collect the rest of the snakes."

Isha picked up the end of the cart again and we began our trek to the menagerie caravan. Metta rubbed her back and then cupped her arms beneath her stomach, trying to support the weight better.

Beatricia used to do that, when her back pained her. She'd probably had the baby by now. A girl, I hoped.

Tears stung my eyes.

I didn't want to go home, back to Yvain. I didn't want to return to that place where I didn't belong, to the family that had lied to me my entire life.

But that didn't mean I didn't miss them. Didn't wonder about them. Had Emile married Elena Caffarelli so she could become a Saldana? Had they found the letter addressed to Marcello in my room in Lilyan?

Had Les recovered?

I swallowed and wiped the tears from my face. Metta looked at me from the corner of her eye. "Sand," I said as way of explanation.

To my left, someone darted behind a pen, vanishing, but not before I'd gotten a glimpse of blond hair, of pale skin.

I stopped and blinked rapidly, clearing my eyes.

Traveler skin ran from olive to deep brown, their hair from sandy brown to black. None of them were blond like me.

Like Lea.

I took off, chasing after the person.

Behind me Metta shouted. I pushed myself forward, my boots pounding on the dirt as I dodged and weaved around pens and paddocks.

Birds screeched, feathers floating in the air as they flapped their wings. I swung left, past a cage of small rodents that scattered into burrows.

Another right and I slid to a stop.

I'd reached a dead end.

My breaths heaved in my chest. I'd been chasing a ghost.

Maybe it had been my imagination, the person with the blond hair. Perhaps my tears had created an apparition.

I'd been thinking about my family. Maybe I'd just missed them so much I had fabricated it all. Besides, if it had truly been Lea, she wouldn't have run from me, from the travelers. She would have strolled into their midst, afraid of no one.

"Allegra."

I spun, and there, hidden in the shadows of empty cages, stood my mother.

Claudia Da Via.

———————

I stared at her, breaths heaving in my chest, blinking to make sure I wasn't imagining her.

But she didn't disappear, didn't vanish as my breath calmed, my heart slowed.

She wore her leathers, bone mask pushed to the top of her head, blond hair plaited down her back.

She took a step toward me. "Allegra," she repeated, her voice little more than a whisper.

"What—" I started, then swallowed. "What are you doing here?"

"I've come to bring you home."

And for a moment my heart soared. Here, here was my way out! It was not Lea who had come to rescue me, but Claudia, my true mother.

But then I remembered the illness that had struck me on the dead plains, making me sicker and sicker the farther I got from Mornia.

I could not leave with Claudia.

I shook my head. "I can't go home with you."

She frowned. "Yes, you can. Forget about Lea, the others. Just come with me right now and we can return to Lovero, to Ravenna. You can become a Da Via, be a part of the Family you were always meant to be a part of. It was what your father and I wanted for you."

I closed my eyes, trying to picture my father. He was dead, though. And no one could really know what he would want.

"It's not that." I studied her features, trying to find every little bit that was like me and every little bit that wasn't. "I cannot leave. There's some sort of magic, a curse from their gods, maybe, keeping me here. If I try to leave, I'll die."

Claudia scoffed. "That can't be true."

"It is," I said. "I escaped once already. I had to return to save my life."

Allegra blinked rapidly, digesting this piece of information. "Why are their gods involved in any of this?" she finally asked. "Why do they care about what happens between a mother and her daughter?"

Meska was a god of motherhood, so I suspected she probably would care about something like this if either of us were devout to Her and not Safraella.

"It's complicated," I finally said, echoing Nev. The wind blew between the slats of the alcove we were standing in, and I thought of Metta and Isha with the snakes. Were they looking for me right now? Afraid I had run off again?

"How did you even come to be here?" I'd tried to escape and had barely made any distance. And yet, somehow, she'd made it to Mornia on her own. She didn't even have a *singura*.

Someone shouted from the caravan and I realized the answer. "You snuck onto the menagerie caravan."

She inclined her head. "I was going to search for you in Yvain, of course. But I never got that far. You turned up missing, and Lea went on the warpath."

I blinked, trying to imagine Lea's rage and what it had meant for the Da Vias, the other Families. She would have never guessed I'd been taken by travelers. The Da Vias would be her first, logical assumption.

"It couldn't have been the Addamos," Claudia continued. "They couldn't have reached you in Lilyan, through all those noble Caffarellis." She said this with a sneer.

"And it wasn't us, the Da Vias, regardless of Lea's wrath and her accusations. I'd seen a small group of travelers leave the menagerie and head into the dead plains before Susten had ended. At the time I'd thought nothing of it. But I knew you'd spent time with the travelers. Had met a boy." She snorted.

"And so I knew you had gone with them. Or been taken. I wasn't sure which, and it didn't matter. When the menagerie left Lovero, I made sure to hide myself in their midst, and they brought me here."

"Allegra!" Someone shouted, the voice drifting through the animal pens and cages. Metta, looking for me.

"You have to hide." I grabbed her arm and pulled her back into the shadows.

"What? From some simple traveler? I'll drop her before she realizes we're here."

She reached for a knife on her belt and I snatched her hand, stopping her from pulling it free.

Claudia's eyebrows drew together in a V.

"Don't," I said. "If you kill her, it will alert the others. And you cannot take all the travelers."

Claudia loosened her grip on the knife.

"You have to hide, to stay hidden from them. If they discover you here, they'll know I'm trying to escape. They'll kill us both." I thought of Nev's little wagon, where we had stored it when we'd snuck back into Mornia. "There's a wagon," I said, and described its location. "It's not much, but no one should search it."

"And then what?" she asked. "Just hide forever?"

"Allegra!" came Metta's voice, closer.

"Just until I figure some things out. If I can undo their god-magic, then we can leave. But until then, stay hidden."

I released her hand and dashed from the alcove, leaving her behind.

I turned the corner and found Metta, searching for me.

Metta stopped and stared at me in the way that she had that made me feel she was seeing all of me, all my secrets, bare and spread out before her.

"I thought I saw something," I offered as explanation for my disappearance. "A loose horse. But it was nothing. Just the sun, playing tricks on my eyes."

Metta blinked and I knew she didn't believe my lie, but after a moment she turned around. "Come, there are still more snakes."

I followed Metta, glancing over my shoulder at the alcove.

Hidden in the shadows I caught a glimpse of white bone mask, decorated with red diamonds.

twenty-nine

†

WE FINISHED UNLOADING THE SNAKES WHILE THE REST
of the travelers attended to their own animals and returning
family.

I thought the animal pens had been loud before, but they
were nothing compared to how they were now they were
full once more.

Animals shrieked and screamed and sang and called to one
another, much the same way the travelers responded to their
own returning members. It must have been hard, to be separated from your loved ones for so long. I'd been gone from
my family for weeks and I felt like scratching at my skin to
relieve the itch of missing them.

But the travelers were probably used to it. They were travelers, after all.

I silently prayed, hoping that Claudia was taking the
opportunity to hide while all the travelers were here with the
menagerie. As the time passed and there was no exclamation

of surprise, no sign she had been discovered, the tension in my body began to fade.

Nev and the others led the cart mule pulling the tiger deeper into the pens and paddock, heading more south than we had for the snakes. There were only six travelers, not counting Isha and Metta, who trailed behind along with me. I glanced at Metta's forearms. They were smooth, empty of the scars showing she cared for the tigers. She must have been more in charge of the snakes.

"How many tigers are there?" I asked.

"Three," Metta said. "But that one"—she pointed at the covered cage on the wagon—"is ours. He is the oldest. The other two are females and belong to other families. One is expecting cubs. If it is a litter, we will get one. We need another male soon, or the line will die out."

"What happens if all the tigers die?" I asked. "Will you have to capture more?"

She shrugged. "No one has traveled to capture a tiger in many years. No one remembers how."

That comforted me, somehow, that they couldn't steal any more tigers from the wild, force them to live in pits, in a cage for all their lives. If they could not get another breeding pair, then these were the last tigers they would cage.

The finality of it all felt right. Nothing should remain caged forever.

Finally, we broke through the maze of pens and paddocks and found ourselves on the southeast side of the animals before the crop fields began.

A pit stood before us.

I wasn't sure what I had expected, but it wasn't this.

The pit was huge. Easily fifty feet across in all directions and twenty feet deep. Inside were two tigers. They looked up at me and pulled their lips back, pinning their ears against their skulls. At the base of the walls of the pit were three holes, each with a metal barred gate suspended above them. Ropes attached the gates to the top of the pit where they were secured. At the east end of the pit stood a large pond, water dripping from what looked to be a trough above.

Metta said, "The water comes from the lake. Tigers like to swim."

"And the gates?" I pointed to the holes.

"Watch."

Travelers walked to the edge of the pit and stopped. Someone unhooked the mule and led him away. A man and a woman went to the edge of the pit and began to shout at the tigers below.

The tigers pinned their ears even tighter and roared.

A man waved a white flag at them and the angry tigers slinked away from the pond, heading toward the holes. They slipped inside and two other travelers loosened the ropes above.

The gates slid in place over the holes with a thunk, trapping the tigers inside.

"Look." Metta pointed to the men who'd loosened the rope. There were grates in the ground, which I hadn't seen before now. The travelers opened the grates, and each of them dropped raw meat inside.

"They feel safe in their holes," Metta said. "They are always given meat. It makes them happy."

Then everyone rushed to the wagon and the waiting tiger there. A wide plank was lowered into the pit, the top resting at the base of the wagon. Someone had fetched a canvas and they draped it over the top of the wagon, and travelers stood at both ends, stretching it out and holding it taut, creating a sort of cover for the end of the wagon and the pit.

Metta ushered me away from the edge and we stood to the right of the wagon.

Everyone fell quiet.

Nev walked to the wagon and slipped beneath the canvas. And though we weren't near, I could hear him speaking softly in Mornian to the tiger.

"What is he doing?" I asked Metta, reading the scene well enough to know that I should at least whisper.

"He is about to release the tiger," she whispered back. "The canvas stops the tiger from seeing the edge of the pit. And from seeing us, so he does not attack someone."

"Won't he see Nev, though? Under the canvas?"

One of her maddening shrugs. "Tigers are dangerous," was all she said as an explanation.

I watched the canvas and Nev hidden underneath, listened to his quiet words as he spoke to the tiger. I couldn't help the lump of fear in my chest, the twist of my stomach.

There was a sound of metal grating against metal. I held my breath.

A thump and a blur of orange as the tiger burst from the wagon and down the plank into the pit.

As soon as it reached the bottom, the travelers yanked the canvas away and Nev and another jerked the plank up, trapping the tiger in the pit.

But the tiger paid them no mind. He waded into the pool, letting the water lap at his belly before he began to drink.

The travelers cheered then, slapping one another on their backs at a job well done.

Nev joined us, a smile on his face. I exhaled a breath I didn't even realize I'd still been holding.

"Now," he said to me, "it is time to celebrate."

———✦———

The travelers knew how to celebrate. It was like Susten Day all over again, but in Mornia instead of Lovero.

There were no stilt walkers and fire breathers, but there was singing everywhere, and music, and dancing and drink and good food.

Children ran together in packs, hands filled with sweets as they tried to steal them from one another, not caring who they crashed into. It made me ache for Lovero, my new home.

But like Lovero, the celebrations meandered and migrated wherever people gathered, though it seemed the heart of it rested in the New Mornia quarters, which was where Nev led me.

He had also borrowed some clothes from Isha for me. I changed out of my ratty dress and instead wore trousers and a sleeveless vest that helped the summer breeze keep me cool. Nev wore a deep red vest that flattered his olive skin.

"Why is this part of Mornia so different?" I gestured to the smooth-walled buildings surrounding us. Many of them appeared to be houses and homes, though some seemed to be businesses.

Night had risen, but there were torches and lamps to light the festival. And the travelers had sung the song of Culda, to keep the ghosts at bay once again.

"Much of the good underground has been used," he said. "New homes collapsed too easily. The clay was not strong. So now they build on top of the land."

I looked at the homes with their colorful curtains for doors and windows. It must have been hard for the first inhabitants to make the change from living below ground to living above.

Nev fetched us some meat, presumably goat, cooked over a fire and wrapped in leaves coated in a sticky, sweet sauce. They were almost too hot to eat, and yet they were too delicious to take our time. I licked every last sticky bit from my fingers.

And everywhere the travelers sang. Mostly it was small groups of people singing, and when they met up, their songs competed or blurred together in a raucous harmony.

But sometimes there would be one loud, chorused song with many people singing together. Nev would frequently join in on those songs, smiling at me. And I couldn't help but smile back, even though I didn't know what he sang of, what the song was about. But the festivities filled me with something, a sort of ache that made me want to laugh and sing, too, and also made me want to weep, to find a corner and cry until all my tears were spent.

Every time I smiled, I felt like a traitor. Claudia was hiding in a wagon, waiting to take me back to Lovero. Lea was on a rampage, trying to discover what had happened to me. I was smiling with the people who had taken me.

"We need to make a plan," I said to him.

He turned my way, glancing at the *singura* around my neck. "Yes."

"Do you have any books or scrolls we might look through, see if there's some forgotten lore somewhere?"

If the *singura* belonged to Safraella, we would go to a church and ask the priests what they knew, what their books could tell them.

Nev shook his head. "No books. Nothing like that. Everything is passed down from *samar* to *samar*. Nothing is written."

That complicated things. "Well, who is the oldest *samar*?"

"Bedna."

"The one who is also the leader?"

"Yes."

I tapped the table. "We should speak with her. She might know things you don't."

"Yes, that is true," Nev said.

Something tugged at my waist.

I looked down to find small fingers, trying to untie my belt.

I snatched the hand and turned to find a girl in my grip, eyes wide, struggling to be free.

I released her and watched as she fled to a pack of children. They jeered at her return and she shoved a few of them before they scurried away.

"They steal as a game," Nev said in my ear, and I turned to find him beside me, shoulder pressed against mine. In his hand he held two glasses of liquid, one of which he passed to me.

The liquid was dark red and I sipped it, expecting wine but instead finding a sweet yet tangy fruit juice.

"She needs more practice, then," I said.

"You caught her, so you have become their new challenge and they will not rest until they beat you."

I sipped at the juice again. "I don't have anything worth stealing." Unless . . .

I clutched the *singura*.

"No. They would not, even in play. It is forbidden."

"But I'm not one of you. Would they not think me below your laws?"

He chewed his cheek, before shaking his head. "Not the children. They would not understand the difference between you and the other *samars*."

The children weren't privy to the more complicated politics at play. That didn't mean the other travelers weren't, though.

I turned to better face Nev. "Which god is the *singura* for?" I asked. "Is it just One? Or all of Them?"

He pointed at the flat disc and the circles with their radiating colors. "Three circles," he said, "for the Three. The outer circle is Boamos."

"Thievery and wealth," I supplied.

He nodded. "The middle circle"—he tapped the middle ring on the stone—"is for Culda. We worship Her proudly tonight." He gestured to a group of travelers as they stumbled past, their singing slightly slurred from liquor.

"The inside circle is Meska."

"She's where you find your status. From the animals and your women."

"Without Her, there is no Three."

Of course, without any of Them there would be no Three, but I understood his sentiment. "How did travelers come to worship three gods instead of one? I mean, in many cities there are more than one god, but people tend to pick a single god."

He leaned closer so he could be heard over the sound of drunken singing. Our shoulders touched, our heads tipped close together.

"A long time ago," he began, "we were three peoples. Farmers and animal keepers, traveling musicians, kings and thieves. Until one day when the longest, biggest *bol* blew across the land, and all the people were forced to shelter together. They were not many, these people, yes?" he asked, and I nodded to show I was following along.

"And they told tales of their lives, and it was not long before the farmers spoke of a longing for their children to see the world, and the traveling musicians spoke of a desire for more wealth, and the thieves and kings spoke of wanting families to care for them no matter the weight of their money pouches.

"And these three peoples knew if they lived together as one people, they could have all their wants and dreams. They could travel through the lands with the animals and bring in much wealth while their families stayed home, waiting for their return.

"So the gods of three people turned into the gods of one people."

The tale had the sound of a fable, something recited often to children. But Nev had told it with flourishes, with smiles and winks that stabbed me in the chest and the heart, until it seemed I was bleeding here and now, and could do nothing to stop it.

Nev's smile faded and he looked at me, his eyes so dark in the night even though the lamp on the table was warm and bright.

"Allegra," he said, his voice no more than a murmur. And yet it rang through me like a bass bell, all echoes and reverberations bouncing off my bones, my flesh, my skin.

A whisper of a touch at the back of my neck. I closed my eyes, remembering how he had loved to run his fingers through the length of my hair. He grabbed my hands now, cupping them in his, the skin of his palms rough against mine.

A tug at my neck.

I snapped my eyes open.

I jerked my hands from Nev and yanked the knife from my belt. I twisted and slashed. Blood sprayed across the top of the table.

Perrin gasped and pulled her arm to her chest, pressing her hand against the slice in her flesh.

Nev jumped to his feet, and when he saw Perrin, hidden in dark corner of the seating area, his eyes narrowed and he snapped at her in Mornian.

She stood, blood seeping between her fingers.

I climbed to my feet as well, and pointed my knife at her. "You'll have to try harder than that."

She ignored me and spat at Nev, responding to whatever he'd said to her.

"It belongs to her," he said so I could understand.

"No," she said. "It is a mistake. She is a *ghoshka*. She should not wear it."

A crowd began to form, their singing fading away as they took in the argument between Nev and Perrin, the blood dripping from Perrin's arm, from my knife.

Metta and Isha appeared so suddenly they had to have been close by. They stood beside Nev, the three of them a concerted front against Perrin, who stood alone. Even timid Isha seemed strong alongside her family.

"The Three choose who is a *samar*," Metta said to Perrin. She rubbed her belly, and though I had seen her do it before,

I got the feeling she did it now to draw attention to her status. That she was about to be a mother and Perrin was not.

"The gods did not choose her!" Perrin spoke so I could understand. She pointed at me with her good hand, her fingers coated in her own blood. "It was stolen from us and now she wears it with no understanding of the gods! She steals our heritage!"

Murmurs from the watching crowd.

Beside me Nev shifted uncomfortably. If Perrin gained support, what would stop them from taking the *singura* from me? From killing me?

Even fully armed, I couldn't hope to stop a mob of such size.

"I am a disciple of Safraella," I said to Perrin, and she looked at me now, returning pressure to her injured arm.

I wiped the bloodied blade on my thigh and returned it to my belt. Let her see that I did not need it. That I did not fear her. Or the rest of them.

"I serve a dark god faithfully, so do not suppose to know me, Perrin. I understand the ways of gods. And I understand enough of your gods to know that even if you manage to take the *singura,* it does not mean it will belong to you."

Perrin glared at me, rage spilling across her features.

Someone spoke loudly in Mornian, and the crowd parted.

An old woman stepped through, her black hair long ago turned to white, her eyes clouding. A *singura* rested on her chest. A *samar,* then.

"She is Bedna," Nev whispered to me as the commotion of

the crowd quieted. "She is Perrin's grandmother," he added.

Great. The leader of the *samars* was also related to the woman who wanted me dead.

Bedna looked between me and Perrin.

"What is happening here?" she asked her granddaughter.

Perrin responded in Mornian, so I wouldn't be able to contradict her story. Nev could, but Perrin held more status than he did, and besides, Bedna would probably side with her granddaughter over Nev.

But whatever Perrin said didn't go over the way she'd planned, because Bedna began to shake her head and finally held up her hand, halting Perrin's words.

"You do not choose who is a *samar*, Perrin."

"But she is a *ghoshka* . . ."

Bedna shook her head again. "We were all *ghoshka* at one time. We were all separate people. Now we are one. It is not up to you to make decisions on behalf of all. The *samars* will decide the fate of this girl, not Perrin."

Perrin scowled and dropped her head, but finally nodded.

The crowd began to disperse, though there were some unsettled mumbles, and more than one traveler shot me a suspicious or dirty look.

Bedna turned to me and another *samar* stepped to her side. "We will sleep off the festival. You will come speak with us tomorrow, Allegra."

I raised my eyebrows, surprised she even knew my name. "How about right now?" I asked. I needed to speak with

Bedna if I wanted to remove the *singura* from my life.

Bedna simply smiled, and she and her companion walked away.

Perrin glowered at us.

"Go home, Perrin," Metta said.

Perrin responded in Mornian.

Metta was a small woman. Shorter than Perrin, not as broad shouldered, burdened under the weight of the child she was carrying. But she held her ground, and looking at her, it seemed only the gods would be able to move Metta and even then, only if they asked her.

"I do not think you will be able to take it," Metta replied to Perrin so I could understand.

I kept silent. It was nice, to have someone else threaten people on my behalf. Even if Metta was still using me as the weight of that threat.

Perrin scowled and left, leaving the four of us alone. I felt strong beside them. We had held our ground, held to one another and prevailed. They spoke so I could understand.

"She will not let it go," Isha said. She fidgeted, tugging at her dress as if it was ill-fitting.

"Perrin is a bully, always," Nev said. "Now she feels she has the gods on her side."

"And the crowd," I said. "Many seemed to side with her."

"Bedna did not." Metta smiled slowly, slyly. "And what matters is what the *samars* believe. Bedna stopped Perrin. And Allegra helped with the menagerie today. Many saw these things."

"Metta will keep speaking with everyone," Isha said, more to Nev than me. "Metta will sway them to us." She smiled at Metta and took her hand.

I thought of Claudia, hiding in the wagon, my mother waiting for me to return home with her. I thought of Perrin, and knew she would try to take the *singura* from me again, with more force. I thought of the dead plains, and how I could not cross them.

It all came down to the *singura*. I had to be rid of it. There had to be a way. If anyone knew, maybe it would be Bedna and the other *samars*. If they were disciples of their gods, then maybe one knew of some long-ago wisdom, forgotten over the ages, that could free me of this burden without sacrificing my life.

thirty

I STEPPED ONTO THE SPIRAL STAIRS AND SLIPPED INSIDE Nev's home. It had begun to rain, putting an end to the traveler festivities. Everyone headed to their homes.

It was dark inside and a moment later the light completely disappeared, sinking me into shadows.

"Nev!" I stood my ground, not wanting to trip over the chairs or table.

Something shuffled behind me and a hand cupped my elbow.

"It is only me," Nev said quietly before I could react. His hand vanished and my elbow was cool in the sudden absence of his skin against mine.

I swallowed.

The lamp flared to life, and Nev set it on the counter in the kitchen, letting its yellow light fill the small space.

Then he reached for my hip. And I let him. Let him place his hand on me, let his breath brush across my throat.

He tugged at my belt and stepped away. In his fingers he held the knife I'd used to defend myself against Perrin. His hands were gentle, holding the knife delicately. It reminded me of how his fingers had stroked my neck, sliding along my jaw, to my throat, before his lips pressed against my skin.

"What is this?" His voice was deep and gruff and spoke of anger and hurt and betrayal, maybe.

"You weren't supposed to find that." I reached for the knife but he pulled it away, taking a step back.

"This is my knife," he said.

"Yes."

"You stole it from me."

"Yes. Would not Boamos be pleased?" It was an unfair remark.

His face darkened. "What were you going to do with it?"

"It's a knife," I said. "Its uses are pretty clear."

"You would kill me?"

"What? No! Nev, I—"

He clenched his jaw, knife still in his hand, though he dropped it to his side. "I welcomed you into my home."

"The knife was for protection," I said. "And welcomed is a bit of a stretch. You took me from my home and family. Your sister made me stay with you while the rest of your people decide whether or not I should die."

"You kill too easily," he said.

His anger was contagious and it spread to me now, coursing through my veins. "Killing *is* easy! People are fragile. And obtuse. And too in love with themselves to see their deaths shadowing them. Our deaths walk beside us from the moment we are born. We are lucky if we reach old age."

"You are a murderer who speaks of death and deals in death but you do not respect it! I said I would help you and yet you keep this knife on you for any opportunity to use it. Life has value!"

"You think I don't know that?" I stepped toward him and it was either a testament to his bravery or his anger that he didn't step back. "You, who sent a snake to kill my uncle instead of facing him yourself?"

"That was not—"

"I cut off his arm, Nev! I cut off his arm to save his life and while I raced to find a doctor, I was taken by travelers, all because I wear a pretty pendant." I flicked the *singura*. "You took me from my family when they needed me most."

"But—"

"Just because the lives and life I value are not the same as yours doesn't mean I don't value life."

The shouting had left me breathless.

Nev turned his back on me. He walked calmly to the shelves and slipped the knife back in its place.

"I am sorry about what you had to do to your uncle. And I would like for you not to kill me. Or Metta or Isha."

"I haven't killed you yet, have I?" I snapped. By the drop of his shoulders it wasn't the response he was looking for.

"Nev . . ." I sighed, trying to curb my anger. "The knife was only for protection. I promise. I would not hurt Metta and Isha. I would not hurt you."

"Because it would not help you," he said bitterly. "Killing us would make your escape harder."

"It would," I answered truthfully. "But that is not why I wouldn't kill you."

I stepped closer to him. "I'm rash," I said.

He turned, confusion on his face.

"What?"

"I'm rash. I do things without thinking about them first. I react. I lead with my emotions. It gets me in trouble, sometimes."

He blinked, waiting for me to continue. "I took that knife because I didn't think about it. I escaped into the dead plains because I didn't think about it. I ran into Ravenna without considering the possible consequences. That one . . ." I paused. "That one was really dumb. Even if it led to answers. It led to a lot of things."

Nev stepped closer, eyes on his feet. "You . . ." he started, then swallowed. "You went with a traveler boy behind the cages in a menagerie," he said.

"Yes."

He looked at me, eyes on mine. "You went with him to his bed."

I stepped closer to him. "Yes, again. That one also led to some unexpected consequences."

He laughed, a quick bark of surprise that faded to a smile.

He was so close. His bruises were fading fast. And his

smile was so much like the smile I'd first seen on him that I didn't even question, didn't even hesitate. I just leaned forward and kissed him.

It was nothing like the kiss in the dead plains. That had been wild and passionate and full of built-up emotions. This one was soft and sweet and quiet and when our lips pulled apart I realized my eyes were closed.

I hadn't been kissed like that in a long time.

"See?" I said. "Rash. I'm sure it makes me hard to be around."

"I do not mind," he said, leaning in for another kiss while above us the rain poured down, blanketing the land, trying to erase us all.

I waited for Nev to fall asleep, listening for soft snores from his alcove, before I slipped outside.

The heavy rain had passed, but it still drizzled, and I walked through the damp and wet night, heading east to where the traveler wagon was stored.

I missed being in Yvain, where night meant people went inside to spend time with their families and to sleep. Where I could spend hours on the top of a roof and trace the constellations, or count the lonely ghosts as they wandered about the streets, making up tragic stories of how they had met their ends.

I'd always thought they'd been boring, the quiet Yvain nights. And I supposed they were, compared to Mornia, and definitely compared to Lovero. But I had spent enough time with them that they had seeped into me, until the absence of them made my bones ache.

I shook my head. I didn't know what I wanted.

Nev's wagon appeared unremarkable. No one would look at it and think someone was hiding inside.

I pushed the curtain aside. And found a knife pointed at my face.

"It's me," I said.

"Allegra." My mother lowered the knife.

I slid inside with her, leaving the curtain open for some fresh air and the hints of moonlight that peeked through the shuffling clouds.

My mother. I was here, alone, with my mother. And for the first time no one was threatening us, or forcing her to hide, or flee.

My eyes watered, and I cleared my throat, trying to control my emotions.

I had so many questions for her. So much I wanted to learn, years of knowledge and mothering and love to make up and it could all start right now, here, together.

"Are you ready to go now?" my mother asked.

I leaned back against the wagon. It seemed Claudia liked to get straight to the point. One new thing I'd learned about her.

Claudia had set her mask, cloak, and most of her weapons at the front of the wagon, but she still wore a few knives to keep them close. Her plaited blond hair was messy, with strands pulled free to hang around her face. She brushed these aside. "Are we leaving?"

I remembered the fear in Nev's eyes when he'd told me how I'd had a seizure as we'd tried to leave Mornia. Remembered the weakness, the hallucinations, the pain. I shook my head. "No, I can't leave."

My mother made a sort of exasperated groan and leaned back against the wall of the wagon. "What is your delay? Do you enjoy it here? This place that stinks of animals? With these people and their incessant singing to keep the ghosts away? Yes, I saw how that works. It's a clever little trick."

"I told you I can't leave. Not until I find a way to get rid of the *singura*." I tapped the necklace hanging from my neck.

My mother leaned closer, examining it in the dark. "Just give it to me, then."

I jerked back. "No. I can't give it away. I would die. That's the problem. If I give it away, I die. If I try to leave with it, I die. And anyway, they need these necklaces to sing the ghosts away. There are only twenty-four of them. If I left with it, they would never stop looking for me."

"Then what's the solution?" she snapped. I couldn't blame her for the exasperation she was feeling. She was hiding in a tiny wagon in Mornia. She was probably miserable.

"I'm going to speak to a woman tomorrow. She's . . . I don't know. A priest mixed with a Family head, maybe. She might know of a way to free me."

"Why don't we just speak to her now? We can sneak into

her house, the two of us, and persuade her to set you free." She tapped the tip of her knife when she spoke, clearly displaying what kind of persuading she would use on Bedna.

And maybe that was actually the solution. Maybe I was being too soft, here in Mornia. One of Lea's favorite sayings was, "Murder is the solution." But even she would admit that sometimes, it just wasn't true. And I felt that in my bones, here in Mornia. That if I killed someone, it would only make things worse for me.

"I don't know where she lives."

"Then we'll kill them all, Allegra!" my mother shouted.

I scoffed. "All the travelers? That's not even possible."

"We'll take a page from that damned Lea. We'll kill all the people with their idiotic necklaces and let the ghosts kill the rest of them. No one will stop us then."

"There are innocent people here. Children."

She snorted. "They're not innocents, Allegra. They're the enemy. They took you from me. Don't tell me Lea has made you soft."

"I'm not soft," I snapped.

She leaned back once more, arms crossed over her chest as she stared at me. "I won't wait here forever," she said quietly.

I blinked. I couldn't untangle what she meant. It seemed a subtle threat, but I wasn't sure if it was for me, or the travelers. Either way, it made my skin crawl.

"I have to go," I said, and slid to the back of the wagon.

"Why? Because someone's waiting for you? That traveler boy you spend your time with?"

I didn't answer.

"Boys come and go, Allegra," she said. "There will be new ones in Lovero. Clippers. Not travelers. The people you belong with."

Belong. She spoke of belonging as if she knew my heart, could see its chambers and how they echoed for me to fit. But she didn't know me. Know who I was. She was my mother, yes, but that didn't mean she knew where I belonged any more than Lea had.

My stomach churned at these uneasy thoughts and I stepped outside. The rain had passed and the night air was cool.

"Next time you come," she said, "bring me some food. And wine."

"They don't drink wine," I said. "Only juice and oil."

"Of course they don't," she sneered.

She closed the curtain, hiding herself from view, and I headed back to Nev's.

thirty-one

†

He was still asleep when I returned, and I sighed in relief. I didn't relish trying to explain where I had been if he had been awake.

I slipped off my boots and climbed back into my warm alcove, chilled from the night air. My blankets were tangled and I shoved them around, trying to get them back in order. My elbow slammed into the wall of the alcove with a thump, and I hissed in pain, holding it to my chest as waves of numbness worked down to my fingers.

Sounds erupted outside my alcove, thumps and shuffling and all at once Nev was ripping my curtain open, knife in hand, searching for whatever had threatened me.

Cool air pooled inside and I took a deep breath, shaking my arm.

"What is it?" Nev asked me.

"A dream," I said. "Nothing but a dream."

He relaxed, knife dropping to his side as he closed his eyes.

"Sorry," I said.

"It is fine." He placed the knife on the table. He wore only a pair of night pants and gooseflesh had erupted on his skin.

My thoughts were unsettled after the conversation with my mother, but the sight of Nev brushed them aside as usual.

"You're letting all the warmth out." I tugged him into the alcove with me and shut the curtain once more.

It was so dark, but my night vision had always been excellent and I could see the rise and fall of his chest as his pulse returned to normal.

I shivered in the chill air and tugged on my covers. "You're sitting on my blanket."

Nev shifted, crawling to sit beside me. I covered us both with the blanket, and the heat that rolled off his body put my own shivering skin at ease.

"Did you think it was Perrin?" I asked. "Come to murder me in my sleep?"

"Maybe." We spoke quietly, as if louder words had no place in this moment. "I would not put it past her."

"I would hear her coming," I said. "I would kill her first."

He nodded and I laughed.

"What?"

"Nothing, really," I said. "We've come so far."

"What do you mean?" He looked at me then, mostly in

silhouette, but his eyes glimmered a touch in the dark.

"When I first met you and you discovered I was a clipper, you were frightened of me."

He scoffed. "I was not."

"And you abhorred my calling," I continued, ignoring his protestation. "But now I can point out our differences, how easy it is for me to think of murder and death as a solution, and you go along with it."

He snorted and leaned closer. His arm pressed against mine, his skin warm, even with the heat of the covers.

"You are not disgusted."

"You never disgusted me," he mumbled. He pressed his lips against my neck.

I leaned into him, reaching for his shoulder, pulling him closer.

He trailed kisses across my throat as I slipped out of my clothes. I slid my hands under the waistband of his pants, sliding them off his hips.

He muttered something to me in Mornian, but even if I could understand the words, they were muffled, pressed against my neck. The sentiment, though, was understood.

The cold air stroked my bare skin and I pulled Nev down beside me, sinking into the warmth of his flesh, the strength of his arms.

I had been lonely in Yvain. And then I'd found Nev in Lovero. And I'd been lonely again, in Mornia. And once again I'd found Nev. His presence always seemed to fill an emptiness in me.

And for a little while, there with him in the dark, the bars surrounding me didn't feel as thick.

—————————

The gray mist rolled through my dreams.

I stood and watched it. And waited for the hidden monsters to appear. They always appeared.

"Allegra . . ." Their echoing voices reached me first, coming from the mist, from everywhere, from nowhere.

Then their shadows, swift and towering, merging and separating so I could never get a true look at them. If they were even real.

"Allegra . . ."

Of course it was a dream. The same dream I'd had every night. Even knowing it was a dream did nothing to change anything. I stood and watched the mist, and listened to the shadows call my name.

A cold breath on the back of my neck.

I spun. Nothing. There was nothing there.

Something brushed my hair. I spun again. Still nothing.

But this was new. This was not the same dream I'd had before. This was different.

"Allegra . . ." the voices hissed. Menacing now, sibilant and empty and yet promising many things.

The gray mist swirled, twisted, and spiraled before me, creating a vortex, a maelstrom.

"Allegra . . ." they said, louder now.

And the maelstrom rose above me, collecting the gray sand below my feet, towering even higher than the shadows, until I had to lean back, stumbling, to see it stretch into nothingness.

And everywhere dread poured over me. Dread and fear and foreboding.

The maelstrom crashed into me.

Something thumped and my eyes snapped open.

Nev was out of the alcove, rubbing his face. He stumbled to the kitchen, lit the lamp, and pulled out the now familiar oil glasses and bottle.

I pulled on a pair of trousers and a vest and slipped out of the alcove, crashing onto a stool.

"What time is it?" I yawned.

He shrugged. "Morning. Afternoon, maybe."

He poured us each a glass of oil and sat beside me. We sipped the oil quietly, the silence between us comfortable.

I needed to refocus. To speak to the *samars* about getting rid of the *singura*.

"Can I speak to Bedna today?" I asked Nev.

He sipped his oil again. "Why?"

"She might know how I can give up the *singura*."

Nev scrunched his face, but only shrugged. "Yes. We will go to her home. First I will have to feed the tigers and snakes."

"Fine." And while he was doing that, I would bring my mother something to eat and drink. I felt ashamed I hadn't thought to bring anything last night.

"Nev!"

Metta and Isha walked down the stairs, and when Metta saw me, she broke into a smile.

"Metta," Nev said. "You will bring Allegra to speak to Bedna today."

"Yes," Metta said. "It will be good. Bedna will see, and Allegra will keep the *singura*." She grinned sharply.

I didn't blame her. She was no closer to her goal of raising her family's status. I would have given the necklace to her right then if I could've. Instead, I would speak with Bedna. She had to know a way to release me from this burden.

Nev went to the kitchen and dug around for a few moments, returning with a tray of meats, cheeses, and bread. He took the knife from last night and sliced the bread into pieces. Then he handed the knife to me.

I hesitated but he continued to hold it out for me until I took it once more.

Metta and Isha noticed the exchange, of course.

Nev cleared his throat. "Perrin will come armed, next time," Nev answered their unasked questions.

Isha shoved bread and cheese into her mouth, concentrating on chewing. Metta just studied us.

"If you kill her," she finally said, "the *samars* will not be happy."

"I don't plan on killing her," I said. "But I will protect myself."

Metta just grunted.

We finished our lunch in silence.

thirty-two

†

the animals before I slipped out of his house. It wasn't that
I was lying to him. I was just keeping Claudia a secret. The
fewer people who knew about her, the better for everyone.

I filled a small bag with a bottle of juice as well as the left-
overs from our lunch, then headed to the wagon.

The sun seemed extra bright this afternoon. It stabbed
into my eyes, until my head pounded with pain. The warm
wind dried out my throat, too, enough that I started to con-
sider cracking open the bottle of juice for me. But if I was
this thirsty, I was sure Claudia was even more so.

I slipped past the cages, avoiding any travelers, though
most were focused on tasks at hand and didn't have eyes
for me.

"Mother," I whispered through the curtain. "It's me." I
slipped inside.

Empty. The wagon was empty. Claudia was gone.

I stared at the empty space. She wasn't here. Which meant she was somewhere else, but where? Where had she gone? And, more important, why?

I thought about what she had said last night. That she wouldn't wait forever. But it had only been a few hours. Surely she wouldn't have left without me . . .

The curtain behind me yanked open, filling the tiny space with afternoon light.

Hands grabbed my arms and they jerked me out of the wagon, releasing me to stumble outside.

I kept my feet and spun.

Perrin stood before me, with a group of six others.

Perrin reached into the wagon and pulled out the sack of food I'd brought for Claudia. She looked inside and smirked, before dropping it to the ground.

"*Ghoshka,*" she said by way of greeting. "Where are you going with this food and drink and wagon and the *singura*?"

Fleeing. She thought I was trying to flee. And the evidence was damning.

I couldn't refute it, not unless I wanted to reveal the presence of Claudia. And even if I did, with Claudia missing, who would believe me?

"What do you want?" I said to Perrin.

Her group of friends laughed loudly. From the other end of the line of wagons, a traveler stepped out to see what the commotion was. He spotted the group of us, then fled, heading west through the animal pens.

"I know you are a *ghoshka*," Perrin replied, "but I did not know you were so dumb."

I blinked, letting her insults wash over me. I didn't care what she said to me. She wanted to goad me into doing something stupid. It was a coward's trick. She had the advantage of numbers. She was in control of the situation. She shouldn't need to goad me at all.

I crossed my arms over my chest, waiting.

Perrin snorted. She looked over her shoulders at her friends who were shouting and laughing at me. They shoved one another around, working themselves up for whatever they had planned.

"You are a *ghoshka*," Perrin finally said. "You do not deserve the *singura*."

"You are like a ghost, Perrin," I said. "You do the same thing over and over again, each time hoping for a different result and each time being disappointed when nothing changes."

Perrin's smile vanished.

Other travelers began to drift our way, drawn by the commotion, maybe. One of them sprinted to the front, shoving his way past Perrin's group to stand by my side. Nev, out of breath.

"What do you want, Perrin?" Nev wasn't even pretending to be pleasant.

Perrin pointed a finger at me. "She tried to flee with the *singura*."

Perrin kicked the bag toward him, and the bottle and

leftover food spilled across the ground.

Nev stared at Perrin. "It is a bag of food. This is your evidence?"

"We found her in the wagon." She pointed her finger behind us.

Nev shook his head. "I see no horse to pull it."

I scanned the growing crowd. Not a single familiar face. No Isha or Metta. No Bedna with her even ways.

Perrin responded to Nev in Mornian and Nev interrupted her with sharp words. I stepped in front of him, facing Perrin.

"Stop hiding and speak so I can understand," I said to her.

She sneered at me. "Poor dumb *ghoshka* doesn't understand Mornian."

"Poor scared Perrin is too much of a coward to accuse me of something to my face. If you have something to say to me, now's your chance." I held my hands out before me.

Perrin scowled. "You are a liar. And a thief."

"You are all thieves," I said to her. "You're just angry that you're not the *samar*. But it seems your gods have chosen me and not you. Who have you angered, Perrin? Meska, Boamos, Culda? Surely it must be at least one of Them if They chose me over you."

Perrin pulled her knife from her belt. It seemed I'd finally pushed her far enough.

I brandished my own knife, the one from Nev's kitchen.

"Perrin, stop!" Nev yelled. But three of the men from the crowd grabbed him and pulled him away. He tried to break free, but they held him too tightly.

"Do not kill her!" he shouted.

"Oh, I will kill her," Perrin said.

But Nev was yelling at me. If I killed Perrin now, it would only make things worse. I had to win this fight, but I had to keep Perrin alive.

Perrin rushed me, reversing the grip on her knife. I reversed my own grip. She stabbed at me. I slammed my forearm against hers, blocking the strike.

I'd spent my youth learning how to kill people. I could kill people with poisons, with swords, with ropes and needles and knives. But we didn't spend much time learning how *not* to kill people with these weapons.

As Perrin struck at me again, my instinct was to return the blow. She'd left her neck open. It would be quick, easy, to stab her in the throat.

I stepped to the right. Perrin lost her balance. She stumbled.

Her eyes narrowed. She'd thought I'd be easy. A fast fight and she'd be the victor. She underestimated me.

Perrin doubled her attack.

And maybe I'd underestimated her, too. She was fast on her feet. Dashing at me, switching knife hands in the way that only someone proficient with the weapon could. I blocked. Spun. Blocked again. Lost ground. Pressed back against Perrin's friends, who had encircled us. They shouted their support of Perrin. Pushed me toward her. I ducked too slowly under an exaggerated slash.

Her knife split the skin on my arm. I hissed and glanced at the wound. Not deep, but deep enough for blood to drip down my arm.

To my left Nev tried to pull free of the men who held him in place. I was done with this fight.

I went on the attack. Perrin's turn to block, to give ground as I pushed her into the center of the ring. Her neck, open again. I slashed, only remembering at the last second to pull back, to halt my follow-through. The knife slid across her skin. Perrin gasped, dancing away. She touched her throat. Her fingers returned coated in blood.

My own fingers were slick from the blood that dripped down my arm. The longer this took, the worse my grip would become. I needed to stop her. I needed to end this.

I was only slightly aware the crowd had grown larger. More travelers had arrived. Metta and Isha shouted and pushed their way to Nev. It was all just noise, distraction from the task at hand.

I dashed at Perrin. She raised her knife and arms. She'd learned her lesson, blocking her throat now. No matter. Perrin stabbed for me. I spun on my heel, twisting behind her.

Perrin swung again, but I leaped onto her back. I was tall, but Perrin was tall, too, and strong. I trapped her free arm beneath my legs as I wrapped them around her waist. I grabbed the wrist of her knife hand. Then I sank the tip of my knife into her chest. A circle of blood appeared on her shirt, spreading slowly.

She froze.

The crowd quieted, their eyes wide at the position in which Perrin had found herself.

"I could kill you," I said to her. "It would be easy for me. So easy. And my god would be grateful. Would thank me for it, Perrin. Should I send you to meet Her?"

The men had loosened their grip on Nev. He shook them off and stumbled into the ring, Metta and Isha followed on his heels.

"Allegra," Nev said to me quietly. Like I was a horse, prone to spooking, or the tiger in the brief moment they'd let him free from his cage.

"You sent a snake into my home," I said to Perrin. "You sent a snake to kill my family. I should end you for that alone."

"No," Perrin said.

"What?" I pushed in the knife just a sliver more.

Her brow broke out in sweat. She swallowed. "Do not kill me."

"You ask me not to kill you," I said slowly, "when you try to kill me?"

"I am sorry," she gasped. Whether she actually was, or whether she was so terrified of dying that she would say anything, I couldn't be sure. Tears leaked from the corners of her eyes, tracing her cheeks.

"What is happening here?" a voice called over the crowd.

People stepped aside and Bedna strode to the center of the

ring. She frowned at me and Perrin.

"She is trying to kill me," Perrin said to Bedna in another ploy to save her life.

All at once I was tired of it.

I unhooked my legs from around her waist and let Perrin go, pulling my knife free from her chest. Only the bare tip was red with her blood. She wouldn't need stitches. It probably wouldn't even scar.

Perrin pressed a hand to her chest, then pointed her knife at me. "She tried to steal the *singura*."

I flicked my own knife free of blood, which arced on the dirt at my feet. Of course, most of the blood was my own, dripping onto the knife from my arm, but the spray of blood still made a few of the travelers in the crowd step back.

I returned the knife to my belt.

"I can't steal something I already own," I said.

"Have you tried to leave Mornia with the *singura*?" Bedna asked me.

"I wasn't leaving," I said.

It was a non-answer, of course. I wasn't trying to escape now, but I had before. It was clear from Bedna's frown that she knew it was a non-answer. She turned her back on me.

"I can sing the ghosts away," I said.

Bedna stopped. Everyone stared at me.

"It is true," Nev said.

"He is lying," Perrin said. "Can you not see he is lying for her? For this *ghoshka*?"

"Perhaps," Bedna said. "But in this we can know the

truth. Allegra, you will sing Culda's song and show us that it would send the ghosts away."

"What, right now?" I asked.

Bedna inclined her head.

Nev's eyes flicked toward me, then away. He didn't fully believe I could make the *singura* work.

"Fine," I said. I cleared my throat, trying to ignore all the travelers who were staring at me, many of them hoping I would fail. Instead I focused on Nev at my side, and Metta and Isha, too. These people who had aligned themselves with me for a myriad of reasons. I was grateful for them, in this moment.

I closed my eyes and sang.

I stumbled on the first line and heard someone snort. Perrin, most likely. But I pushed on, gaining confidence. I had done this before. It would work again. I believed in it.

The necklace grew warm at my chest. I opened my eyes as I finished the verse. The *singura* flashed, and a light jumped from me, stretching out until it reached Bedna and her *singura*.

The crowd was silent.

Bedna stared at me thoughtfully. Then she spoke. "I will meet with the *samars*."

"But I need to speak with you," I said.

"Later," she replied in a manner that brooked no arguments.

And with that Bedna left and Perrin's friends dispersed, except for a few who rushed to her aid.

I strode away, waiting until I was free of their eyes before pressing my hand to the wound on my arm. It would need stitches.

Metta caught up to me, holding her stomach. "You did it," she said. "You can sing the ghosts away."

"Yes."

She stopped and watched me walk away, Nev at my side as we returned to his home.

thirty-three

NEV'S HOME WAS COOL AND DARK AND I SAT AT THE
table while he rushed to light the lamp.

My vest was sleeveless, but my arm had still bled all over it.

Nev pulled his chair over to me and sat down, a bowl of
water, a clean towel, and some bandages in his hands.

My head pounded, even in the cool of his home. I pulled
my blood-sticky fingers away from my arm. "Sorry I
destroyed Isha's vest."

"She will not mind." Nev dabbed at my arm with the
damp towel, cleaning the surrounding skin. "And I will buy
you another."

Something in my chest quivered, and I bit my lip to try to
still it. He treated me as if I was here, now, to stay. It made
me feel . . . something.

I shifted in my seat. "I wasn't trying to escape," I said.

"I know," Nev responded. And that was it. He didn't
question me further, ask me about the food. He believed me.

He trusted me.

I gasped at this revelation.

Nev pulled the bloodstained towel away from my arm. "Did I hurt you?"

"No." I shook my head. "No."

The slash from Perrin's knife was only about the length of my forefinger, but it oozed blood. "It will need to be stitched."

He got up from the table and began to dig through one of the crates on his wall. I took the towel and continued to dab at my wound, feeling the pain as it pulsed through my entire arm.

Nev returned with a needle and thread. He pulled his chair closer. "This will hurt some."

"This isn't my first time being stitched," I said.

I looked away while Nev pierced the needle through my flesh and pulled the thread through to the other side. Stabbings, poisonings, bloody and dead bodies were all things I could handle. But I never did like to watch skin and flesh sewn back together like a piece of cloth.

"What happened your first time?" Nev asked, leaning closer.

"I was seven or eight, and learning about throwing knives. Wasn't paying attention and one slipped through my fingers. We keep all our knives well honed."

I held up my ring finger in the lamplight, the thin white scar mostly faded now. "I only made that mistake once."

Nev grunted in acknowledgment, but then we fell silent

while he finished stitching me.

Finally, he tied the thread off and leaned closer for one last inspection of his work. "It will hold." He looked up at me with a grin.

His stitches were neat, but overlarge, and not very delicate. It made me think of Lea's skills with a needle and how she could make the tiniest stitches in a wound so it wouldn't scar. I missed her skills, right about now. Missed her, actually.

I blinked, sat back in my chair.

I missed her. I actually missed her. Missed her clipper words of wisdom, missed her proficiency in dealing with marks and customers in the shops, missed how she would laugh at Les's jokes.

She had stolen me and betrayed me and lied to me my whole life. And here I was, missing her anyway. Missing my life with my family. Even if I would never belong with them.

Shadows trailed down the stairs, followed by Metta and Isha.

Nev got up from his chair so his sister could take it. She sank down with a soft groan.

"You can really sing the ghosts away," she stated, confronting me without any preamble.

"I told you I could." My head and throat ached. I didn't want to deal with these questions, these doubts. All I really wanted was something to drink and to crawl back into bed.

As if reading my thoughts, Nev set a cup of juice in front of me, and I gulped it down.

"Perrin will not settle for being shamed in front of so

many others." Isha spoke into the quiet, her voice practically a whisper.

"Well," I said, "she'll have to learn to live with it. Or improve her knife skills."

Metta snorted, and her mouth twitched in a small smile.

"It may not be Allegra she attacks next time," Isha said a little louder. "What if it is Nev? Or you or me, Metta?"

I didn't have an answer.

"She will not go after you," Metta said. "Not with your mother and sisters and grandmother's status."

"If she killed you," Isha said to Metta, "there is no one who would stand up against her for it. You have no mother or sisters. You have no status."

"We will have our status back," Metta said, and it was clear from her tone that she meant it. That she was willing to do almost anything to raise their status.

"It is not only you and Nev now," Isha continued. "There is a child. You have brought a clipper into your home. She is a murderer. You throw dice for your status."

"It is for *our* status," Metta said, reaching across the table for Isha's hand.

"And I'm not the one who started that fight," I said. "It was Perrin who tried to kill me."

"She will keep trying," Isha said.

"Well, if she kills me, everything will still work out for you. I will leave the *singura* to Metta and you can get back to your merry little lives."

Metta shook her head. "No."

"You don't have a choice," I said. "And, anyway, the Three will decide if you are worthy or not." I stood and walked to my alcove, digging through my meager pile of belongings until I found the other clean vest and trousers Isha had loaned me.

I went to the kitchen and pulled out a crate, looking for a bar of soap.

"Where are you going?" Nev pushed up from the counter.

"To the lake. To bathe."

"I will come with you."

"No. I'm fine." I straightened. "You should stay and work things out with your family."

Isha scrambled out of my way, clearly back to fearing me after witnessing the fight with Perrin. I climbed the stairs, feeling their eyes on me the entire way.

As soon as I was outside, Nev started yelling at either Metta or Isha, or maybe both, his Mornian harsh and clipped.

I headed northeast, the lake sparkling in the afternoon sun. Most everyone was inside, avoiding the heat, so my walk was uninterrupted.

The west shore of the lake was empty, a blessing I didn't waste. I stripped and waded into the lake, its cold water seeping across my body until I was deep enough to dive under.

It was peaceful under the water. I held my breath until my chest ached and I was forced to kick to the surface.

I scrubbed every inch of my skin, even my toes, only easing my verve around my freshly stitched wound. I used my fingers to rake through my hair and across my scalp. I would have paid good money for a trip to one of Yvain's bath-houses. But a lake in Mornia was all I had.

My mother had vanished, disappeared. But to leave Mornia altogether, she would need a horse and wagon to protect against the angry ghosts, and surely someone would have seen her leaving in that case.

She hadn't abandoned me, then. She was still in Mornia, doing . . . something. My mind drifted back toward her suggestion of killing the *samars* so we could flee, but she didn't know who they were, how to find them without searching every home, killing anyone that got in her way. And once she started killing people, her presence would no longer be a secret.

I couldn't work through her plans, her aims. I didn't know her. Couldn't figure out how her mind worked or what her likeliest move would be.

If it had been Lea, I would've known where to look for her, been able to suss out her plots and go from there. Lea I understood. My mother was a stranger to me. And now that she was acting strange, I was lost in the dark.

Bedna was speaking to the *samars* about me right now. Telling them what I had done. Hopefully it worked in my favor, but maybe using their magic would simply anger them more, and they would vote to finally kill me and be done with the whole mess. I couldn't guess at that, either.

Everywhere I looked, shadows greeted me in return, hiding the plots in motion around me.

My stomach churned from the cold water and these dark

thoughts. I climbed out of the lake and dressed in the loose-fitting vest and trousers. They were very comfortable, the fabric soft and supple. I tied my hair into a tight braid and headed back to Nev's. I'd been gone long enough that hopefully everyone else would have left. I needed time without Metta and her schemes, and now Isha and her judgment. My headache had eased some after the bath, but hadn't vanished completely. And now I was cold from the swim and craved my bed even more than before.

Nev sat at his table, oil waiting for us beside a large dinner.

I should have been starving, but instead the sight of the food just turned my stomach. I sat on the edge of my alcove.

"You are not hungry?" he asked.

I shook my head and then leaned it against the clay wall. The coolness seeped into my skin and I groaned. "When I sang," I said. "Will that make them stop wanting to kill me?"

Nev sighed and sat back in his chair. He poured himself a small glass of oil and sipped it before he spoke. "There are some who will never accept you. Will never accept you as a *samar*."

"People like Perrin. Because I'm a *ghoshka*," I said.

He winced. "They do not understand why the Three would choose you over one of us. Seeing you makes them upset and fearful."

"I've always been feared," I said. "I wear a bone mask and creep through the night. Being feared is nothing new for me."

"But the people who feared you in Lovero did not want

343

you dead. The fear you create here will cause people to side against you. They will press the *samars* for your death, even if you can sing the ghosts away."

"Then I should leave. If I'm not here, then they won't have to be confronted by their fears." My head pounded and the light from the lamp only seemed to make it worse.

Nev shook his head. "You cannot. We already tried."

"Then we need to try again. I can't stay here, Nev."

I should have been worried about my mother, but I was too tired to give it more thought. She was capable of taking care of herself. I would look for her again later, after I had rested.

I climbed into my alcove and pulled my blanket over me. Its warmth sank into my skin, easing my shivers.

Nev stood beside my alcove. "You are sure you are not hungry?"

"I'm too tired to eat." I yawned to make my point.

He studied me suspiciously, but finally nodded. It was late afternoon, but perhaps he was tired, too, because he changed and climbed into the alcove with me, pausing only to blow out the lamp.

"We will speak to Bedna when she is done with the *samars*," Nev said quietly. He pulled my curtain shut, sinking my alcove into darkness to help me sleep.

thirty-four

I AWOKE IN THE MIDDLE OF THE NIGHT DYING OF THIRST.

I crawled out of bed, stumbling from the alcove to where Nev kept a carafe of water. My head pounded and my eyes—sleep blurry though my vision was—burned. I gulped water, not caring as it poured down my chin, my neck, my chest.

I drank until the water sloshed around in my stomach and only then did I stop. My hands shook when I set the carafe back down. My whole body shook. I was so cold.

I tripped over my feet on the way back to the alcove, lacking the strength to pick them up. I shoved past the curtain and crawled under the covers until I reached Nev. He was so warm. I pressed myself against him, shivering.

Sick. I was sick. It was the only thing that made sense. But why? I wasn't in the dead plains, fleeing from Mornia. I was right here, *singura* still around my neck.

My thoughts twisted around each other until I couldn't unravel them.

"We fit together," Nev said quietly, pressing his face against the back of my neck.

"What?" I said. "What?"

He mumbled and pulled me closer, pressing my body against his.

Sleeping. He was talking in his sleep about how our bodies fit together for sleep. It didn't mean anything.

I closed my eyes, and clenched my teeth together to try to stop them from chattering. I pulled my knees to my chest and squeezed ever farther under the heat of the blankets.

And at some point I stopped shivering enough to fall asleep again.

"Allegra."

The whispered calling of my name made me snap my eyes open, sure it was the monsters in the mist, coming for me. But as my vision cleared, I saw Nev, leaning over the bed.

I moaned and turned away. But Nev tugged at the blanket, uncovering me. I gasped at the cold air that poured over me, slapping at Nev's hand, but he held firm to the blanket.

I sat up. "What are you doing?" I meant it to be a yell, but my voice only emerged as a croak. The light beyond the curtain made my eyes ache and I narrowed them to tiny slits.

"Eat this soup I made, and you can return to bed."

I scowled, but with my covers removed, the idea of a warm soup heating me from the inside seemed like a good plan.

I crawled out of bed and staggered to the closest stool. I sat down heavily, but then Nev put a spoon and a steaming bowl of soup in front of me and I forgot the call of bed.

The soup was a meat broth, salty and thickened with something that had a slight spice to it. Not that it mattered. I barely tasted it as I scooped it into my mouth as fast as I could. Nev watched, frowning.

When I'd finished the soup I pushed the bowl away. My stomach felt full and warm, but my limbs still shook from cold and my entire body ached.

I climbed back into the alcove, dragging the blankets with me.

"Thank you for the soup," I managed to mumble.

If Nev responded, I didn't hear him, but I thought I felt a hand resting on top of me over the blankets before I fell asleep again.

Nev left me alone after that, only waking me once, accidentally, when he climbed into bed with me, whispering an apology as he jostled me awake. It was the only reason I knew I'd slept through the entire day.

When he left the bed again in the morning, I didn't even wake.

"All day yesterday," a familiar voice murmured, its quiet words scraping over me until I cracked my eyes open.

The shadows were talking about me. One leaned closer.

"Allegra," it said. And then I knew them for what they

were. The monsters in the mist that called my name, that wouldn't let me sleep, that poured a maelstrom of fog and sand over me, drowning me.

"No." I pushed away from the shadows.

But one grabbed me. Its hand pressed against my forehead, cold like ice, and all at once I realized how hot I was. I was burning up. The maelstrom was burning me up.

"She has a fever," the shadow said.

"I'll go into the market, buy some medicine."

"We'll go to Bedna."

"Someone should stay here."

"She'll be fine by herself for now."

Then the shadows left, disappearing into the gray mist surrounding me.

I slipped back into the darkness until once more a shadow appeared. This one silent. It leaned over me, all quiet breaths and soft movements.

I whimpered, trying to press myself away from it, but I was too weak.

"Shhh," the shadow said. Something cold and wet pressed against my forehead.

I tried to force my eyes open, to see the shadow monster for what it truly was, but a light blinded me. The scent of tullie blossoms wafted over me.

Home. Somehow I'd made it home.

"Lea?" I mumbled, closing my eyes once more. "I'm sorry. I'm sorry."

"You're safe," the shadow said. "I'm here for you. I'll always be here for you, now."

The shadow held my hand, familiar calluses rough against my skin, and I tumbled once more into the darkness.

I was lost. Lost in the gray mist. Lost away from home, where no one could find me.

Not even the shadow monsters were here. Not even the maelstrom.

Something tugged my arms. I was moving, sliding for a moment before I was flying. Soaring through the air like a bird, like a ghost in the night, maybe.

But I couldn't stay a bird forever. I turned into a canal boat, rocking back and forth, bumping up against another boat that was warm and solid and pressed me close to its hull.

I tried to shove myself away from the other boat, groaning. It only pulled me in tighter.

"I have you," the boat said. But it wasn't a boat voice.

My eyes fluttered open. Sunlight poured into them, sending spikes of pain through my head. Footfalls sounded below me. Maybe I was walking.

I forced my eyes open again, prepared for the sun. And found a shadow. I was always surrounded by shadows now. This one carried me, pressed against his skin, his chest rising and falling with heavy breath. Other shadows paced on either side of us.

Something splashed around me, and then I was sinking

into water, getting deeper and deeper, until the water covered me completely. I had turned into a boat again, but I was sunk, drifting to the bottom of the canal.

No. I had never been a boat. I had always just been me, Allegra.

My eyes snapped open.

I was underwater, completely submerged. I thrashed, kicking my legs until I was jerked up, breaking through the surface of the water. I took a deep breath, water streaming across my eyes, into my mouth.

I was pressed against someone. Nev. Nev held me in his arms, shirtless, just as soaked as me.

"What?" I said.

"We are at the lake." He turned and carried me back toward shore where Metta and Isha waited. "We had to bring your fever down."

He had walked into the water with me, pushing us both under the surface until my mind had returned to me.

I remembered the shadows, the voices. They were Nev all along. Metta and Isha, too. "I've been sick."

"You still are sick," he said.

And when he said it, I realized he was right. Maybe my mind was clear again for the first time in . . . I wasn't sure how long, but my breath wheezed in my chest and I shivered in Nev's arms.

Back on shore Isha draped a blanket over us, but Nev didn't stop walking, carrying me north while Metta and Isha paced us.

"Where are we going?" I asked.

"To Bedna," Nev said. "She will help."

I leaned my head against his chest. I was just so tired.

"Where did you find the tullie blossoms?" I mumbled.

Nev looked at me in concern, but I closed my eyes and let him carry me away.

———※※———

Nev set me carefully on a bed. A real bed, too, made of wood, not an alcove dug into the wall of an underground house.

We were in a building, with windows and doors. New Mornia.

Bedna hovered over me, looking closely at one eye, then the other. She held her warm palm against my throat and pursed her lips as she counted the beats of my heart. Then she leaned back and covered me with a blanket.

She faced Nev. "How long has she been like this?"

"Three days," he said. "It came on suddenly."

"From her arm wound perhaps?" Bedna suggested, but Nev shook his head.

"It's not infected. It's clean and healing. This is something else. The fever hasn't broken. Not with rest or medicine. Not with cold water."

"He carried me into the lake," I mumbled in explanation.

Nev and Bedna both turned to stare at me.

"She understands Mornian?" Bedna asked quietly.

"No." Nev shook his head. "Very little."

They spoke in riddles and mysteries, twisting and turning

351

me around until I couldn't find myself anywhere.

"How soon after she sang Culda's song did she fall ill?" Bedna asked.

Metta stepped beside him. She pressed a dry shirt into his hands and he pulled it over his head. "She complained of being tired right after the song."

I coughed, deep in my chest.

"She woke feeling worse," Nev said. "I let her sleep until afternoon, when I made her eat something."

"Soup," I supplied.

They stared at me even closer then. Nev's eyes were wide with concern.

"She's understanding more than just a little Mornian," Metta said quietly.

I pushed myself up on my elbows at that. "Are you speaking Mornian?" I asked.

They glanced between each other, but their non-answer was an answer of its own.

I coughed some more, the sharp pain in my lungs contrasting with the fear snaking through my chest. "What's wrong with me?" I asked. "What's happening?"

"Lie down." Bedna pushed me onto the bed. She pulled another blanket over me and I couldn't deny that the extra warmth was something I craved.

"Also." Nev spoke slowly. "This is not the first time she's been ill . . ."

"When?" Bedna asked him.

He looked at me, apologies in his eyes. "In the dead plains.

She tried to go home. But the farther she traveled from Mornia, the sicker she got. When we turned back, she recovered. We thought—well, we didn't know what it meant but we suspected it had something to do with the gods. She had displeased Culda, maybe, so she couldn't travel."

Bedna made a thoughtful noise in her throat and disappeared into the kitchen.

"You were leaving with her?" Metta exclaimed.

Nev faced her. "Yes. I was."

"This is not the time for squabbles," Bedna snapped.

I turned on my side, watching them. But they fell silent. Finally, Bedna disappeared around a corner.

Metta stepped closer to Nev and they began to whisper to each other so Bedna couldn't hear them.

"How could you do that? To me? To our status?"

"All you care about is your status!" Nev whispered harshly. "You don't care about me. You have Isha. You will have the child. You will have your status back and what of me? You'll continue to send me away, to travel forever with the tiger, gaining wealth to help our status even more?"

"You like to travel!" she shot back.

"I was alone, Metta! I was alone until Allegra. She is the best thing that ever happened to me, and we are the worst that ever happened to her. Look at her! She is like this because of us. But no, all you care about is your status."

Nev was out of breath. I'd never heard him speak that way to Metta before. To anyone, really.

"I care about more than just our status," Metta finally

said. "It is because I care about you, and Isha, and the child that I try so hard to raise our status. To make a better life for all of us. I don't want Allegra to die."

"Only because if she does, you're worried you won't be able to hold the *singura*."

"No," she snapped. "That is not why I don't want her to die, Nev. I see she makes you happy. I see she is strong, that she is not afraid."

They glanced at me then, and Metta sighed, then walked away.

Nev pulled a chair beside my bed and sat beside me.

"Tell me what's going on." I kept my voice quiet, mostly to prevent more coughing.

Nev shook his head. "I do not know." I would have accused him of lying to me, but I could read the fear in his eyes.

I couldn't speak Mornian, past the few words and phrases I'd learned from Les. But if Nev and the others had really been speaking Mornian right now, then something had changed, because I had understood each word. Hadn't even realized they were speaking Mornian.

Bedna returned, a steaming cup in her hands. "Drink this, Allegra."

I struggled up onto my elbow and took the cup. The warm steam poured over my face. "What is it?"

"It is a tea," she said. "It will help lower your fever." She placed her fingers on the bottom of the cup and tipped it to my lips, until I had to drink or risk the tea spilling over me and the bed.

It tasted terrible, like she had soaked sticks in hot water and added some bitter leaves for fun. I tried to stop, but Bedna shook her head and kept tipping the cup.

"Drink all of it. Then take another nap. We will be here when you wake."

I finished the tea and she took the cup from me. "I don't want to sleep," I said. "I've been asleep too long. And there are monsters in the mist."

But even as I spoke, I realized how wrong I was. My eyes were heavy, and my head bobbed. I did want to sleep.

I slipped down onto the bed and closed my eyes. Nev brushed my still damp hair away from my face, and then I was asleep once more.

thirty-five

†

MY DREAM RETURNED. I'D BEEN SURROUNDED BY SHAD-
ows for days now, but they had been false, hallucinations
brought on by my fever, my illness.

Now, standing before the gray mist again, seeing the
shadows dart behind it, merge and separate before me, I
wondered how I could have ever mistaken Nev and Metta
and Isha for the shadows that towered over me, here in my
dream.

"Allegra . . ." they called, their familiar voices returning
the dread to my bones.

The mists twisted and spun, the maelstrom returning.

My hair whipped around my face. I pushed it from my
eyes.

"What do you want?" I yelled into the maelstrom as it
rose above me.

"What belongs to Us," the voices said.

I stepped back. It was the first time they had spoken to

me, other than to call my name.

"What belongs to you?" I yelled into the wind. But I was too late. The maelstrom crashed down and I woke with a gasp.

Nev sat across from me in the chair and he leaned forward, worry on his face.

"Nightmare," I croaked, struggling to a sitting position. I felt . . . not cured. Not well, but better than I had before I'd drunk the tea. Lucid and clearheaded.

I turned, sliding my feet off the edge of the bed.

Nev pushed his hands forward, trying to hold me in place. "Allegra."

"I need to use the bathroom," I said, and he lowered his hands.

Isha appeared from somewhere and stood beside Nev. "I will bring you."

She grabbed my arm and pulled me to my feet. I wobbled, unsteady.

She walked me out of the house and around back, to Bedna's bathroom. The hot sun warmed my skin and I closed my eyes, savoring it.

Isha paused at the door. "Do you need help?"

I shook my head and freed my arm. It was slow going but I managed to make it to the toilet without falling down.

"I'm surprised you volunteered to help me," I said to her past the curtain door. I emptied my bladder, then used the wall to pull myself back to my feet and hobble to the door. I pushed the curtain aside. "Aren't you worried I'll kill you?"

Isha pursed her lips and didn't respond, only taking my arm and helping to lead me back to the front door.

"I'm joking," I said to her.

"You are too weak to kill anyone right now," she finally said. And I caught the twitch of her lips as she tried to hold back a smile.

I snorted. "I wouldn't bet on it."

Back in the house I sat on the bed with a groan. Bedna stepped from around the corner with another cup of tea.

"No," I said. "No more tea. No more sleeping."

"This is *ahlo kheel*."

She passed the cup to me, and I looked down to see the thick, green liquid staring back up at me.

"It will help your strength to return." She pulled another chair over and sat beside Nev, next to my bed.

I sipped the oil. It had a fragrant herb flavor that left a fresh taste in my mouth.

"Are you speaking Mornian right now?" I asked her.

She glanced at Nev. "No."

"But you were earlier. And I could understand you?"

"Yes." She sighed.

"What's going on? I need answers."

"You have been sick," Bedna started. I passed the cup the Nev and scooted closer to her.

"I know. But you think it was something different. Not just a normal illness. Why?"

"Because you are still ill. Because you are improving, here, but you are not free of it. And because . . ." She paused.

"And because I could understand you when you spoke Mornian."

"Yes." She nodded. "And because it happened before. I believe it is a spiritual sickness. When you tried to leave, you pulled away from the Three and closer to your god in the west. So you fell ill."

"Spiritual sickness," I stated. She wasn't even speaking Mornian and I was having trouble understanding her. "The gods are making me sick," I said. "Why?"

"I do not speak for the Three."

"You're a *samar*," I said. "If not you, then who?"

Bedna exhaled through her nose, and then nodded. "It was a mistake for you to take up the *singura*."

"So I've been told."

"Yes, but it was a mistake for *you* to take it up. You are already a *samar* for your own god," she said. "To take up the *singura*, to sing the ghosts away, it is a pledge, to be a *samar* for the Three. But you are not. You have not given up your own god."

"No." I shook my head vehemently. "I am a disciple of Safraella. I am Her mortal hands in this world. I do Her dark work."

"Yes." Bedna nodded. "And that is why you are sick. Because the gods, your god, the Three, are jealous gods. They do not share."

"They do not want to share," I said, "but they won't let me give the *singura* to someone else. I am trapped. I either serve the Three or I die. How can I escape from that?"

Bedna didn't respond. She had no answer.

There was no way out for me.

"And what if nothing changes?" I said. "I cannot give the *singura* away, but what if I keep it, and still serve Safraella?"

"The illness will consume you," she said.

"I'll die?"

She shrugged. "It is only a suspicion."

"But I wore the *singura* for days before coming here. I was never ill in Lovero." Never had the nightmares.

"I believe it is because your god shielded you. She is the patron of Lovero. You are Her *samar*. She protected you."

"Until I left. Until I arrived here."

"Yes."

I closed my eyes. Gods. My life had become a battle between gods.

How had I even gotten here? I wasn't anyone special. I wasn't Lea, the chosen of Safraella. I was just a girl who had received a necklace from her uncle for her birthday. And now my life had become this: choose to serve different gods, or die.

But Safraella was a god of death and murder. Even if I chose to set Her aside, which everything in my being rebelled against, there was no saying She would not find a way to kill me, the way She had when the Da Vias had turned to another god. At the very least, if I stood before Her at the end of my life, would I be confident She would provide me a new, better life?

Nev called my name, softly, and I opened my eyes again.

"You should have never brought me here," I said to him.

He inhaled sharply.

"Do not blame the boy," Bedna said. "Bringing you here is not what set these trials into motion. The pieces were in place long before either of you were born. Bringing you here was a kindness he did for you. At least now you know what you face."

"My death."

Bedna scowled. "Would it be so bad, to turn to the Three to save your life?"

"Would you?" I asked her. "You, who are Their disciple. Would you give Them up, turn to another god just to save your life?"

She clasped the *singura* at her neck. She didn't answer, but I read the truth in her eyes before she turned away from me.

"It would be a hollow faith," I said.

I leaned my back against the wall of her house, pulling my legs up on the bed. I would not be controlled in this. I was done. I was done letting people, or gods, make decisions in my life. They would not force me to change gods outside of my will. If I died, then I died. But at least I died because of a choice I made. I would not be caged.

"Allegra," Nev said.

I shook my head. "No," I said. "No."

I lay down on the bed, facing the wall, my back to all of them.

And because I was still ill, it didn't take me long to fall asleep.

I woke in the night, the house quiet and empty except for Nev. He crawled into bed with me, and I pressed myself against him, his arms wrapped around me.

"We fit together," I said, remembering what he'd said in the night, before I fell too ill.

I felt him smile against my neck. "Yes. I think so, too."

It was unfair to blame him for bringing me here. It wasn't his fault any more than it was Les's fault for giving me the necklace, unaware what it meant, what would happen. We were all just trying to do the best we could with the knowledge we'd had at the time.

"I'm sorry," I said. "For what I said before. I don't blame you."

"I know," he said. And that was it.

"Where is everyone?" I asked

"Metta and Isha are resting. The baby will be born soon. Another ten days or so. Bedna is out. She will meet with the *samars*. Ask them to search for a solution."

A solution. There was nothing they could do. They had no real influence over the gods, no more than I did over Safraella, anyway. The only one who had ever claimed anything like that was Lea, and she wasn't here.

"What about your tiger?" I asked. "Shouldn't you be taking care of him?"

"I am taking care of you." He kissed my head.

"I'm serious," I said. "He's stuck in that pit. You're responsible for him."

Nev chuckled, and irritation wormed its way through my chest. "He is fine."

I couldn't stop thinking about the tiger, though. Maybe he dreamed of something different. Of the jungle, hunting his own meat, finding his own home. Or maybe he'd been caged so long that he couldn't even dream of his freedom, of the home and life he'd lost. Maybe his chest ached, empty for something he'd never even had.

"Please go take care of him," I said, my voice cracking. "Please."

Nev looked at me in confusion, but finally nodded. He climbed off the bed. "I will be back soon."

He slipped through the door and was gone, and I tried to ignore the disquieting churn of my stomach. Dread surrounded me. Like the maelstrom in my dream made reality.

Bedna pushed her way into the house and saw me, staring into space on the bed.

"You are deep in thought," she said. She poured me a glass of oil, then sat across from me.

"I have much to think about," I said. "Nev shouldn't have told you that he tried to help me escape."

"He was trying to help you now, as he was trying to help you then."

I closed my eyes and exhaled slowly. "Dumb," I said. "He's so dumb."

"He is young. And in love. Men are never smart when it comes to matters of the heart."

In love.

I had hurt Nev. I had turned his life upside down. And yes, it wasn't my choice to come here, but still. "I have done nothing to engender such devotion from him. He has no reason to love me the way he does."

Bedna smiled a small, knowing smile. "That is not always the way of things."

We fell into a thoughtful silence. I wondered if there had been a man in Bedna's life, at one time, who did stupid things because he loved her too much for his own good. And I wondered if I would do the same for Nev, if our situations had been reversed. Did I love him enough to risk my own life for his?

I didn't know. My feelings for him were complicated. They were so wrapped up in all the things that had happened to me. I suspected it would take me a long time to unravel them all. And I would take the time to do so, but a long time was not something I had left anymore.

A thought came over me, and I focused on Bedna. "Did you know my uncle?"

She looked at me, eyebrow raised.

"He was born here. Lived here as a child. Alessio."

Bedna nodded. "Yes. I remember him. I did not know him, but I did know his mother."

"The mother who brought him to Yvain to be rid of him, you mean."

Bedna pursed her lips. "Helna was a . . . troubled woman. She was a *samar*, but she did not feel close to Meska or her mercy. She never wanted a child, never wanted to be

364

a mother. And then she fell pregnant on a travel. She was ashamed. Not from her family, or anyone else, but she shamed herself. And then when the child was born a boy, she was more shamed. She resented him. Her mother and father tried to reason with her, but she would not listen. She wanted to find the child's father and give him to the father to raise. So she and her own father traveled to Yvain. But she did not return. Her father left the boy there because it was her wish, and she was a *samar* and a mother and his daughter, who he loved. He did not realize the boy had taken the *singura* until it was too late."

"He left my uncle on the streets of Yvain, for the ghosts to take."

Bedna exhaled slowly. "I did not know this. It was a wrong thing, what was done to your uncle. Plenty of people would have taken the child. But she was too shamed. She did not want to see him anymore." She paused here. "I am not glad he took the *singura* and kept it from us so long, but I am happy to know he found a good life."

It was an apology of sorts. Not that I was the one who needed it. But it was still nice to have, anyway.

She sighed and leaned back in her chair. And all at once she looked old. She *was* old, of course. Her once-black hair was white. Her skin was wrinkled and soft. She was probably older even than Marcello. But she gave off such an air of power. Of being in charge, of fairness and verve, that until this moment I'd forgotten that she was, indeed, a woman near the end of her life.

"What happens to you?" I asked. She looked at me, eyes full of questions at the change of subject. "When you die, I mean. When I die," I said, "I will stand before Safraella, and She will grant me a new life. A good life, if I have served Her well."

I thought about all the people I'd sent to meet Her, the lives I'd ended, the coins I'd slipped into mouths. Maybe I'd made a mistake by putting this necklace on, but I hoped She would take pity on me, see the work I'd done in Her name, and decide I had done enough to be worthy of a good, new life.

But, then again, She had never been a god of mercy.

Bedna exhaled slowly. "We do not know."

I left my thoughts behind and looked at her. "You don't know?"

"No. I will die and stand before the Three and what happens after that is a mystery."

I shook my head. "Why . . ." I paused, trying to tread carefully. "Why would you worship gods who promise you nothing? Who leave you in the dark? Even Acacius in Yvain offers His followers a chance to become one with the land."

Bedna shrugged. "We do not worship Them in order to be granted boons at the end of our lives. We worship Them because we have always worshipped Them. Because it is our way of life. And They give us daughters and sons, wealth and music, safe travels and nights free from ghosts. That is enough for us. What happens when our lives end is a mystery, yes, but one I seek gladly. The stars are no less beautiful simply because we know not where their light comes from."

I couldn't decide if that kind of unknowing blindness was terrifying or comforting. But I didn't think I would have the strength to face my oncoming death so easily, had I not known what waited for me afterward.

Because as my death approached, I didn't fear. I only felt sadness that I would never get to say good-bye to my family. To tell them I loved them.

And forgave them.

Bedna stood from the chair, groaning. "I return now to the *samars*. Nev will return to you soon."

"I'm fine," I said, aware it wasn't actually the truth. But I would be safe by myself.

Bedna hummed, and left me alone.

I closed my eyes, but a moment later the whisper of the curtain sounded and someone entered the house.

"Allegra," they called.

And I opened my eyes to find my mother, bone mask over her face, no longer missing.

thirty-six

†

"MOTHER," I SAID. "I WENT TO VISIT YOU BEFORE BUT you were gone."

She slid her bone mask to the top of her head and sat down on the chair next to my bed. "I couldn't stay in that wagon for another day. I needed space. I found where you've been staying, though. I visited you while you were sleeping."

The tullie blossoms. I thought I'd imagined them.

"You're looking better, Allegra. It's time for us to leave."

I shook my head. "No," I said. "I can't leave. I already told you this."

"Safraella will protect you. You are Her disciple. She'll stop whatever god curse these damn travelers have placed on you."

"It's not their fault," I said.

"Who cares whose fault it is? Just come with me now. We can take one of their wagons, return to Lovero. Start over. Be mother and daughter like we were meant to be."

I squinted at her.

"What?" she asked.

"It's just, you're so convinced Safraella will protect me, when you yourself didn't even follow Her when you were younger. You told me in Ravenna how it was the grace of your other god that gave me to you."

My mother leaned back in her chair. "That was a long time ago. I'm devoted to Safraella now."

"I don't doubt it," I said.

"She protected me and Val when Lea brought the ghosts to our home. She will protect you now, too. You are a Da Via. You are my blood."

"But I have always been devout, and when I tried to go home, I wasn't able. I don't think you'll overcome that any more than I could."

My mother shook her head. "This is nonsense. Come now, get up. I'm your mother, I know what's best for you." She reached out for me.

I leaned away. "What?"

"You'll come home with me and be a Da Via. You'll take your place at my side, where you always should have been. No one will look at me with pity anymore. And the two of us will be the strongest mother–daughter pair in the Da Vias."

I studied her. Really studied her. She looked like me, so much like me, that I had forgotten she wasn't actually me. She was her own person. With her own agenda. Her own goals. And that was bringing me back to her, to her life, fitting me into the life she led.

"What if I don't want that?" Because what she was describing sounded a lot like another cage. A gilded one, maybe, but a cage nonetheless.

"What?"

"I don't . . ." I paused, trying to work through my thoughts. I coughed. "I spent my whole life as a Saldana feeling like I didn't belong," I said.

My mother leaned forward. "You were always meant to be a Da Via."

"Maybe," I said. "That's what I thought, anyway. And I've spent my whole time here in Mornia trying to get back to Lovero, so I could become a Da Via, so I could finally fit."

"Yes!" she said.

"But how is being a Da Via any different than being a Saldana?"

Skepticism spread across her face. "Because we're Da Vias. We live in Ravenna, the greatest city in Lovero."

"It's just a place," I said.

"And you'll be with family," she countered.

"The Saldanas are also family," I said. "And they raised me."

"They raised you because they took you from me!" she snarled.

"Yes," I conceded. "And they lied to me. Kept me caged with them. But they did it because they loved me. Because they didn't want to lose me."

"I didn't want to lose you, Allegra. And in Ravenna you'll be with me. Your mother."

All my life I'd dreamed of having a mother. And here she

was before me, when I was sick, when I was dying, trying to get me to leave with her.

Lea had taken care of me. Had taught me, loved me. What was a mother other than that?

"It's the same," I said to her. "Da Via. Saldana. It's all the same."

Ravenna or Yvain. Da Via or Saldana. It didn't matter where I made my home. Who I called my Family. Whichever I picked wouldn't change who I was. I needed to fit with myself, first. "Ravenna and Yvain, they're just different sides of the same coin."

"And what is this place, then?"

"A different coin."

"That's nonsense. Come. I'll take you home."

"You can't take me anywhere," I said. "You can't take me."

Behind my mother, the curtain to the house pushed open and Bedna stepped inside.

She paused, staring between the two of us. Silence, heavy and thick, full of deadly promise.

My mother pulled her mask over her face.

I exhaled. "Dammit."

Claudia dashed toward Bedna, unsheathing her sword so fast I barely registered it.

"Stop!" I shouted.

And they both did. Bedna, freezing by a chair, my mother pausing with her sword aimed at Bedna's heart.

"Bedna," I said quietly, trying to keep things calm so no one ended up dead. "Please, take your seat. And Claudia, please put your sword away."

Bedna did as I asked, lowering herself carefully into a seat. Her eyes were wide with fear, but her lips were pressed together tightly in anger.

Claudia stared at me, her expression hidden behind her bone mask, but she did as I'd asked and sheathed her sword. Not that Bedna was out of danger. It was going to take a fair bit of skill to keep her alive for the next few moments.

Claudia slid her mask to the top of her head. Bedna glanced between the two of us, noting our similarities.

"Allegra," Claudia said, her voice all at once soft and hard, speaking of anger and something else. A wistfulness, maybe. A wanting. "I came here to bring you home and that is what I'm going to do."

"To your home, you mean," I said.

She didn't respond, but she didn't need to. Claudia hadn't managed to find her way to Mornia only to return me to the Saldanas, the people she hated most in the world.

"You know I can't," I said. "I can't."

"You're getting better!" Claudia argued. "You've improved so much. Soon you'll be fully recovered."

"No," I said. "Even if that were the case, I still would not leave with you."

"How can you say that?" Anger leaked through her voice, but mostly it seemed she tried to disguise her pain. I'd hurt her, this woman I barely knew. She had chains wrapped around her heart, and I'd put them there and hadn't even known it.

Nothing hurt us more than love.

"I'm tired," I said, and held up my hand, forestalling her interruption. "I'm tired of everyone taking me from people, from places. I've always been stolen against my will. I'm done with it. No more. I make my own decisions now."

Claudia took a deep breath. "Then choose to come with me." She held out her hand, palm up, asking me to take it.

And it called to me. My fingers even twitched, begged me to slip them into her own, to lace them together. She was my mother, the mother I'd always wanted. The mother I'd desperately wanted to know. And she was begging me to do all that, to go with her. To let her be my mother. It would be the easiest thing, even if it meant giving up everything I'd ever known. Meant giving up Nev. No more arms wrapped around me in the night, whispered words in my ear that I couldn't even understand. He'd stood by me from the very moment we'd met. We fit together. I belonged with him.

I released the blanket I'd been clenching, smoothing it out with my fingers.

The brightness in Claudia's eyes dimmed. She read my answer in my face, my body. Her arm dropped to her side.

An inhale of breath was the only warning she gave.

Claudia yanked out a dagger and lunged for Bedna.

I kicked at Bedna's chair, connecting with the seat. The chair slid backward, Bedna still seated in it, until it hit a rug and toppled over.

Claudia's knife passed through the empty space.

"Stop!" I climbed to my feet.

"You're coming with me," Claudia snarled. "Even if I have to kill every last traveler in Mornia."

She dashed for Bedna again.

I jerked the blanket off the bed and whipped it at Claudia's feet. She stumbled, allowing Benda enough time to scurry away from the chair.

"This is madness!" I shouted at Claudia.

"You know nothing of madness," she said, then yanked her bone mask onto her face.

Weak. I was too weak to stop her. If she was driven to kill Bedna right here and now, I wouldn't be able to stop her. Not alone. Not even with help, maybe. Claudia had held her own against Lea in the Ravenna market. Even at my peak I doubted I'd be able to slow her down, determined as she was.

Claudia slashed at the blanket around her ankles, cutting herself free from it.

Bedna scurried behind her kitchen table and snatched a broom. She swung the handle at Claudia's head. Claudia knocked it away, turning to face Bedna once more.

The warning horn sounded outside.

We paused, listening. It came a second time.

I looked at the curtain covering the door. It drifted listlessly in the night air. No wind. No storm.

Pounding footsteps outside. Nev shoved his way through.

"Bedna, Allegra we need—" He stopped mid-sentence, catching sight of Claudia before him.

Claudia didn't hesitate. She swung around, dagger whipping with her. Nev jumped back, but not before the dagger caught him below his throat, cutting across the jut of his collarbone.

If Claudia had aimed a little higher, or Nev had been a little slower, she would have spilled his life's blood.

Instead, Nev hit the back wall with a grunt. He slipped off his feet, crashing to the ground. Claudia darted for him.

I leaped onto her back, wrapping my legs around her waist. My hands grabbed her wrist with the dagger.

Claudia spun. I lost my grip, slipping off her and landing on top of Nev. Claudia's dagger tumbled to the ground. I scrambled for it. My fingers closed around the warmth of its hilt.

I held it before me, protecting Nev. I began to cough, a hack, deep in my throat, my chest.

"Stop," I said in between coughs. I tried to catch my breath, tried to stop the pain that tore through me with each cough.

Claudia stood over us. Her chest rose and fell rapidly.

Finally, my coughing eased and I was able to take a deep breath.

"Stop," I said once more.

Claudia took a step away from us. Another. Until she hit the wall and leaned against it, the fight gone from her.

She pushed her mask to the top of her head once more and took a deep, shuddering breath. Tears had dampened her face. She wiped them away with her gloved fingers.

"You will never be mine, will you?" she asked, her voice breaking slightly.

I untangled myself from Nev and he scrambled to his feet, pulling me up with him. I let my arm with the dagger drop to my side, but I didn't give up the weapon.

"I belong to me," I said, "and me alone."

She nodded once, pushing herself off the wall. "It's unfair."

"Yes," I said. Because she spoke the truth. Lea and Les had taken me from her when I was an infant. They'd thought they'd been doing the right thing, probably had been doing the right thing, really, but it didn't mean people didn't get hurt. That Claudia hadn't lost a daughter she would never get back. That I hadn't lost a mother, too, even if I'd gained another one.

I thought about Nev, kidnapping me from my family to try to keep me safe. He rested his hand on my hip, prepared to jump back into a fight with Claudia, if needed.

Sometimes we hurt the ones we loved the most when we tried to do the right thing.

The horn outside blew again and Bedna lowered her broom.

"The *bol*?" Bedna asked Nev.

I stepped away from him, one eye still on Claudia, who seemed to mostly be ignoring us as she pulled her mask back into place.

"It is not a *bol*." He shook his head. "That is why I came back for you. All the *samars* are needed."

"What?" Bedna set her broom down. "Why?"

"What is it?" I asked.

"Ghosts," Nev said. "An army of ghosts, coming this way."

thirty-seven

GHOSTS. AN ARMY OF GHOSTS. HEADING STRAIGHT FOR
Mornia.

I should have been confused, like Bedna clearly was, as
she shook her head and asked Nev to repeat himself. But I
wasn't.

I knew what this was, had lived through it before, even
though I had been too young to remember. An army of
ghosts could only mean one thing.

Lea Saldana.

I spun to face Claudia, because she would understand the
meaning of it, too, would know who drove the ghosts toward
the barrier protecting Mornia. But Claudia was gone, having slipped away while I'd been focused on Nev.

She'd heard him, though. The only question was, was she
fleeing, or did she go to seek Lea in the night?

"I have never seen so many," Nev was saying to Bedna,
who scrambled around her kitchen table to Nev. Blood

coursed down his chest. He patted at it absently, wincing when his fingers connected with the wound. It was long, but shallow.

"The barrier will keep them out." Bedna pushed Nev into a chair and had him lift his arms while she pulled his shirt off, being careful around the pieces that stuck to the wound.

Once free, she took a damp towel and dabbed at the wound.

"No," I said.

They both looked at me. I squeezed the dagger in my hand.

"What?" Bedna asked.

"The barrier," I said. "I don't know that it will hold."

Bedna set the towel down and began to wrap a bandage around Nev's chest. "The barrier has always stood up to the ghosts," she said. "Culda's song is strong. She, and the Three, have always protected us from the ghosts."

"The ghosts do not come of their own will, or because of coincidence. They are being driven. They come to break down your barrier, to flood your streets with the angry dead."

Bedna and Nev stared at me.

"How do you know this?" Bedna's voice was quiet, edged with fear.

"Because it is my aunt who brings the ghosts to Mornia. She is Safraella's chosen and the ghosts are Her wayward children."

Someone screamed in the street outside of Bedna's house.

She jumped, then finished tying off Nev's bandage.

The scream was followed by more shouts, yells. Pounding footsteps. The sound of fear working its way through a crowd of people. The ghosts were coming and people were afraid.

"Come." Bedna strode from her house. Nev and I followed on her heels and I was glad she was too old to run because I was too sick to move quicker than a walk.

Nev put his arm around my waist, helping me to move. Normally I would have pushed him off. I didn't need his help. I could walk, for now, anyway, but this was not the time for my pride. This was the time for action.

Lea had said she would never use the ghosts as a weapon again. She had seen what it had done to the Da Vias, when she had opened the doors to their house and invited the ghosts inside. The Da Vias had turned their back on Safraella and Her punishment had been ruthless.

A group of women and men ran past, heading southwest like us through the streets of New Mornia.

But the Da Vias had deserved it. Mostly. They had killed the Saldanas in order to gain power and to keep their secrets safe. Maybe the head of their Family had been at fault, but they had followed her and it had led to many of their deaths.

The travelers here, in Mornia, had done nothing. Yes, Nev had taken me. Yes, he had sent his beloved snake to try and kill Les. But that was not the fault of everyone. The vast majority of these people hadn't even traveled to Lovero with the menagerie. They were innocent.

We broke free of the buildings of New Mornia and the dead plains spread before us.

And there, in the west, drawing closer, was an army of shrieking, screaming ghosts.

We stopped. All three of us, shocked by the vision before us. The ghosts were whipped into a frenzy, spinning, circling, wailing. But they weren't focused on their destination. Instead, they were focused on a figure in their midst. She was too far away and it was too dark to see, but I knew it was Lea, in the center of them, pushing forward through the ghosts.

"*Dost ba ebal Culda,*" Bedna gasped out. *Culda save us.*

We pressed forward again, heading for the barrier along with everyone else.

The travelers stood in a line, like they normally did at night to sing the ghosts away, but there were so many of them, now. Everyone had come to stand at the boundaries and sing. They had already taken up the song by the time we reached them, and we squeezed into the line, Bedna on one side of me, Nev on the other.

I didn't even have to sing. The *singura* around my neck picked up the song surrounding it, glowing for a moment before it flashed, connecting with Bedna's and then traveling down the line. It didn't end, though. The light kept glowing, holding the barrier strong as long as the travelers kept singing.

Behind us, Metta and Isha appeared. "What is happening?" Metta yelled over the song; then she saw the spectral army pressing toward us and gasped.

Isha wasted no time, stepping beside Nev and picking up the song. Metta followed quickly after her, and together we watched as the ghosts drew closer. And closer.

When the ghosts reached the barrier, I didn't know if it would hold. Maybe the ghosts would be pushed aside, the same way they were pushed away from Lea when they got too close. Or perhaps the barrier would collapse against the strength of so many ghosts.

There were hundreds of them. They must have been following her the entire way. Days and days traveling through the dead plains, collecting the angry dead as she went.

The ghosts were close enough now that details began to emerge. They were no longer a writhing mass of glowing, spectral light, but instead were individuals—this one a man, that one a woman. A child. An old man. All of them wailing in their hunger to reach what was in their midst.

We could see her now, too. A figure in black riding a bay stallion, bone mask strapped to her face, the left half so black it practically disappeared in the darkness. Travelers gasped when they saw her, and truly she was a terrifying figure.

But she was just my aunt. Just Lea Saldana, who loved beautiful fabrics and hand pies stuffed with lamb. Who hated the scent of goldencones or hot days without a breeze.

Who had died once, and returned stronger.

She was the chosen of Safraella, yes, but she was still just my family.

When she drew close enough, she stopped. Another horse

walked beside her, a black stallion who pawed at the ground. She'd brought Night with her, to take me home.

I looked at Nev then. Blood spotting his bandage, hat pressed to his head, singing beside his family.

"I'm glad," I said to him over the sound of the song, the sound of the ghosts. He looked at me.

"I'm glad I'm here," I said. "With you."

His eyes softened.

Lea slipped off Kismet's saddle and walked to the barrier. The ghosts circled her but kept their distance, having learned if they crept too close, or tried to touch her, they would be pushed back by an invisible force.

One of them bumped into the traveler barrier and the ghost was shoved away, much in the same manner.

Lea stopped, and watched a few more ghosts as they were pushed away from the invisible barrier.

She turned toward the travelers again, and though her face was covered by her bone mask, I felt her eyes lock on to mine.

"I have come for what is mine."

Her voice was not loud. She did not yell, and yet she could be heard, clearly, over the shrieks and cries of the ghosts. Over the traveler song.

"You would bring ghosts into our home?" Bedna shouted to her. The ghosts moaned. "You would kill us all for one girl?"

"For my family I would murder the world."

It wasn't her.

It looked like her. It sounded like her and moved like her.

But something was wrong. It was not Lea. Not the Lea I knew.

Lea pressed forward and the travelers sang louder and when she reached the barrier, she pushed against it and it glowed brighter, but kept her out.

She wasn't a ghost. There was no reason for her to be unable to step through the barrier, and yet she couldn't seem to get through.

Lea pressed against it again, and it glowed once more, casting shadows onto the dead plains, and behind Lea was the largest shadow of all, stretching out behind her like the shadow of an oak or a tower. She stepped away from the barrier and the light dimmed, plunging us into night once more.

"Did you see that?" I asked Nev. He nodded, once, quickly.

The wind picked up, whipping my nightgown around my legs.

"She's not herself," I said.

"It does not matter," he replied. "She comes to kill us all."

The wind tossed my hair into my mouth and I spat it aside. "The ghosts will vanish with the sun," I said. "I can reason with her after that."

Nev looked at me, doubt spreading through his eyes, but he picked up the song once more, singing loudly with the other travelers, keeping the ghosts out.

The alarm horn sounded again. I glanced up at the tower and the man who stood there, blowing the horn. Almost everyone was already here, holding the barrier in place. There was no reason to sound the alarm.

Dust blew into my eyes and I wiped them clean. Behind Lea, on the horizon, the stars began to disappear.

I blinked rapidly, in case the dust had ruined my vision, but no. As I watched, more and more of the stars began to vanish.

"What is it?" I shouted to Nev.

"A *bol!*"

A dust storm, now of all times. Maybe it was coincidence, but I had a hard time believing there wasn't something bigger happening that we were blind to.

The *bol* would come, and some of the travelers would leave the line, to secure their animals, their livelihoods.

Lea pressed against the barrier again, testing it for weak spots.

If enough of the travelers left, Lea would break through the barrier, I felt it in my bones, and the ghosts would wreak havoc on anyone still present.

The sun would rise. Maybe in an hour. Maybe less. Could we last that long? The *bol* was still so far away and seemed to be moving slowly, but would it be fully upon us before the sun? Before our adrenaline failed us and our strength turned to weakness, to fear? Until we fled for safety from the ghosts?

Lea stood across from me now, palm flat against the barrier, watching as light flared out from the pressure.

"You'll kill everyone," I said to her. And even through

the wind, the song, the screams and cries of the ghosts, she heard me.

"You're the only one who matters," she said. "They attacked us in our home. They deserve to die."

"Like the Da Vias?" I asked, and thought of Claudia, my mother, hidden somewhere in the dark.

"I returned the Da Vias to Her. It was what She asked of me."

"These people are innocent! You would murder children in your wrath."

She blinked behind her mask and dropped her hand from the barrier. In her darkest rage, I knew Lea would never intentionally harm a child. It was the whole reason she had stolen me in the first place. To keep me safe. From the ghosts. From the Da Vias.

From the world.

But I couldn't be kept safe from the world. It was everywhere and bad things happened and that was just the way of it all.

Behind her, the brown dust from the storm bore down on us. If I could see it, it meant the sun was rising. I glanced over my shoulder and saw the thin line of black sky turning purple over the horizon. Only a few more minutes, then the ghosts would be gone.

I faced Lea. "There has been enough spilled blood."

I remembered Les's blood, pouring across the table. All of this because I had sought comfort in the arms of a traveler boy.

I reached over and took Nev's hand. He squeezed my fingers.

Lea missed nothing.

"They took you," she said. "They took you from us."

The wind gusted behind her. Night whinnied, loud and high.

"You took me once, too," I said.

Her head jerked, like I'd slapped her.

She stepped back and the tension seemed to ease from her. Her chest rose as she took a deep breath.

"All right," she said. "All right."

Then she walked away from the barrier, the ghosts following after her.

Beside me I could practically feel the relief as it rushed through Nev. Lea was bringing the ghosts away from the barrier, pulling them with her, waiting for the sun to rise.

The *bol* struck.

And the barrier shattered.

thirty-eight

†

THE WIND GUSTED INTO OUR FACES. PEOPLE STUMBLED or turned away, protecting their eyes.

And it was enough for the barrier to collapse.

As if someone had taken a mallet to a glass bowl, the light flashed before us, then crackled in spider webs and suddenly was gone, vanishing like a candle, snuffed out in the wind. The light from the *singura* at my chest died, and even though many of the travelers kept singing, the light didn't return.

"What . . ." I managed to say, before someone screamed, the *bol* whipping her voice instantly away.

She'd probably screamed once she'd recognized how much danger we were in, with the ghosts so close.

But screaming only attracted them.

Even through the wind and sand and dirt, the ghosts were apparent, their spectral glow gleaming through the storm. Almost as one they turned away from Lea and toward Mornia, and the travelers who stood at the border, trying to keep their homes safe.

"Run!" Someone shouted, and only later would I realize it was Lea, her voice reaching us even through the storm.

I turned to my left but Bedna was already gone, rushing away with the rest of the travelers, heading for the nearest home, whether it was a building in New Mornia or a hole in the ground in Old Mornia.

The ghosts screamed and streamed toward us.

"Allegra!" Nev shouted, yanking on my arm. But we wouldn't make it to safety in time. The ghosts would catch us, would rip our souls from our bodies until we, too, were ghosts wandering the plains.

We needed protection.

"This way!" I pulled him forward, stumbling toward the ghosts that rushed at us.

Nev held his ground and my fingers slipped from his and suddenly he was gone, disappeared in the dust and the sand that swirled around me.

"Nev!" I shouted into the wind. "Nev!" But if he answered, the wind stole it from me.

A ghost materialized to my left. It screamed, its open mouth black and empty and hungry.

A flash of light in front of me and the ghost vanished, replaced by Lea.

I stumbled to her. She caught me in her arms, and never before had I held so tightly to someone.

A ghost appeared behind us, but Lea's power deflected it away.

Lea pulled back and looked at me, her face covered by her stark bone mask, wind bellowing around us. "I have you," she said to me.

"I know," I said over the wind.

And the sun rose.

Even in the midst of the *bol* the ghosts vanished, leaving everyone safe once more.

From the storm a shadow rushed us.

Lea shoved me aside with just enough time to yank her sword free and block the attack by Claudia Da Via.

I fell to the ground, the wind pelting me with sand and dust. I held my hand in front of my eyes, trying to protect my vision.

I expected Lea and Claudia to talk, to shout things at each other like they had the last time they'd been together, standing on either side of a street that separated Ravenna and Lilyan. But they were utterly silent, and that was more frightening by far. They couldn't waste the energy and effort words would cost. They were in it to kill each other.

"Stop!" I shouted, climbing to my feet.

Thunder approached, and shadows. Night and Kismet galloped through the dust, eyes wide as they fled toward Mornia.

A gust of wind caught me straight in the face and I fell, my hand pressed against the sand on the ground, trying to stay on my feet.

The fall saved my life.

Perrin slashed her knife where my face had been. She lost

her balance and staggered away a few steps.

"The gods were wrong when they chose you!" she shouted over the roar of the wind. "It is just you and me now, *ghoshka*."

And she was right. I'd lost Nev in the storm. Behind me I caught a glimpse of Lea and Claudia dueling, their leather-clad forms dodging in and out of my sight like sand wraiths or storm ghosts or some other myth.

Perrin charged.

But I still had the knife I'd taken from Claudia and I raised it now, to defend myself.

I'd beaten Perrin before in a knife fight. But that had been days ago, before I'd fallen ill. I should have killed her then, and none of this would have come to pass.

Perrin slashed at me and I ducked, twisting around her. The wind buffeted my hair into my face. I hastily brushed it aside. Visibility was bad enough with the sand.

Perrin stabbed for my ribs. I slammed my forearm onto hers, shoving her knife down. She grunted. I jumped back, panting. My chest pounded with every breath. My vision spun. I didn't have much to give.

Lightning flashed above us, static from the sand. And in the brief illumination shadows loomed over me, taller than trees. Three of them. Or four. They were gone almost immediately. Perrin rushed me.

I feinted right and she bought it, placing her foot and stabbing. I twisted left and slashed with my own knife.

It bit into the flesh of her arm. Perrin jerked free, dancing away until the sand swallowed her from my sight.

I coughed, and then coughed again. And then I couldn't stop. The cough brought me to my knees, hand pressed against my chest, eyes watering from more than just the sand and dust.

A figure in the storm. I raised my knife, prepared for her next attack.

But the figure appeared and it was Nev, followed by Metta and Isha. They held hands to keep from getting separated, and all three wore scarves around their mouths and noses, protecting them from the sand.

"Allegra!" Nev shouted, his voice muffled behind his scarf.

"Perrin!" I tried to yell at him, to warn him away. But my voice emerged as a croak and I coughed again, until I was forced to use both hands to keep me upright on the ground. My vision blurred, darkness creeping on the edges.

They dropped beside me, and Isha tied a scarf around my nose and mouth, blocking out the sand. I continued to cough, but after a few moments I was able to catch my breath, to ease the tightness in my chest, to clear my vision.

Nev grabbed me under the arms and pulled me to my feet.

"Perrin!" I croaked out. He leaned closer, trying to hear me.

Perrin dashed out of the storm, smashing into Nev. Her shoulder connected with his chest and I heard him grunt, his breath bursting out of him before he fell, yanking me off my feet with him.

Perrin and Nev tumbled to the ground, but Perrin recovered quickly, jumping to her feet.

Isha rushed to me, trying to help me up.

The wind gusted around us, the sand pelting our bare skin.

"Perrin!" Metta yelled. But Perrin ignored her. She kicked Nev in the head and he collapsed, unmoving.

Perrin strode to me, switching the grip on her knife.

Isha stepped in front of me in a moment of bravery I would have never expected from her, but Perrin shoved her out of the way, and Isha's dress wrapped around her legs, tripping her.

I stumbled away from Perrin, breath wheezing in my throat, knife held before me. I couldn't beat her. She would kill me, here in the storm, on the dead plains.

I backed toward Nev and Metta, who was on her knees beside him, trying to revive him. Perrin hadn't tried to kill him, and I didn't think she would injure either Metta or Isha. The only one she truly wanted dead was me.

From the corner of my eye a shadow flitted past us. It vanished before I could do more than register its speed as it coursed low to the ground.

Perrin charged. She stabbed for my right side. I blocked.

She flipped the knife to her left hand for the same attack. I blocked there, too. I staggered backward, the sand shifting beneath my feet, keeping me off balance.

Perrin pushed at me again, relentless in her attacks. Calm and confident.

Her knife caught me across the knuckles, then again on the forearm.

My blood dripped into the sand at my feet, staining it red only for an instant until the wind and dust blew it away.

She was trying to bleed me, to wound me so much that I would lose strength with every drop of blood.

Another nick. This one across my cheek. I tasted blood as it soaked into the scarf covering my mouth.

The shadow again. A quick flit of . . . something. It wasn't human. It moved too fast to be human.

Perrin attacked again, in my moment of distraction. She stabbed straight for my chest. I brought both arms up, crossing them in a block, but the strength of her stab was enough to force me off my feet. I slammed to the ground, the sand and dust exploding around me before it was whipped away by the wind.

I couldn't catch my breath. Couldn't find the strength to get to my feet.

Perrin loomed over me. The look in her eyes was bright, wild. She'd won.

Lea dashed out of the storm.

Perrin had only enough time to jump back. Lea swung her sword in a fast arc, catching Perrin's knife hand. The knife, and one of her fingers, spun off into the storm.

Perrin shouted in shock and pain.

A shadow exploded from the spinning sand. I had a quick glimpse of stripes, orange and black, with a white-tipped tail, and then the tiger leaped at Perrin. She screamed and

393

the tiger crashed onto her, mouth around her throat.

She thrashed but the tiger dragged her away, disappearing into the swirling sand of the storm.

My breath exhaled in a cough, and Lea dropped to her knee before me.

"How bad?" she asked, and I realized she saw the blood coating my hands and arms and face and thought that was the danger, that I'd been wounded. But it wasn't a wound that was killing me, but how I couldn't catch my breath. How my heart pounded, how I was on fire, burning up.

Claudia Da Via dashed from the sand.

"Look out!" I managed to cough.

Lea spun, but not quick enough. Claudia blocked Lea's sword and slammed a knife into her side.

Lea gasped and the sword tumbled from her grip.

Claudia danced away. She looked at me, expression hidden behind her bone mask, and then she was gone, disappearing once more.

Lea fell beside me, hand pressed to her side. But blood seeped through her fingers, dripping off her gloves onto the sand below her.

"Lea!" I shouted.

Metta and Isha and Nev were behind us and Metta crawled over to me now, hand on her stomach as she reached us, Isha lifting Nev's face out of the sand that threatened to bury him.

And still the storm raged. The sand twisted, whirling faster and faster.

Lightning flashed again, and the shadows were still there, three on one side, a fourth across from them. Huge and stretching into the sky.

The sand spun, whipping away in a cyclone, a column of wind and dust.

And I knew it for what it was. This storm, this *bol*. The maelstrom from my dreams.

It towered over us, spinning faster and faster until it crashed down.

thirty-nine

†

THE STORM VANISHED.

But not my nightmare.

I opened my eyes in the sudden quiet. The wind had vanished. The sand. The dust. Everything, except for Lea beside me, who stirred in the silence.

Pale light flowed around us, watery and gray. I pulled the scarf from my face and the air felt stale and stagnant.

A gray fog rolled in and out of the empty space surrounding us.

Lea pushed her mask to the top of her head, her hand weak and feeble. I pressed my own hands against the wound in her side. It was fatal. This I knew. Claudia had meant it when she sank the knife into Lea's side.

"This is a dead place," Lea said. "But at least I'm clothed this time. I must not be actually dead yet."

"Shhh," I hushed her.

My dream. A dead place. Somehow I had brought us here.

The *singura* felt cold against my chest.

Lea snorted and then coughed, her lips staining with blood. "I've spent your whole life quieting you and now here, at the end of mine, you try to quiet me?" She chuckled. "It's almost poetic."

She shifted, trying to push herself up, but she paused and then groaned.

"Don't move," I said.

"Twice Claudia Da Via had a hand in my death," Lea said. "I suppose that's kind of poetic as well."

Above us a boom sounded. I gasped.

The fog swirled and spun rapidly and to the left it suddenly parted, vanishing like a wisp of smoke blown away with a breath.

A forest of bones had been hidden by the fog. Bone trees stretched upward, swaying slightly, white and bleached.

Lea shifted again. "Allegra," she said, but I kept my gaze on the bone forest. There was movement among the trees. I narrowed my eyes, peering into its depths.

"Do you see that?" I whispered. "Something moves . . ."

Lea grabbed my chin, her fingers slick with blood, and turned my face to hers.

"Do not look," she said. "Do not stare upon Her face."

"What?" I asked.

And then She was there, appearing from the folds of the bone forest, taller than the tallest tree, dark and empty and faceless but for the bone.

"Don't look at her!" Lea yelled.

But how could I not look at Her? Not look at Her terribleness? Her beauty? Not hear Her breath, like the baying of a thousand hounds, not hear Her heart, like the crack of a tree in a storm.

She was everything and I—I was nothing. I was empty, hollow. I was—I was—

Lea yanked my face away.

I inhaled sharply, my mind clear again.

Another boom echoed around us and the fog across from Safraella swirled and vanished. But instead of a bone forest stood a desert, white sands stretching on endlessly.

"They come," Lea said.

And They did. The Three. *We sing a song about the Three, of Meska, Culda, and Boamos. Boamos gives us wealth and thievery, while Culda sings us safely home. And great Meska with her animals wraps us in our mother's warmth.* Gods of the travelers. I did not look upon them, but They cast shadows on the ground before us, as did Safraella.

"Leave." A voice spoke, masculine, deep like the ocean, maybe, or the heart of a mountain. Boamos.

Safraella's shadow shifted on the ground.

"I have come for what is mine." Her voice was soft and quiet, like a final, whispered breath. The kiss of a corpse.

Safraella was a jealous god. This we knew. This we had learned from the Da Vias folly. She would not let me go. She would not let me be stolen by these other gods.

"It was her own will." A third voice now, bright and

sweet, like birdsong, or a hymn, hummed in the dark. "She wears the *singura*."

"She is mine," Safraella said.

"No." Boamos.

"Then I will take her."

There was a noise, a screech and crack, as if a tree shattered. Safraella had ripped one of the bone trees from the ground. It was long and straight and sharp.

She cast it at the Three.

From the shadows I saw the bone spear strike Boamos in the chest. He screamed, an unearthly sound, the sound of mountains tumbling into the sea, or boulders shattering into sand.

We screamed as well, pressing our hands to our ears, trying to drown out the sound, the unbearable wail.

The shadows launched themselves at one another.

The ground trembled. The air thundered. Ripping and tearing noises surrounded us as the gods battled.

Lea's blood was warm and slick on my hands. The *singura* weighed heavily on my neck.

"Allegra," Lea said, and I pulled my vision away from the shadows of battling gods. Her skin was pale. Her eyes glassy.

"You should have been mine." Her voice was barely more than a whisper.

I pressed my forehead to hers. "I was always yours."

And it was true. Maybe I was meant to be a Da Via. Or maybe I was meant to be a Saldana. It didn't matter, in the end. Names were just names, and didn't make us who we were.

Lea squeezed my arm, her grip light, weak. The gods stormed above us.

We were not meant to witness this. This battle. This war. This was not for our eyes. This was a dead place, Lea had said. And we would die here. It was a certainty I felt in my gut. In Their rage at one another, They would destroy that over which They fought.

Lea closed her eyes.

The spiritual sickness hadn't left me. I was dying. Lea was dying. The *singura* swung from my neck before me. If I didn't have the *singura*, none of this would have happened. If I didn't have the *singura*, we wouldn't be here, in this dead place, Lea dying.

I was still caged. Caged by the gods.

I grabbed the *singura* with my fist, coating it in blood, and pulled it from my head.

"I don't want it!" I shouted at the shadows fighting above us. "I give it away willingly to Metta!"

I hurled it away from me, into the fog of the dead place.

It was no longer my burden to bear. I belonged to me now, and no one else. And so I would die, but I would die free, with Lea at my side.

Silence fell over us, a blanket over our heads, or like sinking beneath the cool waters of the lake.

The shadows of the gods stilled, and though I couldn't be sure, it seemed They looked down upon us, seeing us for the first time, perhaps.

Lea's breath wheezed in and out of her.

And mine didn't. I felt light and unburdened. Uncaged. Free.

The gods stirred, and their shadows separated, pulling apart from one another, returning to their sides.

"Come, daughter," Safraella said. And though She could have been speaking to either of us, I knew She spoke to Lea.

"No," I said. "No."

"Everyone owes a death," She said. "Oleander Saldana was granted a resurrection once. That is more than most."

"You can save her again," I said.

Lea's eyes were closed. She struggled to breathe. I clutched her to me.

"Please," I said. "I need her."

I knew what it meant, to serve a dark god. To do Her dark work. To serve. But for an instant I wished for a god of something kinder, maybe, to answer my prayer.

"Death is the only kindness I offer," Safraella spoke, as if she'd heard my thoughts. "I am not a god of mercy."

The shadows shifted, then one stepped forward.

"I am."

Meska, god of animals and motherhood, Her voice soft like the down feathers of a bird, warm like a mother's love, like a child cradled in devoted arms.

Maybe sometimes love hurt us.

The fog and pale light floated away, washed aside in the gentle, warm breath of Meska as it enveloped us all.

But maybe sometimes it saved us, too.

forty

I SLIPPED OUT OF THE DARK ALCOVE, INTO THE DARKER room, and closed the curtain behind me. I slid my feet across the floor, then stepped up the stairs, one after another.

The morning sun burst over my head, warm and welcoming and bright.

I shifted the bag from one shoulder to the other and headed north to Bedna's house, where I knew she was waiting for me.

People went about their business, and though many of them looked at me, none scowled or glared like they had in the past.

I reached Bedna's home and pushed my way inside. She sat at the kitchen table and waved me to take a seat.

"How did you know it would work?" Bedna asked.

I sipped the oil she served me. It was light and fruity and her favorite, so she said.

She spoke of the *singura* of course, and passing it to Metta.

"I didn't," I said.

I'd woken in the dead plains, outside the border of Mornia. The morning sun streamed down on us, its warmth like Meska's warmth, before She sent us away from that place where gods battled.

And we'd lived. Even Lea—though her leathers had been soaked in her own blood—got to her feet with the rest of us, her wound healed by Meska's mercy. Lea wasn't my mother, not truly, but maybe that small distinction didn't really matter to a god of mothers. After all, She had brought Nula and Bema back to life, in the story Nev had told me, so what was a little mortal-wound healing to a god like that?

Bedna had found us, Metta, Isha, and Nev as well, too shocked or frightened to speak. But Metta wore the *singura,* the one that should have always been hers had Les not taken it as a child, a single memento of his mother.

By the grace of the gods no innocents had died. The travelers had fled from the ghosts, through the *bol* bearing down upon them, and all had managed to find shelter or outrun the ghosts until the rising sun had saved them. The only true death was Perrin, her body dragged some distance away by the tiger until he had abandoned her.

The tiger was nowhere to be found, and the people agreed that Perrin had angered Meska by her ill treatment of the tiger, and so She had taken her.

Later Nev and I would walk over to the pit. We found a mound of sand pressed against one of the walls, tall enough for the tiger to free himself.

The other two tigers had remained in the pit, too accustomed to their cage to want anything else.

I finished off the oil Bedna had poured me. "Lea said it was a dead place," I continued, "and Nev had told me the *singura* could only be passed on in death. And, anyway, I had nothing to lose."

"You had your life to lose."

I shrugged. "Yes. But it's just a life in the end. What is it worth if you're not willing to give it up to save the people you love?"

Bedna made a small noise and passed me a bottle of oil, which I added to my bag. "You were fortunate."

I did my best to imitate one of their traveler shrugs. Her lips quirked. "I am alive," I said. "And free. That was the most I could hope for."

Outside, the morning was bright and the sky was blue. The *bol* that had arrived with Lea had vanished in an instant, suddenly dying with our return. Whether it had been a natural storm or not, I didn't suppose anyone would ever be able to say.

Metta had lost their tiger, and their status had taken a hit. But she had gained a *singura,* and in the next few days she would have a child and would become a mother.

"It is enough to work with." She grinned, grasping the *singura* around her neck.

The travelers were still wary around me, but now it was less because I had stolen something from them, from their gods, and more because I had returned it, and lived. And seen the gods, of course. At the very least, it was no longer something only Lea and Les could claim.

Les.

"He's fine," Lea had told me. "Well, as fine as can be expected. It was close for some time, but he was awake when I left, mad as hells that he couldn't come with me, driving everyone crazy. Marcello is loving every second, taking care of him. And the baby, Malia. He was never this helpful when you and Emile were children."

Nev was waiting for me outside of Bedna's. He took my hand, fingers wrapping around my bandages, and together we walked out of New Mornia to the western border where Lea waited, loading Kismet with supplies.

Her mask rested on top of her head and she smiled as we approached. She tightened her saddle bags and came around. Nev gave us space.

"You won't come home with me?" she asked again as I passed her the final bag of supplies for her journey, even though she'd been asking me constantly.

"If I did," I said, "nothing would change for us. We could try to do things differently, but it wouldn't last. We would fall back into old patterns. This way, at least, I can come visit whenever I want."

"And leave again," she said, a touch of bitterness in her voice.

"Yes," I said. "But you knew I would, one day."

"My wild one," Lea said. "Exploring the world."

"We will travel north to Fazia first," Nev said. "Then

after that, Yvain. They will be happy to see the menagerie."

"Good," Lea said. "Because Les and Beatricia will hold me to it. Don't leave me to their wrath."

"I won't," I said. "You can tell them at the least I'll need to collect my things."

Lea smiled. Then it vanished and all at once she was hugging me and I was hugging her in return.

"Maybe it was a mistake taking you," she whispered to me. "Maybe I was wrong. But I'm not sorry for it. I'll never be sorry for it, no matter how many knives Claudia Da Via sinks into me. And I would do it again."

I nodded, not trusting my voice or the tightness of my throat.

Sometimes, we did terrible things in the name of love. Sometimes, family and loved ones hurt us the most. But sometimes, those we loved were the easiest to forgive.

Lea stepped away from me, holding me at arm's length. "I'll see you soon."

I nodded. "Soon."

Then she climbed onto Kismet's back and made her way west, toward Yvain and home and family.

Nev stepped beside me, taking my hand again. "You have your freedom now," he said. "Is it what you thought it would be?"

I shook my head. "No," I said. "But then, I guess that's the way of things, sometimes." I faced him, and took in his new bruises from Perrin, the scratches and cuts from the storm. But there were no longer any bruises from me. And his smile was as wide and bright as the first time I met him. My heart thumped.

"And anyway," I said, "I'm not exactly free. I'm still stuck with you."

He laughed. "We have made a terrible mistake."

"Awful," I agreed.

"Yes."

The menagerie would leave in a few days and we would travel with it. I would see the world with Nev, and then we would return to Mornia and Metta and Isha. Or go to Yvain and Lea and Les. And I would never escape from my family, the people who had caged me.

But maybe I didn't need freedom in order to be free. Maybe I'd just needed to find the right cage. The one of my choosing.

My hand slipped into Nev's.

It fit perfectly.

Acknowledgments

Authors always say the second book is really hard to write. But of course no one (me) really believes them. Because it's not like this is actually the second book I've written, so how hard could it be, right?

But, alas, it turns out that I am not a special snowflake after all, and this book was just what authors who had come before me said it would be: really, really hard to write.

Good thing I had some great people helping me along the way.

For starters, my agent, Mollie Glick, and her team of awesome peeps, who are there at the drop of a hat if I need anything.

And my editor, Alex Cooper, who writes me really long edit letters but somehow makes them seem totally doable and not scary at all—even if she thinks it would be a good idea to cut entire characters and make the book one hundred pages shorter. She's pretty much always right. And of course Alyssa Miele and the rest of the HarperTeen team who make things happen so seamlessly.

To Anne Ahiers and Jennifer Coats, who really quickly read early drafts of this book and managed to convince me that, no, I hadn't forgotten how to make sentences or actually write words in general. (What am word? You tell me, Anne and Jennifer. You tell me.)

To cheerleaders Austin Gorton, Hannah Oman, Ryan

Spires, Jessica Kirkeby, Molly Beth Griffin, Megan Atwood, and Tricia Conway. And the staff, faculty, and students of Hamline University's MFA in Writing for Children and Young Adults, especially my final two advisers, Phyllis Root and Swati Avasthi. And of course my Front Row cohort, Jessica Mattson, Brita Sandstrom, Josh Hammond, Zack Wilson, Jennifer Coats, Anna Dielschneider, Gary Mansergh, and Kate St. Vincent Vogl. You are all excellent people.

To my dogs, who can't read this and sometimes bark at me when I should be writing but keep me from being lonely while typing away. Hopefully they know how much I love and appreciate them.

And last again is my family: my mom and dad, and my siblings Anne, Patrick, and Cassie. They say things like "I just wish Sarah had a new book coming out every month"— and actually mean it.